ANGIE'S PULSE POUNDED SO HARD IT WAS TOUGH TO FOCUS ON ANYTHING ELSE.

The hellscape that spread out past the frame of the tree was a barren, rocky landscape, all black rock and lava rivers. In the distance, volcanos belched thick red lines of lava and smoke. The sky overhead was red, casting strange shadows and weird lines across the landscape. In the distance, she could already see demons flying over the top of the volcanos. And their screeches sent a shiver of terror down her spine.

Beside her, Sebastian said, "Are you okay?"

"Not even a little bit," she said with a sound that would have been a laugh if she weren't so scared. "You?"

"Been better," he said.

Going into the hellscape wasn't something humans survived. That both she and Sebastian had survived this horror didn't make it any easier to face.

"The demons haven't noticed us yet," Aidan said quietly. There weren't any signs of fear in her voice, but Angie wasn't sure she'd ever heard Aidan speak so…quietly. "We need to go now if we're going."

"We're going?" Sebastian asked Angie, one last time.

She didn't take her gaze off the breach. "We're still going," she said.

Bone Lantern Witch

Spiderweb Witch

Storm Shadow
Witch

Darkling Mist
Witch

Apocalypse Witch

APOCALYPSE WITCH

A DEMON WITCH NOVEL

KAT SIMONS

T&D PUBLISHING

Apocalypse Witch

For my family. Always and forever.
And for my muse who figured out how to finish this series!

CHAPTER ONE

*A*ngie Jordan stared at the people sitting around the giant, black lacquered conference table and tried not to lose her temper. It was a very close thing.

She wasn't sure if they were trying to push her buttons and force her to lose her temper—after all, Morty had been trying to do that for months now—or if it was just the irritating buzz of the florescent lights overhead—someone needed to change that one fucking bulb—but whatever it was, they were getting on her very last nerve. And she was not a happy witch.

Not that she'd been particularly happy the last few months. Outside of having the love of her life back in her life, the rest of this demon stuff could hang.

The entire demon hunter council could hang too. Even Gabriella. And Angie sort of even liked Gabriella.

"We have to go," Angie said again, slowly, between one

calming breath and the next. "I have to go. There's no negotiation here. We didn't come here to ask permission or argue. We're here to let you know what's going to happen. So you all understand."

She hated everything about this conversation. Especially because, according to both Aidan, sitting to her left, and Sebastian, sitting to her right, even twenty years ago this wouldn't have been an issue. There would be no sitting around a conference table under an irritatingly humming florescent light trying to convince the demon hunter council that Angie and the other two hunters *were* going into a demon realm, and it was a thing that was going to happen whether the council liked it or not. She and the two hunters would have just done it. And then reported back to the history keepers if they survived.

The *if they survived* part poked holes in her confidence and determination, so she pushed that thought away.

In the last few decades, though, the council had gained more influence and power, moved into more of a governing body, made rules and demanded check-ins and forced agendas. And generally screwing things up for everyone. Demon hunters were, by nature, an independent lot, who did things when they were called to do them, not when some council told them to. And it rubbed wrong, particularly against Sebastian, that this council kept trying to gather more power to a central body.

Aidan mostly just ignored them or worked around them. What the legendary hunter did and did not do, what she had done and what she knew, were all pretty much mysteries. To

Angie, but also, as far as she could tell, to everyone else, too. Council included. Which just had to irritate the hell out of Morty. That part did make Angie happy.

For this meeting—confrontation?—they'd gathered in a conference room in the demon hunters' suite of offices in Midtown Manhattan, instead of the room with the giant fireplace where Angie had first met this council. She figured since she now knew for sure the giant stone fireplace was actually a portal to another location, Morty probably didn't want her anywhere near that room anymore.

The conference room was nominally more comfortable. She'd had to stand during that first meeting and here she got to sit. There was a coffee service down the center of the large conference table, silver pots of steaming back coffee, little ceramic bowls of sugar cubes, and a few tiny ceramic pitchers of milk. There was even one silver pot with hot water and a tray with artfully arranged tea packets—a gesture for Sebastian, she imagined. But weirdly, none of it was within easy reach of any of the participants because of the sheer size of the table. Given the size of the room, the table fit perfectly. It was just too big for their group.

The entire council was here this time, unlike the first meeting, when two of their members were missing. Since then she'd met one of the two. Morty. And he'd tried to kill her, or at least arrange for her to die, so that was where they stood. He sat at the head of the conference table, directly opposite Angie, Sebastian and Aidan, and he spent a lot of the meeting either smirking at her—he thought she was dying and was delighted with that turn of events—or scowling at the two hunters bracketing her.

The second hunter she'd never met before was remarkably quiet throughout the meeting. Remarkable because none of the others had been shy about voicing their opinions. She'd been introduced as Tabitha, though of course that wasn't her birth name. None of them used their real names. Real names were dangerous around demons—both real demon names and real human names—so none of the hunters used the names they'd been born with and none of them told anyone those names. Even Sebastian. Angie was in love with him, and she had no idea what his birth name was. To be fair, she'd only learned a bit over a week ago how he'd become a hunter, so there were some holes in their knowledge of each other. She didn't mind. She understood.

Tabitha was an interesting contrast to the rest of the group. On the one side, you had those like Gabriella and Morty, wearing business attire—Gabriella more casual Fridays and Morty more big meeting with his full suit jacket and tie—but then you had the other side with Steven and Jess in more casual clothing. Jess tended toward more colorful extravagance in their silky wrap jacket and purple pants. Steven's esthetic was more the jeans and sweater kind. Karen, someone Angie also didn't like and whom she suspected would have been happy if Morty's murder plot had succeeded, actually showed up in yoga pants and a sports bra, like she'd just come from the gym.

Angie respected people's right to dress how they wanted.

She wasn't going to insult Karen's dress sense. But the outfit, frankly, looked out of place and *cold* in the conference room.

Tabitha, on the other hand, wore a high-necked dress, simple flower patter, long sleeves, skirt to her ankles. The pale material against her dark skin was beautiful, but she looked out of another era. Reminded Angie a little of the *Little House on the Prairie* TV show. Tabitha even had sturdy boots under her dress instead of modern flats. Her dark hair was pulled up into a tight, smoothed bun, and the dots of red in the depths of her deep brown eyes were more prominent in the florescent lighting that the others. And she was, quite frankly, stunning.

Most of the hunters—outside of Sebastian—cultivated appearances that let them blend in and look relatively bland. Even Sebastain tamped down his appearance when he needed to look innocuous and unnoticeable. Aidan was so good at blending in she could quite literally vanish until she wanted people to see her. And Jess's artistic bent fit well in New York and wouldn't draw much attention here. The average hunter was a chameleon, ensuring no one looked at them twice. But Tabitha, at least here in this conference room, didn't appear to blend in even a little bit. That was curious enough to draw Angie's attention right after they'd been introduced. Since then, though, Tabitha had only spoken once, in a very quiet voice, to offer them coffee or tea and ask if they'd all recovered from their last demon fight.

They had, mostly. Enough to start planning this expedition into the demon realms. Which was why they were here. Listening to the rest of the council argue about it.

Most of the argument wasn't so much that *Angie* intended on going into the demon realms. On purpose. Though there were the usual, "You'll release a plague of demons!" arguments that were getting really old.

No, the big argument, the real pushback from the council, was the fact that Sebastian and Aidan intended on going with her.

According to the demon witch they were going to find, Sebastian and Aidan *had* to come with her, or everyone would die. They needed Carmen, too, but that was a different story and not something they could discuss in front of the council.

"Angela," Jess said, their neutral smile calm in the midst of all the arguing, "you need to see this from our point of view. You're talking about taking two of our strongest demon hunters with you into realms where… Well, not to be too blunt, but it isn't likely any of you will return."

"I returned once from a demon realm already," Angie reminded them. Actually twice. Both times with Sebastian's help.

"And brought back powers that are killing you," Morty reminded her.

"And whose fault is that?"

Technically, it wasn't Morty's fault. A hunter named Jacob had pushed her into the demon realm. He'd had a pragmatic reason for it—to prevent a plague of demons getting through—and hunters were often pragmatic to a fault. But she still blamed Morty. Mostly because she liked blaming Morty even if he wasn't the reason she'd been trapped in the hellscape.

Morty, however, would not take the unearned blame. "Jacob's. And I'm sure he doesn't regret it, given what you can do now."

"All the more reason for her not to go into a demon realm," Karen said, looking at the council instead of Angie.

The way Karen often insisted on talking to the others instead of directly to her was one of the more irritating aspects of this meeting. Angie didn't like being talked down to, and Karen talking around her felt a lot like the hunter was treating her like a child. The whole "hush, the grownups are talking" attitude in this contentious crowd was laughable as well as insulting. Especially coming from a woman dressed like she'd just come from the gym.

"Her ability to kill demons is exactly what we need," Karen said.

Angie took a deep breath through her nostrils, let it out slowly. Reined in the sparks of magic threatening to break out along her fingertips. She half-closed her eyes to ensure all her magic was as it should be, well controlled and each part staying in its own lane.

The spiderweb of her powers—the image she used to visualize all her various magics—was stable and intact. Mostly blue with her witch magic. A little bit of purple, where some magic had blended at one stage. And three distinct lines of red. One, her demon witch magic, the magic that let her open portals into demon realms, had always been there. It was the bane of her life. But that power had brought

Sebastian to her, so she couldn't entirely begrudge it. The other two lines of red had come with her out of the demon realm Jacob had pushed her into. Those were made up of magic she'd somehow taken into herself and incorporated into her web while stuck in the demon realm. Demon magic itself. And it allowed her to do something no human could do. Not even the hunters.

Kill demons.

But it also might be killing her.

Her ability to kill demons now had had some…not good repercussions. It put a target on her back that most of the demon world would aim for, hoping to eliminate a human who could kill them. And it made her valuable to all the wrong people—including the demon hunters. Everyone who found the skill useful wanted her to use it to go around murdering freed demons. Trying to convince all those parties that she was *not* in fact an assassin was proving difficult.

Her preference was to get rid of that extra magic. To return to her own magic, and only that magic. If she could get rid of the ability to open portals and just go back to being an ordinary witch, she'd do that, too. But that wasn't an option at the moment. Might never be again.

"I am not going to go around killing demons," she said to the council, her gaze on Karen, who didn't look at her. "And, once again, I'm not here to ask permission. I need answers. Those answers are currently living in the demon realm. That means I need to go."

"And we're going with her," Sebastian said, his soft

English accent broking no arguments—even though the council was big on arguments.

"You have not been giving permission," Karen snapped. Then pressed her lips together when Sebastian raised a brow.

"Since when do demon hunters need permission to hunt demons?" he asked quietly. The menace and annoyance in his voice wasn't lost on the people in that room.

Angie suppressed a grin, but only barely. She liked him like this. And she liked seeing the council temporarily put in its place.

"You're not going to hunt demons," Morty said, trying to sound reasonable and adult. "You're going to save your girlfriend. And no one survives the demon realms. Not for long."

"But we did that part already, Morty," Angie said. "And the person we're looking for has done that for years." Centuries actually, but time didn't work the same in the demon realms, so Betha hadn't actually lived for centuries, even though centuries had passed on Earth.

Discovering another demon witch, knowing there was someone else out there like her, gave Angie mixed feelings. On the one hand, Betha might just have the answers Angie needed. On the other, she had no idea if she could trust a witch who'd been living in the demon realm for so long.

"I'm not sure how often we need to say this," Steven said, "but we cannot afford to lose both Aidan and Sebastian. We can't afford it. Their loss could mean the entire world overrun with demons."

"Then the rest of you are not doing your jobs," Aidan

said. One of the few comments she'd made during this contentious meeting. "If the world rests on the shoulders of two demon hunters, there is a bigger problem than if Sebastian and I die in a demon realm. Eventually, we will both die. Then what?"

"By that time," Morty said, "we'll have more demon hunters. People to replace you. But we don't yet."

"And if we die tomorrow?" Aidan said. "It's always a possibility that we will not survive a demon fight. That's our jobs." She let her gaze travel over the council. An ordinary gaze in the face of an ordinary woman. An exterior that hid an actual legend. The red in the very depths of her brown eyes flared a little. Or that could just be a trick of the flickering, buzzing florescent bulb. "Our job is always dangerous and death always possible. That you're relying on us so heavily is bad. And it's time you started to fix that problem."

"And in the meantime," Sebastian added, "we'll be going with Angie. Because none of us *want* to die."

Angie didn't smile, because she knew it would appear smug and condescending. But she was feeling a touch smug. Or maybe just glad that she had two such strong hunters on her side, guarding her back. The way she'd guard theirs.

The conference room fell silent after Aidan and Sebastian's comments, the members of the council looking at each other expectantly. No doubt looking for some argument that would keep Angie and the others from doing what needed to be done.

Angie glanced at the coffee on the giant black table and

considered getting up to get a cup, but really, she just wanted this to be done so she could go home. They had to prepare for this expedition, and she had…things to do before they left.

After some shuffling and throat clearing, Karen finally said, "You only have the word of someone who could very well be a demon herself. Someone who can't be trusted. And likely lied. There's no reason to think if Angie went alone and no one else was there, that the rest of you would die."

A Hail Mary attempt to at least keep Aidan and Sebastian from following her. "She wasn't a demon," Angie said. She'd be inside Betha's head, in a vision. She knew the woman.

"But there had been a Khymir demon in that fight," Morty pointed out, being so reasonable she wanted to kick his leg. Good thing he was so far away, she might have been very tempted.

"More than one," Steven reminded the group pointlessly.

"And Khymir are extremely tricky," Karen said.

"Yes. I remember." The shapeshifting demons could look like anyone, sound like anyone, and were very difficult to spot. They'd caused a lot of trouble in that last fight. A lot. "This wasn't a Khymir." She raised a hand. "And before you say the Khymir fooled me with other guises, I realize that."

One Khymir had even disguised itself as Carmen, and when another demon killed that one, Angie thought Carmen had been killed.

But Carmen was a different story.

"This wasn't a Khymir," Aidan said. "In fact, she showed us the Carmen Khymir."

"A very good trick for one of the shape-changing demons

to use to gain your trust," Karen said. She glanced at Aidan but still didn't deign to look at Angie.

"And you must admit," Gabriella said, "that this isn't the first time a demon has…lured someone into a demon realm by pretending to be something or someone they're not."

Gabriella didn't look at Sebastian when she said that, and Sebastian didn't react to it. Angie wasn't even sure if Gabriella knew how Sebastian had become a demon hunter. But that comment struck very close to home.

And Gabriella was right. Sebastian had been fooled once, tricked by a demon who'd manipulated his mind. But he'd been a teenager then. Grieving lost parents. He wasn't a child anymore. And he had years of demon hunting under his belt.

That Gabriella agreed with something Karen and Morty were saying, though, gave Angie pause. She'd *known* in that moment that the person who'd stepped out of the demon world, the person who was responsible for killing a demon and his gangster minion, *was* the demon witch Betha. She'd lived in the other witch's head through two visions, using her blood in the last vision. She'd known Betha from *inside* thanks to that blood link. Angie was certain, in those moments, that she was meeting a centuries old witch.

Who…should have died centuries earlier.

And fuck it all, Gabriella was right. This absolutely could be a trick. A trick to kill Aidan and Sebastian and her and even Carmen.

This could all be a lie.

But even if it was… "We'll know soon enough if it's a lie if the person we think is Betha tires to kill us," Angie said.

"All the more reason to have two strong demon hunters and a demon witch working together. If it's a trick, we'll just… open a portal and leave. That's what I do. Remember."

She held Morty's gaze with this last. He had threatened her family once. He'd been working to try and get her killed for months now. He was certain she would one day go crazy and release a demon hoard on the world.

And, like it or not, he had valid reasons for that fear. The history of demon witches was littered with blood and death and destruction.

A direction she did not want to go. One she was actively trying to avoid.

She was never going to convince Morty of that, though. But according to Morty, she was dying. "Besides," she said, still holding his gaze, "I'm already dead anyway. Aren't I?"

He gave a shoulder shrug. "And if you die before you can open a portal and send Aidan and Sebastian home?"

That was a terrifying thought that she tried hard not to let sink in. She hated, on my levels, that Morty made any salient points at all. But this was one. "I'll have two hunters with me to prevent demons from killing me," she said. "And if I feel like I'm dying of this…other thing, then I'll send them home immediately."

She wasn't sure Sebastian would go and leave her behind in that situation. But they'd cross that bridge if it came.

"What if you come out with even more of this new demon magic?" Steven asked. "What if going into the demon realm is what this…possible demon witch wants because it will make you even more dangerous than you already are?"

That was a horrifying thought. Angie wanted to get *rid* of what she'd picked up there, not gain *more* of the terrible magic.

"And what if, like Betha, you can't come back?" Gabriella asked quietly. "What if this becomes a one-way trip?"

Angie couldn't think about that. "Betha only stayed because of Eloise. It's Eloise that can't come back, not Betha."

Gabriella nodded. "And we don't know why."

True. But that was one of the questions Angie intended on getting answers to. One of the many things she needed to understand and wouldn't without talking to Betha.

"Three hunters are going into this," Jess reminded them gently, their gaze on Angie. "If we lose any of you, we lose a hunter."

Angie was forever forgetting she was supposed to technically be a hunter, even though they all agreed she was bad at it. Her talents lay elsewhere.

"Some of you don't mind losing me, though," Angie said with a shrug. It was true. No point in them dancing around it. Everyone sitting in that room knew what had happened in New Mexico.

"None of this changes anything," Sebastian said, his voice deep and his attention arrowed in on Morty. But he skimmed his gaze over the rest of the council. "As Angie said, this isn't a request. We're going. This Betha might have a cure for Angie's…condition. Or at least some answers. If it's a trick, we'll deal with that. Prepare for the possibility before we go in. But if there's even a chance for answers, we're going."

"All of us," Aidan added.

"Doing so will be suicide," Karen said. "Reckless suicide."

"Not if I can help it," Angie said. Karen still wouldn't look at her, so she made eye contact with the rest of the board. Tabitha and Gabriella were the only ones not frowning. Even Jess frowned, though their frown was more sad and gentle than an angry scowl. "And I will do everything—and I mean everything—in my power to ensure we all get home. We all know my power is not insignificant."

Not before New Mexico, but even more significant since.

Because Angie could kill demons now.

CHAPTER TWO

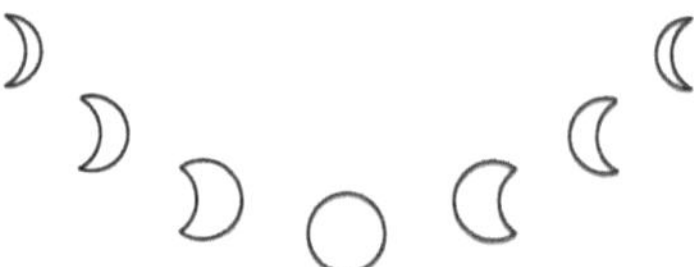

When Angie and the others finally walked out of the conference room, they'd succeeded at convincing absolutely no one that this was a good idea. And in fact, Angie had more doubts now than she had going in. She'd been so intent on getting answers, and *knowing* those answers lay with Betha, she hadn't considered all the possible dangers and drawback.

She'd considered the dangers of going into a demon realm, of course. Her worst nightmare, and she was walking right into it. Only her need for answers and resolution could hope to overcome that fear. But now she worried that who she thought of as Betha might not actually be the centuries old demon witch with answers.

"What do you two think?" she asked once they were safely ensconced in the midday pedestrian traffic in Midtown Manhattan.

The crowds pressed in around them without getting too close, probably thanks to Aidan and Sebastian *willing* the people to give them some room. The midday heat warmed Angie's skin. Summer was close and soon the humidity would envelope the city. But for the moment, the breeze was strong enough to keep the temperatures manageable. Half a block away, a food truck sold coffee and bagels to the tourists, but the smell of warmed bagels and roasting coffee grounds was lost amidst the smell of hot tarmac and too many cars in one place.

Without discussing it, they all turned to walk downtown, which took them in the direction of Angie's small apartment in Greenwich Village. Though she suspected Sebastian would swing them all into a restaurant along the way to ensure Angie ate. She'd eaten before the meeting, because she did not want to go into that confrontation hungry and irritable. She'd still ended up irritable, so that part didn't work. But she hadn't been starving during most of the meeting. That was good.

She was hungry now, though. And she'd need to eat soon. But they could walk for a while and talk before her body demanded some calories.

"Do we think we should still go?" she asked. "I hadn't really considered that Betha might not be Betha. How would a demon have known to take her form? How could any of them know?"

"Demons are manipulative," Sebastian said quietly.

They were holding hands because she'd locked down her touch psychic sensitivity and they could. She had had enough rest and recovery time to ensure she didn't read anyone on accident anyway. Which was nice because she liked being able to hold his hand.

"Yes, but…when? When would one have thought to use the Betha form. And then show us the dead Khymir that wasn't actually Carmen. And before that killing all the other demons."

During that fight, one very powerful demon and his human minion had been killed by energy that came out of a portal Angie had opened. A portal into a demon world she'd never seen before. A portal she hadn't been able to close after, because, at the time, she'd thought the demon witch who came through had held it open.

She'd assumed the woman who came through, who looked like the demon witch from the sixteenth century, was *the* demon witch because she'd killed dozens of demons.

Humans couldn't kill demons. It wasn't possible. Only demons could kill other demons.

Or so everyone thought. But when Angie had accidentally incorporated demon magic into her web of powers, after being stuck in a demon realm with Sebastian and Carmen, she could suddenly kill demons. In her quest to find a way to get the demon magic out of her, to fix whatever it was she'd done to herself, she'd spent several sessions in the hunters most secret archive, going through all they had on demon witches—which wasn't nearly as much as they'd wanted her to believe they had—and discovered that another demon witch, a very long time ago, had opened multiple portals and had taken in demon magic, and could kill demons.

Very little of that was actually *written* in the records. A lot of information about this witch, Betha, Angie had gleaned from visions. Right down to knowing what Betha even looked like and knowing her name. Those things weren't written down. The hunters had had no idea *who* she was until Angie's visions.

So why would a demon assume Angie would know?

When she said as much to her companions, Aidan said, "There are mimic demons who can slide into your thoughts if you're not prepared to lock them out. You were pretty busy in that moment and you thought you'd just watched a…an acquaintance die. You would have been vulnerable to that kind of thing."

"You think that's what happened?" She glanced at the legendary hunter strolling beside them.

Aidan wasn't a person who stood out in a crowd. On purpose. A smidge taller than average height—so shorter than Angie—not too thin, not too fat, not too pretty, not too *not-pretty*. Dressed casually in jeans and a plane black t-shirt. If you didn't look deep into her brown eyes and spot that tiny flash of red, you might not realize Aidan was anything but ordinary. Though the aggressiveness of the ordinary might give her away to someone paying attention. If that didn't, the red in the eyes surely would. At least for those who knew what demon hunters were. Ordinary, mundane humans might just think that red was a trick of the light.

"No," Aidan said. "I think we spoke to a centuries old demon witch." She shrugged. "But the other is a possibility. The problem with that logic is that the demon would have to have gotten into my head and Sebastian's head as well as yours in those moments."

"Neither of you knew what Betha was supposed to look like. Why would the demon need to worm into your heads?"

"Because if not, we'd seen through the guise." Aidan glanced at her, smiling faintly. "We'd see a demon. It is sort of what we do."

"There was no demon inside my head," Sebastian said. "They haven't been able to do that to me since I was a kid."

The reminder of his past, of the time when he'd become a hunter, made her heart hurt for him a little, so she squeezed his hand. She'd only just learned his origin story. Most hunters never talked about it. Sebastian had been no exception. But he'd told her just before their last demon fight. And now, she had a deeper understanding of the impact the demon world had had on him.

Because when he was only twelve, he'd had to watch his parents run into a demon realm and never return. When he'd gone in after them to try and rescue them, in the split second before Aidan had pulled him out, a demon had latched onto his mind and buried a bit of itself there. Two years later, it convinced an angry, scared, fourteen-year-old Sebastian to let it out of the demon realm by pretending to be Sebastian's father.

The manipulation and duplicity of demons was something he was intimately acquainted with.

Angie hated that this situation would bring those memories up for him. But on the other hand, he was in a unique position to *know* what it was like to have a demon manipulate him into seeing and hearing what he wanted to see and hear.

Angie hadn't exactly *wanted* to see and hear a real Betha in real life. She'd been good with attempting visions to get her answers, having assumed the witch had died centuries ago. But having access to the real person was definitely a bonus.

But she just couldn't believe a demon would have been able to pull off that ruse. Especially with two demon hunters right there, one who'd *had* a demon mess with his mind before. Sebastian would have recognized the signs. Right?

"Maybe," he said. "I would have if the demon had tried to mess with me. But that doesn't mean one couldn't have been messing with you."

"Well this is just irritating." She hated when the council had a valid point. They were already pains in her ass. She didn't want to deal with them also being smug.

"Something that was inside that world was strong enough to kill Fredericks," Aidan said. "A Khymir couldn't have done that. And it wasn't just the realm itself being incompatible with all those demons that resulted in them being destroyed every time they went through that portal. Powerful blasts were coming *out* of the realm. If this is a demon trying to look like Betha, it would be a very neat trick. And it wouldn't be a beast like a Khymir. They're strong and dangerous, but not higher-level-demon, like Fredericks, dangerous."

That was oddly reassuring. In a weird way. Except for the

part about it potentially being a demon stronger than Fredericks that was pretending to be Betha.

Angie sighed. They'd spent a week, all three of them, recovering and resting and getting themselves ready to try this. They'd had numerous discussions about *how* to do it in a way that protected them all. And they'd talked about the possibility that Betha wasn't their friend and had some nefarious purpose in store for them.

They hadn't considered this wasn't even Betha.

But... Angie needed to take this chance. So far, she wasn't dying because of the magic she'd absorbed. But there had been no direct answers in the hunters' secret archive. Just more questions. They had to look elsewhere. Though most everyone else thought her being able to kill demons was great, she did not. And Sebastian did not.

The ability put a target on her back. The other demons would be coming soon.

And there was still the looming possibility that it would kill her. How could a human possible hold demon magic and survive?

She wanted the magic out. To get rid of it and return to her ordinary witch magic. She'd even tolerate her demon witch ability. Though, being honest with herself, she was looking for a way to get rid of that, too. With no more demon magic, or demon witch magic, she could return to being just a witch.

Except...

Angie's greatest fear wasn't actually that Betha was really a demon in disguise. Her greatest fear was that Betha—who was still living in the demon realm and killing demons and had not in all this time gotten rid of her ability to do so—might not have any answers at all. Or her only answer was that Angie was stuck with all this power.

Thinking of that left Angie breathless and panicky, so she shoved it aside. One thing at a time. One worry at a time.

"We're still doing this?" Aidan asked.

"We're still doing this," Angie agreed. "But maybe we keep the possibility that she's really a demon in disguise in mind."

"Fair enough."

"We still need to find Carmen," Sebastian pointed out.

Carmen was the fourth person supposed to go into the demon realms with them. Betha had warned that if all four of them didn't go together, they would all die. Angie had no idea how that was possible, and she didn't trust Carmen as far as she could throw her. But Carmen *had* helped Angie's friends and work colleagues when they'd needed it, saving lives in the process, so Angie had to accept the woman wasn't all bad. Just mostly bad.

Angie was still processing her feelings from when a Khymir demon had fooled her into thinking Carmen had been killed. Those had been very bad, complex moments.

"You know Carmen," she said. "She'll show up last minute like it was all part of some plan." Mostly just to irritate Angie.

"She'll be there," Aidan said. "She's as curious as the rest of us. And less restrained about following her curiosity."

Angie snort-laughed at that.

Aidan nodded to a half-empty Italian restaurant. "Let's eat. I'm hungry. And there's no hunts tonight."

Angie needed food too. And then she needed to go to another meeting. One she was dreading even more than the meeting with the hunters.

A meeting with her bosses.

CHAPTER THREE

Because this wasn't the sort of conversation Angie wanted overheard by the other employees, she'd requested a meeting with her bosses on neutral ground, expecting them to pick a café or restaurant in the area. Instead, they invited her into their home.

She'd never been to Dana and Omar's apartment. She'd worked for them for almost three years now, and in all that time, they'd been excellent bosses, but they kept a certain distance between themselves and their employees. She couldn't really blame them. Despite the casualness of Dana's Cauldron, a place for all things witchy and pagan, it was still a business. And they were still the bosses. Great bosses, to be sure. Protective and understanding and kind. But still the ones signing the paychecks and having to do the hiring and firing when necessary.

For most of the time she'd worked as a psychic at Dana's,

she'd had no problems and had only had to even call out sick once, with a cold. She'd been a model employee, mostly because she loved her work so much. It wasn't difficult to go in every day.

But when she could no longer run away from her demon hunter issues, when Sebastian and the hunters had come back into her life, things had gotten more complicated.

She still tried never to miss a scheduled work day. And if she had to, she made up for it. She never called out when she had regulars booked. And she covered for any of the other psychics if they needed time so that she earned herself goodwill.

Going to New Mexico had been a long trip, though. She'd needed to retrain her magic, to regain control of it. And fortunately, her bosses had understood that. They were both witches too. She hadn't gone into all the details. There were things about the demon hunters she couldn't tell them even if she wanted to. And there were things about her own magic she didn't want them to necessarily know—especially this newest ability to kill demons.

They'd given her lots of time off while she'd needed to be in New Mexico. And they'd been very patient with her since she got back. They'd even kept her employed after her demon trouble spilled over into their place of business and endangered their employees and some of their customers. They had her back, went out of their way to look after everyone, and they hadn't fired her on the spot.

She suspected Dana and Omar actually knew more about her and the demon-related world than she'd admitted to them.

Dana hadn't even hesitated when Angie told her a Khymir demon had snuck into the store. The older witch had known exactly what that demon was, and the danger it posed, and gone into action.

Angie had never been so grateful for an employer before in her life.

Which was one of the reasons, the many reasons, she was dreading this meeting.

Their home was the entire top floor of a building that had gone through many iterations but was now mostly retail space and a handful of offices. Dana and Omar had held on to their loft, because after living above their own business for the first ten years of its existence, they were keen on keeping some distance between them and the business now. Not that their home in Soho was all that far away from Dana's Cauldron's location in the Village, but it was far enough.

The loft was huge, two stories tall and almost entirely open. It was also almost industrial looking in its details, which Angie hadn't expected. There were exposed steel beams, and an entire brick wall to one side. The circular staircase up to the bedroom loft was silver steel. The loft itself was walled in with wire and clear plexiglass. The couch and chairs and coffee table that made up their "living room nook" were all modern and sleek and thinly cushioned. The giant, floor-to-ceiling windows that looked across Houston Street gave a spectacular city view on one side, and a view all the way to the Hudson River on the other. The kitchen was open and filled with shiny new silver appliances. And the art on the walls was very modern abstract.

The aesthetic was so different to Dana's Cauldron it was a little jarring. The only thing in the place that looked even remotely like it might fit into their business was the handwoven rugs scattered around the polished, hardwood floors and the two distinct altars set up against the brink wall, underneath the bedroom loft.

The place was sparkling clean, there was no clutter, and Angie's footsteps echoed when she walked inside, before stepping onto one of the woven rugs.

Dana had opened the door for her, and when she saw Angie scanning the loft, she grinned. "We've been trying something new. I kind of like the minimalism. Definitely feels different to the store."

"Yeah it does," Angie said. There was the faint scent of incense in the air, once she was inside, and the smokey warmth of candles just blown out. That, at least, was something she could associate with her bosses.

Omar stood in the kitchen, a stove-top kettle in hand. "Tea or coffee?" he asked.

"Anything is fine." Angie's stomach was tight and her palms sweating. She'd been worried about this for a week, and now that the time was upon her, she was too anxious to think about food or drink. Which was a definite sign of her nerves since Angie always needed to eat.

Omar gave her a wink and put the kettle on the stove. "I'll surprise you. I've been working on something."

Dana led Angie to the thin-cushioned couch in the living room nook. "Don't worry, he's quite good at these little experiments. And I've tried this. It is good."

"Tea?"

"Chai, but with his own spice blend."

That actually sounded amazing, and if she weren't so nervous, Angie would be looking forward to the drink.

"Sit." Dana waved to the couch. "What can we do for you?"

Angie settled on the uncomfortable looking couch, weirdly grateful it turned out to be as uncomfortable as it looked because it was easier to sit straight and she was always going to be sitting on the edge of the cushions anyway.

But when she opened her mouth to speak, nothing came out at first. She scowled. Where did she start? She'd thought through some of the things she wanted to say, needed to say, but she hadn't really planned how to actually *start* the conversation.

Which she said aloud as Omar joined them, handing her a handmade mug with a starburst on one side of the blue glazed ceramic and another mug with a pentagram on the red background to Dana.

Dana smiled up at him as she took her mug. She'd settled in one of the plastic chairs bracketing the couch that looked as uncomfortable as the couch, but she seemed relaxed enough. Omar settled on the coffee table, facing Angie. Since the coffee table was made of see through plastic, the position worried Angie for a moment until it was clear the table was stronger than it looked.

Her bosses were both in their late sixties, though Dana might be pushing seventy—she waved away age as a concept and didn't admit to anything. They were dressed casually, Dana in wide-legged linen trousers and a red turtleneck shirt that suited her light brown complexion. She had immaculate makeup on, subtle and flawless, highlighting her hazel eyes. And she had her long white hair wound around her head in a messy, fall-over-any-minute bun. The contrast between perfect makeup and messy hair was a very Dana look.

Omar's full beard and mustache were neatly shaped and trimmed short, full silver to match his thick mane of silver hair. His dark tan skin showed his age around dark brown eyes, but his strong features seemed made for this era of life, giving him both gravitas and the sort of character that drew people. He was a kind man, who looked like a retired warrior monk. He wore a pair of black silk pants under a green silk robe embroidered with branch and vine patterns. Neither of them were wearing shoes, but Dana had waved off Angie's offer to remove her own shoes when she came in, and Angie was too nervous to argue.

"Why don't you just get to the meat of it," Omar said, with a gentle smile. "No need to pretty things up for us."

Angie let out a small chuckle, glanced out the huge windows. The day was bright and she knew there was a lot of traffic below on Houston, but none of the sound traveled through those huge windows.

Okay. Straight to the meat of it. "I… I'm going to need more time off," she said bluntly. "But I don't even know how much. I have no idea how long I'll be gone." Or if she'd come back at all. But she was afraid to even suggest that out loud. "So I completely understand if this means you can't hold my job for me. I've already taken advantage of your generosity enough. I know that. And then I went and brought demons to your store, and endangered your employees, and now I need to…leave again. It's not fair to you, or the other psychics or employees, so… So. Yeah."

Dana frowned over her mug. "Are you handing in your resignation?"

"I don't want to quit," she admitted. "But I can't ask you to hold my job."

"Why not?" Omar asked, reasonably, smiling.

"I…" She hadn't been except that response. She had no idea how to answer it. Mostly because what she'd just said should have made the answer obvious.

Omar chuckled. "Angie, you are an excellent psychic. One of our best. And most requested. Your regulars miss you when you're gone and would be very disappointed to hear you'd quit. Worse yet if we fired you! Now, if you gave us reason, we would fire you. Of course."

"Of course," she said hoarsely.

"But you've never given us reason."

"The demons…"

Dana waved that away. "We run a store for witches. Do you think this is the first time demons have come into our store? Why do you think we started drawing the circle around the place?"

One of the things Angie had loved best about Dana's Cauldron was that every year, Dana and Omar built a special circle around the store. It made anyone who came in intending harm to anyone inside the store restless and itchy to leave. It grated against them until they couldn't stand to be inside and left quickly. Occasionally, dangerous people did walk into Dana's, including demons. But they walked right back out again.

And until they did, there were a whole bunch of witches around to defend the mundane humans and take care of each other.

She'd felt at home in Dana's the instant she'd walked into the place. And the added bonus of it being a safe space made it her home away from home.

The demon that had gotten through just a week ago, disguised as a customer, had been jumpy and restless even before Carmen had pointed out it was a demon. It had only stayed inside the store so long at that point because a fight started.

That was the incident Angie had been sure would result in her being fired. That they'd kept her on after had been such a relief. And now, here she was asking for more time off.

"It's not fair of me," she said.

"Fair." Omar huffed. "If life was fair, there'd be no starving children and there would be world peace. Fair is an aspiration, but not current reality."

"That's very pessimistic of you, my love," Dana said fondly.

He grinned back as if she'd just given him a compliment.

Angie raised her brows.

Dana chuckled. "What we're telling you, in our own way, is that you have yet to do anything that we either haven't seen before or are not prepared to deal with. Our store, and our lives, are not…mundane. And we do not expect our magical employees to function the way a mundane human can function."

"It's a shame we can't sometimes," Omar said. "But it is what it is."

Angie looked between them, her throat thick with emotions she was working very hard to hold in. She didn't cry in front of people if she could help it. Certainly not her bosses! But she'd just broke down and bawled in front of her friends and coworkers at the store last week, so maybe this was her now.

"I don't know what to say."

"Tell us if there's anything we can do to help," Dana said.

"No. I can't even really talk about it."

"Then we won't pry," Omar said. "Privacy is as important as flexibility in our world."

"Just know, you have a job when you get back," Dana said.

Omar nodded. "And if you need someone to look after your cactuses while you're gone, just let me know. I quite love cacti."

Angie shook her head and didn't try to hide the single tear that slipped over her cheek. "Thank you. I was dreading this conversation because I didn't want to quit."

"Glad we could put that worry to rest," Omar said. "Now, for the important part. How is that chai, and should we serve it in the café?"

CHAPTER FOUR

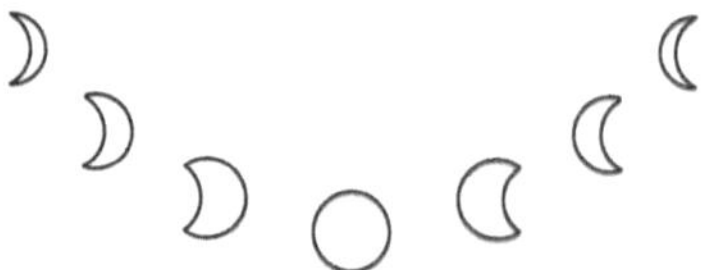

Angie was staring at the medallion her mentor Esmerelda had given her in New Mexico when her doorbell rang. She wasn't expecting anyone, and no one had rung up from downstairs to be let in. Sebastian was out settling some things—she hadn't asked too closely what he had to settle—and then picking up food. Aidan had disappeared to do Aidan things—Angie didn't ask. She didn't get people dropping in, not even work people, without prior arrangement. And her neighbors only rang her doorbell unexpectedly if they'd picked up some of her mail on accident. When that happened, they often as not just slipped the mail under the door—she knew and was friendly with her neighbors, but they all went about doing their own thing and rarely interacted. She liked that about her building.

She considered ignoring the buzz, because she wasn't in

the mood for small talk with a neighbor who was trying to be more friendly, and she wasn't in the mood for dealing with someone who wasn't supposed to be in the building.

And if it was someone dangerous, well, she had wards on her door and was, even now, reciting a shield spell. She didn't want to deal with dangerous unexpected either, though.

Angie needed to call her parents and her brothers. Because if she didn't come back, she didn't want to just disappear on them. She wanted to say a few baby words to her niece, make sure both her brothers were doing well, check in with her dad to see how his soccer teams were doing since the season was ending, and then she wanted to have a nice long talk with her mom.

Whether or not she'd tell them about all this…

That's why she was staring at Esmerelda's medallion. Hunting for wisdom. The conversation with her bosses had gone remarkably well, and she was still a little emotional over their support. But they were witches, and as they'd pointed out, used to the supernatural world. Outside of Angie's mother, who was more kitchen witch with small magics and a close coven of friends who liked to meet a couple times a month to chat and exchange recipes, the rest of her family were mundane. Perfectly ordinary people who'd normally have no idea demons were real and magic the likes of which Angie could do really existed.

Her family did know about her magic, and her ability to open portals, and outside of her younger brother Christopher who wanted nothing to do with supernatural things these days, her family was quite accepting of who she was. No one had ever made her feel scary or abnormal or dangerous or wrong. Or like she didn't belong in the family. She was loved unconditionally, and she loved them the same way. Even her brothers who could bug the shit out of her at times were the best brothers and she'd fight anyone who said differently.

The thought of disappearing into a demon realm and they never knew what happened to her was horrible. Not something she wanted to do to them. Or to herself.

But explaining what she was about to do, on purpose…

That was going to be a difficult conversation. As bad as the one she'd anticipated having with her bosses. Worse, because she couldn't quit her family to keep them safe from getting hurt.

The doorbell buzzed again, insistently this time. Someone holding it for a long time before releasing it. Then through the door, she heard, "Angie, I know you're just sitting there. Answer the door."

Gabriella?

Okay, that was not what she'd been expecting and it was very weird. The older hunter was not someone who dropped by unexpectedly. Gabriella knew where Angie lived, but she'd never been here. And they'd said all they needed to say at that frustratingly pointless meeting with the council. She couldn't imagine what Gabriella would want.

Given Angie's very recent experience with a Khymir, though, she didn't take the identity of the person on the other side of her door for granted. She was much more… leery of people she was supposed to know who she met unexpectedly since the last demon fight. Probably she should have been all along. It surprised her how unguarded she was sometimes, given the world she lived in. Even when she thought she had herself well guarded and insulated from surprises.

She had a shield spell up and had stacked an illusion spell and a confusion spell in the wings by the time she'd made her slow way to the door. She peeked out the little peephole and sure enough, Gabriella was standing outside. Looking impatient and annoyed.

She was also carrying a large cloth reusable shopping bag with pictures of fruits and vegetables decorating it.

That was…unusual. The last time she'd seen Gabriella with a reusable shopping bag, she'd been collecting a dangerous artifact from Sebastian.

Angie opened her three locks and slid the chain off the hook. When she opened the door, Gabriella was scowling at her.

"Why have I been waiting for ten minutes out here in this hallway?"

"Because you didn't text me ahead of time to tell me you were coming, I don't get unexpected guests, and my last fight involved Khymirs."

Gabriella's mouth flattened but she gave in with a shrug. "I didn't text because I want no evidence of this visit. I didn't know you didn't get people dropping in, though I should have expected that. And I forgot about the Khymirs. I need to come inside for this, though. So I will give you permission to touch my hand and reassure yourself I'm not a demon. For ten seconds max. If you can avoid it, don't read any deeper than that."

This was a big deal offer from a demon hunter. They avoided her touch because they knew she could see far more than they wanted her to. She didn't blame them. She didn't want to see too much into most hunters lives and psyches either. The entire council had purposefully never allowed her to touch them in case she read them. Either on purpose or, occasionally lately, even possibly on accident. That one of them would allow it to reassure her they weren't a demon meant that Gabriella really wanted to come inside and had something very serious to talk about.

Angie's gaze dropped to the bag Gabriella was carrying. Then she said, "Put your hand out, palm up. I won't need more than a second. I barely had to touch the one who'd disguised itself as Carmen.

And that wasn't an experience she hoped to repeat. But eliminating the possibility now was important.

Gabriella held her hand out in front of her, palm up, her mouth as tight as her bun, hiding her emotions otherwise. Angie didn't abuse the trust. She set her fingertips against Gabriella's skin for a second, no more. She really didn't need much to know the person standing in front of her was a person and not a demon.

A person who could will her not to know much about them. So again, the openness was telling.

And, if Angie were being honest, a little scary.

She stood back and let Gabriella. "Would you like some coffee, tea?"

"No thank you." Gabriella moved from the short hallway, past Angie's closed bedroom and bathroom doors, into the main room of the apartment and looked around.

The kitchen was open to the living room, separated by a counter where Angie had her microwave and some stacks of protein bars and tea. One wall of the apartment was brick, a detail Angie loved, and the fireplace in that brick wall, though blocked off and not a working fireplace anymore, had made a great space for her cactus garden. The windows at the far end of the apartment looked out over a side street in the Village, giving her a nice view but not too much traffic noise. And her neighbors' windows were far enough away, she didn't have to worry about people looking in through her open curtains all the time. She kept her altar under that window, the small wooden cabinet currently cleared of any ceremonial paraphernalia. But the smell of candle and incense and tea lingered in the air of her space, not unlike it had at her bosses' loft.

Angie loved her little apartment. But she wondered what Gabriella saw when she looked around. It was small, and nothing like the grand mansion in the city where visiting hunters lived. Angie didn't know what sort of place Gabriella lived in. Maybe it was a simple apartment. Or maybe she lived in a fancy place on the Upper East Side. Angie wasn't really sure she wanted to know. But she was passing curious about what Gabriella saw when she looked at Angie's living space.

"It suits you," Gabriella said with a shrug. She didn't

smile, but she didn't scowl either, so Angie took the comment as a compliment.

"Would you like a seat?" Angie gestured to the couch.

"No. I can't stay long. It's important no one knows I've been here."

"Even Sebastian and Aidan?"

"I doubt they'll say anything to anyone, and they are going with you, so I suppose they must know, but... It will complicate my life significantly if anyone, on the council specifically, finds out about this meeting."

"You're freaking me out, Gabriella."

She lifted the shopping bag. "I've brought you something that I think will be useful in your quest. I still think it's a bad idea. But if there's something I can do to help you get home safely, well... We still need Sebastian and Aidan quite a lot."

Angie rolled her lips into her mouth so she wouldn't smile at that. "And me?"

"You're very useful too."

"Such a flatterer."

Gabriella snorted. "Do you want my help or not?"

"So long as it's not putting you in danger."

Gabriella blinked at that. And Angie wondered why she looked so surprised. Did she seriously think Angie would *want* her endangered? She'd assumed Gabriella thought better of her.

"Yes. Well." Gabriella shoved the bag in Angie's direction. "These are delicate. Be *careful* with them." She let out a sharp breath through her nose. "Well, as careful as you can be, given where you're going."

Angie took the bag gently, frowning. She wasn't entirely sure what she expected to find—some secret demon hunter weapon, a collection of magical artifacts, protein bars so she didn't pass out trekking through demon realms—but what was inside the bag left her breathless.

A small, simple book with a plane outer cover, and a portfolio folder filled with yellowing pages. Angie looked up at Gabriella in time to see the small red dots in the depths of her brown eyes flare.

"This isn't…" Angie took a deep breath. "I thought these couldn't leave the archive."

"They can't. They haven't." Gabriella lifted her chin.

"I see." Angie looked into the bag again.

The small book was a diary. A diary written by a woman several centuries ago, about her lover—a demon witch who opened multiple portals onto the demon world and was looking for some sort of "medicine." The portfolio folder filled with documents… Angie was sure those were the records of a demon hunter's encounter with a demon witch several centuries ago. A witch who killed a demon in front of him and who opened portals into demon realms.

Thanks to Angie opening her psychic senses to each of these documents, she learned they were about the same demon witch. She even learned her name.

Betha.

Until her visions, the hunters hadn't known these two documents were related or described the same witch. They had an idea of the time period for the demon hunter Yusuf's record of his fight with the witch—which it turned out hadn't been a fight—but they didn't have any specific date for the diary.

Thanks to these two documents, Angie knew that not only had Betha opened multiple realms, not only had she absorbed something in those demon realms, she could and did kill demons. Despite being human.

Gabriella had told her, after the fight with Sokolov's demon, that Yusuf claiming the witch had killed a demon had always been considered…literary license, even though Yusuf couldn't "literary" if his life depended on it. The hunters had dismissed the idea that the witch had *really* killed a demon because they *knew* humans couldn't do that. Yusuf had also been wounded and this record taken down while he was in hospital, so his recollection of what had happened was taken with a grain of salt.

But in Angie's visions, she'd *known* Betha could kill demons. From inside Betha's perspective.

She'd also learned that the "infection" Betha had picked up in the demon realms, the infection that she thought she'd passed to her lover Eloise and that was killing Eloise, was what allowed Betha to kill demons.

The links were impossible to ignore.

Angie ensured her psychic senses were well controlled before she reached into the bag to pull out the diary. Eloise had written this. Before the "infection" had taken her. She'd been very vague about the incidents she was writing about, and for good reason, so a lot of what Angie knew about her had come from the visions. She'd even seen Betha through

Eloise's eyes, seen Betha open multiple portals in a way Angie hadn't even know was possible.

There as a lot she hadn't known was possible until these two documents.

"Why are you giving me these?" she asked quietly, looking up at Gabriella."

"Because I think some of the answers you seek are in there…somewhere. Buried in the document and the thoughts of the people who wrote them. Things that only you can find and decipher. The documents aren't helpful in the archive. They might help you. And if they do, if they bring all of you back unscathed, or at least only scathed enough you still survive, then it will be worth the risk of you taking them."

"And if I don't come back?" she asked quietly.

"Then they'll be lost," Gabriella said pragmatically. "And I'll probably have to deal with the consequences of giving them to you. But the hole in our knowledge of demon witches will not be much worse than it is now."

The demon hunters had wanted her to believe they knew everything there was to know about demon witches. But they didn't. They knew more than Angie. But after she'd been allowed to see everything they kept in the archive finally, it turned out they didn't know nearly as much as they'd claimed.

"You might also need…help in dealing with this witch," Gabriella said. "Can't hurt to have some evidence of your knowledge." She didn't meet Angie's gaze as she said this, her gaze skimming over the apartment again.

"I'll bring these back to you," Angie said.

"Don't make promises you can't keep." Gabriella straightened her shirtsleeves. "I have to go now." She turned toward the front door without waiting for Angie, but turned back at the hallway. "Take care. Stay safe. You would be… missed, if you didn't return. And not just because you're a horrible but useful demon hunter."

Angie stood in place contemplating Gabriella's last words long after the apartment door closed behind her.

CHAPTER FIVE

"Ican't believe she let these out of the archive," Sebastian said as they sat on Angie's couch, contemplating the diary and documents Gabriella had brought her, spread out on her coffee table.

Angie had her legs folded under her, her hand wrapped around a mug of chamomile tea, as she resisted the urge to touch the documents with her psychic senses open. Getting sucked into a vision while in her own home, with Sebastian and Aidan both there, wouldn't be too bad. But the last time she'd gone into a vision with Betha, she'd accidentally opened a portal into a demon realm and nearly loosed demons onto the archive. Gabriella had had to hold them off while *also* trying to pull Angie from the vision. Not a fun afternoon.

Aidan, from the kitchen where she was bumping around

making pasta for their dinner, said, "I can't believe she hasn't insisted on going with us."

"Why would she do that?" Angie asked. She kept her gaze on the secret documents because she was a little afraid if she looked away they'd somehow vanish.

"Couple of reasons, not least is curiosity," Aidan said, dropping penne pasta into a big pot of boiling water. "Why do you think she's spent so much time in the archive herself."

"I have no idea," Angie said honestly. "She hasn't been very chatty about herself with me."

"Gabriella loves information. Lives by it." Aidan gave the pots and pans on Angie's stove a satisfied nod, then came around the cabinet to stand over the coffee table. "Morty wants everyone to believe he knows everything, but Gabriella has spent more time in the archive. She's learned a lot more about…well, everything, than Morty has ever bothered to do. He assumes because the archive is secret from most hunters, they won't know enough to know he's lying."

"But Gabriella does."

"Gabriella does."

"Then why doesn't she call him out on those lies?"

"Politics." Aidan shrugged.

"I hate politics," Angie said with a scowl. "At least I hate political machinations and deceit."

"Welcome to the club," Sebastian said, raising his mug to Aidan in a solute.

Aidan smiled and nodded down to the documents. "I think Gabriella would love to know…everything about this history. It's been a lost element in our knowledge. And if she weren't afraid of you opening another portal, she probably would have let you back into the archive to read more of these there. But with us going into demon realms voluntarily now… That wasn't something she'd get past the council."

"She said you'd been to the archive. A few times." Angie finally glanced up to look Aidan directly in the eyes.

"I have." Aidan nodded. "The history keepers over the years have been more…accommodating."

"Where you looking for something in particular?"

"Sometimes."

Angie waited for her to elaborate. In vain. She sighed and glanced down at the documents again. "I would like to open to these again before we go into this little adventure of ours. But I'm afraid to."

"Afraid of another portal opening?" Aidan asked.

"Afraid I'll see Betha's death."

"That would save us a trip," Aidan said.

"And destroy any chance I have of actually getting some answers."

"Not necessarily. There are a lot of documents in that secret archive. Probably plenty of secrets your psychic talents can uncover. I'm sure Gabriella would accommodate that so long as you agreed to share what you learned."

"But the rest of the council will not go along with that."

Aidan sighed and nodded, heading back into the kitchen. "They'd be…trickier."

"I think…" Angie paused before saying, "I need to tell

you both something before we do this. It's important. I don't think it'll affect us because…well demon realm. But. It's important."

Sebastian frowned at her, turning on the couch a little to give her his full attention. He'd long since finished his tea and set the empty mug on the floor near the couch.

She glanced at him, then at Aidan, then back to the documents. "I'm getting really tired when I don't use my magic," she said, going right to the point of things. "If I don't tap all that power regularly… I'm getting really tired."

Aidan paused in mid-stir in the kitchen to stare at her. Sebastian's frown turned fierce.

Angie winced. Yeah, she'd known this wasn't going to go over well. She'd mentioned it to Esmerelda when she'd noticed it first, right after coming out of the demon world with this new magic. They'd hoped it was just a temporary thing. Which was why Angie hadn't mentioned it to the others. But it was still a thing, even if it proved ultimately to be temporary. And they were about to go into a very dangerous situation. Sebastian and Aidan both needed to know where she was at, magically speaking.

"It's a bit like the way I used to get tired when I overextended using magic. The first time I tapped the demon witch magic directly and then had to sleep for a day. When I was first training and I'd push too hard in spellwork until I exhausted myself. Like that. After the incident in New Mexico, though, I wasn't exhausted. Despite wielding a lot of magic, tapping the demon magic, the demon witch magic, killing two demons… I wasn't exhausted. And I haven't been getting tired after using my magic, even when I use a lot of it."

"You were completely wiped out after that fight with Sokolov's demon and the other demons. You used a lot of magic then, all three kinds, and then nearly fell asleep in the café at Dana's Cauldron after." Sebastian pointed out all the obvious points.

"But I didn't collapse, did I? I didn't actually pass out. I just got sleepy. And that was emotional exhaustion. Worry and fear and terror of what almost happened with my friends." She looked at Aidan over the counter in her kitchen, then back to Sebastian. "I had used a *lot* of magic that day. Two visions, one of which opened a demon portal. A challenge with a demon that required will, opening two portals for the first time. Fighting a hoard of demons with you two using both witch and demon magic while also holding open two portals with demon witch magic. What I did that night was like nothing I'd ever done before."

She let out a breath and shrugged. "And the exhaustion afterward was normal, ordinary, emotional exhaustion. The exhaustion of adrenaline finally settling and the danger being over." She tightened her grip on her mug. "I was not exhausted from the magic use. And I should have been. I shouldn't have been able to stay awake until we reached Dana's that night. Not after...everything."

"What does this mean?" Sebastian asked.

Angie gripped her mug tighter. "I don't know. I don't know if it's permanent. I don't know if it's... If it's a sign I am dying. I don't know. I just know that *not* using any of my magic leaves me tired. Exhausted."

Aidan turned back to the stove to manage the various pots and pans, her back to Angie when she said, "You use your magic all the time, though, right? In work with the psychic readings…"

"That seems to…count. When I work, I feel energized. It's… There's more energy that comes when I tap the demon magic. But tapping any of my magic does the trick." She flicked a glance at Sebastian. "This week, while I've been… resting and recovering. I've been doing little spells to keep using my magic, to put off the exhaustion. Sleeping is fine. I feel rested after I sleep. And I've been careful not to brush up against the demon magic. Obviously I haven't been opening portals. But I've been regularly tapping into my witch magic and doing little things…increasing the warding spells around my doors and windows. A little illusion spell no one would see. Reading random objects around my apartment, things I know won't have anything to them that I don't already know. That kind of thing."

"How often?" Sebastian asked. "Do you have to do this constantly?"

She shook her head. "Just when I start to feel the exhaustion coming on. Happens…a few times a day if I haven't been at work. The more I use my magic, the better I feel, the longer I go before the exhaustion sets in. So if I do something small a few times a day, I'm fine."

Sebastian looked toward the kitchen. "This is bad, isn't it?"

Aidan kept her back to them as she drained the pasta. "Not great, no. But also maybe not horrible. And maybe temporary."

"We're going into a demon realm," Sebastian pointed out. "Maybe more than one. That's not a time for Angie to have a weakness."

"Not a weakness for the purposes of what we'll be doing," Aidan said. She poured the pasta into the pan with the red sauce and started gently stirring everything together, still not looking at them.

Angie finally unfolded from the couch, taking hers and Sebastian's tea mugs back into the kitchen, and retrieving three large bowls for the pasta. "I'll have to use magic the entire time," she said. "Sheild spells, portals, maybe the demon magic if…when demons notice us and attack."

She tried not to shudder at the idea, but Aidan still gave her an assessing look from the corner of her eyes so Angie knew she'd made some sort of telling gesture.

She ignored Aidan's look. "I'll be constantly using magic while there, so I'll have plenty of energy—so long as I have food and water. There won't be a pause in magic use long enough for this to be an issue."

Setting the bowls out on the counter between the kitchen and living room, she looked across to Sebastian. "I'll be fine. But…it is a thing and if we're doing this, it's a thing you should know about. Just…probably more of a thing for us to worry about when we get back."

This time she left the "if" off. They'd get back. They had to.

She still hadn't told her mother what she was doing.

Once Gabriella had dropped off the documents, Angie had spent the next two hours, until Sebastian arrived and then Aidan, staring at them, wondering if she should read them. She'd reread Yusuf's records of his time with the demon witch, but there were a lot of things missing, and implied, in that record that hadn't actually happened—which Angie only knew because of her two visions. She'd stared at the blood on the last page, blood that was Betha's, and wondered again how it had gotten there. She'd been considering an ordinary reread of Eloise's diary, without the psychic element, when Sebastian had arrived, and she'd decided it was better to have dinner before attempting that.

Aidan had arrived a few minutes later with grocery bags and announced she was cooking because she wanted pasta. Angie hadn't had the energy to argue and had been a bit grateful when Aidan waved off her offer to help.

The pasta smelled glorious, so she was glad Aidan had done the cooking. Even with her worry, her body thought a giant bowl of pasta and red sauce filled with garlic and mushrooms and onions and sausage was an excellent idea.

All the distraction meant she hadn't bitten the bullet and called her family, yet, though. That was something still hanging out there, waiting for her to face.

But after dinner. She could worry about that after dinner.

They sat around the coffee table, Angie and Sebastian on the couch, Aidan in the one cushioned chair Angie had. Angie's apartment was too small for a proper table, so she always ate on the couch or at the kitchen counter. But she only had two bar stools there.

The pasta was amazingly good—she wasn't sure why but she never thought about Aidan cooking and was a little surprised to discover the hunter was so good at it—and settled in her stomach well, despite her anxiety.

But the looming call to her parents and the absence of Carmen weighed on the meal.

CHAPTER SIX

As Angie did the dishes with Sebastian, with Aidan sitting at the kitchen counter flipping through a pagan magazine Angie got from work, Angie brought up, again, one of the bigger problems. "We still don't know where Carmen is, do we?" She glanced back from the sink to Aidan.

She'd gotten the impression, that night after the fight with Sokolov's demon, that Aidan and Carmen knew each other. But Aidan had never commented on the relationship, not since and never before. Angie was very tempted to ask now, with everyone full on pasta and relaxed—the relaxation before the storm—but she didn't want to deal with a non-answer from Aidan when there already felt like there were too many unanswered questions on the table.

"She'll show," Aidan said. "She said she would."

"She did?" Angie turned, water slopping onto the floor from the mug she was washing. "When?"

Aidan didn't even look up from the magazine. "That night in Dana's café, after the demon fight. I told her we were going looking for the demon witch and she'd have to come with us or die."

"Why didn't you tell me you'd talked to her about this?" Angie dropped the mug back in the sink gently then turned to face Aidan. She didn't trust herself to have a delicate piece of ceramic in her hands at that moment.

Aidan finally looked up. "Carmen is unpredictable in a lot of things. And not someone you should trust. I didn't tell you, because I wasn't sure she'd actually show up. I wasn't sure she hadn't lied. I didn't want that to come as a surprise right before you were about to open a portal and walk into a demon realm on purpose. Rather you think she might not show and she doesn't, than you're counting on her showing and she doesn't."

Angie scowled. There was some logic in that, but that didn't make her feel better. Or less ticked off with Aidan. "Why are you telling me now then?"

"Because she found me today and said she'd meet us. Knew the time and place. I figured she meant it or she wouldn't have gone out of her way to find me."

"She found *you*."

Aidan grinned. "I did make myself available to be found. But yes." She gave Angie and Sebastian both a look. Sebastian for his part, hadn't stopped drying the plate in his hand, but he also hadn't taken up a new dish, and he was frowning at his mentor too. "There's a lot of history and complicated feelings between the three of you. That's going to be an issue."

She didn't ask, Angie noticed. "Probably."

"Okay. Then you should know, Carmen was a hunter at one point. A long time ago. And not for long."

"I knew it!" Angie said before she could stop herself. She felt a little silly for the response, but it was nice to have guessed right from all the dropped hints and implications.

"You were right," Aidan said. "There was even talk, when she'd first found the history keepers meeting, of her eventually become a keeper of the history. She used that as leverage to get into the archive. She is a very good actress and conwoman with an extremely strong will. And almost immediately after finding the meeting, she decided she didn't want to be a demon hunter the way the rest of us were. She wanted something else."

"Revenge."

"Revenge."

"On someone in particular?"

Aidan bobbed her head from side to side. "There were a couple of people initially. But it was always going to be revenge on the world. I know it's hard to believe, but she does have a moral compass of sorts. It's just…a little skewed."

Angie snort-laughed at that and went back to washing the last few dishes in the sink. "She kept Sebastian captive in a circle, struggling all day to keep a demon from ripping the head off a gangster. That is not moral."

"She had her reasons."

"She *always* has her reasons. But her reasons put innocent people in danger. Did Sebastian tell you about Ellen and Mara Grant?"

The first time they'd met Carmen, she'd been pretending to be a live-in maid in the mansion of a rich man who was dealing with demons. She'd had some scheme going with him, using the Molder demon Carmen may or may not have been enthrall to, and that scheme put the life of his infant daughter in danger—he nearly sacrificed the baby to a demon, for nothing more than wealth and power. Years after that, the same little girl and her mother ended up in danger all over again. All because of what Carmen was doing.

Then she'd used a father's love of his daughter in another scheme just as a test for Angie and Sebastian. That test as well as what Carmen had done with Sokolov had led directly to the fight with Sokolov's demon. But it was more than that, it was the way she'd used Sokolov's brother-in-law and his love for his sick child to manipulate him into doing something that could have gotten him killed.

Angie's distrust toward Carmen, her anger toward Carmen, had never just been about what she'd done to Sebastian. Angie couldn't forgive that, but she also couldn't forgive what Carmen had done to Ellen and Mara. What she'd done to Sokolov's brother-in-law, Ivan. What Angie was sure she'd done to countless other people over the years.

Carmen's moral compass was bent. And she did really shitty things as a result.

Aidan sighed and nodded when Angie said that part out

loud. "Yes. That was always Carmen's problem. The will of a hunter. The pragmatism of a hunter. The moral compass of a vigilante. The ability to nearly fuck things up in so many ways… I think that's her superpower."

Angie snort-laughed at that, but without much humor. "If Betha hadn't said we'd all die if it wasn't the four of us on this journey, I wouldn't *want* Carmen along. I can't trust her. We can't trust her. And there's every reason to believe she'll betray us for some pragmatic reason of her own that has to do with whatever revenge she's currently planning."

"All true," Aidan agreed with a nod. "Except for the part where she'll betray us."

When Angie threw Aidan a disbelieving look over her shoulder, Aidan said, "She wants you a live to kill demons. She's gone out of her way to ensure that happens. So she won't actively *try* to betray us inside the demon realms. But sometimes, what Carmen considers help is…not."

"I've noticed." Carmen had considered the Sebastian and Sokolov incident a way to "help" Angie finally tap her ability to open portals without needing trees.

Angie handed Sebastian the last mug and looked at him closely. He'd been very quiet during all this. "How do you feel about her coming along?"

"I'm not happy about it," he said. "I'd prefer to leave her behind. I don't trust her. And I don't really like her. But…" He met her gaze. "But I will do whatever it takes to ensure *you're* okay, and if that means a temporary alliance with Carmen, I can do that. I've done it before." He sighed and put away the last mug he'd finished drying. "I don't want to see her dead. I'd just love it if she wasn't part of our lives anymore."

"That was never going to happen once she learned Angie was a demon witch," Aidan said with a sigh of her own. "She's been obsessed with them since those first months when we all thought she'd still be a hunter."

"Why?" Angie asked, baffled. "What could she possibly want with someone who could open portals like I can, someone who could release a plague of demons by accident or design? She should have been terrified by that like all the other sane hunters."

Sebastian rubbed her back with a gentle hand, though she wasn't sure if he was trying to reassure her or himself in that moment.

"You'll have to ask Carmen," Aidan said. "That's the one thing I've never been able to figure out. And she's never told me."

Angie sighed. Carmen wasn't likely to tell her either. There was a lot Carmen didn't tell her. "Do you know her real name? I mean…even a name she used before Carmen?"

"No," Aidan said. "But then, there are very few hunters whose real names I know. Just like they don't know mine. It's better that way. I doubt she can remember hers well anymore. I certainly can't."

"But you're a lot older than Carmen, aren't you?" Angie challenged, her eyebrows raised. Waiting for Aidan to come clean.

Aidan grinned. "Thanks for doing the dishes. I have to go."

Angie straightened from the sink when Aidan stood. "Wait, we still need to talk about... About what we're doing."

"We've already done that. Tomorrow night. The Ramble. Plenty of good trees there. Carmen will meet us. We'll go from there. No point in discussing details we've already settled. Besides you need to call your family." Aidan's gaze jumped between her and Sebastian. "And you two need a night alone together."

Angie tried not to hear the implication of that comment, but it was still there, hanging in the air. She and Sebastian needed a night alone together...

Because it could be their last.

CHAPTER SEVEN

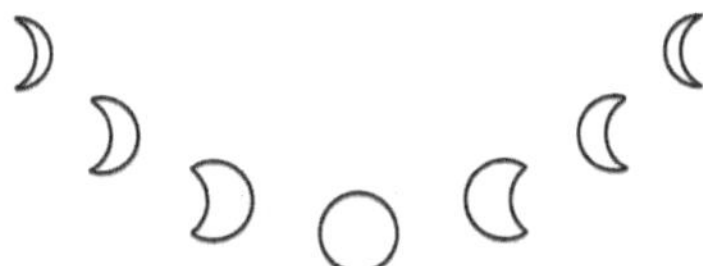

The Ramble during the day was a delightfully wooded section of Central Park with thick forests of pine and maple trees, easy dirt paths and walkways, some benches for sitting and admiring the quiet, few traffic sounds from outside the park, and infrequent people disrupting the peace. At night, when the park itself was not a place to travel lightly, the Ramble could be downright scary. Dark, shadowed, isolated, the trees rising up along the path hiding all manner of thing…

Except when you were a powerful witch and your two companions were people who regularly hunted demons, the threat of mundane robbers and murderers went down substantially.

Still, Angie held a shield up in front of herself, Sebastian, and Aidan, and kept two defensive spells queued up and ready to cast should she need them. None of them needed the hunters to waste their will and effort on a mugger. Not with what they were about to do.

She supposed they could have gone somewhere that wasn't in the middle of the big city park, or even to another park—which honestly wouldn't have been much safer. But this place felt like it offered up enough trees to choose from, and also it weirdly reminded Angie of the woods in her visions of Betha and Eloise. Not quite as extensive and thick. Even without being able to hear the city often, she could still catch the occasional sound of a bus passing on Fifth Avenue. Still, the feel was close enough, and in magic, feelings counted.

She had her giant purse slung over her head, the strap across her chest, the bag heavier than normal with water and protein bars. She'd also thrown in a small first aid kit because last time she'd had to use tissue and hand sanitizer to clean a wound for Carmen, and she'd only had ordinary Band-Aids, which had had to do as a weak sort of butterfly stitch. This time, she wanted to be better prepared.

Sebastian had a backpack too. His had the diary and the rolled up pages of the hunter report on Betha inside. Just that, though he'd wanted to stock more water and protein bars, too. But they'd all decided it was a better idea to keep the documents from the archive safe and not messed up with melted chocolate if a wrapper burst in the heat. Instead, Aidan had another light canvas backpack filled with water and bars and some other snacks—mostly for Angie. Neither hunter ate much when they were on a hunt. Demon hunters didn't want to throw up at inopportune moments and eating before being exposed to some of the smells that came with demon hunting could do that to even the best of them.

Which was why there were also bottles of regular soda inside Aidan's bag—one of the few sources of calories she'd take in on a hunt.

Angie wasn't sure how long they'd be in any given demon realm. She wasn't sure how to open a portal specifically to where they wanted to be—not least because she didn't know *where* they needed or wanted to be specifically. She wasn't even sure which realm they needed to be in. This was a journey that could take time, or they could get lucky and find Betha quickly. They could also return to this realm any time they needed to.

She hoped.

She'd never done this on purpose before. And only once opened a breach while inside a demon realm. Now that they were here, in the woods, surrounded by trees—some of which were safe, with solid trunks and no natural Vs, others with thick branching trunks and the exact V-shape she needed —and Angie's doubts and fears roared to the surface.

What if she could get them into a demon realm and then couldn't get them out?

What if she couldn't control which realm she opened after all?

What if she opened dozens of realms and they still couldn't find Betha?

What if the realm they had to go to to find Betha— whichever one that was—what if that realm wasn't compatible to a human? Betha would be there, so Angie had to assume there'd be air to breathe and the heat or cold would be manageable, but still. Betha wasn't quite human anymore. So judging the survivability of a realm by what Betha could survive probably wasn't the most accurate marker.

So much could go wrong. So much could fail. And failure here meant more than just not finding Betha and answers. Failure in this could mean death.

She thought back to her conversation with her parents last night. A good one, but hard. She'd told them in the end what was going to happen and why she was doing what she was doing. She couldn't tell them about the hunter council—she physically couldn't, there was some sort of preventative compulsion inflicted on all hunters to prevent them talking about the council to any non-hunters—so she couldn't tell them about the documents and the secret archive. But she could say that some of what had happened when she was last home required she make this journey. That it was important. And that she'd have Sebastian and Aidan with her.

When Angie's mother had heard Aidan was along for the ride, she'd stopped asking so many questions and, if not exactly relaxed, seemed to at least accept that Angie had the backup she needed.

Aidan had smiled when Angie told her this. "Your mother is a smart woman," she said. "Always has been."

The darkness closed in around them, even the faint lamplights on most of the park paths and the surrounding city lights were blocked in the area of the Ramble. Looking up, just darkness overhead. Cloudless so not even the orange glow from reflected city light to reveal they weren't in the middle of nowhere. It was almost eerie how isolated and distant from the real world this place felt. Like they'd already walked into another realm.

They stopped going deeper into the woods when Angie found a tree that would work well for opening a breach between realms. She didn't need the tree anymore. She could have done this in her apartment if she'd been willing to risk the safety of all the people in her building if a demon got out —which she was not. But she wanted at least one tree available to start this search. A sort of security blanket, she supposed.

The branching maple was perfect, with a very solid V shape in its thick, tall trunk. Its branches were filled with thick green leaves, but high and out of the way, leaving the V exposed and maybe a little too easy to look into. There were other trees around the maple, of course, some even with that specific and required shape in the trunk, but the one she'd selected felt the best for creating a solid portal.

She'd never tried to create a portal that would be solid and stable. She'd never needed to. Opening portals had only ever been something she did on purpose during those early years when she'd worked with Sebastian, and the few times she'd helped him and Aidan on a hunt. She'd done it in the months since becoming a demon hunter, of course, and finally trained the skill a bit more, learning to both hold the portal open and close it on purpose, in her own time instead of opening it on accident and getting stuck.

But that had always been in service of pushing a demon *back* to the demon realms.

She'd *never* opened a portal with the intent of going through it. On purpose.

Her breathing sped and she could feel the panic flowing through her. Why was this necessary again? She didn't want to do this. She could go the rest of her life without doing this. Did she really need answers? She could just…not kill demons, not use that magic. And then it could stay in its little threads and leave her alone.

Except… There was still the hanging specter of threat that this would kill her. That she would not, could not contain the magic from another *realm,* and that magic would destroy her. She didn't feel like she was dying. Betha had apparently not died. So maybe not.

But Betha also lived inside a demon world. She said it was for Eloise, or at least she had in the visions, that Eloise needed to stay in the demon realms to survive. If that were true, Betha could have lived here? Maybe lived out her life with the demon magic and die naturally.

Not likely for a demon witch. At least according to the records. But no one besides Yusuf knew about Betha, so maybe.

Angie closed her eyes and took in a deep breath, trying to calm the rising panic. She'd decided this was necessary because she wanted answers. She wanted to reverse what had been done. Get the demon magic out of her. Being able to kill demons, even if she didn't *want* to use the ability, put a target on her back—demons wanting her to kill their enemies, demon hunters wanting her to kill demons, Carmen wanting her to use all these new skills for Carmen's own nefarious reasons. But almost worse, it put Sebastian in the crosshairs too.

His job was always dangerous. But adding the fact that he could be used to get to her had made things infinitely worse.

And if she were being honest with herself, what she really wanted, what she was looking for, was a way to stop being a demon witch all together. She wanted to know if she could cut off *all* the demon related magic for good and just…be a witch.

She'd hoped for those answers in the hunters' secret archive, but all she'd gotten there were more questions. And this lead. This one, solitary lead.

She opened her eyes, blinking away the panic, or at least banking it so it wouldn't make her hyperventilate. She'd thought about this, for more than a week now. She couldn't afford to miss this chance, couldn't afford to let this chance at information and answers slip away.

This might be her only hope.

Sebastian came up beside her, close but careful of touching her. She had shut down her psychic skills solidly, and she wasn't exhausted and stretched too thin now, so she took hold of his hand, letting him know the touch was fine.

"You okay?" he murmured.

"No. I don't want to do this," she whispered back. "But I know I have to. I need to. I need to. I just don't wanna." She said the last with an exaggerated pout, and he humored her by smiling at her weak joke.

"We can always leave," Aidan reminded her. "Any time you want to, we can just come back here."

She was right. This wasn't like the other times. This wasn't her going into a demon realm on accident and getting stuck there. They didn't have to stay. She could always just open a portal and get them out. Any time she wanted to. They weren't going to be trapped this time. They could come back.

The panic banked a little more, though it was still there, lurking just below the surface. She let out a long stream of air, letting the deep release calm her nerves. She wanted these answers, so she needed to do this. And she could always return.

She glanced around the surrounding trees. "Can't go anywhere without Carmen, though. Where is she?"

"Right here, chica." A voice from behind the maple tree with the V. Carmen moved around the trunk and smiled at her.

Angie scowled. "How long have you been there?"

"About a half hour. Took you long enough to get here."

"How could you know to meet us in this exact spot? I didn't even know we were going to be *here* here."

Carmen patted the maple. "Good tree."

Angie huffed. That Carmen had picked out the same tree for Angie to use as Angie had picked out for herself was beyond annoying.

"So are we doing this or not?" Carmen asked, looking at all of them with her brows raised.

Carmen was a chameleon of a woman, the kind of person who could blend into her surroundings, and took advantage of people's preconceived, even bigoted, notions to be whoever she needed to be in any given moment. At that moment, she was the Carmen she liked to show Angie, though Angie wasn't sure if this was the real her or just another act. She could never tell with Carmen.

The witch was dressed in black leather pants and a leather jacket, with her dark brown hair pulled up into a tight bun. Angie would have taken the look as an aggressive style choice except she realized the leather would be good in the rough terrain of a demon realm. Hot and maybe sticky, but effective at blunting the glass-sharp lava rock of the hellscape. Angie didn't have any leather clothing, so she'd gone with her usual jeans and t-shirt, her light spring jacket not likely to help much against fire and the rocky landscape. But it was too late to rethink her own style choices.

Carmen also carried a small backpack over one shoulder, which Angie nodded to. "I hope you brought your own water."

"Plenty of it," she said with a nod. "Not gonna get trapped without supplies this time."

Angie's gut tightened at the reminder of the last time. "You sure about this?" she asked.

Carmen had been just as terrified, just as panicked about being trapped in a demon realm as Angie had last time. And she didn't have the same compelling reason Angie did to go this time.

But maybe Carmen had her own reasons for this journey. Probably reasons that would make Angie balk at taking her along. Reasons that had nothing to do with Angie finding a way to get rid of all her demon related skills. Carmen wanted Angie to kill demons.

So… What was in this for Carmen?

A question she asked aloud.

Carmen shrugged, her gaze skimming around the surrounding trees. "Chance to meet a legendary demon witch who's still alive. Someone who kills demons regularly? How could I pass that up?"

"That's not why you're here," Angie said.

"Maybe not," Carmen said, meeting her gaze again and not saying any more.

"Not going to tell me?"

"Nothing I need to talk about."

"I could leave you behind."

"And we'll all die if you do." Carmen nodded at Angie's narrow gaze. "I know the deal, chica. Whoever that was who came out and told you to find her… She said we'd all die if the four of us didn't do this. Since I don't want to die, I'm here."

Angie snorted at that. But she didn't believe Carmen completely either. There was no reason to believe Betha's prediction would come true. Carmen was nothing if not contrary, and she didn't like doing what other people wanted her to do. Angie wouldn't have put it past Carmen, even knowing what Betha had said, to simply not show up and risk the consequences.

But Carmen liked information. That's what Aidan had said. And Carmen definitely liked knowing more than the people around her. According to Aidan, Carmen was also obsessed with demon witches. So maybe that was all she wanted. To meet the infamous witch who killed demons regularly. Angie wondered if that was enough motivation to get Carmen here.

Even if it meant walking into a demon realm.

"Do you think the woman is who we think she is?" Angie asked, curious if Carmen had considered what the council had considered and Angie hadn't thought about. "Or do you think she'd a demon trying to trick us?"

"Little of both," Carmen said. "I think she's this demon witch of yours. But I also think this is a trap."

"And yet you're still here."

Carmen smiled.

Angie sighed. She couldn't trust Carmen even a little bit, but the woman was still alive, despite making enemies all over this realm and the demon realm. She wouldn't be here if she thought the trap was an automatic death sentence. Or if it was, that she couldn't still manage to wiggle her way out of that death trap.

"Fine," Angie said after looking to Aidan and then Sebastian. She nodded. "Let's do this."

She reached instinctively for the pentagram charm that normally hung from her wrist on a white beaded bracelet. The very first present that Esmerelda had given her. A charm to help her ground, to help her control her ability to open portals, or more importantly, close them when she'd accidentally opened one. But she'd taken that bracelet off when she got back from New Mexico and tucked it away in her altar. Wearing it while she was channeling demon magic had felt…odd. Wrong? That wasn't quite the right word. But something, some instinct, had her putting the bracelet away and making herself a promise. When she got rid of the demon magic, she'd put the bracelet back on.

Instead, she pulled the silver medallion from the pocket of her jeans, letting the silver and turquoise chain hang between her fingers, the small circular pendant in the palm of her hand. She flipped it one way, then the other, and realized it felt right with the owl pointed upward. An instinct she didn't argue with. When it came to witch magic, she did a lot on instinct. She closed her hand over the medallion and looked up.

"Okay. Wherever the tree takes us first. Then we see what the medallion tells me to do." Betha had said to use the medallion to find her. So Angie would use the medallion to find her.

They'd talked about trying to go into the last realm Betha had been in, but Angie got the feeling that wasn't her home realm. If it had been, Sokolov's demon wouldn't have been eager to escape into that realm. He would have run toward the lava and red sky hellscape Angie had also opened into that night. He'd seemed relieved to see the other realm, with its purple sky and black vines creeping over gray rock. So Angie and the others had concluded that wasn't the place Betha spent most of her time.

Angie had to hope their logic held. Otherwise, they were about to waste time going into the red sky hellscape that haunted Angie's nightmares.

"Everyone ready?" she asked, once again glancing around at her companions.

"Sebastian through first," Aidan said, her gaze on the tree now. "Then Carmen, then me, then Angie."

"And we move fast," Sebastian said, "so no demons have a chance to notice the breach and try to sneak out."

"Once I come through, the portal will close. That's the kind of opening I'm creating." She met Carmen's gaze. "You sure?"

"I'm sure." Carmen slipped her other arm through the backpack strap, settling it firmly on her back.

Angie closed her eyes and took a deep, cleansing breath, filling her lungs with the scents of loamy earth and pine and maple. Let the sounds of the distant city and the night birds and the humming insects settle her. Let the soft soil beneath her feet ground her. Home. And she could come back whenever she needed to.

She checked her magic, the stability of her web.

Then she opened her eyes and looked into the V in the maple tree.

Into the lava belching hellscape beyond.

CHAPTER EIGHT

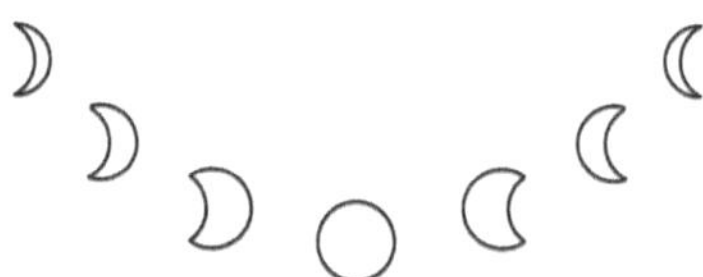

Angie's pulse pounded so hard it was tough to focus on anything else. The adrenaline rush of knowing she wasn't just holding this portal between realms open but was going to, *on purpose*, walk into that land was absolutely terrifying. Especially that realm.

The hellscape that spread out past the frame of the tree was a barren, rocky landscape, all black rock and lava rivers. In the distance, volcanos belched thick red lines of lava and smoke. The sky overhead was red, casting strange shadows and weird lines across the landscape. It wasn't as dark as it was sometimes, but it wasn't bright either. In the distance, she could already see demons flying over the top of the volcanos. And their screeches sent a shiver of terror down her spine.

But at least there were no chittering demons yet. The chittering demons were the worst. They set Angie's teeth on edge and filled her with so much primal terror she couldn't breathe. Not because they were the worst or most dangerous demons. They were horribly dangerous and deadly, brutally efficient at tearing through their victims. But not a higher order demon who could be smart and cunning as well as vicious. Angie was still, in her most primitive lizard brain, so terrified of the chittering demons, though, it went beyond logic.

They were the demons who'd attacked her the first time she got pulled into a demon realm and nearly trapped.

That chittering sound made her guts turn to mush. And even knowing she could scatter them with lightning using just her ordinary witch magic, or, if necessary, kill them with her newest magic, didn't dissipate the primal terror she experienced when she heard the chittering. She wasn't sure anything ever would.

So the fact that the chittering demons weren't nearby, hadn't noticed the breach yet, was the only saving grace as she stared into the depths of the hellscape.

Beside her, Sebastian said, "Are you okay?"

"Not even a little bit," she said with a sound that would have been a laugh if she weren't so scared. "You?"

"Been better," he said.

An admission that, weirdly, made her feel better. Sometimes the hunters—especially Sebastian and Aidan— were so confident and in control when they faced demons— because they had to be or they'd get killed—that she forgot they could also be scared of anything demon. But of course, in this case, Sebastian was probably reliving his worst nightmares and primal terrors too. Watching his parents vanish into the hellscape. Watching her get sucked in. Going in on purpose to save Carmen only to end up stuck there with Angie and Carmen.

Going into the hellscape wasn't something humans survived. That both she and Sebastian had survived this horror didn't make it any easier to face.

"The demons haven't noticed us yet," Aidan said quietly. There weren't any signs of fear in her voice, but Angie wasn't sure she'd ever heard Aidan speak so...quietly. "We need to go now if we're going."

"We're going?" Sebastian asked Angie, one last time.

She didn't take her gaze off the breach because that would close this one. At least, she thought it would. It had always done so before on this type of portal. And she hadn't had to push it open. Just look. And there it was. She chose caution over experiment in this.

"We're still going," she said, nodding. She was gut-churningly terrified. There was a scream trying to crawl up her throat. And she was certain the stench of sulfur leaking out from the breach was going to make her want to throw up when she stepped into the middle of it. But she was still going in.

She saw Sebastian nod from the corner of her eye. Then he stepped forward, in front of the breach. He couldn't see the hellscape beyond. Not yet. He wouldn't until he moved into it. But they all knew it was there.

Because this was a portal in the frame of a tree trunk, he had to hop up onto the edge of the V. Seeing him crouching on the trunk, the hellscape beyond, left her breathless. She wanted to jerk him backward and close the portal before he went through.

In the distance the flying demons screeched.

Sebastian glanced back at her. She couldn't look directly at him because she'd risk closing the breach, but she felt his gaze and gave a little nod.

He slipped through the break in the tree trunk.

Into the hellscape.

Angie swallowed the scream that was still trying to claw its way out of her throat. "Carmen."

Carmen stepped up to the tree and braced her hands on the trunk, leaning in through the V. "This is the stupidest thing I've ever done," she murmured. "And I have done some stupid shit."

"Yup," Angie agreed. "Don't leave Sebastian in there alone."

Carmen snort-laughed, sounding almost genuinely amused. "So fucking arrogant. You're lucky I like you."

She didn't give Angie a chance to respond before she heaved herself up onto the tree trunk, slung one leg into the demon world, half in and half out for a moment, still staring in. She took a deep breath and slung her other leg over the trunk, jumping through the breach.

Angie felt Aidan come up beside her. "I'm going through now," the hunter murmured. "Sebastian and I will wait on the side to help you through. You sure you can do this?"

"I have to," Angie said. She wasn't sure she would have

been able to do this without having Sebastian and Aidan with her, though. "Thank you."

"We've got your back," Aidan said. She approached the maple tree trunk and let out a long breath. Then without even looking back at Angie, she hopped up onto the trunk, standing in the V for an instant before stepping through.

Angie wanted to blink, but couldn't now that she was caught in this…well, she used to think of it as a trap, holding open the portal. She wasn't sure what to call it when she did it on purpose. More, though, if she blinked and looked away, she'd close the portal and trap her friends inside.

She stepped up to the V, placing her hands on the trunk, the bark rough against her hands. The scent of maple did nothing to dampen the stench of sulfur. The distant demons screeched. And she thought she saw dark shadows moving on the horizon, black shapes against the red glow of lava.

Fuck fuck fuck fuck.

The litany ran through her head as she pushed herself up onto the cradle of the tree trunk, her feet scrambling at the bark as she got into a position to move through the breach. Not nearly as graceful as either of the hunters, but she was trembling too hard to care. She took a deep breath, full of a mix of her real world greenery and earthy dirt with the stench of rotten egg brimstone from the demon realm. Her stomach bottomed out. She took a rapid series of panicked breaths.

And dropped into the hellscape.

She landed on the hard, black rock with an awkward thud which would have been embarrassing if she weren't so terrified.

Sebastian was beside her instantly, helping her back to her feet. She blinked hard at the rocky, jagged landscape around her. The demons in the distance screeched again. And the line of demons she'd seen moving across the horizon had turned toward them.

Shit.

It took her a beat, maybe two, before she realized she needed to make sure the portal had closed. When she turned to face it, all she could see was more of the hellscape spreading out around them.

Their escape home had closed the instant she turned her gaze from the portal.

They were committed now.

"There are demons headed this way," Carmen said, attempting to sound calm, but Angie heard the strain in her voice.

She related very strongly to Carmen in that moment. The panic was clawing at her throat too.

Facing the line of approaching demons, she realized they were running toward them now. Fast. Sebastian released his hold on her and faced the columns of approaching demons. Aidan took up a position at their backs. When Angie glanced over her shoulder, she realized more demons were coming from that direction.

This was a bad idea. Such a bad idea.

Panic made it difficult to think. So she pulled in a deep, sulfur-scented breath, and when she let it out, she thought, *Demons first. Track Betha second.*

Murmuring a spell under her breath, she reached for all

the surrounding electricity. There was not enough moisture here to bring rainfall. But there was plenty of electricity.

Thunder rumbled in the distance.

Angie looked up to the sky, and pulled down the lightning with a final word of her spell. She grabbed hold of the streaks and electrical bolts in the air, and rained them down on top of the approaching demons. In front of her. Behind her. Lighting strikes falling into the middle of the charging hoards.

Demons scattered. Reformed their lines. Race toward them. She rained more lightning. Bolts with multiple branches, hammering into the lines of demons. Scattering them again. And again.

She'd done this here before, pulled the lightning, thrown it down onto charging lines of demons. Multiple times now. It felt weirdly easy, weirdly familiar. That familiarity and ease would scare her when there weren't so many fucking demons racing toward them.

The others shouted things over the noise. She felt some movement around her from the other three. Backs to each other. Focused outward and protecting each other.

Not alone, she reminded herself. Others. Hunters. Strong enough to defend against demons.

But also people she wanted to protect.

She shouted up at the sky and pulled down even more lightning, strands of sizzling electricity filling the air with such a strong burnt ozone smell it overpowered the sulfur. Overpowered the sounds of the demons. The chittering. Even the shouts of her companions. Only that electric zing and the claps of thunder as light cut the air.

A touch on her shoulder, too familiar to scare her. She looked back at her surroundings and realized the demons had stopped charging.

But they hadn't run away.

The last time they'd been here and she'd rained so much lightning down that Sebastian had to pull her out of the process with a gentle touch she'd scattered the demons completely, sent them running away. That had given her group a much needed reprieve to deal with the fact that they were trapped and she was too exhausted to open a portal home and needed rest.

She wasn't exhausted this time, though. That part was really starting to scare her. All that magic—regular witch magic at that—all that power, and she felt…good. Strong.

Closing her eyes very briefly she checked her web. No, she hadn't pulled in any extra demon magic. Still just those two threads bracketing her demon witch power. The rest, a healthy glowing blue. In a metaphysical sense, she got the impression of her blue magic glowing more brightly, almost overpowering the red threads, which was odd. And the strands of purple that remained woven throughout the web were pulsing.

She got the oddest feeling of…happiness from those threads. Which was so disturbing she popped her eyes open and looked at Sebastian.

"You're okay?" she asked.

"We're all fine. None of them got close enough for us to have to fight." He frowned a little. "Are you okay? Tired? Need food."

"Not yet." She swallowed, then admitted, "I'm feeling really good and energized actually."

"Even after all that?"

"Even after all that."

His jaw worked as he studied her face. "Your eyes aren't red."

His, on the other hand, were more red than usual. She suspected if she looked at Aidan, that spark of red in the depths of her eyes would be stronger now too.

"The demon magic?" he asked.

"Seems to be quiet. It seems to be my witch magic that's so happy right now. And that blended purple stuff that I'm not entirely sure what it does."

He nodded, but his frown didn't lighten. "Okay. A bit worrying but while we're here it works in our favor, so we'll deal with that later."

"Agreed." She let her gaze travel over the landscape. "But they haven't run away."

"They're back here still too," Aidan said.

Angie glanced over her shoulder. Sure enough, the demons that had been attacking from that direction had also moved off, but hadn't run away. They were all holding at a distance. A pretty far distance, too. Even racing at top speeds, it would take them minutes to reach the humans. Enough time for Angie to act, to call the lightning again.

"This is weird, right?" Carmen said, her voice quiet. She sounded strained but calm.

"This is definitely weird," Angie agreed. "They should be attacking or running away. Not just…standing there."

"Waiting to attack again?" Carmen again.

"Or watching to see what we do," Aidan said. "Humans who can defend themselves like Angie just did don't often come here."

Often? Didn't Aidan mean *never*?

"We should check the medallion," Sebastian said.

Angie shook herself out of the appalling thought that people sometimes did enter this realm on purpose, and she pulled the medallion from her pocket. The silver felt cool, almost like water in her palm. Such a contrast to the hot, dry air around her, she wanted to set it against her cheek.

Flipping the medallion over so that the owl side was facing upward, she whispered the spell Esmerelda had taught her and asked the medallion to find Betha. She even visualized the woman in question though she wasn't sure that was necessary. But with her magic, visualization could help spells form correctly.

For a long moment nothing happened. She could practically feel everyone holding their breaths, waiting. Even the distant demons felt like they were waiting. Though they were a long ways off, she still swore she heard them shuffling around, their feet making the sharp, black lava rock crinkle. Or maybe that was just the lava rivers moving across the rocks.

Then the little medallion sent a shiver into her palm. The barest of movements. Just a little rocking. Not a pull in any direction yet, but still a reaction.

She waited, hoping it would do...something. When they'd used it to find Carmen, it had vibrated and sort of *leaned* in a direction. And when they were close to her, the medallion had tried to race ahead of Angie, hovering over her hand and moving in a very definite direction, only linked to Angie's hand by the silver and turquoise chain looped around her fingers.

It wasn't doing that now, though. Just vibrating on her palm.

"Either we're in the wrong realm or it can't decide where to go," she said quietly. "I'm going to start walking one direction and see if it reacts in any way."

"That a good idea?" Carmen asked. "We still have a pretty significant audience out there."

"Not sure what else to do," Angie said. "It's...reacting. Vibrating. But not showing me a direction." She walked a few feet to the left. The vibrating tugged her back the way she'd come. That was a good sign. So she walked in the opposite direction, past her group again.

But then the direction of the tugging reversed, too.

Bringing her right back to her companions.

She frowned. She had said Betha's name. Not anyone else's. This was weird.

Scowling at Carmen, she said, "Your real name isn't Betha, right?"

Carmen shook her head. "Never even used it as a fake name."

"Aidan?" Angie asked.

"Beautiful name. Never used it. Definitely wasn't born with it."

"Sebastian? Do you have a name somewhere back that the medallion could think is Betha?"

He shook his head. "Not even a nickname." He glanced into the distance, his gaze running over the demons. "My mother's name wasn't even close. Her name was Henrietta. My dad sometimes called her Henri for short."

Angie's soul hurt at the story, at all the nostalgia and loss she heard in his voice. She wanted them to have room and time for him to tell her more about his family. Finally. So they could share the heartbreak of those memories and he wouldn't be burdened anymore.

But this wasn't the time.

"Why are you asking about names?" Carmen shuffled closer and looked around Angie's arm at the medallion in her palm. "That thing not working?"

"It's doing something weird. I walk away from you all and it tugs me back to you. Either it thinks one of you is Betha, or it's still caught up on finding Carmen, and I don't know how to change its target. Which would be odd since Betha told me to use it and Esmerelda said nothing about it being a one-shot deal."

"Is it pulling toward me?" Carmen asked.

Angie took a moment to study the feeling in her palm. She moved the medallion away from Carmen, moving closer to Sebastian. It didn't do anything. So she moved closer to Aidan. Still nothing but the humming vibration in her palm. Finally, she moved toward Carmen.

Nothing.

"No," she said, looking at her companions. "When I'm

standing with you all, it hums gently in my palm. It only tugged at me when I walked away from you, but it calmed as soon as I was back with you.

"That's not how it's supposed to work, is it?" Aidan asked.

"Definitely not."

"Without it, we have no way of finding this other witch, then, do we?" Carmen said.

"She wanted us to find her though," Angie said, frustrated, "and said to use the medallion."

Sebastian moved closer, but his gaze remained on the distant demons. "Wrong realm maybe? Could it be telling you to open another portal, into another realm?"

That…was actually a good thought. It wouldn't lead her anywhere in this realm if they were in the wrong place.

In the distance, the chittering started up. That sound that set her teeth on edge. They'd fallen silent after the lightning strikes. But apparently whatever had kept them quiet wasn't an issue anymore.

"They're starting to move," Aidan said.

The ones in front of them were too. Angie glanced back the direction Aidan was watching. Then to the rows of demons in front of her. They were moving slowly. Not racing or running toward them. Inching forward really. But still. Moving toward them again.

"They'll try to get through if I open a portal, won't they?" she whispered.

"They will," Sebastian said, also quietly. "But it won't be the first time we leave with demons right on our tail."

"We did that once. And it sucked. And some of them almost got out. And you ended up exhausted."

"Open into another demon realm," Aidan said. "Not into our realm."

"Right," Carmen said. "We don't care if one kind of demon moves into another kind of demon's realm."

That was true. Angie cared a lot less about that. She had to open a different kind of portal to get them home anyway, which meant she could just as easily open a portal into a different realm.

The terrifying knowledge of how to do that was in her head thanks to the visions of Betha. What Betha had known about opening portals into different realms had implanted in Angie's brain during the specific vision when she'd touched blood on the old document and watched Betha open multiple portals onto multiple realms. And then into the demon gods' realm.

Angie didn't want that kind of knowledge in her head, but there it was. And in this case, knowing she could get to another realm meant she could get them out of their current predicament without endangering her own world.

"Remember the rings," Aidan said. "We're probably going to need to move deeper."

Yes. The rings. Apparently, the demon realms were organized in concentric circles that moved "deeper" to the center which was the god realm. Similar to what Dante had described in his Inferno poem. But more layers. She'd gotten a crash course in the idea from Gabriella right before the fight with Sokolov's demon. But afterward, during their week of rest and planning, Aidan had explained the whole theory to her.

Some other demon witches had discovered those layers too, the layout of the realms. Whether they'd been there or not, Angie wasn't sure. No one was. But the witch who'd been killed by her coven in the seventeenth century in the US had definitely had knowledge of the way demon realms were organized. And Angie suspected Betha had that knowledge too. But *that* wasn't something Angie had absorbed during her vision.

Getting through the layers, moving deeper into the demons' planes of existence, was only possible for some demons. Higher order demons could move close to the god realm. Few could cross into that realm. Lower order demons couldn't move between realms at all.

And apparently, demon witches could access all those worlds. Even the demon god realm.

She pulled in a deep breath and let it out slowly as she let the knowledge she'd pick up from Betha flow forward from the dark corners of her mind where she'd shoved it so she didn't have to think about it. There were no clues in those memories as to where Betha was now. But there was knowledge of realms she'd gone into frequently looking for a cure for her and Eloise.

Unfortunately, Angie couldn't tell which of those was the realm they'd been living in all those centuries ago. Betha had moved through too many planes. But there were a handful she moved through a lot. Angie would start there.

"Okay," she said, her gaze on the slowly moving line of

demons. "I'm going to access one of the places I think Betha went. The minute I open the portal, the hoard will rush us."

"And there will likely be trouble on the other side," Aidan added. "Because…demons."

Angie sighed. Always fucking demons. "So we'll have to move fast. But stay aware," she finished.

"I'll go through first this time," Aidan said. "Then Carmen."

"Angie and I will go through together," Sebastian said, before anyone else could comment.

They'd done that the last time they'd been here, too. Because Sebastian hadn't been prepared to leave her without cover. And she wasn't going through the portal without him.

No one objected and Angie didn't look at the other two to see their expressions. This point wasn't something either she or Sebastian would compromise on anyway.

"You'll see this portal," Angie said. "The outline of it anyway." Carmen and Sebastian had seen the last one she'd opened inside this realm. Another thing that was different about the treeless portals. "As soon as I say go, go. No matter what."

A screech in the distance, over the belching volcanos. Those demons were winged and dangerous. Angie didn't want to give them time to reach her group.

She tucked the medallion back into her jeans pocket and closed her eyes, trusting the others to watch the demons.

She gripped a metaphorical hand around a line of blue magic to ground and balance her.

Then reached for the demon witch line of power in her magical web.

CHAPTER NINE

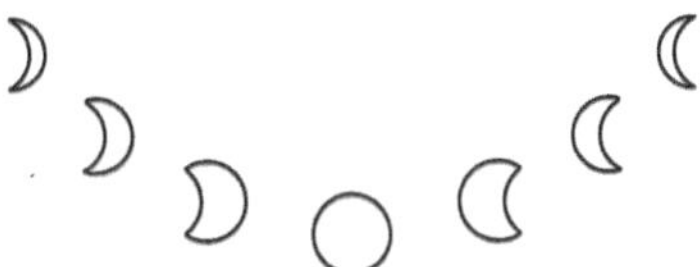

The power slammed into Angie, roaring through her blood. She hadn't had to access this magic directly when using the tree. Now, the only way to open a portal to somewhere else, she needed the direct contact.

And the direct contact filled her with so much power and strength it left her breathless. This wasn't the magic she'd absorbed in this realm. This was all her own. Just her own.

Her own was so fucking strong.

She heard the demons in the distance, the sound of the chittering getting closer, the screech from the flying demons near the volcanos. She heard Sebastian near her ear. "They're moving. They're coming."

But most of her was inside the magic now, absorbed, filled up with, taken over by.

She wanted to smile and that was terrifying, so instead she focused on that knowledge Betha had somehow managed to pass to her through centuries. Focused on opening a portal into one of the realms Betha had visited often. This wasn't the one from which Betha had emerged during the fight with Sokolov's demon. This was one Angie had never seen before, except in Betha's mind.

The portal whirled open, a circling line of light like fire surrounding it.

Beyond lay a desert landscape, but the sands were black and twinkling in a hazy gray light. Nothing that looked like plants. But also no lava or volcanos that she could see. There was still the distinct stench of sulfur, though.

"Go," she said, her voice deep as the magic flowed through her.

Neither Aidan nor Carmen waited. They leapt through the ring of fire so fast, Carmen practically bumped into Aidan on the way through.

Angie moved closer to the opening. "Sebastian."

"With you."

There was strain in his voice. Angie wanted to look around to see what he was seeing, see how close the demons were, but she was afraid she'd get overwhelmed or lose focus.

Holding his hand was risky in this moment, but she grabbed his arm anyway, and together they stepped through the portal.

Dry, hot air blew across her cheeks, scalding hot, and sandpaper rough, but breathable and manageable. Behind them, Angie could still hear the chittering. And the screeching.

She faced her portal, releasing her hold on Sebastian, and focused on closing the breach. The demons on the other side had reached the break now, but to her amazement, they weren't rushing through. The chittering demons, with their multiple limbs and long claws and spike tipped tails and round heads and teeth filled mouths clustered around the opening, but didn't make an attempt to go through.

As she swung the doorway closed, giving it the nudge to seal it off, one of the flying demons from the volcanos flew through, diving into the new realm just as Angie got the breach sealed.

Fuck. She turned to look up…

As something very dark and large swooped out of the gray sky and swallowed the flying demon whole, cutting off its screech in an instant.

The dark shape was a gray that blended into the swirling cloud cover overhead so well that she lost sight of it instantly. She was sure that hadn't just been the clouds though. There was definitely another monster up there.

"Uh," she said, because her brain was well and truly into panic mode now. The entire sky could be filled with those gray monsters and they'd never know. Terror clamped down hard around her chest and throat.

"Fucking hell," Carmen muttered, then she started cursing in Spanish.

Angie knew most of those words and felt every single one of them in her soul. She'd never agreed with Carmen about anything more.

"I thought the lava realm was horrible," she whispered.

"Don't trust the sand either," Aidan said. She sounded… ominously neutral.

"Wait," Carmen said, her voice a squeak. "Are you telling me we could be standing on a demon now, it blending into the sand the way that thing blended into the clouds?"

"We could," Aidan said. "More like they'll be under the sand, though, not so much looking like the sand. Although…" She gave a little shrug.

That was not a reassuring shrug.

Fear crawled along Angie's legs from her feet, making her want to leap up into the nearest tree to get away from the sand and whatever the hell might be underneath it. Except there were no trees. And somehow being high up in a tree felt like it would bring her closer to the cloud monster. Or monsters.

A scream lodged in her throat. Where the hell had she taken them? How the hell had Betha come here so often.

She was afraid to move and draw attention to their little group, afraid to even speak loudly. But she managed a choked, "Keep a lookout and I'll check the medallion."

If the medallion led them deeper into this realm, Angie was going to piss her own pants. She was so scared of what could be beneath her, what was *definitely* above her, none of which she could see, that she almost missed the obvious and very visible chittering demons.

Goddess, she never even imagined she'd think anything like that.

Carmen pushed up against her back, not quite touching her, but close enough she was crowding Angie. "Take out the medallion," she said, her voice hushed and urgent. "Please tell me we can move somewhere else from here."

The ground beneath their feet rumbled. A vibration that made the sand shift. Something overhead roared. The clouds—or whatever—shifted and rolled.

Angie wanted to scream so badly she had to clamp her mouth shut.

She fumbled with the medallion when she took it out of her pocket and nearly dropped it into the shifting sands. Which gave her a heart attack. What if she lost the medallion? Shit, what if it fell into the sand and was swallowed up?

Then she'd go home and forget all about this idiotic quest, that was what. Standing here, terrified to a level she'd thought she'd reached but apparently hadn't, this whole thing felt remarkably pointless.

She gripped the medallion harder, wrapping the chain around her fingers so she wouldn't drop it. Then whispered the spell with Betha's name again.

The charm vibrated on her palm almost immediately and Angie's fear that it would lead them deeper into this realm grew. "I'm going to walk away to see if it'll give me a direction," she said, even though the thought of moving made her gut tight. Moving meant creating vibrations and vibrations might draw attention. She felt like a tiny, scurrying lizard trying not to be noticed by the eagle circling overhead or the snakes slithering over the sand.

Sebastian and Aidan said nothing. Carmen said, "Hurry."

A quick glance at Sebastian and Angie realized he had the

very intense look he got when he was exerting his will on…
something.

The scream locked in her throat inched upward. If he and
Aidan were exerting will, it meant they were holding off
something very bad and that meant there was something very
bad nearby. Some monstrous demon or something as
monstrous as a demon. Maybe something that ate demons.

She blinked hard and shoved away all those thoughts
because she just couldn't stay focused and do what she had to
do if she continued down that direction.

The churning gray overhead made her skin crawl and
moving even a little sent a rush of fear-fueled adrenaline
through her blood, but she did it. Watching the vibrating
medallion on her palm. It lifted off her skin a little, wavering
in the air as she moved away from her group. Far enough
away that Angie started to feel very exposed.

She glanced up. Churning grayness that she was going to
pretend were just clouds. Muted light that wiped out all
shadows. The black sand and gray sky all felt so
monochrome, the blue on the medallions chain from the
turquoise looked odd, like those black and white pictures
with just one thing on them colored.

And for some reason that was even more terrifying.

The medallion continued to hover over her hand, pulling
her neither one way or another. Not even back to her group
for a long moment. As if it was trying to decide which way
to go.

A grunt from Sebastian drew Angie's gaze back to him.

The medallion jerked in her hand, tugging at the chain

she'd wrapped around her fingers, and pulled her back toward her companions.

She didn't argue with it this time, just hurried back to them, her legs shaking.

When she reached Sebastian, she realized there was something poking out of the sand not more than fifty yards from him. A stock of some kind. It could have been a plant, except that it was black. And scaled. And had waving tendrils on the top. Pulsing tendrils that seemed to be gulping at the air through little suction-cup lined openings.

She wanted to ask what that was, but realized whatever it was, Sebastian was holding it off because he was staring at it with such concentration he wasn't even blinking.

She glanced back at Aidan and realized Aidan was doing the same focused stare, but she wasn't looking at a waving stock with pulsing tendrils at its tip. She was looking at a place where the sand had bulged up into a small mound, sand falling down the sides of the cone-shape.

Shit shit shit. None of this was even a little good.

"Medallion brought me back here after waffling," she whispered. "Next realm?"

"Next realm," Carmen said. "Why the fuck did I come with you?"

"Curiosity," Angie said as she searched her memory for a realm Betha had known and been too often.

"I am not this curious."

"Yes you are." Angie found another realm in her memory that seemed to be a place Betha went a lot. Found the way to opening into that realm. "The instant I get this portal open we are all going through at once. Got it?"

A grunt from Sebastian. Nothing from Aidan. Carmen said, "Hurry."

Yeah, Angie was going to hurry.

She grabbed hold of her demon witch thread, balancing with the witch magic, and opened the portal. So fast, it actually made her a little breathless. But tapping her magic this way, metaphysically "holding" it, also filled her with a great sense of strength and power. A feeling that raced through her blood, hot as the last realm they'd been in, making her feel electric and indestructible.

That feeling almost wiped away her fear it was so startling. Almost. Because she heard Sebastian grunt again. And Aidan made a sound like a hiss. And Angie realized there was something very large they were willing back and that was very very bad.

"It's open." She grabbed Sebastian's arm and Aidan's so she could maneuver them without them having to take focus from what they were doing. Touching them while she had so much magic coursing through her was probably a bad idea, but she'd worry about that later. No inadvertent psychic visions came through at least. She'd locked that part down, but with so much happening…

She walked Sebastian and Aidan to the portal, trusting Carmen to stay close. When they were standing right in front of it, she said, "We're going through. Get ready for the transition."

"You're going to have to close this the minute we're through," Carmen said.

"Yup." Angie tugged Sebastian and Aidan over the threshold, Carmen crowded close behind. And then Angie swung the portal closed, the swirl of fiery light closing down rapidly.

But not before she saw a blast of sand and something very dark rise up through that cloud of shining black crystals.

Something with a lot of teeth lunged. And the portal snapped shut.

CHAPTER TEN

Angie's brain couldn't process the monster she'd just glimpsed. Trying to "see" it would probably break her brain, so she settled for the impression of horrible and let the details go. Horrible and with lots of teeth was enough.

How the hell had Betha spent *time* in that realm. How had she survived?

Questions Angie would ask if they ever found the witch. A big question Angie wanted to ask was *why*. Why go into a place like that? There was nothing but sand and gray clouds and monsters that she'd been able to see.

Though, she supposed that the "nothing but monsters" part described most demon realms.

When she was sure the gateway was closed, she eased her grip on her magical threads and finally scanned her new surroundings. Adrenaline and terror were still racing through her blood, so she was jumpy already. Which was her excuse for why she squealed when a tree branch waved in front of her.

Sebastian's hands came up to her shoulders when she jumped back into him, steadying her.

"We're okay," he murmured, his voice sounding hoarse. "There's nothing nearby at the moment. Unless you count the foliage."

The foliage was bad enough. For once, this wasn't a barren realm. There were vines and trees and creeping plant stems everywhere. They were all red and looked horribly sharp. But at least it wasn't an empty landscape.

The sharp, red plants closed in around them. Not moving toward them or away from them. Not like the plants were reaching for them. Just waving in a breeze. But with all the sharp thorns, and hairs, and bits, she didn't fancy accidentally brushing against anything.

"I wouldn't touch any of the plants," Aidan said, her voice quiet and muted. "But we have some breathing room before being attacked."

"We did not in that last realm, did we?"

"No," Aidan said. And didn't say more.

She looked very serious and not nearly as relaxed as Angie was used to seeing her. That was as spooky as whatever that last monster had been.

Angie looked at the medallion. She'd left the chain wrapped around her fingers as they'd passed through the portal, not even bothering to put it back into her pocket. The silver disk twisted gently as she lifted her hand to look at it.

"I have no idea how Betha survived that last realm

visiting it so much," she said. "But this is another one she seems to have gone into a lot. At least, that's what's left in my mind from my vision of her." She flipped the medallion onto her palm. "Let's see if this takes us anywhere." Without the pressure of demons bearing down on them, Angie whispered the spell again, murmuring Betha's name.

This time, there was a definite pull on the disk. A sort of leaning in one direction. Angie frowned and started to carefully walk the way the medallion leaned. And found it definitely vibrated in that direction.

"Okay," she murmured. "Guess we're going for a walk this time." She glanced at the press of red vines and tree limbs. Walking through this forest of…well, she wasn't sure but it was probably deadly, was not going to be easy. "How do we get through all this without touching it?"

Sebastian glanced around, then set his backpack down and pulled something out of the depth. A very large knife. A machete. With a long handle made of silver that was etched with symbols.

"What the hell is that?" Angie asked, her eyes widening as he lifted the huge knife up.

"Gabriella gave this to me," he said. "Seemed to think we might need it. It's what it looks like. A big ass knife. But it's got some spells worked into it to make it resistant to…demon taint."

"That's…" Angie started.

"Surprising," Carmen finished, her eyes narrowed.

"Gabriella helping, or the knife itself?" Angie asked, though her gaze was still on the knife.

"Both," Carmen said. "But also the knife. That hasn't been let out of the archive in…a hundred years?"

Angie did finally turn to look at Carmen. "You've seen this before?"

Carmen managed her first smirk since they'd started jumping through demon realms. It was almost reassuring, that smirk. "It'll slice through the plant life," she said, ignoring Angie's question, "but what do we do about the stuff that comes out of the plants."

Angie frowned and looked around. Then groaned. Because of course the plant life in a demon realm wouldn't just drop harmlessly to the ground. Of course there'd be something deadly likely to come out. Poisoned sap. Or acid.

Or blood.

"You're a telekinetic," Aidan pointed out to Carmen. "Move the stuff away from us as we walk."

Carmen made a face, then nodded. "If we move slowly, I think I can manage."

Aidan snorted, almost a chuckle. "You can manage."

Carmen rolled her eyes. And again, Angie was struck by the fact that the two of them must have known each other before all this. At some point, they'd known each other well enough that Aidan knew about Carmen's telekinesis. Angie would really really like to know more about their past acquaintance.

One day, she intended on badgering Aidan into some answers.

That day was not this day. Because they were surrounded

by potentially deadly plants and the medallion was definitely pulling them in a direction here that, she hoped, led to Betha.

Sebastian glanced at Carmen. She gave him a nod, and he sliced through the nearest red vine tipped with sharp barbs. The knife cut through the plant easily. And predictably, the plant spewed…something. It was thick and red, like blood, which was what Angie had been afraid of. But it was a dark red, almost black color, and for some reason that made it worse. Thick, and viscus, it didn't spray out far. More sort of glumped out, oozing toward them.

It smelled weirdly like rotting detritus rather than blood or brimstone. A sort of sweetly rotting smell that was, in its own way, as nasty as the smell of rotten eggs. That stench got stronger when the black blood stuff oozed out.

Carmen grunted, flicking her hand at the sludge. The glump of blackish blood oozed in a different direction.

"Huh," Carmen muttered. "That takes will."

"Not usually a part of your telekinesis?" Angie asked as they started moving in the direction the medallion indicated. Slowly. Very very slowly.

"Not usually," Carmen said as she gestured at the next oozing line of blackish blood. "Usually just… It feels physical. Like, I think about moving something, then move it with a gesture, and my mind, but there's no…will behind it."

Angie nodded, though most of her attention was divided between the medallion in her palm so she assured they were still going the right way, and Sebastian carefully cutting away at the vegetation.

Most of the vines and branches dropped easily away from the knife. So easily, it was like he barely had to make effort. The blade was a hot knife through butter. An analogy that wasn't too far off, she realized, when she noticed the ends of the plants being cut were smoking as well as oozing blood, adding a scent like burnt meat to the sickly sweet detritus smell. And the knife in Sebastian's hand was glowing now, white hot.

"That's not hurting you, right?" she asked.

They moved in a clump, with Aidan taking up the rear, Sebastian in front, and Carmen and Angie more or less shoulder to shoulder in the center. The formation wasn't too difficult to maintain through the forest, so long as they stayed close together. And it meant Angie had a very good view of the knife.

"I can feel the heat," he said, cutting another plant, "but not in a way that's hurting me. The hilt isn't getting hot."

Carmen eased some hanging branches to the side with a sweeping gesture she made with both hands. "The hilt is fine, but I wouldn't touch the blade. It won't hurt Sebastian, while he's wielding it. But it'll slice through our limbs."

"Ew," Angie said.

Aidan chuckled.

"You sound more relaxed now," Angie commented to her.

"No demons nearby," she said. "Don't need as much will to keep the plants at bay."

Angie scowled back at her. "You're using will to keep the plants away?"

"Just a little." Aidan glanced down at the ground and Angie realized some of those vine tendrils were inching closer to them, then coming up against an invisible barrier. "They aren't moving toward us on purpose, by the way. Just…moving. It's what they do. That's why it's not taking as much will to keep them back."

"Ah." But also yuck. The fact that she might inadvertently have stepped on one of those vines without realizing because it had moved into her path made her legs feel that same dancing, anxiousness that had crawled up her limbs in the black sand realm.

Carmen pushed another spray of blackish blood back into the other foliage after Sebastain cut a particularly thick vine blocking their path. "Notice the…stuff isn't hurting the other plants? I thought it would burn them or something."

"They must be adapted to it," Angie murmured. "They're of the same realm. Just bad for us strangers." The medallion in her palm started to lean a slightly different direction. "We need to angle more right," she told Sebastian.

"There's a path here," he said. "Overgrown, but definitely a path. Someone else has cut through here before. Multiple times."

"Animal?" Angie asked hopefully.

"Demon," Carmen said with a grunt.

"The witch," Aidan said, sounding certain.

"I'd ask how you know that but I'm a little afraid of the answer," Angie said as they followed Sebastian, still cutting away the overgrowth as Carmen telekinetically caught and tossed away anything that sprayed.

"Demons don't make paths like this," Aidan said. "Too human and contained. Not chaotic enough. Not enough damage."

"Huh." Angie nodded. "You know, I thought you were going to say some hunter instinct or some other demonic sign."

"The witch is a human, even if she is a demon witch."

Angie gave Aidan a scowl that did nothing to ruffle the hunter's calm.

"She was here looking for something, right?" Aidan continued.

"Right."

"So she'd have had to work her way through all this too. And would have done it the way we are, cutting and avoiding the splatter. A demon adapted to this realm probably either doesn't care about the splatter or doesn't care about the thorns. Or dies if it gets into this forest." She considered their surrounds, nodding a little. "And maybe that's why there aren't any demons around. The forest would kill them."

"Oh good. Walking through the middle of something that kills demons. That's comforting." Angie tried not to shiver.

"I'm walking next to *someone* who can kill them," Carmen said. "Don't see me bothered."

Carmen's turn to receive the sour end of Angie's scowl. "I can't tell if that was an insult or not."

"I like that you can kill demons," Carmen said, before grunting and thrusting away a big spray of…something dark green and more liquidy than the blackish blood, which also smelled distinctly more like rotten meat. "Consider it a compliment."

"Right." Angie was feeling very complimented. She watched the little medallion as its vibration turned a little more to the right, but before she could tell Sebastian, he was already heading in that direction. "Following the path still?"

"Following the path."

"It's exactly where the medallion is leading."

"Is that good or bad?" he asked.

"Hopefully good." It meant they were nearing the person they'd come here to find. That had to be good, right? If it only took three realms and this one was their last—one without hoards of demons baring down on them to boot—then she'd take it.

She considered their location as they eased through the deadly foliage. If she had to move to a demon realm, to save the love of her life, she'd want a realm where they could live without being constantly attacked. They wouldn't have been able to survive constant attacks. Eventually, Betha would wear out.

Angie had assumed Betha had simply killed enough demons to scare the others into leaving her and Eloise alone. But maybe she'd done something a little less taxing.

Sebastian cut away another vine, and the path in front of him opened up into a kind of clearing. Not huge, but large enough for them to all stand together and have room. A spot the creeping vines seemed to be avoiding.

Just to be sure she asked Aidan.

"I'm not stopping them. They are circling around this clearing all on their own."

Angie looked up at the sky, now clearly visible above the red leaf and thorn canopy. It was a hazy sort of orange-pink color. Like sunset. The physics of demon realms was not the same as the physics of the human realm. Which meant things like sunrises and sunsets weren't a given. Angie had never once seen the red sky in the lava realm change more than a few shades, darkening a little and lightening a little. But every time she'd opened a portal into that realm, the sky had just been red.

Was there a sun in this one? Was it sunset right now? Or sunrise? Or did the sky just always look orange-pink. And if so, how the hell could they survive in this atmosphere?

"Pretty," Carmen commented, sounding a little sour. "Why aren't the vines moving into this space? What's wrong with it?"

"Good question." Aidan sounded more fascinated than sour.

"Which direction is the medallion pointing?" Sebastian asked quietly.

Angie nodded to a small break in the surrounding vines. A place that looked like it had been cleared before. There were three of those breaks in the surrounding foliage. Three places where they could follow an already cut path.

"Traps?" she asked Sebastian, but loud enough the others could hear.

"Possible," he said. "Or possible she was just searching in different directions while here."

"You sure about the direction?" Carmen asked. She moved closer to stare down at the medallion.

"That's the way it's leaning." But it wasn't just the medallion, Angie realized. There was a… She wanted to call it giddiness but that felt like a weird word to use while in a demon realm. But there was an eagerness in her gut, a sort of pull toward that direction that wasn't just from the medallion.

The sensation was so strange, she closed her eyes to make sure her web wasn't acting up. Adding more demon magic or something.

What she saw made her adrenaline surge. Not new lines of red, thankfully. But the two lines of demon magic, the two red lines that she'd picked up in the lava realm and that allowed her to kill demons… The two lines were stretching. Pulling toward…

The direction the medallion was leading them.

"What the hell?" she muttered.

Those same lines of power had done something similar in the fight with Sokolov's demon. She couldn't remember if she noticed that before or after opening the portals she'd opened during the fight but she did remember they'd been acting strange, just like this, stretching toward something.

Or maybe someone?

"Oh shit."

"What's wrong?" Sebastian, sounding intense and worried.

She popped her eyes open. "It's okay. I think. It's just… The demon magic? It's sort of pulling toward the direction the medallion is indicating too. It did that during the fight in the church as well."

Sebastian frowned.

"I think it's drawn to…Betha."

"You think your own magic is pulling you toward her?"

"Not mine. The demon magic," she said, because despite it being integrated into her web of magics now, she didn't—couldn't—consider it part of *her* magic. "None of the witch or demon witch threads are affected. It's just the magic I absorbed in the lava realm. It's not hurting me or anything. It's just… It's like it's reaching toward something."

"And you think that something is Betha."

She shrugged. "Maybe?" She looked to Aidan and Carmen, then back to Sebastian. "Or maybe it just likes being here?" If it was that last, though, they should probably take that as a warning. Demon magic being comfortable someplace probably meant that someplace wasn't comfortable for humans.

"We'll know if she's waiting for us at the end of this path," Aidan said, pragmatic as always. "Won't know until we get there."

Sebastian was still frowning at Angie, his brows lowered, the red light in the depths of his eyes a little brighter. "You sure you still want to do this."

"I'm worried about the magic thing too," she said. "But yes. We've come this far."

And honestly, she was worried about the return trip. She knew she could get them back to the human realm, because Betha had and that was in her mind. But this realm was "deeper" than the other two. A level farther removed from the human realm. And Angie wasn't sure she could get them directly back, even with the knowledge of how to in her head. If they found Betha, Angie could ask the other witch, make sure she knew exactly how to get everyone home directly.

That as much as anything else motivated her to keep going forward.

"Are you ready to start again?" he asked Carmen.

She nodded, but she was frowning at the ground around them. "Sure would love to know how this spot is so clear."

"Magic?" Angie asked.

Carmen shrugged. "Not that I can see. You?"

Angie tried looking at the area from her peripheral vision. Even made an attempt to see any auras in the area. But demon auras were still beyond her skill level. And apparently so were demon realm plants. She couldn't see anything magic or otherwise when she looked. At least not anything that stood out as different from the surroundings.

"Nothing." She shook her head.

Carmen's quiet grunt wasn't reassuring. Angie was curious about the mechanics of this clearing as well. But the giddiness and pull toward her destination was intensifying. And the little medallion was vibrating hard in the same direction.

"I think we'd better getting moving," she said, her gaze on the path barely blocked by a few red, thorny vines.

Sebastian gave her a look, but then moved toward the path and started cutting away foliage again as Carmen ensured the spray went in the opposite direction, and Aidan kept the creeping vines from creeping too close, while the scent of sickly sweet detritus and burnt meat wafted around them.

Angie kept an eye on the medallion. But she knew they were on the right path now.

The demon magic urged her on.

CHAPTER ELEVEN

The medallion on Angie's hand rose above her palm and started to float faster forward as they crept through the trees. Angie wrapped her free hand around the chain attached to the medallion, even though her fingers on the medallion hand were already looped through the silver and turquoise. With the medallion trying to race forward, she didn't want to risk losing it.

The red plant life and rotting detritus smell was still thick around them, but the path Sebastian was cutting with the glowing hot knife Gabriella had given him was less cluttered with branches and vines now. A more obvious path that hadn't been fully retaken by the jungle yet. Her group still remained in a clump together though, no one wanted to risk brushing against one of the thorns on the plants.

With the more opened path, though, they were able to

move a little faster, able to keep up with the medallion as it tried to fly to its destination.

"We have to be very close," she murmured. "It did this same thing when we were hunting for Carmen in the desert."

Carmen didn't comment but she did give the medallion a side glance before deflecting another spray of blackish blood from a vine looped down across the path.

Angie started to hunt their surroundings for signs of Betha. Obviously the medallion thought she was close. There had to be evidence of…something. Or maybe this was just where the demon witch would meet them. It was hard for Angie to imagine Betha would want all these strangers showing up at her door and endangering Eloise. Yet the signs of someone having been through here relatively recently couldn't be denied.

The thought that it might be another human, someone *else* living in this place, made Angie a bit panicky. One human—or rather two humans—living in a demon realm was bad enough. More than that would horrify her.

Since the medallion was reacting so strongly, she also checked those threads of demon magic in her web. They were still *leaning* the same direction as the medallion, but they weren't leaning more or pulling harder, the way the medallion was. Just stretched in that same general direction.

The sense of giddy excitement filling her was not what Angie would have expected in this place and contrasted sharply with her lizard brain's signals that this was all very bad and she should run away.

The path opened up in front of them again, this time onto

a much larger clearing. One that encompassed a small house, a patch of the red-brown earth with stalks of…something growing in it, and a strange sort of gazebo built to one side of the house, with a red roof held up by thick pillars of a wood that looked almost purple. Angie hadn't seen any plants in the jungle they'd passed through with wood like that, but that didn't mean the trees didn't exist somewhere. Probably just not along the path they'd taken.

The area was quiet but for a small bird-like creature sitting on the top of the gazebo. It made a cawing noise that was a cross between a crow and one of the flying demons that lived above the volcanoes in the lava realm. The sound poked sharply at Angie's ears, making them hurt a little. Not enough to cover them. The call wasn't loud. Just… discordant.

The creature cawed again, then took flight on black leathery wings, it's yellow and orange feathered body almost instantly blending into the strange sky. The light from that pink orange sky hadn't changed since she'd last saw it, so if this was sunrise or sunset colors, the process took much longer than it did in her realm.

After the bird left, the clearing fell silent. No one came out of the house. Or out of the jungle surrounding the house. The medallion on Angie's palm had stopped flying forward and now rested against her skin again, vibrating quietly, as if content. The air around the cabin was significantly cooler than it had been under all the trees and vines, with a chilled breeze that was almost cold. Not what she'd expected in a demon realm so she was glad of her jacket. Carmen's leathers seemed an even better idea now too. Not just because they'd have protected her from the thorns and vines inside the jungle, but they'd be comfortably warm in the cold breeze.

Angie glanced at her companions. Aidan was watching the surrounding jungle, her full attention on the plant life—which was not creeping into the clearing at all, but was being stacked up against a border the way it had grown against the circular border in the first clearing. Sebastian watched the house and gazebo, his eyes narrowed, the spark of red in their depths a little stronger now, but not flaring. Carmen was spinning in a slow circle, taking it all in, hands on hips as she scowled.

"This the place?" she asked Angie. "I mean, it has to be, doesn't it? Don't imagine demons live this way." She paused, then shrugged. "Though honestly, I've never thought about a demon house. They live in houses in our realm, though, don't they."

"That's because we do and they wouldn't be able to blend in otherwise," Aidan said absently, her attention still on the jungle. "But for the record, some demons do build and live in homes that would be familiar looking to humans." She shrugged. "Others build and live in monstrous castles and pavilions. Some live in caves. Some just wander the plains. Depends on the species."

"You know a lot more about demons than even the council does," Carmen commented.

"I do," Aidan agreed. Without explaining further.

Angie was very tempted to allow herself to get distracted so she could ask Aidan all the questions she wanted to ask her in that moment. But this wasn't the place to do that. Getting distracted here could get them all killed.

Instead, she concentrated on the house, small as it was, and the fact that it was so silent. Did she just…go up and knock on the door? The medallion seemed to be indicating that they'd reached their destination. That meant Betha was close. She had to be around here somewhere or the medallion would have just led them past the cabin and directly to her.

Just to be sure, though, Angie whispered the spell and Betha's name again.

The medallion continued to vibrate against her palm. And she got that weird sense of happiness or giddiness in her stomach. But she wasn't being pulled anywhere. She made sure the others were watching their surroundings, then closed her eyes briefly to look at her web. The two threads of demon magic were still slightly stretched. Not relaxed and settled into the rest of the shape.

Pulling toward the house.

Okay. Guess she went up and knocked on the door.

She started toward the house, hunting the area as she moved, watching the windows inside the small structure. There were only two in the front of the house, not large, but not arrow-slit small either. Large enough to let in the weird lighting. Small enough to block off with boards if needed.

No one looked out, though. Not that she could see.

If this was some demon's home and she knocked on the door, she was going to be as embarrassed as she was terrified. The whole idea of *knocking on a demon's door* seemed so absurd she wanted to laugh. And also run screaming back into the jungle.

Once again, she asked herself why they were doing this. She'd had good reasons. At every opportunity to back out, she'd insisted they go forward. And yet there was still a part of her wondering if she shouldn't have just stayed home and tried to enjoy her life before a demon killed her. Running *to* the demons and their realms felt like rushing the "demons killing her" part of her life.

No one peeked out the windows. No sounds came from inside the house. If Betha was in there, she was being extremely silent. And Eloise. What of her? Inside? Dead? But if Eloise weren't still alive, Betha would have no reason to remain in a demon realm, so she had to be around here somewhere too.

The silence was oppressive and as frightening as knocking on the door would be. Angie fisted her hand around the medallion, still humming happily in her palm, and knocked on the door using that hand. The wood muffled the sound, rather than it echoing, like her knocks were sinking into dirt. It was a strange sort of disconnect from what she'd excepted. Opposites world, she thought. Or maybe just weird world.

Noisy homes were quiet. Knocks were muffled rather than loud. What else would be opposite or weird? Maybe food was sniffed instead of eaten?

She waited for a few moments, her gaze jumping back to the others, still standing in the open, then to the door again. She looked around from the corner of her eye, trying to spot magic of some kind at work, but didn't see anything that looked like witch magic.

And maybe there wasn't any witch magic. She'd used hers in the demon realms, to call down lightning. But she had no idea what kind of *witch* Betha was. Only that she was one because all demon witches were witches. Also, they all seemed to be women, or at least female presenting. And in this one case, Angie had a strong suspicion that Betha was also a touch psychic like herself.

But there was nothing she'd come across in the demon hunters' archive or in Betha's thoughts to indicate that all demon witches had to be strong *witches* with strong *witch* magic.

Angie happened to be. But she had no idea how common that was among demon witches.

It was funny she'd never thought about that before. She kept compartmentalizing her various magics. But they were all integrated into her web of power. Which meant they fed into and support each other. They were integrated even if the threads were distinct. Each one affected the others.

So the fact that she had very strong *witch* magic probably affected the other kinds of magic in her web.

A strangely interesting epiphany she'd have to think about soon. Or maybe even discuss with Betha. It'd be really nice to be able to talk about all this stuff with another demon witch.

If they actually ever found her.

If this wasn't a trap.

The thought snuck in under her skin, though she had been

trying not to think about possible betrayal. It was hard enough moving through the demon realms, and she was still jumpy and horrified by the two previous ones—that someplace could be so much worse than the lava realm it made her miss the lava realm had not been a fact she'd considered before taking this journey—and thinking about this being a trap, a betrayal, was too distracting.

But now that the thought was there, in this weirdly quiet clearing with no signs of life in the house even though her medallion said Betha was here... Angie couldn't shake the worry.

She lifted her hand to knock again, but a voice from just beyond the clearing stopped her, hand in the air.

"You actually found me."

CHAPTER TWELVE

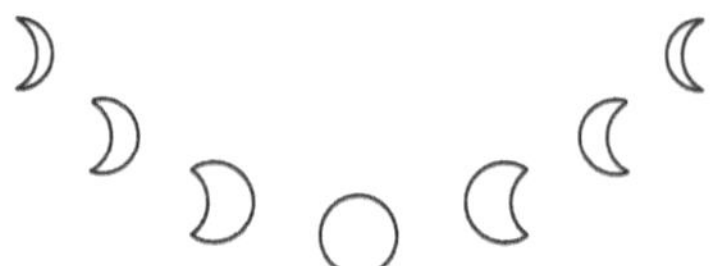

ngie turned slowly toward the voice that had come from the jungle, her heart thumping. A shield spell automatically rose to her lips and she found herself murmuring the words and making the distinct finger gestures to create the shield. Except she wasn't standing next to the others, which meant she wouldn't be protecting them. She edged away from the door so she'd be able to defend the others if needs be.

She still wasn't sure if she would be protecting them from a demon or not.

A woman stepped from the vines and trees, just to the edge of the clearing. She was dressed, neck to toe, in a sort of jumpsuit made of shimmering scales. The scales themselves were a dark dark blue, the shimmer over them sparkled almost purple. The combination was fascinating to look at. And reminded Angie of the gloves Betha had worn when she'd come out of the portal into the old church turned warehouse after they'd defeated Sokolov's demon. Gloves, Angie realized, that Betha had stuffed into a pocket in the jumpsuit.

Her long dark hair was pulled back into a bun today, twisted to the back of her head tightly. She was older than she'd been in the visions of course, but not as old as one might expect of a centuries old woman. Thinner, though. Her cheeks hollow. And eyes that Angie knew had once been brown were now very red.

A demon's eyes.

Betha blinked and the red vanished.

But Angie saw the way her mouth moved and her fingers twitched before the red disappeared so she knew Betha had cast an illusion spell to hide the red.

Betha used magic the way Angie did—the spells requiring a combination of words and hand gestures. She was a touch psychic the way Angie was—at least Angie was pretty sure of that based on her visions. And Betha was a demon witch who could now kill demons.

That so much of their power was the same couldn't be a coincidence. Angie was *sure* of it.

But this could still be a trap.

"Thank you for recommending I use my mentor's medallion," Angie said. "We wouldn't have found you otherwise."

"Even with the information I left in the blood?"

"Left in the blood?"

Betha smiled faintly. "Obviously we have a lot to talk

about." She glanced behind her. "And things are quiet at the moment. Why don't we go inside. It's safe here in the clearing."

"I noticed." Angie gestured to the cleared circle. "How do you keep the vines out?"

"Blood. Everything here is always about blood." She sighed. "Eloise is sleeping. We'll have to be quiet. But she sleeps very soundly these days."

"She's still with you." Angie nodded. She'd wondered, and half worried, Eloise had died. But if she had, there'd be no real reason for Betha to have remained here all these centuries. Except maybe to kill demons.

"She's…not good," Betha said. "But she's better here."

"Should we talk outside. I don't want to disturb her."

"The sleep is…deep. We'll be fine inside."

There was more there Betha wasn't saying. Angie hoped for better answers once they settled.

Betha glanced at the others. "There's room inside for us all." She gestured at the house, and her scale covered suit shimmered in the weird orange-pink light. "I know it looks small. It's bigger on the inside." Her gaze flickered to Carmen. "You're real this time." She nodded and then went to the house door without another word, leaving the door open as she went inside.

"Real?" Carmen asked.

"Not a Khymir demon," Angie said. "That was the last version of you Betha saw."

"The dead Khymir? That's disturbing."

"Not the only thing," Angie murmured with a sigh.

Sebastain stepped close. "Should one of us stay out here?"

"It'll be very obvious if someone does that we don't trust her," Angie said.

"We don't," Sebastian pointed out.

But she'd been trying not to make that too obvious. Though Betha probably knew they didn't trust her already. Or any of this. There were demons about. A smart witch didn't trust anything in a demon realm.

"I'll stay outside," Aidan offered. She nodded to a chair just outside the front door. "I'll sit and keep an eye on things."

"We'll leave the door open if Betha doesn't object," Angie said.

She still had her shield spell up, hesitant to drop it, even though the woman who appeared to be Betha hadn't done anything threatening at all. In fact, she'd been pretty matter-of-fact that they'd found her. Not necessarily pleased, but not upset. In fact, Angie really hadn't been able to read Betha's expression. There was a neutrality to it that was... disconcerting.

That emotional disconnect, the lack of emotion, had Angie keeping her shield up as she led Sebastian and Carmen into the house. Carmen hesitated at the door, glanced at Aidan as she sat in the purple-wood chair, then followed close to Angie and Sebastian.

The interior of the house was larger than it looked from the outside. There were levels below the main floor, though how many Angie couldn't see at a glance, with the top floor being mostly open space with some wooden chairs, a single couch, and a small hearth opposite the door. The floor and walls an orange-red sandstone-like stone, with a few windows letting in the strange orange-pink light from outside. The center of the room was a circular staircase going down. The hole in the floor was surrounded by a low wooden fence-like banister that Angie still thought looked pretty unsafe.

Betha gestured at the staircase. "There are two more stories below this and the stairs can be blocked off. Those levels can be made secure from demon attack. Though we don't get much of that now. And not here. But it's not wise to take that for granted."

"Why *here* specifically?" Angie meant why live here, in this jungle, in this realm, and was glad she didn't have to clarify for the other witch.

"The jungle. The demons have a hard time entering it. Most of them are vulnerable to the thorns and would die or be seriously wounded by the sap that comes out of the plants."

"Most?"

"The ones who aren't vulnerable are just as dangerous to other demons as the plant life. There are…two kinds of demons who can enter this jungle. The Aminore and the Helavitee demons. But they don't come into my territory anymore."

Those weren't demons Angie had heard of before. "Because you can kill them?"

Betha nodded, showing no real expression to Angie's

comment. Just the matter-of-fact nod. "Do you want some tea? I brought some back the last time I went into the human realm for supplies that is really good."

"Water?" Angie asked, curious how Betha and Eloise had managed even the basics of survival in a land designed to destroy humans.

"There's ground water here. Go deep enough and it's purified. There's a well at the base of the house that we use." Betha set a hanging kettle on the hook inside the hearth, over a low fire. "We can burn the wood as long as we let it dry long enough for all the sap to dry up. It's not dangerous to us when its dried and burns. Actually smells kind of nice. And has the added benefit of driving off demons when they smell the smoke."

Betha gestured to some of the chairs scattered around the hearth, arrayed in front of the couch. "Make yourself at home." She snort-laughed, the first real expression she'd allowed. It was a bitter sound as far from a real laugh as a sound could get.

She went to a cabinet by the nearest window, a window that looked out onto the jungle behind the house, and plucked out four mugs. Then paused. "Will your friend outside have a cup of tea?"

"Probably not yet," Sebastian answered for Aidan. "She doesn't like to drink or eat much if she's going to be in a demon fight. The smells." He shrugged.

Betha nodded. "Smart. We probably won't have to worry about demons, but with two of us now…" She shrugged and brought the mugs, all four at once, to a small bench set to one side of the hearth. The bench also had some red clay jars on it, and an anachronistic plastic food storage box with a clip-on lid. The clear plastic box was full of tea bags.

"Two of us?" Angie said.

Betha glanced at her. "Demon witches." She winced. "Apocalypse witches."

"Apocalypse witches…?"

Angie frowned at Betha's back as the other witch dropped tea bags into the mugs, then went to retrieve the now whistling kettle from the fire. She used a metal hook to remove it and a tea towel to hold the hot handle while she poured water into the mugs. She kept her back to them was she waited for the tea to steep and then took the bags out with a spoon, dropping them into a waiting bowl. She didn't offer sugar or milk, but Angie could hardly blame her since tea was more of a luxury here than she'd expected.

She watched Betha's tea-making process with some interest, but most of her mind had gotten caught on that term Betha had used. Apocalypse witch. That's what Sokolov's demon had been afraid of. He'd been trying to escape the coming apocalypse witch. And that was who had killed him. Well, Betha had killed him—at least the person they were looking at right now who Angie *thought* was Betha—and that was what the demon had called her.

But it wasn't a term Angie had heard before. When she'd asked Carmen about it, Carmen had been cagey. So had Aidan. Sebastian hadn't heard the term.

To be fair, none of the hunters had used the term demon witch for her either. Early on, Sebastian had said the hunters referred to people who could do what Angie did—opening portals—as realm splitters. Angie had only learned the term demon witch because of Carmen.

But now that Angie had seen almost everything the hunters had on people like her, she knew the term apocalypse witch wasn't in their books and papers. Which meant whatever Carmen and Aidan knew about it, it wasn't from those records.

The term had invoked a boogeyman of such horrifying proportions it had terrified a powerful demon. A *very* powerful demon. Scared. Of someone who wasn't another demon.

Angie's brain still couldn't quite make that make sense. Yet she'd witnessed it. And witnessed Betha easily killing that powerful demon.

She had so many questions, she wasn't sure where to start as Betha handed around the mugs of tea and then sat on the couch across from the various hardback wooden chairs they'd taken. Sebastian gave his tea a subtle sniff and his expression revealed his surprise, though maybe only to Angie since she knew his face so well. He sipped the tea hesitantly. Then gave a small nod. Angie smiled into her mug.

"Good?" Betha asked, also smiling faintly.

"Perfect." Sebastian was sincere in his compliment.

"You're surprised."

"I'm a tea drinker who lives in the US most of the time. I'm always surprised with a good cup of tea."

"Tea snob," Angie added, just to be clear.

He gave her a look and she grinned back, unrepentant.

Betha watched them, her thoughts hidden behind a neutral expression. "The US is…an interesting historical development."

"That's a very politic way to put it," Angie said.

Betha shrugged. "I've seen a lot of changes over the years. Usually in leaps and bounds. Time is…odd here."

"To you, how long have you lived here?" Since Betha seemed inclined to talk, Angie would ask questions. And this seemed a relatively easy place to start.

"Hard to say," Betha admitted. "I don't have a calendar. And the days and nights… Well, it can be hard to tell them apart sometimes. Things don't change that much for a long time. Then they do. If I had to guess, I'd say a day and night here go on for the equivalent of a month in human time. But I don't age a month in that time. If I had, I'd have died a long time ago. I think."

"You aren't sure?"

"The…" Betha shook her head, pulled in a deep breath. Sipped her tea. "We're getting ahead of ourselves a bit. First, how much do you know about…your situation?"

"Depends on which part of it you mean," Angie said. She wasn't sure if she should reveal everything to Betha, but getting answers would require some quid pro quo. Some trust. On both their parts.

So she told a brief and edited version of getting caught in the lava realm with Carmen and Sebastian. That she'd only learned a few months before that that she could open portals without needing trees. And that, in the process of getting out of the lava realm, she'd accidentally pulled in some of the realm's magic and incorporated it into her own powers.

She didn't get too specific about her visualization for all that power, the web she used as a reference point. And she didn't go into all the details around how they'd been trapped. Who had trapped them. But she did talk about what had happened after she'd absorbed the magic.

"I didn't even believe it myself the first time," she said. "A human can't kill a demon."

"Until they can," Betha said with a nod. "When did you believe?"

"After I killed a second demon, and there were witnesses to confirm…what had happened."

"My newfound ability arose in a moment of pressure and panic, too." She considered Angie, her eyes narrowed. The red was still hidden behind whatever spell Betha had used, but Angie had a hard time not seeing it if she glanced at Betha from a certain angle. "You're able to read things with touch, aren't you?" Betha asked. "You can pick up…images, knowledge through touch?"

Angie gave a jerking nod. "You can too."

"I can. That's why I left the blood."

"The blood?"

"On the document Yusof and I composed. He needed it for his people and we couldn't have them knowing the truth but… But by that stage I'd heard of the apocalypse witch and knew… I knew another would rise. Sometime in the future. But it wasn't clear how long I'd have to… How long that would be. I couldn't be sure I'd still be alive and I wanted to leave her as much information as I could. The blood seemed the best way. So much history and emotion and knowledge in the blood."

There had been. "The…apocalypse witch has to be a touch psychic?" Angie asked. "You knew that would be a prerequisite?"

"I did. It's complicated. But yes. I knew the witch in question would have to have a certain configuration of powers. A very specific combination. There were a few who've come close over the centuries, but no other witch reached the level of being able to kill demons. Or, at least they didn't survive long after they reached that level. Surviving it is the real trick."

Angie's head spun with the information, the implications, and the fact that other witches *had* died after absorbing demon magic and being able to kill demons. That had happened, not just with Betha. At least, that seemed to be what Betha was implying. And it meant Morty hadn't been wrong to expect and assume Angie would die.

But how had Morty known since that wasn't in the records anywhere?

"There was one with such anger," Betha continued, "I thought for sure she'd be the one." She frowned. "I'm not sure how long ago she lived, in your time, exactly. But it was when your country was not even a country yet. Just settlements where Europeans had stolen other people's land."

Angie nodded. She knew the witch Betha was referring to. No one used her name. She was the witch who'd supposedly had maps of the demon realms. And whose coven had had to kill her when she'd loosed a demon plague on the world in retribution for the witch trials.

That had happened in the seventeenth century. According to Gabriella, that happened about a hundred years or so after Betha's time—based on the period Yosuf, the demon hunter, had been active. There were no dates in Eloise's diary to indicate *when* Betha and Eloise had lived exactly. Only that it was written in English, though an older word choice and cadence. Angie still wasn't entirely sure where Betha had lived before living here in the demon realms.

"I've read of her," Angie said of the witch whose coven had killed her. "At least, a little. What the hunters have been able to get. There's apparently more information about her that a witch historian is keeping."

"That is information better kept in witches' hands anyway," Betha said, her gaze flicking to Sebastian and then away. Settling back on Angie. "She was angry, and so powerful. I thought she'd be the one. But...no. No. She was a strong witch. And a strong enough demon witch to travel the realms a little. But she wasn't a touch psychic. Her psychic abilities took a different form. Card reading. Divinations through scrying."

"I can scry," Angie said. She had several ways of accessing psychic visions. The touch was just one of them. But it was her strongest. Easiest. The other ways required actual spells to make them work. She didn't need to do anything with her touch skill except control it.

"Yes, so can I." Betha nodded. "With a spell. But I can also get those visions through touch. That other witch could not. She didn't have that one element to her mix of powers. And she never managed to take in the infection. Her coven killed her before I could figure out why she seemed to be immune."

"Immune? You still talk of the ability to kill demons as an infection?"

"What do you call it?"

Angie shook her head, frowning. She probably should explain her web of magic to make this conversation easier. She still hesitated a moment longer, though, worried that she was giving too much away. But if she wanted answers of her own, this might be the only option.

Finally, she said, "I have a visualization for my magic, for the various magics woven together to form my powers. A spiderweb. I pulled in magic in the lava realm and incorporated that into my web. Two strands of that magic run through the rest."

Betha sat forward, her head tilted, the first signs of real emotion in her expression. An eager interest that hadn't been there before. "A web, you say. That's fascinating. I don't have that. It's all just nebulously there. An…aura if you like. But I can't see the parts distinctly."

"Discovering I could was an accident. During a spell casting. But…I needed that view to start opening portals without trees."

And goddess wasn't it nice to talk about this out loud with someone who *understood*. Not just in an abstract way, but in the bone deep way of someone who could do all these things. Even her other witch friends, who she could talk to about anything magical, didn't understand at the level of experience what Angie was dealing with daily. The freedom of knowing she'd be understood made it difficult to restrain, to hold back. She wanted to just spill everything with Betha and get answers in return.

The thought that this still might be a trap of some kind, that this wasn't actually Betha, was still hovering in the back of her mind. Made her wince internally when she eagerly blurted out personal things. But she couldn't seem to help it. Betha *understood*. Angie didn't have to *explain* everything in metaphor or abstracts. When she talked about opening a portal without a tree, Betha *knew* what that meant.

"I found that skill on accident too," she said, "though not in a vision."

"The ability to open treeless portals happened during a demon fight, not during that vision," Angie clarified. "But I found if I held the thread in my web that's the demon witch magic, and held a line of witch magic for balance, I can open and close portals any time."

"You needed the balance of the two to get it to work?"

"I can control it that way. I don't go around accidentally opening portals. I need to grab that particular magic to open treeless portals, and to keep from getting swept under by it all and letting a hoard out, I use the witch magic as balance."

"I see." Betha's gaze turned inward but she didn't comment.

Angie wanted to ask her more about how her portals worked, though she sort of knew from the visions of Betha.

Angie would love to hear more in detail. But a beat passed and it looked like Betha wouldn't offer the information.

And Agine found herself spilling out more of her own experiences without meaning to. "Before I incorporated the magic from the demon realm into my web, I could close those portals by simply looking away, the way I did with ordinary tree portals. Now, I have to shove open the portal and shove it closed. It's easy. A well hinged door that swings open and shut with little pressure. But it stays open and only closes with that little push."

"Yes! Yes. For some time after I was infected, I could still close a tree portal simply by looking away. The others required that push. Then after…" She swallowed and blinked hard a few times. "How much did you see when you touched the blood I left for you?"

"A lot, I think. Are you talking about *that* night?"

"*That* night. Yes."

The night she'd opened a portal onto the realm of the demon gods. A realm not accessible for even most demons. A realm where actual gods lived and which, even in the secondhand vision, had been so horrendously unknowable, Angie's head had hurt in her real body. She'd also accidentally opened a portal in the archive during that vision, but that was a story for later.

"Since then," Betha said, skipping the details of the night in question. "Since then I need to shove a tree portal closed too."

Angie could still look away and close portals if she created them using a tree. But she worried about a time when that wouldn't be enough. "Why do you think being a touch psychic is necessary?"

Betha shook herself out of her thoughts. "That's part of the legend," she said. "With the one whose anger ruled her, I thought… But no. The legend is right. The apocalypse witch must also be able to get visions through touch."

Angie blinked. "Legend? What legend?"

"The demons' legend. The one prophesizing the apocalypse witch. The legend that they think spells their doom."

CHAPTER THIRTEEN

*A*ngie sat with her cooling mug of surprisingly good tea between her hands as she let Betha's statement sink in. A legend. She supposed that made some sense, given Sokolov's demon's reaction to Betha, his fear. But the demon had also seen Betha in action. So Angie hadn't considered his fear was more than that at the time.

But the demons had a whole legend around Betha. Except… From what Betha just implied, the legend was there before she was. It didn't arise from Betha's ability to kill demons. It predated that.

Angie glanced at Sebastain, who glanced back, but his expression was carefully neutral—likely more for Betha and Carmen's sake than Angie's. She looked at Carmen, too, whose expression was also closed up, but Carmen, her eyes narrowed, was staring at Betha where she sat across from them on the couch. And Angie got the impression Carmen knew more than she'd admitted—not a stretch, Carmen always knew more than she admitted. And hid behind a cocky smirk when she didn't know more.

Carmen had been enthrall to a demon once, though. If there was a legend prophesizing the doom of the demon realms, Carmen had probably heard it.

"Can you tell me more about the legend?" Angie asked Betha, facing her again.

"Give me just a minute," Sebastian said, rising and setting his empty tea mug on the stone floor beside his chair —the tea must have really met his approval. "I just want to make sure Aidan doesn't need anything."

That was strange. Angie watched him go to the front door, turned back to Betha, and realized Betha was watching Sebastian with narrowed eyes.

"A demon hunter, hm?" she asked Angie quietly. "That's…unexpected with someone like you."

"I get that impression," she said.

"You love him?"

"Yes."

"Love is dangerous for witches like us."

"I've gotten that impression, too."

"It will leave you vulnerable to bad decisions."

Angie almost snort-laughed at that, but swallowed the reaction. Betha's comment was an understatement. "Makes him vulnerable to bad decisions, too. We…do our best. And talk it all out."

"Sometimes even that won't help," Betha said quietly, her gaze steady on Angie's.

Angie wasn't sure whether to take that statement as a threat or just a warning, especially given what had happened to Eloise, so she took it as both. She could feel Carmen's gaze on the size of her face, but didn't turn to face the other witch, just continued to hold Betha's considering gaze.

When Sebastian rejoined them, he said, "She's fine and said so far no sign of any demons."

Betha nodded. "As I said, we shouldn't get any here. But having a hunter at the door will help."

"Why don't the demons come here exactly?" Angie asked. "Outside of the jungle being a bad place for so many of them. There are still a few who can roam this area. You said they don't come here anymore. Because you can kill them. The smoke from your fire? Or is it the blood circle? What *exactly* keeps them away?"

"All of it. It's taken a lot to carve out some space here. But mostly… It's the blood, yes." She made a small gesture with her head and shoulders that could have been a shrug. "I guess I can tell you. I use blood from a demon kill and set some circles in the area. The one around my house that protects us and keeps the vines out. A few in the jungle where my paths intersect so I can remember where I'm going. I use the blood similarly to how you might use salt to form a protective circle. The blood circles are protective as well, but not like ordinary magic circles. We can pass over them without breaking them. They're just circles of blood buried in the dirt. And that keeps both the vines and the prowling demons away. Mostly. I have to reenergize them with new blood every so often. Or the vines start to creep in again."

"Can a demon get past the circle or does it just drive them away?"

"Drives them away. They don't like the smell. Means we're mostly safe, but there are some who might try…getting past the stench to attack anyway. I live—We live with that threat out there all the time, so we have other protections in place." She gestured to the stairs going down. "But the circle gives us some peace."

"Fair enough." Angie frowned a little. "Every time I've killed a demon they vaporize. Where are you getting blood?"

"I've developed different ways of killing. Not just the bolt from my hand. Things that are just as deadly but leave enough behind for me to drain their blood."

The thought made Angie's stomach turn, but she kept that reaction to herself. There wasn't a lot of blood involved in her kind of magic, but she didn't like to judge the witches who needed more for their workings—unless they proved themselves untrustworthy or evil. But the idea of using a lot of blood in her magical spellwork had always bothered her. That wasn't made better by the blood being demon blood, she realized.

"Did that take long?" Carmen asked, her first comment the entire conversation.

Betha glanced at her. "To learn how to kill them in different ways? You could say so from a certain perspective. But my measurements of time are distorted, so I can't say for sure. It seemed like it happened relatively quickly for me. But for the passage of time beyond this realm…" She shrugged.

While this was all fascinating, Angie wanting to get back on track. Since she didn't want to live in a demon realm, being able to form a circle of safety using demon blood wasn't knowledge she needed immediately. "Can you explain the legend to me now?"

"The legend." Betha sighed and nodded. "A myth. So they thought. No one I've…talked to has been able to tell me how old the legend is or when it arose. I know it was there before me because one demon called me that just before I killed it and that was too early in my ability to kill demons for the source of the legend to be me."

"I was wondering that," Angie said quietly. "What does it say, exactly?"

"There are various versions, but they all come down to a human witch will arise who can do what no other human can do, and she will destroy all the realms, even the god realm, until there are no demons left."

"That sounds…" Angie huffed and set her now empty tea mug on the small table between them. "That sounds impossible." In the vision, Betha's brain had nearly shattered just reaching a hand into the god realm to retrieve some sand for what she thought would be a cure for Eloise. Pushing her human hand into that world had been excruciatingly painful. Betha having the power to *destroy* that realm seemed absurd.

Betha said, "I think that last part is hyperbole. Exaggeration to really scare the demons. I think most of it is hyperbole, honestly. But… There are elements that are not exaggerations."

"Like the fact that you as a human can still kill demons."

"That, yes. But there's more."

"What more?"

"The more is the reason I left the blood behind, knowing you would need it. Knowing you'd show up and need the information I'd gathered over that year. Knowing we'd need to meet." Betha's gaze jumped from her to Sebastian, then back again. "The legend says that, after the appearance of the first apocalypse witch, a second would arise. And then a third. When the third arose, all would be doomed and lost."

"I'm the second?"

Betha nodded. "I've been waiting for you for a long time, Angela Jordan. I planted the seeds, hoping you'd find them when you finally came into your powers. And after all this time…here you are."

"But… But I thought you were looking for a, a cure for the demon magic you've pulled in. I thought you were trying to rid yourself of it." Angie hadn't known that for sure. She'd only known, through Eloise's diary, that Betha was looking for medicine. And because of the vision of *that* night, Angie knew at least some of that cure was for Eloise. But Angie had hoped…

Angie wanted was a cure. She wanted a way to take this target off her back and not be able to kill demons anymore. She didn't want to be an apocalypse witch. She just wanted to go back to being a witch.

"The medicine I sought, that led me to *that* night," Betha said, "was for Eloise. I'm sure you saw that."

"That she can't leave the demon realms without getting sicker, yes. But what about you?"

Betha shrugged. "I started out looking for some way to rid myself of this curse. But after a while, I decided it wasn't a curse after all. Killing demons, destroying something so evil… There are worse ways to live."

Angie had to resist the urge to look around at the house built in a demon realm with safeguards and lockdown levels to protect from a constant threat. No time to relax completely. No friends or family besides Eloise. Only occasional comforts of home. Angie knew there were worse ways to live, but this ranked right up there for her. A life she did *not* want.

Betha obviously read Angie's reaction in her expression because she shrugged. "I'll allow, this isn't a great lifestyle." She gestured at the house. "But when it's this or my love's life, I'll take this. And if I couldn't kill demons, I couldn't keep her safe here. So it worked out in the end."

"In the visions, you thought you'd been the one to infect Eloise. But you know that's not what happened, not how it could have happened, right?"

Betha's slow blink made Angie worry. That after all this time, Betha still thought she could pass on the demon magic to a human who wasn't even a witch.

Then Betha said, "It took me a long time to accept that, and I still blame myself. Not for…infecting her. Technically. But for putting her in a position to get infected. I brought her here, to escape those hunting us. It was a temporary move. Here and back, I thought. Just long enough for the men to get confused and go away. But… Being here was not good for her. Bringing her here was a very bad decision. Caused the problem."

"How could you have known?" Angie said quietly.

"That doesn't comfort me when I see her suffer." Betha waved a hand. "But it hardly matters anymore. Our situation is what it is."

"Do you know…how she was infected?" In Eloise's case, the term seemed more applicable than what had happened to Betha and Angie. Sort of. Angie did still feel like she'd picked up an infection of some kind, only it would take more than antibiotics to get rid of it.

"We're still not entirely sure. When she's here, though, it seems to remain in balance enough that she functions fine. She's only in real danger when we go back and stay in the human realm too long. She reacts the way one of the weaker demons might at leaving its own realm. Some just can't go anywhere else without suffering, even dying. Their… chemistry is the word, I suppose, is not compatible with the human realm. That's good for humans. None of those demons try to worm their way into the human world. Bad for Eloise, since she seems to now be like those demons."

"The cure you made that night, for Eloise. Did it help at all?"

"For a time." Betha pulled in a deep breath, let it out slowly. "She seemed to be recovering after. Stronger. Able to withstand being in the human realm. I thought we'd be able to go back." Betha rolled her lips into her mouth. Then, "But we still can't stay for too long. She can return with me for longer periods now, if she wants to. She can be there. But she's… more comfortable here now. Her body is physically happier while she's here. Being in the human realm drains her. Exhausts her after a time." Betha glanced at the stairs. "She doesn't go back often now. She doesn't like the way it feels."

"And you've found no other way to cure her?"

Betha's gaze flickered before she met Angie's again. Something in that expression made Angie's pulse pound, and she wasn't entirely sure why. An instinct that was deep and went right past her logical thoughts to her lizard brain.

"Nothing," Betha said.

But she was lying. Angie couldn't read her aura—it was either too big or Betha knew how to block it from an aura reader—but Angie didn't really need to. Betha was hiding something. She wasn't telling them something.

And Angie was certain that *something* was not only important, it meant the difference between life and death.

She just wasn't sure for who.

CHAPTER FOURTEEN

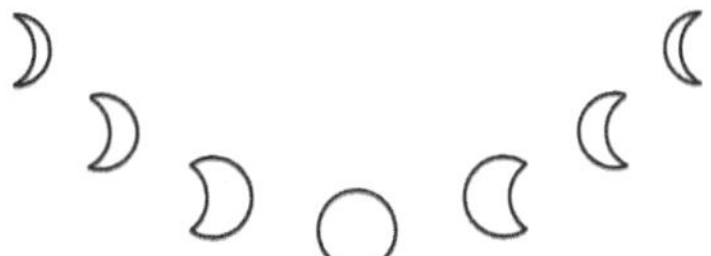

ngie wanted to press the topic, push Betha more, but Aidan walked inside the house at the same time as Angie heard someone coming up the stairs. Aidan didn't join them. She stayed by the doorway, staring at the stairs, her expression very neutral.

Frowning, Angie glanced at Sebastian, but he was frowning at Aidan, too. Something strange was happening.

"That'll be Eloise," Betha said, leaning back in her seat, cradling her mug of tea. Angie had seen her sip that tea, swore she'd seen her drink some of it. But there still seemed to be a lot in the mug, and for an instant, that left Angie feeling a bit queasy.

Something wasn't right. She just couldn't put her finger on it.

The footsteps coming up the stone stairs sounded heavy, heavier than Angie would have expected from Eloise, based on how she'd appeared in the visions. But the only time Angie had seen the other woman, she'd still been very sick and wane from whatever aspect of the demon world had made her ill. She'd been almost hollow looking. Gaunt, her cheekbones sharp, her eyes sunken, her skin almost gray. And her eyes, very very red.

The person walking up the stairs sounded neither gaunt nor hollow.

Angie glanced at Betha and frowned. Betha's expression gave nothing away. She didn't look eager to see Eloise, but she didn't look nervous or worried either.

Finally a crown of light brown hair topped the circular hole in the floor and a woman came into view.

A woman who looked like a perfectly ordinary human woman. Her light brown hair pulled back into a long braid that draped over her shoulder. Dressed in a simple purple skirt and a long-sleeved purple t-shirt. Unlike Betha's scaled jumpsuit, the clothing looked ordinary and comfortable. The sort of thing a person would wear around the house. Her skin was pale, but there was color in her cheeks. Freckles strung across her nose and onto her cheekbones, which weren't hollowed out or wane looking, like the vision version of her that Angie had seen. She looked healthy—healthier than Betha actually.

And if it weren't for the fact that her eyes were demon red, Angie would have assumed the woman was an ordinary human.

Those eyes though. Similar to what Betha's had been when she'd come out of the jungle, before hiding that red behind an illusion spell. Redder than what happened to demon hunters. Hunters were exposed to demons and the demon world so much, they took a tiny bit of it in, that red in the depths of their eyes. Not much. With brown-eyed hunters, it was easy to dismiss that red flare even. But it was still there.

With Eloise, there wasn't just a slight flare, a little red in the depths. She looked more demonic than Sokolov's demon had in his human form. The red eyes so bright and distinct, Angie shivered.

"Eloise, come meet our guests," Betha said. Her voice sounded loud in the otherwise quiet room.

Angie stood to greet the other woman. She wasn't as tall as Angie was, and she wasn't particularly thick or heavy. The heavy tread of her footsteps coming up the stairs seemed incongruous with the woman smiling a greeting at Angie.

"Angie Jordan," she introduced.

Eloise's eyes widened and she looked past Angie to Betha. Then she erupted into a huge smile and said, "The other one! You've arrived. Finally. Oh, we have waited so long for you."

"Eloise," Betha said quietly. A warning in her tone.

A warning that set off alarm bells for Angie again.

Eloise's smile dimmed a little but not completely and she said, "I get a little carried away. Forget where I am sometimes. But we are very glad you're here." She glanced at the others, turning to see Aidan still hovering by the door. "And you've brought friends."

Angie made the introductions. Sebastian stood and

reached out a hand to shake Eloise's. Eloise blinked at that and smiled, shaking his hand hard enough it looked like she was trying to pull him off his feet. Sebastian was just over six foot tall and muscular. It took a lot of strength to pull him off balance.

Carmen also offered a handshake, which Eloise returned in a way that looked much gentler. Aidan just nodded when she was introduced, a small, polite smile on her face. She kept her hands clasped in front of her, though. And Eloise didn't make a move to approach her for a handshake.

When Eloise faced Angie again, Angie was very tempted to reach out and shake her hand as well. And to read her. Except that Angie didn't do that without permission if she could help it. It felt like an invasion of privacy, an assault. Unless it was an accident—and accidents did happen—she didn't read people without their permission. She might get answers faster if she did here, but it would also violate a trust she wasn't prepared to violate.

Yet.

The feeling that something was off, something wrong, didn't let her go. Something about all this wasn't as it seemed and she couldn't put her finger on what was wrong. Betha's reaction to Eloise joining them? Some of the things Betha had said. Eloise's red eyes coupled with a pleasant and even eager greeting. The fact that Eloise, who Betha said was still not well, looked healthier than Betha.

Things weren't adding up right, and yet Angie couldn't see where she was getting the math wrong.

But she didn't offer her hand to Eloise, just nodded, like

Aidan had, in greeting and smiled. "It's a pleasure to meet you in person. I feel like I know you a little. Your diary…"

Eloise rolled her eyes. "The hunters kept it? It was mostly nonsense."

"Except the parts that weren't."

"I should have left those details out." She sighed and came around to kiss Betha on the cheek. "I just…needed to talk about things. I tried to be vague."

Betha reached up and patted her hand when Eloise rested it on her shoulder. "You were, love. Vague enough."

"Not enough," Eloise insisted, "or that diary would have been burned a long time ago."

"We needed it to be found," Betha said. "Remember. That's why I ensured Yosuf had it."

Eloise's expression blanked for a moment, then cleared and she nodded. "That's right. I forgot. It's been a very long time."

"Do you still keep a diary?" Angie asked in an attempt to keep things on a light social level for a few more minutes. The interaction between the two women was fascinating, the way Eloise's face had gone blank at the reminder of what had happened in the past… There was something there too.

"I don't," Eloise said as she turned to make herself a cup of tea. "Doesn't seem much reason here. And at least here I don't have to hide anything from prying eyes. No one finds us here." She spun around and smiled widely again. "Except you! You've found us. Isn't that marvelous."

She returned to making her tea. The water in the kettle

still steamed when she poured it out even though it had been off the hearth for a while.

Angie glanced at Betha. The other witch was still sitting on the couch even though the rest of them had stood. She was watching Angie closely as Angie spoke with Eloise, and there was something in her gaze that triggered that lizard brain reaction again, that nervousness that made Angie certain she was missing some vital piece of information.

Glancing back at Eloise, Angie said, "I hope you don't mind us dropping in and talking. I've never met another demon witch before. We have a lot to talk about."

"Demon witch." Eloise tisked. "I've always hated that term. But it could be worse. Apocalypse witch! Horrible moniker. But she insists we must face it."

Since Eloise's back was to her, Angie glanced at Betha again when she asked Eloise, "What would you prefer?"

"Oh, I don't know. I'd prefer no labels. They don't help anything." She sighed and faced them again, her own mug of tea in hand. "But we have other things to talk about, don't we? My opinion on terms hardly matters. We have this situation to deal with."

"Situation?" Angie waited until Eloise had sat on the couch next to Betha before taking her seat in one of the purple wood chairs. She watched Eloise sip the tea and make a humming noise in the back of her throat that reminded Angie strangely of Sebastian when he tasted a proper cup of tea.

"Well, having the second apocalypse witch come finally. We've waited a very long time. I think it's been a long time. I can't really remember…" She trailed off and her face went blank again. Then she blinked and settled back into herself. "Has it been terribly painful for you?"

Angie's turn to blink. "No." In fact, it was more painful for her to not do magic than it was to do magic. She felt stronger when she was actively tapping her web of power now. "It hasn't caused me any physical pain," she clarified. The mental turmoil was real. But physically, she was fine.

"It hurt my Betha at first. But she's adapted. It doesn't hurt anymore, does it, love?"

"Not anymore," Betha said in a soothing tone.

"It did at first, though?" Angie asked.

"It…burned. Like my blood was too warm for my body. Not… It wasn't anything I couldn't handle. Not even as bad as menstrual cramps." She smiled a little as if making a joke.

But Angie wasn't laughing. "I never had that. The… demon magic didn't hurt me."

"That's because you weren't the first," Betha said. As if that answered the question.

"Was this something that was in the legend?"

"The first will burn, the second will savor, the third will bloom. And all will die." Eloise recited the phrases in a sing-songy voice, like she was repeating a children's rhyme or a poem. She gave her head a little shake and looked at Angie. "That's what one version of the legend says."

"All will die?"

"We assume since it's a demon myth," Betha said, "the demons are talking about themselves."

Angie nodded. "So…what am I supposed to be savoring?"

Betha shrugged. "I'm not sure. The power maybe."

"Do you savor this power?"

"I don't mind it now. It doesn't burn anymore. I'm not sure savor is the word, though."

"I wouldn't consider this savoring either. And I don't savor killing demons."

Betha nodded. "As I said, there are many parts of the legend. This is just one version. Since it caused me some physical pain the very beginning, Eloise clings to the rhyme."

Eloise didn't react to this statement. She just smiled and sipped her tea.

"How long did the pain last?" Angie asked.

"A few months. It eased when I started moving between realms, looking for a way to get rid of the magic. Searching for answers. After Eloise… Well, I stopped caring about answers for myself, but we needed an answer for her."

"We found one," Eloise said.

"The… That night?" She looked at Betha for confirmation. But Betha had already said that night, whatever she'd created from the god realm hadn't permanently cured Eloise. They wouldn't still be here if it had. But Eloise also looked a lot healthier than Angie had been expecting.

"That's the night. I was so sick. I felt a *lot* better after. But…" Eloise frowned and her face blanked again. Then she blinked and gave herself another little shake. "I don't remember much about that night. Except that I was scared for

Betha. There was someone else there, wasn't there?" she asked Betha, turning a little on the couch to face her.

"Yosuf. The demon hunter."

"That's right! He was there to help us. I was sorry for what happened to him."

"What happened to him?" Angie asked quietly. According to the hunters' records, Yosuf showed up in a hospital with a mark branded into his chest and near death. The mark was a triangle inside a circle. He claimed the demon witch had given it to him when they fought. He'd survived the wound. But given he and Betha had created the document accounting for their "fight" together, and that Yosuf had really been helping her when she'd breached the god realm, Angie wondered if that brand hadn't come about some other way.

The last thing she'd seen in her vision of that night was Betha realizing the portal into the god realm wasn't closing. And there was something coming. Then Angie had been forced out of the vision by a very irritated Gabriella to attend to the portal Angie had opened on accident in the archive.

She'd never learned what had actually happened that night.

"You didn't see?" Betha asked, frowning a little.

"I was forced out of the vision before most of that night played out."

"Forced out? How?"

"The...person with me, making sure I was safe... Well, she had to force me out because I accidentally opened a portal and a demon was trying to escape."

Betha straightened a little. "You opened a portal while you were in a vision? That's…"

"Not something I'd ever done before. No. I'm still not sure how or why it happened."

"Was this… Were you touching my blood when this happened?"

Angie nodded.

Betha's frown deepened and she looked at the orange-red stone floor, at the single woven rug under the table between the couch and chairs.

"Do you know why I opened that portal?" Angie asked.

"No." Betha shook her head and looked up. "No. Something to do with the blood. It's always fucking blood."

"Language," Eloise said, sounding prim and cheerful. As if they weren't sitting in a demon realm, talking about blood and magic that burned.

Betha sighed and gave Eloise a fondly exasperated look. "There is no one here who cares if I curse."

"I do. It's crass."

Angie made a mental note to mind her language around Eloise, even though Angie was not someone who flinched at cuss words or flinched from using them. But she'd keep them in her head while she was around the other woman.

"Eloise," Angie said, focusing on her. "You're not a witch yourself, are you? Not a magic wielder?"

"Oh no. No. Not me. I can mix some medical herbs and brew some healing teas, but none of it is real magic. Just… Oh, they'd call it science now, wouldn't they? I like the idea that I am a scientist."

So, Angie hadn't been wrong about that part. Eloise wasn't a witch of any kind. Not even a kitchen witch with the kind of small magic Angie's mother had. An early chemist, and that might have gotten her labeled a witch in different eras, but not a real witch. Which meant her pulling in demon magic, getting linked to this realm, made even less sense.

Angie met Betha's gaze. "What happened that night?"

"With Yosuf?"

"I'd like to hear more about that, too, if you're willing, but I'm talking about the other night. When the men with torches were chasing you. When you took Eloise into a demon realm. What happened?"

Betha sighed and glanced at Eloise, who was busy sipping her tea, looking unbothered. "Death and destruction," Betha murmured. "Death and destruction."

CHAPTER FIFTEEN

"I suppose, after all this, I should start from the beginning." Betha readjusted her position on the couch so that Eloise was leaning against her arm, drinking her tea, smiling contentedly.

Angie glanced around, and then finally sat back down. Sebastian and Carmen followed, slowly. Aidan remained standing at the door, leaning against the wall, seemingly comfortable and at ease. Outside, the wind had picked up and Angie could hear it blowing through the reeds or plants or whatever that was that had been planted in the small patch of churned earth. The light never changed, but some shadows shifted as the breeze blew the jungle at the back of the house.

Betha glanced at Eloise's head. "It started before the torches, before the fight with Yosuf. It started…several months before that." She sighed and looked at Angie again. "In my day, witches were not looked at kindly. Some were

"

ignored because they could do things for their community, but the church, and more importantly, some prominent leaders of the churches did not like women of agency."

Her fingers gently stroked Eloise's shoulder. "There were other things they were not overly fond of either. But as women, we could live together as 'good friends' and unmarried aunts, and be content. Eloise made the occasional healing remedy for our village women. We delivered babies and helped women through pregnancies and after birth. I used some of my magic to help heal when I could. I'm not a technically a healer, but it was one of the ways I could use my magic that wouldn't call too much attention to us. When needed, I might give 'advice' prompted by the 'spirits' or 'God' to those who sought clarity from me in exchange for small gifts. It was this last that eventually brought the trouble to our doorstep."

"It wasn't your fault," Eloise said, her voice firm but quiet. "It was a bad situation and the mayor was a very very bad man."

Betha shrugged. "I knew what he was capable of. I should have...tempered my advice."

"He beat and raped her." Eloise glanced at Angie. "His wife. He was terribly abusive to his wife. The entire village knew. No one did anything. She was his wife. No one believed a wife could be raped at that time."

"Some still don't," Angie said, also quietly. Her anger sparked at this long dead man's crimes, but she held the reaction in check and was grateful her control of her magic was solid. From the corner of her eye, she saw Sebastian's hand twitch, as if he'd reach for hers, but he kept his hand fisted on his thigh. Probably for the best. They needed to be ready for anything. But she wouldn't have objected.

"The wife came to me for advice," Betha said. "Well, no, actually first she came to us for some healing creams and a brace for the injury he'd done her wrist. She, at first, claimed the injury was due to a household accident." Betha's mouth flattened. "We all knew, but when I touched her wound, I knew the details and I…had trouble stomaching them."

"A hazard of that particular gift," Angie said.

Betha grunted agreement. "I asked if she needed more help. At first, I just meant with her injuries, but her eyes got wide and she asked if I'd divine her future. She couched the request in appropriate religious terms, but no one in that room thought I'd be asking 'God' for advice." She shrugged. "We spoke aloud the way we were required. I wanted to turn her down. Her husband was powerful in our small community. And Eloise and I already lived on the edge of respectability and forbearance. We healed the local women and ensured their babies were safe—as much as we could— and we occasionally fixed issues with cattle or crops in ways that everyone deemed acceptable because—" she waved her hand in the air, "—it was really God listening to prayers. Excuses were made and we were allowed to live as we pleased because we contributed to the village in a way no one was prepared to give up."

"And we would have grown old that way if not for this man," Eloise said with a snarl.

"When I gave his wife maybe too honest advice, and she

returned to a family that was more accepting of taking her in and protecting her than most families of the time, I was, of course, blamed for 'bewitching' his wife."

"The torches?"

"Not yet." Betha sucked in a long breath. Eloise snuggled closer into her side and rested a gentling hand on her knee. "I knew of my ability to breach demon realms through trees before this, of course. But I was mostly very careful not to because of the worry that the demons would get out. They had once, when I was a child, and a man whose name I never got came and ensured the demons were sent back and advised me on how to avoid doing that ever again."

"A hunter."

Betha nodded. "I only learned about them later, when I grew up and started to…look into that talent more. I had started opening realms on purpose, looking for answers. I summoned two demons to ask questions. They were clever and evil and sneaky, and the first nearly fooled me into releasing it. I learned my lesson very well that day, though, and did not make those mistakes again. My dealings with the demonic world were, up to that point, academic. I wanted to learn, but I had no real interest in pursuing a life entangled with demons."

Angie had that in common with Betha. In fact, even the discovery of her demon witch powers and the rescue by a demon hunter were similar. It made her wonder how many demon witches had simply flown under the radar and never shown up in anyone's records because, after that first mistake, if they survived, they refused to have anything to do with demons ever again. Probably more even than the hunters knew.

"The mayor didn't take kindly to his wife leaving him, and being supported in that process. She was his possession, you see. And he thought he'd been robbed. He blamed me. And, as you may well assume, he was a very violent man."

Eloise made a slight humming sound under her breath and her hand on Betha's leg tightened. Betha patted her shoulder as if to comfort her.

"When he and some other men accosted me while I was alone in the woods around the village, collecting some of the herbs we didn't grow, I did not take the attack…easily. I was not what they were expecting."

Angie snorted at that. No Betha would not have been. And the attackers deserved whatever it was they got.

Betha's mouth lifted a little in a very faint smile at Angie's reaction. "At first, I used my witch magic, but the way mine works, it takes…time. Spells require time. They aren't instant."

"Mine is similar. I have a few spells so well memorized I can activate them quickly. But most take at least a few seconds, more often minutes, to compose."

Betha nodded. "So while I had power to defend myself, I was not given enough warning to use that power. So I chose instead another option."

"You opened a portal."

"There were several suitable trees. But once I'd opened one and let a demon loose, I panicked and looked away from the tree. Closed the portal. Trapped the demon in our realm.

And had no convenient hunter nearby to help me get the bloody thing back where it came from."

Betha was describing one of Angie's worst nightmares. Opening a portal and releasing a demon on her own realm. Even one was one too many.

"I…panicked," Betha said. "The creature killed several of the men. But I hardly cared about that in the moment. I didn't want the thing to get out into the world." She glanced at Eloise. "I didn't want it to find its way to the village. So I opened another portal. I thought maybe the portal would… suck it back in or something. I'm not sure." She sighed and looked off to one side, her attention turned inward. "I had to look away to defend myself from the demon. Closed the portal. Opened another. Had to look away. The third portal I opened, another demon got out before I could look away." She closed her eyes. "I thought… We are all dead and it is my fault."

Angie couldn't offer platitudes or comfort because Betha's guilt hit so close to home she could feel it in her bones. She could *feel* that guilt as if it was her own. The panic Betha must have felt in those moments. Angie might as well have been inside a vision of that moment, feeling all the things Betha was describing because Angie knew those feeling so fucking well.

Betha dragged in a ragged breath and opened her eyes, looking at Angie. "I don't really talk about that night. I've only retold the story to Eloise. But I think about it all the time."

Angie nodded.

"I thought you might understand," Betha said quietly. "I can't remember how many portals I tried opening and closing to get the demons back in. Or how long it took before I accidentally just…opened a portal in mid-air. I was so scared and panicked and terrified of what the demons might do, I just opened a portal in front of one. No tree. No idea how I'd done it. And it was a lot harder to wrench my gaze from that one. To look away and close it. The demon I'd opened it in front of went into the realm, but I couldn't enjoy that moment of triumph because there were others around me still and the men were dying and…" She blinked and shook her head. "Some of this is…fuzzy. The timeline is jumbled. A hunter did arrive during all this. Late, the bastard. And he had the gall to curse me as if I'd done all that on purpose."

Angie's gaze jumped to Sebastian. He was watching Betha closely, silently. Aidan didn't comment either. Angie wondered if they knew who this hunter was. "It wasn't Yosuf," Angie said, just to confirm. This had taken place earlier than Betha meeting Yosuf. Eloise was already infected by the time Betha had met Yosuf.

"It wasn't Yosuf," Betha confirmed. "This hunter…he didn't survive this night. There were too many demons. I don't know how many got out. One…one brushed against me when it escaped and its memories, its thoughts… For a while, I thought that brief contact with that particular demon was what infected me. It was very powerful, more powerful than anything I'd ever encountered, and it gave me the vision of —" She snapped her mouth closed, but held Angie's gaze. "Later, its thoughts guided me on that other night."

Angie nodded. The demon who'd revealed the god realm to Betha. It had escaped that night. "Did you ever encounter that demon again?"

She shook her head. "It was one I thought would destroy our world, but it obviously never did. I'm not sure what happened to it. Disappeared into our realm never to be heard from again."

"For such a powerful demon that seems odd," Angie said.

"It does. I've never had an explanation for it."

Angie glanced at Sebastian, then Aidan. "Do you know who it could have been?"

"Lot of very powerful demons were given sanctuary in our realm over the centuries," Sebastian said. "Probably one of those."

Betha nodded. "I was caught up in my difficulties afterward, I didn't have time to hunt for it. And when it didn't destroy our world, I figured it would be one of the quiet ones. Or the hunters would go after it. I had other things to worry about."

"The infection," Angie said.

"In all the chaos, after the hunter arrived, I at least had someone at my back while I opened portals. But there were several freed demons. I'm not sure this hunter was… No, I'm certain this hunter wasn't strong enough for the chaos he'd stepped into. I opened another portal in thin air for him to force demons back through. And he got a few in. But then another got out. It was…" She shook her head. "Anyway, somewhere in all this, I opened a portal and the hunter shoved me inside."

Angie wanted to curse. What was it with hunters pushing people *into* demon realms?

"I'd never been *inside* the realms I could open," Betha said. "There were more demons there, of course. Later, I'd remember it was the lava realm. Later, I'd have nightmares about those moments. But in the moment, I couldn't even think enough to consider how terrified I was. I just acted. Drew down power and tried to keep the demons off me. And somewhere in that fight, I picked up the infection for real because I killed a demon. Power shot from my hand like nothing I'd ever had access to before, and the demon vaporized in a red mist. This sent the other demons scattering. Left me enough breathing space to remember I could open a portal home even without trees. I still wasn't sure how I could do it, but I did it."

Betha shook her head hard and said, "The details are mixed up after all this time. I don't remember how long any of this took. I got back to the woods, to the fight, to see the hunter had been killed while I was gone and there were still three fucking demons. The woods were strewn with the bodies of the men they'd killed. All of them dead. I found out later one man had escaped, but when I stepped back out of the demon realm, I didn't know that. I thought the demons had killed everyone." She shrugged. "So I killed them."

Meeting Angie's gaze, Betha looked like she was daring Angie to comment on the morality of what had happened, or condemn her for not sending the demons back. Angie wasn't sure why Betha thought Angie would. Maybe others had? But Angie knew Betha's panic and fear in those moments as if it were her own, and while Angie didn't want to become some kind of murdering demon assassin, she could absolutely see Betha using the one real power she had in that moment to end the destruction and save the world from the mess she'd created.

Well…not started. The mayor and his band of men who'd attacked Betha started this all. That was where the blame actually rested. Betha might have gone the rest of her life without learning she could open portals without trees, without pulling in the magics that allowed her to kill demons. If not for the attack, none of this might have ever happened to her.

When Angie just nodded without comment, Betha's shoulders visibly relaxed. "I had to kill all three that night," she said quietly. "The hunter had managed to get some back, I think, but like I said, details are fuzzy. There were three left and I killed them. Any that had escaped into our world were either later caught by hunters or hid themselves from everyone because I never heard from or saw them again. None attacked the village. Which was really all I cared about." Her gaze jumped to Eloise again, then back to Angie.

"A hard night," Angie said. "What happened when you got back to the village?"

"I cleaned up and tried to pretend none of it had happened. Or at least that I'd had nothing to do with it all. I didn't even tell Eloise what had happened at first."

"And that was a silly mistake," Eloise said. "She should have trusted me." Eloise's turn to glance at Betha, her frown holding years of irritation.

"I should have," Betha admitted. "The man who'd escaped, he was delirious for a while, screaming about demons. The bodies in the woods were found and about half the village thought this man had done the deed. Been possessed by a devil or demon—since he kept screaming about demons—and gone on a killing rampage. It was probably two months later before anyone started pointing fingers at me. And it took another several months for that finger pointing to take hold and for the men of the village to see me and Eloise as potentially dangerous witches."

"Eloise isn't a witch, though."

"She and I were close and lived together and she helped the village women with her 'potions.' Of course they thought she was a witch too."

Angie sighed. So many centuries of misunderstandings had led to a lot of evil.

"I spent most of that intervening time hunting for information. First, in my realm. I traveled to some of the larger churches around our area, looking for books, none of which helped much. So I then started looking for answers in the demon realm. The books kept by the priests did give me one detail I needed. I will admit that. I learned about the strength of a triangle inside a circle. Those powerful shapes combined were extremely protective. I used that to draw protective lines around any area I intended on opening a portal. It kept the demons from escaping and kept Eloise safe."

"She started joining you?"

"She was in danger and I didn't want her far from me. Otherwise, I wouldn't have involved her."

"You would have been hard pressed to keep me away," Eloise said primly.

This brought out a small smile from Betha.

"The demons I…spoke with during my hunt for a cure for what I'd picked up in the realms were unable to tell me how to reverse the infection. But I did learn the myth of the apocalypse witch during those months. I dismissed it as a legend and not related to reality. Demons lie of course. So I didn't trust anything they said. I was just looking for hints. My blood was burning and I was desperate for a cure, so I thought I might find some clue in whatever stories they told me."

"All that demon work drew attention," Aidan said. It was very nearly her first comment since they'd entered the building and the sound of her voice startled Angie into glancing back at her.

That Aidan was still standing at the door, inside the house, and had been since Eloise came upstairs, was still worrying. Angie wanted to ask her why, but of course couldn't yet. She also wanted to hear more of Betha's story. They were here for just that. But Aidan standing at the door, when they were in a demon realm, and there were demons in the jungle, and they could walk through Betha's circle of blood even if they didn't do it often, meant Aidan saw something *inside* the house as a bigger threat than those possible demons outside.

And that was very very strange.

It was Eloise. Something was wrong with Eloise. But what?

"The demon work attracted attention," Betha said, in response to Aidan. She gave the hunter a shrug but didn't seem bothered by the fact that Aidan was weirdly still standing at the door. "Not from the hunters at first. That surprised me."

"The demons weren't on the verge of escaping," Aidan said. "Hunters show up when demons might get out. When you summoned them in the human realm instead of talking with them in their realms, they were securely trapped. But you mostly talked with them in their realms, didn't you?"

Betha's gaze narrowed just a little at Aidan with that statement. But she said, "I did. I thought it was safer. I might get killed if I couldn't control them, but no one else would be hurt because they wouldn't be able to get into the human realm. Eloise wasn't happy with that plan."

"No, I was not." Eloise's mouth flattened and she gave Betha a look.

Betha mostly ignored the look. "But it was safer. I only brought demons into the human realm when their realm was incompatible with my existence."

There were demon realms where humans couldn't tread. Actually, most demon realms were places humans got killed almost instantly, but there were a few where it wasn't the demons that did the killing but the atmosphere of the realms themselves. Just like some of those realms were incompatible to the existence of demons from other realms.

The god realm was incompatible to everyone's existence but for a select few demons. And, of course, the demon gods.

"It wasn't the hunters that caused the problem," Betha said. "It was human men. Not the village men. The ones who'd sided with the mayor, most of them died that night with him. And there were a lot of people who thought he got what he'd deserved and didn't try too hard to investigate what had happened to him and the others. There were rumors in the village they'd brought the demons on themselves and been killed by them. The rumors started to circulate that the mayor had been in league with the devil for years, and this was just his comeuppance. No one looked to me and Eloise. Or if they did, they kept it to themselves. Most of them anyway. We helped heal their illnesses and saved their women and children during childbirth. We'd earned some grace and so most looked the other way."

"Even if they thought we were in league with the devil ourselves," Eloise added.

"Even if," Betha agreed. "So it wasn't the people in our village that…escalated things. It was men from outside the village, from some of the neighboring communities, who'd been of a similar vein and thought as the mayor. They were the ones to start pointing fingers at me and Eloise, to claim we were unclean women, witches, dealing with the devil, all that rot."

"Well you are a witch," Eloise said, giving Betha a fond look.

"The only thing they got right," Betha agreed with a small smile. She grew serious again as she said, "Eventually, they came for us with torches and ropes and there was a pyre built, waiting for us. We ran. They chased. And when we were surrounded and I knew we were in trouble, I made the biggest mistake of my life."

"It wasn't," Eloise insisted. "They would have killed us."

"And I didn't?"

"Are we dead yet?" Eloise pointed out reasonably. "We are not."

"We're not exactly alive anymore either."

"Hush. What nonsense." Eloise set her empty tea mug aside, turning away from Betha as she did and scowling. "We are alive. We are together. The rest is just…life."

"Life." Betha quietly huffed and shook her head. At Eloise's glare, she gave in with raised hands. "Let's not argue about this again."

It was obvious this had been a long-standing argument, with Betha blaming herself for Eloise, and Eloise refusing to let Betha blame herself.

Betha asked Angie, "Did you see it, in the vision?"

"You taking Eloise into a demon realm? Yes. I…I jumped out of the vision before the portal closed on you." Actually, she'd felt pushed out of the vision, as if Betha herself had shoved Angie out before the portal closed so Angie wouldn't have to experience that nightmare.

"A demon got out and killed the men who'd come to burn us," Betha said. "That wasn't my mistake. I wanted them all to die. And I didn't care if they died by demon at that stage. But taking Eloise into that realm was a huge mistake."

"We still don't know why I was changed there," Eloise

said. "Centuries of Earth time later, and we still don't know what happened." She sounded resigned and almost accepting of the fact, as if the answer didn't really matter to her anymore.

"But being in the demon realm changed you," Angie said.

"It did. Being back in the human realm now is like…it feels like it's seeping into my skin and rotting me when I'm there. More so in the beginning. After Betha's potion, I can tolerate the place for a while. But eventually, I start to feel the waning, the rotting, and I have to come home."

Betha flinched when Eloise called this place "home." Angie couldn't blame her. She'd nearly flinched too. How any human could refer to this realm as "home," unironically, Angie wasn't sure. But since it was the only place Eloise could be comfortably, how else would Eloise think of it?

"That was the night that brought Yosuf to the hunt," Aidan said quietly. "It took him some time to track you down, though. You… You killed that demon you loosed on the men with torches. Making it harder for Yosuf to find you."

"I never left the demons in the human realm long," Betha said. "And killing them was as easy as sending them back."

Aidan nodded. "That night wasn't the only time you loosed demons."

"Because that wasn't the last group that came for us," Betha said. "That night…changed everything. We were hunted after that. More men. Some claiming to be from the church. Others just sadistic people who sought violence and liked destroying women. We had little rest from these attacks, and our own neighbors wouldn't intervene. They might not have wanted to destroy us themselves, but they weren't brave enough to defend us either. In between all the attacks, I was trying to find a cure for Eloise. It was a difficult time."

"I imagine it would be," Angie said. "When did Yosuf arrive?"

"About a month into all this. Maybe more? I don't remember for certain. Between the centuries and the intensity of the time, I don't remember the details well. Yosuf showed up when I let more demons out to take care of yet another group of men attacking us. He had to struggle to get them back to their realms, so I used his distraction to disappear with Eloise. But… By that time, I'd learned of a possible cure. I needed to get the last ingredient and I needed to do it from the human realm. We'd had no peace or time to do what needed to be done, though. It wasn't something I could risk being interrupted during. The demons I loosed on the group Yosuf tried to save, I did that to buy myself a few nights, some time so that I could do what I needed to without interference. There was always a gap between the attacks and when new attackers showed up. I thought, if I turned the demons loose on them, that would buy me another of those gaps before the next attack."

"But you went back and saved Yosuf when you knew he hadn't rid this realm of all of the demons?" Angie had seen that part in the vision and she suspected, had she touched Betha's blood earlier, she would have seen more of that night.

"I came back to check all the demons were banished. I

didn't come back for the hunter." Betha lifted her chin, staring at Aidan. Daring her to disagree.

She didn't. But Eloise did.

"That wasn't why you went back," she said quietly. "Stop trying to make yourself a monster. You're not the one who became a monster in all this."

"I kill regularly, often. What else would I be?"

"Killing demons to protect people is not the same as becoming a monster," Eloise said firmly. "And that night, we returned because you said the hunter would be overwhelmed and you wanted to make sure he survived. The last one who'd tried to intervene had not survived. Because you couldn't kill demons at that stage. You might not want to admit it, but I saw how guilty you felt that the hunter had been killed, even if he was an arrogant prick."

Carmen snort-laughed at that. "Most of them are," she said. Then glanced at Sebastain and winked, "Not you, handsome."

Sebastian grunted a non-response.

"What about me?" Aidan said, with a small smile.

"You are definitely an arrogant prick," Carmen said.

Aidan chuckled.

Angie watched Betha and Eloise through this exchange. Eloise seemed amused. Betha looked on with her eyes narrowed, her expression difficult to read.

"We went back to try and save Yosuf," Eloise insisted. "We weren't sure we'd be able to, and Betha didn't like bringing me into the human realm for long. I couldn't stay.

But she insisted we check on the hunter and the demons. She always cleaned up the demons after loosing them."

"At least, I tried to," Betha said quietly. "With that first hunter, that first time being trapped in a demon realm... I missed some of those. The one who...who showed me the way to the realm I needed for Eloise's cure got away. But more besides might have. I didn't destroy the world with those loosed demons but I didn't want to risk any of the others I let out doing that."

"So you always went back and made sure they were banished or killed," Angie said.

"I did. And that's all it was that night with Yosuf." She looked at Eloise with raised brows, as if daring her to argue the point.

Eloise rolled her eyes and shook her head, sighing. Another old argument, Angie guessed.

"Why did you tell Yosuf what you planned?" Angie asked. She had an idea because she'd been in Betha's perspective during that vision. But she wondered if Betha still felt, after all this time, that her motive was the same as it had been then.

"To protect Eloise," she said. "What I was going to do was...not something that anyone should do. I needed to. To help Eloise. But there was a high probability that I would fail. Or worse, loose something truly disastrous onto the human world. Something that could have gotten through my protection barriers. Having a hunter who'd been strong enough to survive several freed demons, and send them back to their realms guarding Eloise would ensure the worst possible case wouldn't happen. Or at least, there'd be hope if the worst did happen. I was counting on Yosuf to be an exceptionally strong demon hunter with a will unmatched."

"He nearly was," Eloise said quietly.

"Yes," Aidan said, "he nearly was."

Aidan spoke sometimes as if she knew Yosuf personally. But since that would make Aidan something close to five hundred years old, an age she'd have reached by sheer will alone, Angie balked at the idea. She wanted to think Aidan had just read a lot more about Yosuf, knew more about him from some other source, than that she was really that old.

"He didn't die that night," Angie said. "But he was wounded. I had to leave the vision after you…retrieved the sand. What happened then?"

"What happened then…" Betha looked off into the middle distance for a few moments before meeting Angie's gaze again. "What happened was my worst nightmare. And none of us should have survived."

CHAPTER SIXTEEN

$\mathcal{A}$ caw from outside the house broke through the quiet that followed Betha's statement, a quiet Angie had been reluctant to disrupt for fear Betha wouldn't tell them the rest. She wasn't sure why she thought the events of that night were important, but she knew they were. Knew there was something there that she needed to learn.

The caw distracted everyone though, and all eyes turned toward the front door of the small house.

The door was open still, the temperature inside cool and comfortable with that cool breeze blowing into the house. Aidan hadn't left her post by the front door. At the caw, she ducked outside without a word. Sebastain followed her, also without saying anything.

Angie hesitated long enough to glance at Betha. Both Betha and Eloise had straightened in their seats on the couch and were staring hard at the front door.

That was enough to push Angie into gear and she followed the hunters outside. Noticing only when she was out in the clearing that Carmen had followed her outside, too.

Aidan and Sebastian were standing near the center of the clearing, turning in slow circles, scanning the surrounding jungle. The strange bird-like thing that had been sitting on top of the house when Angie and the others had first arrived was back, perched on the roof again. It's yellowish feathered body and black webbed wings bright against the red foliage behind it.

It cawed again, a sound like a warning klaxon in the otherwise quiet clearing, and ruffled its leathery wings.

Angie stood closer to the house, but scanned the jungle. Something was out there. Coming toward them. The bird-thing was warning them. Intuition screamed at her to prepare some spells. She didn't argue with the wisdom of her intuition, stacking two defensive spells and holding them on the edge of casting.

In this realm, she thought she'd still be able to call the lightning. And because there was moisture and water here, probably rain too. Though she worried about the kind of rain that might fall in a demon realm from a sky that was orangish-pink. Probably not the best option. But lightning always seemed to help.

And illusions did an excellent job of distracting demons during an attack, giving the hunters—and anyone else around—time to deal with the demons or run away. So the illusion spell was Angie's go-to when dealing with deadly foes.

The silence across the area was deeper than it had been

when they'd first entered the clearing. There'd still been the sounds of the breeze moving through the jungle then. Even with the way the door had sounded weirdly muffled when she knocked on it, she'd still heard sound. Now, except for the weird bird's caws, she couldn't hear anything else. Her ears felt stuffed up with cotton, and it left her weirdly disoriented.

She glanced back at the house, wondering if Betha and Eloise would even come outside, or if they were so used to this, they'd remain inside. No one came and closed the door. Whatever was happening wasn't something that sent them into lockdown.

But Aidan and Sebastian were on high alert, scanning their surroundings, their expressions deadly serious. Angie glanced at Carmen. Carmen gave a little head shake, frowning at the jungle vines piled up against the protected clearing.

And then Angie felt it. A vibration through the soles of her feet. Faint, but there. Like a low-level earthquake.

Or something very large moving this way.

She sort of hoped it was an earthquake.

Angie started back toward the house, to ask Betha what was coming, just as Betha stepped outside. She was scowling and staring into the jungle opposite the house.

"What is that?" Angie asked.

"Irritating," Betha said. "And also not unexpected."

"You expected a ground tremor? You should have warned us."

Betha raised her brows. "You really think that's just a ground tremor?"

"No," Angie said.

"But a woman can hope," Carmen muttered.

Angie nodded. That she was in such agreement with Carmen was annoying. "What's coming?"

"I was afraid of this. With two of us here…" Betha shook her head. "It was never going to be easy. They let us talk longer than I thought they would."

"Who?"

"The demons."

"Which ones?"

"Most of them."

"That sounds really bad," Carmen said. "How many is most of them?"

"Of the two species that can enter the jungle?" Betha shrugged. "There are…about three dozen in total. They aren't like some demon species where there are hundreds of them."

"Thirty-six still sounds bad," Angie said.

"Thirty-six is more than enough," Betha said. "These are not the demons you're used to."

"Meaning?"

"Let's put it this way," Betha said, coming out to stand next to Angie. "The demon gods? They sometimes harvest these demons for their personal guards."

That sound very very bad.

"Thirty-six, you say?" Angie turned in a circle, because the vibration in the ground seemed to be coming from everywhere, yet she couldn't hear anything moving through the jungle. Couldn't tell which direction the threat was coming from.

"At last count. They are slow breeders."

"And the jungle doesn't bother them."

"Very little bothers them."

"You can kill them?"

Betha was quiet a moment.

Angie frowned at her. "You can't kill them?"

"It takes a lot to kill one. It's not just a single shot and they explode."

"That's just one?"

"Uh huh."

"So…if there are more than thirty approaching?"

"If it's most of them, we will have a much harder time killing them. Even with what you and I can do."

"Fuck." Angie glanced back toward the house. "Where's Eloise?"

"Locked in the safe room at the lowest level of the house."

Angie nodded. Then glanced at Carmen. "You want to go into the basement with Eloise?"

Carmen startled at that. "You're gonna need me to fight these things."

"Probably. But this isn't what you signed up for."

"You really do care if I die. That's sweet."

"Shut up. Go into hiding or don't. Up to you." Angie let out a breath. She would have sent everyone into lockdown, herself including, if she thought that would help. But she knew Sebastian and Aidan wouldn't hide. And she had every intention of having their backs. What Carmen did was up to her.

But after watching someone she thought was Carmen die once… Angie wasn't sure she wanted to live through that again. Even with Carmen. Who she didn't even like.

The people she did love… That was even harder, waiting, knowing they'd be in danger.

"How do you kill the demons?" she asked Betha. "The usual way, just more of it?"

"The usual way, but more of it," Betha said.

"They're coming because there are two of us in one place, right?"

"Right."

The ground trembled harder.

"Will they go away if we leave? If I go somewhere else and come back later." It was a weird hope, but any option that saved lives was something she was willing to try.

"Now that they know for certain there are two of us? They'll never stop coming."

"Fuck," Angie muttered again. "They'll want to kill us both."

"They've tried to kill me before," Betha said. "They haven't succeeded. But it's never been so many of them at once. They aren't…cooperative with each other."

Angie scanned the jungle again. "How do you know it's so many of them?"

"The bird caws. And the silence."

"The silence?"

"One of their weapons. You won't know they're here until they're on us."

"Oh good." Angie looked at Sebastian, who glanced at

her briefly, his expression serious and unreadable. Then he turned back to the jungle. "What happens if I draw a circle around us?" She faced Betha again. "Can we use a protection circle against them?"

"If we want to linger inside it forever. Sure."

"Get Eloise."

Betha glanced at her sharply. "Why?"

"We're getting out of here."

"Where to?"

"Not here," Angie said. She hadn't quite thought ahead to *where* yet. But not here seemed better than here. And she wasn't about to leave Betha and Eloise to face this threat alone. "Hurry."

She started the spell to draw a protective circle.

"Get closer," Carmen called to Aidan and Sebastian even as she stepped up to Angie's back.

Betha glanced at the jungle, looked at Angie, then shook her head and raced back into the house. Angie wasn't sure how long getting Eloise up here would take. They'd have to do their best to give Betha the time she needed.

Carmen started toward the house. "Don't stop. I'll help her get Eloise."

Angie continued her spell, giving Carmen a brief nod. She couldn't argue with her while mid-spell and Carmen was right. Angie couldn't stop.

The vibrations beneath her feet were stronger, but the silence around them seemed denser, thicker. Like she was trying to hear through water now while still having cotton in her ears. It was nothing she'd experienced before and was almost enough to distract her from the focus she needed for her spell.

Almost.

Instead of a usual circle, Angie used some of the knowledge she'd picked up in the visions from Betha and drew a triangle first. She walked the shape, forming the lines in the soft red dirt by dragging her foot as she chanted the protection spell. Without thought, she mentally touched her blue magic on the metaphysical plane, letting the magic flow into her, through her. Fed into her spell all the power she had to bring.

She stopped the triangle before closing it, leaving enough space for the three women to move into the protective shapes. Then she moved outside it and drew a circle, again drawing the shape by dragging her foot through the sand, pouring power into the protective chant.

"They're almost here," Aidan said quietly.

Angie was halfway through the circle. She glanced at the house. No sign of the others yet. She kept going, trusting Aidan and Sebastian to warn her if anything emerged from the jungle while she was focused on her spell. She got to the apex of the triangle, and again, left a gap in the circle, not closing it yet.

Then she looked at the house. She wondered if she'd be able to hear shouts from inside the house, if she'd know if the others needed help. She could hear the other humans speaking just fine. It was just all the other noise that seemed absent. But if she could hear the others talking, surely she'd be able to hear any cries for help?

She wanted to shout for them to hurry. Stopped herself. She wasn't sure they'd even hear her. And she worried she'd give their plan away to the approaching demons.

"They're close," Sebastian said, his voice deep. "We're out of time."

"I'm not closing the circle with the others," Angie said.

"We'll hold them off as long as we can," Aidan said. She glanced at Angie. "But these aren't the kind of demons that move into our realm, that hunters normally fight."

"Are you telling me your will won't be strong enough?"

"I'm tell you we don't have much time."

Angie cussed again. She was doing a lot of that. "Okay, we need to buy the others as much time as we can."

She had no idea what was taking so long, but then, she didn't know how deep the house went and how long it took to get there and back and what sort of lockdown protections they'd have to get through to get Eloise back up here. Her anxiety made each second feel excruciatingly long. The others could be on the way up now, only a few minutes could have passed since Carmen went into the house.

"Ah shit," Aidan said.

Angie turned, slowly, her heart hammering, her fingers sparking with magic as fear coursed through her blood.

The jungle trees and vines were shivering, moving, shifting. All around them. Every part of the jungle.

The vines began to sizzle and burst open, spraying their bloody sap at the edge of the circle. It splattered across the circle that kept the vines out, landing onto the red-brown dirt inside Betha's protected clearing.

The stench of blood and rot and sweetly decaying detritus filled the area. Angie only realized then that the stench of the jungle hadn't permeated the clearing, that the immediate area had smelled relatively ordinary. Now the stink of the jungle rushed over her. Bringing a cold wind that seemed at odds with the approach of demons.

The bird-like animal on the house roof cawed again, so loud it sounded like a gunshot in the silence.

And then the jungle trees and vines began to part.

Revealing the demons.

CHAPTER SEVENTEEN

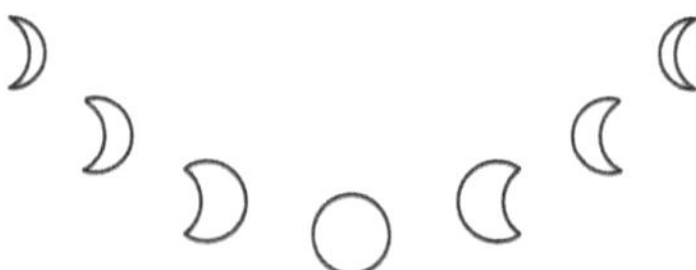

Angie had confronted many demons in her lifetime, an unfortunate number of demons for someone who'd rather not deal with demons. They were all horrifying. All the stuff of nightmares. Even when they presented a relatively bland human front like Sokolov's demon had. The presence of the sand burrowing demons and the sky fog demons in the realm they'd passed through to get here had been some of the most terrifying monsters she'd experienced because they were so difficult to see. Knowing they could come at her and she'd never see them coming.

So she thought seeing yet another horrible, terrifying monster would just be…another horrifying, terrible monster. That what stepped out of the jungle would be the stuff of nightmares and add to her list of things that lingered in the darkest parts of her brain.

On one level, she'd been right. What walked out of the

jungle would absolutely haunt her nightmares. What she hadn't expected was that these monsters would be…

Beautiful.

Beautiful in a very alien way. Not like an Adonis sort of way. These were still monsters. But they were the kind of demons that humans thought of when they thought of the demons that seduced. There were six of them surrounding the clearing that Angie could see. All stood as tall as the uppermost trees in the jungle, making them absolutely huge. Not the more than thirty Betha said were coming, though that could just be because they weren't visible yet. The half dozen that Angie saw were more than enough.

Each one was unique looking, but in general, they had red skin that blended remarkably well with the surrounding jungle, a variety of jewel toned eye colors that was not something Angie had ever seen in a real demon before, and physiques that were muscled and curvaceous at once. If this species had genders, they sort of blended together different elements that a human might consider gendered traits, making them strangely attractive in both a male and female way all at the same time. And also in a neither way. There were thick, black feathered wings on some of them. Black curving horns on most of their heads. The ones without wings seemed slimmer and curvier than the ones with wings. They had four arms and two legs, the arms all ending in long fingered hands tipped with slim, sharp nails.

The horns on their heads curved up out of generous waves of black and red hair that actually had shimmery gold strands through it. Their facial features were sharp boned and weirdly easy to look at, like majestic creatures that almost, but not quite, looked human. Compelling. That was it. She was compelled to look upon them and feel awe.

No fucking wonder the demon gods took some of these beasts to be their personal guards. If they were vain gods, a vanguard made up of these entities would definitely suit that vanity.

The sheer size and magnificence of them was probably one of the more terrifying things Angie had ever seen. Because this was a monster she could see stunning their prey so long the prey wouldn't realize they should be terrified, wouldn't realize they were about to die until they were already dead.

"Uh," she managed and then had to swallow hard. Blink hard a few times to remember what she was supposed to be doing.

Fending them off. Giving Betha, Eloise, and Carmen enough time to get up here. Right.

"Are you seeing this the way I am?" she asked her two demon hunter companions quietly.

The silence surrounding the monsters and the clearing was still profound. Almost complete. She couldn't even hear the bird-like animal on the top of the house cawing anymore and it was right there. It was like she'd lost her hearing and the world was now silence. Except she heard her own voice out loud. Heard her words clearly.

The others must have heard her just fine as well, because Sebastian grunted and said, "Not demons I've seen before. You?" he asked Aidan.

"No," she said. "Though I've heard about them. They don't leave the inner realms, fortunately."

"Yes. Very scary," Angie said. "But also…are you seeing them as beautiful? The way I am."

"That," Aidan said. "Yes. Horrifyingly beautiful."

"Sebastian?"

"In a way that is difficult to explain," he agreed.

"But are they mesmerizing to you? Is this weird beauty something you're feeling drawn toward?"

"Are you?" Sebastian asked.

"Very strangely, yes. But the feeling is scary."

He stepped up to her back and touched her wrist briefly, a quick brush of his fingers over her skin. The sensation was one of those that sent a little shiver through her body. One of the places he could touch her and start her blood pumping harder and her heartbeat thumping and her skin sparking with desire. The touch that could easily turn into a kiss that turned hot that turned into something more.

She caught her breath, her eyelids fluttered, and she glanced back at him. His dark eyes were darker than she'd expected. She'd thought to see the red flaring brighter with the surrounding threat. But no. Just Sebastian's dark brown gaze and a small smile that left her breathless.

He leaned in and whispered close to her ear, "Nothing is ever as attractive to me as you are."

Well. If that didn't readjust her brain in a blast of heat and love. A shiver went down her spine. She found herself breathing in Sebastian's familiar scent, that rich spicy soap she loved so much. The gentle warmth of his body heat that made her want to wrap herself around him. In that moment, all the years of love and lust gathered into a warm tightening in her chest. She sighed.

Whatever weird spell the surrounding demons had started to weave shattered instantly.

She blinked as Sebastian leaned backward. Then narrowed her eyes. "What just happened?"

"Redirection," he murmured.

That was a word for it. "You and Aidan don't need that?"

"Will," Aidan said.

As if that explained anything. But since it was their power against demons, maybe it did.

Angie would ask for more of an explanation later. For now, when she turned back to face the demons, she realized her fascination wasn't so overwhelming, she didn't feel so compelled to study the beautiful creatures. She didn't feel the need to get closer.

When she realized she had been feeling a need to get closer, her stomach dropped. Holy shit that was scary. She glanced down. She hadn't moved. They were all still standing inside her incomplete protection barriers—Sebastian and Aidan in the triangle portion and Angie just outside the triangle, but inside the circle. So she hadn't moved toward any of the demons.

But she had been feeling the desire to get closer to them. She hadn't even realized, hadn't had any alarm bells going off, would have moved closer to get a better look without even recognizing the danger if Sebastian hadn't broken the spell.

That was very scary.

The jungle behind the six creatures stirred and more of them came into view, clearing the jungle to stand just outside Betha's circle. The vines that had piled up against the edge of that circle continued to burst open and spew their blood-like sap into the clearing.

Yet the demons didn't step over the line of blood Betha had buried in the sand.

Angie thought they might be able to. But Betha also said they didn't like the smell and so didn't come this way much anymore. Was it just the stink of blood keeping so many of them back. Or was it something else.

"Are you two willing them not to enter the clearing?" Angie asked quietly.

"Not yet," Aidan answered.

"They aren't trying to enter yet," Sebastian said.

That was strange. Very strange.

"They're waiting on Betha to come outside, aren't they?" she said.

"Appears so," Aidan said.

More of them moved into view. A dozen now. Maybe more. They didn't stand very close to each other. And Angie watched one swipe a clawed hand at another that did get too close. They seemed to make a noise at each other, their mouths moving and a sharp forked tongue flickering out from one. That gesture made another lean in with its teeth exposed, a lot of sharp black teeth.

But no sound reached her.

That was as scary as the fact that she found the creatures

so beautiful. The more that appeared, the stronger that impression, though she no longer felt quite so compelled to study them. The beauty was more frightening than attractive now.

Like facing down an entire herd of beautiful, deadly tigers. Only these beautiful, deadly beings were the size of a two-story house.

Not being able to hear where Betha and the others were was maddening. Angie's heartbeat hammered so hard she could barely breathe. And she wanted to close off her triangle and circle because her self-preservation instincts were screaming to protect herself and Sebastian and Aidan. But if she closed the spells now, she'd have to break them for the others, and then start over. There wasn't time for that. Not with dozens of house-sized demons just waiting at the edge of the clearing to attack.

A few ruffled their feathers in the cold breeze. But still no sound. Some teeth baring at other demons who got too close. Those shockingly beautiful alien faces staring at Angie and the hunters as if they were all bugs about to be smashed.

And the waiting! The waiting was making her body shake as adrenaline surged through her blood with nowhere to go because she couldn't *do* anything yet.

She didn't dare attack, or try to kill one of these creatures. Because that would start their attack. She'd have to close her protection spells. Betha had said it would take more than a single shot with these demons, too. She just couldn't do this alone. Could the hunters even *will* demons like this? Was that even within the realms of possibility for humans?

Angie had seen both Sebastian and Aidan do amazing things. Things that looked like magic. Things that other hunters simply couldn't. But this was different. These were demons who could survive the god realm, could serve the demon gods. Even one of these would have been difficult for them to handle.

And there were dozens of them.

A subtle movement from Aidan had Angie swinging toward her, worried something was happening. But the demons on Aidan's side of their triangle hadn't moved into the clearing yet.

Aidan said, "The others are coming."

"You can hear them?" Angie still couldn't hear anything beyond her companions' voices.

"No."

Angie waited, but Aidan didn't expand on her answer and Angie didn't have time to grill her. She trusted Aidan to know.

Angie scanned the creatures surrounding them, all those beautiful monsters just lingering and waiting, and then studied her holding spells. A few words and gestures would close the circle, another couple of gestures would close the triangle. She needed to buy the others time to get from the house to the circle, and time for her to close everything up before the demons attacked. Or come up something that would hold them off if they did attack.

Okay. Okay. Illusion spell it was. And maybe the water spell. To Aidan she said, "Tell me the instant the others are on the ground floor and heading toward the door."

Aidan grunted in agreement.

"Ang?" Sebastian asked.

"Got a plan to buy running time," she said.

A grunt from Sebastian.

They might not be able to hear the surrounding demons—or anything else for that matter—but that didn't mean the demons couldn't hear them. Angie wasn't going to be too specific out loud. And maybe that's why Aidan had been so vague too.

Angie waited, her gaze on the two demons closest to her, both of them stunning, winged creatures with features cut from marble, their red skin sparkled with golden light that just shouldn't have been so damned beautiful for a being that was about to try squashing her.

Aidan said, "Now."

And Angie triggered her illusion spell.

CHAPTER EIGHTEEN

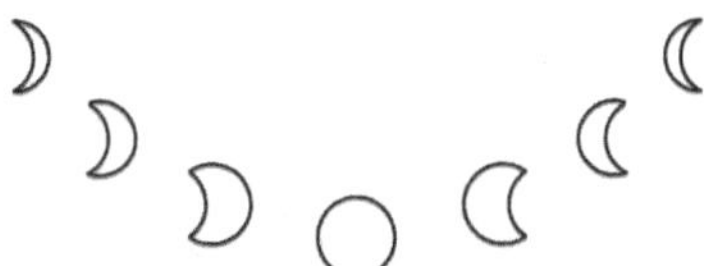

The sky around the clearing filled with flittering, fluttering, colorful lights. Lights in neon colors that didn't belong in this world. Flying creatures the size of Angie's head diving around like demented fireflies above the demons standing at the edge of the clearing.

At first, Angie didn't think the distraction would work. The encircling demons didn't react to the flittering lights immediately. Her gut tightened and she almost cursed aloud.

But then one of the illusions swarmed right at a demon's face before fluttering up into a swarm over the demon's head. And the demon looked up.

It frowned, heavy brow lowering, the wings along its back fluttering black feathers as it turned to follow the lights. Then it reached up with one huge, long fingered hand and casually swiped a claw through the gathered swarm of light.

The lights scattered. Reformed. Dove at the demon's head.

The demon swiped at them again.

Angie murmured another few words, adding to the illusion spell, triggering another series of lights. These more aggressive. Diving and swarming around all the demons.

More of the surrounding beasts swiped at the attacking lights. Frowns. Some open mouths and teeth displays. She still couldn't hear them but she got the *impression* sounds were made at the "attacking" lights.

Distraction. They had distraction.

She glanced at the house. There in the doorway, Betha looked out, watching the light display. She glanced at Angie, brows raised. Then gave a little nod and ushered Eloise out of the house ahead of her.

Eloise sprinted toward Angie as Angie waved her quickly into the circle. Carmen came next, her eyes wide, frowning deeply as she raced into the center of Angie's protection shapes. She gave Angie a glance on the way past that carried a lot of meaning, meaning Angie would have to sort out later.

Betha continued to hover at the door, her gaze moving around the clearing.

Angie wanted to shout at her to hurry the fuck up, but she didn't want to alert the distracted demons to what was happening. None of them had seemed to notice the extra humans yet. She didn't want to do anything that drew their attention away from the swarming lights.

Why the hell was Betha waiting? This was the time to go!

She waved a hand at the other witch, a hurrying gesture she knew couldn't be misinterpreted. Betha still hesitated.

So Angie cursed in her head and muttered the end of her rain spell, calling down whatever moisture was in the sky overhead—more than existed in all of the lava realm—and sent it pouring down onto the surrounding demons.

Uncertain what that rain might do to her and the other humans, Angie concentrated on holding the rain beyond Betha's circle. This was a lot harder, took more magic, was a more complicated spell than just making it rain. It took concentration to keep the rain focused.

But the concentration worked. The surrounding demons threw their heads back in open mouthed gestures she took for howls or yells or something. And then a lot of swatting at the rainfall. It didn't seem to be doing them any damage—and why would it necessarily. This was their realm, they should be used to rain in the jungle if they could move through the jungle that other demons couldn't. Still, the rainfall seemed to irritate them. Between the still ducking and diving lights swarming around their heads and the rain pummeling them just outside the clearing, none of the demons paid any attention to the humans.

Exactly what Angie needed.

Betha threw her another look. Then finally sprinted from the house. The instant Betha was past the first line Angie had drawn, Angie shifted her concentration to closing the circle. The rain stopped falling as she let the spell go. But the illusion spell continued, not needing her focus to play out.

As the demons continued to swat at flitting lights, Angie

got the circle sealed. She moved into the triangle and finished that spell just as the demons started to realize something was wrong. Two of them faced her as she murmured the last words and made the last hand gestures to close the triangle.

Both of the demons started across the clearing, heading toward them. They snarled as they stepped over the blood circle, and one of the two actually covered its nose and mouth with a clawed hand. The other wrinkled its nose and its lip lifted, revealing its sharp black teeth. The one with its hand covering its mouth fluffed out its feathered wings like it intended to take flight.

Then more demons were moving across the clearing line, ignoring the light displays fluttering around their heads and dive bombing them as Angie's illusion spell continued to play out.

She murmured the final word and brought her hands down in the final gesture. The triangle closed.

And suddenly the area filled with sound. Roars and screeches and a language that hurt her ears. She heard their wings flapping and their feet scraping over the dirt. She heard the shouts and hissing and when a demon nearby flicked out its tongue, Angie heard the rattle sound like a rattlesnake.

Woah. "What's happening?"

"You've created a strong enough protection barrier their tricks aren't working," Betha said, or really shouted over all the noise that now pummeled them from every side. "Smart to draw the two shapes together. A circle wouldn't have been enough."

"When we have time, I want to talk more about these shapes together. In the meantime, we need to get out of here."

"We're safe in the circle. We could wait them out." Betha shrugged.

Her lack of fear in the face of…all of this was disturbing on a basic level that Angie couldn't explain. That she wasn't scared, that she just seemed annoyed, was…confusing.

"Are you not telling me something?" Angie asked. "This should be scary to you. Eloise is in danger."

Betha shrugged. "What I've seen? I don't really get… scared anymore. Not like I did centuries ago. It doesn't seem to be an emotion I can access."

"She worries," Eloise shouted above the noise. "She doesn't fear."

"And you?"

"I'm terrified!" Eloise scowled at the surrounding beasts.

Eloise looked annoyed, too. But despite her words, she didn't look terrified. Just harried. Like she'd rather be somewhere else, but wasn't panicking.

And why would she, Angie supposed. They *lived* here. With the creatures roaming the jungle. This was the place they called home. The place Eloise actually felt most comfortable.

Maybe Angie was reading things into their reactions that she shouldn't. Maybe they were just so jaded and used to this, it wasn't as horribly frightening as it was to Angie.

Or maybe something was wrong and Angie just hadn't figured it out yet.

But whatever was going on, what she did know was that

they couldn't remain indefinitely in this clearing with beautiful monsters bearing down on them. The first few had reached the outer edge of her circle and were already testing its limits, poking at it and hissing when the circle flared blue and forced them back a step.

"The triangle and circle are strong enough to hold them off for a while," Betha commented.

"But they'll find a way through eventually?" Angie asked.

Betha sighed and made a short of head shaking gesture that wasn't quite a nod but not really a shake either. "It's a very strong protection pattern."

"Did it work *that* night? When you opened *that* realm?"

Betha's mouth flattened and she didn't comment.

That was enough for Angie. They couldn't stay here. They had to go elsewhere and come back when the monsters left.

"How long will they remain waiting here if we leave?" she asked Betha over the noise.

There were more demons surrounding them now, poking at the shield, getting jolted back a step or two. Angie had very carefully built this circle and triangle so she wouldn't be linked to it, so this sort of testing wouldn't hurt her. But even without the link, her imagination conjured up fantom pain for each of those tests, and that was not comfortable.

The noise, if possible, was worse now, with all of their snorting and snarling and hissing and roaring—at each other as much as at the shield. Angie suspected the only saving grace here for the humans was that all the beautiful monsters didn't much like each other either.

"They'll wait for a while," Betha said. "I think. I've never had to wait out so many. They might scatter fast after we go. Try to hunt us down in whatever new location we land. They don't like being around each other this much, with so many of them."

"Yup." Angie watched three swat and hiss at each other when they got too close together to test the circle.

"So they probably won't stay long waiting for us to return. They'll go hunting. They're beautiful and dangerous and more intelligent than some demons, but not as much as real higher level demons. These are very clever predators who know two apocalypse witches are bad news and should be killed." Betha paused. "Unless someone is manipulating them."

"Who could do that?"

"One of the gods." Betha shrugged.

That would be very bad, Angie thought as her stomach bottomed out. But that was a later problem. Their current problem involved getting out of here and hoping the demons scattered.

"Okay," Angie said, wincing as the noise level rose with a fight between two of the demons. "Anywhere in particular, or just away?"

"Particular," Betha said after a moment. "Somewhere that will be safer and also okay for Eloise to stay for a bit."

So. Another demon realm for sure. Angie would have loved to have brought them back to the human realm and hung out in the comparative safety of New York City, but for Eloise's sake, they had to stick to demon realms.

Which weren't any safer, but at least they weren't here with all these powerful monsters baring down on them.

"You have an idea where?"

Betha nodded, though her gaze, and her frown, were still directed at the surrounding demons. Then she turned and with a concentrated stare, started to open a portal in the very center of the triangle.

The others all backed up behind Angie, even Eloise to Angie's surprise. Sebastian had his back to Angie's to watch the demons and guard her. Aidan did the same. Carmen stood just behind Angie's shoulder watching the portal swirl open, a light of red spiraling wider. Until Angie could see into the new realm.

"You see inside that one?" she muttered to Carmen, though it was half a shout over another demon screech.

"Not any more than I've been able to see inside yours," Carmen confirmed.

That much was the same at least.

Close to Angie's ear, Carmen said, "You trust her?"

Angie gave a small headshake, but she was very aware of Eloise standing just behind them. And actually, she wasn't sure if Carmen was referring to Betha or Eloise. The two women were still hiding a lot. And there was something strange about Eloise that Betha was definitely hiding.

But again, a later problem. If they died here, Angie would never get her answers. And she didn't want to die.

The realm beyond the circle of red light wasn't one Angie

had seen before, which wasn't surprising. From this vantage, all she could see were shifting shadows and dark gray rocks. Nothing much beyond that, though.

"Here first," Betha said. "Then we'll jump to the next realm. That should be enough to confuse them."

"Wait, can they come after us into another realm?" Shit, that hadn't even occurred to Angie. She'd been in flight mode, prepared to run away for some breathing room, wait the demons out.

"They'll try," Betha said, matter-of-factly. "But hunting between realms is harder than hunting inside a single realm, so we should be able to lose them."

Angie's gut tightened and the tea that had been so soothing earlier churned like acid in her stomach. So much of this was terrifyingly not good, she wasn't even entirely sure what to worry about.

But running was better than staying, even if they had to run to a few different places to lose the demons.

"Go through," Betha said. "I'll come through last. Open another portal once you're there and we'll hop immediately to the next one." She looked away from the portal and it remained open. "We'll have to move fast, jump a few realms. But with two of us, that should be easier."

"Okay. Any particular place next?"

"Dealer's choice," Betha said with a small smile. It was a remarkably modern idiom for a centuries old woman who spent most of her time in demon realms.

Angie nodded. To Sebastian, "I'll go through first. I need either you or Aidan to come through last with Betha."

"I will," Aidan said. "Sebastian, go with Angie. She'll need someone at her back."

He didn't comment but Angie had a feeling Sebastian going through the portal with her immediately had never been in question. They walked up to the portal together, Sebastian's gaze moving over the surrounding demons the entire time.

Angie started into the new realm, which was so dark and shadowy, she really couldn't see much past the few rocks just beyond the breach. She couldn't hear anything over the sounds of the surrounding demons either. So she couldn't tell if there were chittering demons here.

Even with all the other terrifying things she'd experienced lately, she really didn't want to see, or *hear*, the chittering demons.

She pulled in a deep breath. Grabbed Sebastian's hand and squeezed tight and briefly, then they stepped into the new realm together.

CHAPTER NINETEEN

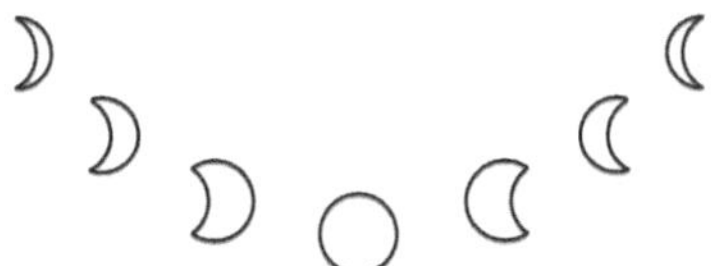

blast of hot, brimstone-laced air hit Angie in the face, a sharp contrast to the cold breeze that filtered through Betha's clearing. Angie and Sebastian moved back to back immediately, and scanned the area. Shadowed landscape of rolling hills, mostly rocky and without the surrounding vegetation that had filled Betha's jungle. A dark sky overhead with moving gray clouds that skittered over the blackness. No stars. No visible moons or light of any kind in that sky. Angie wasn't even sure where the light to see her surroundings came from, but she could see.

And all she saw was shadows.

The others followed through the portal fast. First Carmen, who moved close to Angie and Sebastian and put her back to them so the three of them formed a circle to keep an eye on the surroundings. Eloise stumble through the breach a beat after Carmen and look around like she was annoyed more than scared.

Another longer beat. Two. A hesitation that had Angie's teeth on edge. And then Betha and Aidan stepped into the new realm.

The portal swirled shut behind them, started to swirl shut even as Betha stepped through, so that it closed fast. Winked out of existence. Left them in this new realm.

"You'll have to teach me how to close those that fast," Angie said. Both impressed and eager to learn. Closing a portal faster meant less chance any demons escaped.

"As soon as we're out of this realm," Betha said.

"Dangerous demons?" Angie went back to scanning their surroundings.

"Hardly any here. Three species maybe. It's not the demons that are the problem. The…darkness has a weight that will seep in if we don't leave soon."

That was new to Angie. But then a lot of this was new.

Betha glanced behind her. "And it will only take them a few minutes to figure out which realm we escaped to."

Angie tried not to let the panic show in her voice. "Okay. Where to now?"

"Anywhere you can get us next. I'll open the portal after that. That should confuse them enough we'll be good."

"I'm hoping for an explanation for that later too," Angie said.

But she didn't wait for one. She dragged up a memory of one of the realms Betha had opened into before, another memory she'd picked up from her visions fed by Betha's blood. Then she grabbed hold of her demon witch thread and her witch magic and spun open a portal.

The process went fast, the portal opening into a gray world with black vines and a purple sky. This was the realm Betha had come through into the human world when she'd killed Sokolov's demon. A realm Angie at least knew she and the other humans could survive in.

Betha hesitated when she saw the realm though. Her eyes narrowing. But she didn't comment, instead going through first this time, with Eloise right behind her. The others followed, except Sebastian who only went halfway through the portal, waiting on Angie to join him.

She stepped through with him, then made the effort to close the breach. Her process went much slower than Betha's. When the portal finally spun down to a dot and winked out of existence, Angie swore she saw something glimmering in the other realm, something *looking* into her portal.

"What was that?" she muttered.

"The darkness," Betha said. "Too close." She let out a breath. "But that's a difficult realm for the Aminore and Helavitee demons to move through. They might not even try to follow us through there."

"Why is it hard for them?"

"The darkness." Betha turned to scan their current surroundings, and Angie finally looked around too.

A plain of black grass on gray rocks spread out around them. Twig like trees of gray that blended with the rocks, and black foliage that looked more like moss than leaves covered the limbs. Black vines crept across the rocks. And the purple sky overhead churned. That sky looked a bit like twilight, the light of the realm that dusk gloom that was hard to see through even though there was technically enough light.

In the distance, a volcano puffed smoky gases into the air instead of lava. And their immediate surroundings smelled weirdly of flowers instead of sulfur.

"You weren't happy about me opening this realm," Angie said to Betha. "Why?"

"Too close to the human realm," she said offhandedly. "Too easy to get there from here. I don't like Eloise being this close."

"Will she be okay here?"

"Here? Yes. For now." Betha walked over to Eloise, who was looking around and didn't seem particularly distressed about their new location.

"There's something weird going on there," Carmen muttered to Angie, her voice low.

"Yup," Angie said. She just wasn't sure what it was yet. "Did anything happen when you went to get Eloise?"

"Betha didn't seem in a huge hurry," Carmen whispered. "Eloise was locked into a room I wasn't allowed to see into. She took her time coming out and seemed more resigned than scared."

"Neither of them seems particularly scared. That's weird, right?"

"Maybe," Carmen said. "They do live there."

"Were you scared?"

"Terrified. But I don't live in a demon realm."

"You dealt with a demon regularly."

"He was always inside a containment circle," Carmen said as if that should be obvious. "And a Molder demon isn't a Aminore or Helavitee demon."

The fact that Carmen was more afraid of the demons they'd just faced than she was her Molder demon meant the beautiful monsters were as scary as Angie had thought they were.

"Did Betha or Eloise say anything coming back up?" Angie asked, keeping her voice so low, she wasn't sure Carmen would even hear her.

Carmen murmured, "No. Nothing at all. Betha didn't even explain what was happening to Eloise as they came up the stairs."

Something was definitely very strange there.

Sebastian gave Angie an unreadable look. He'd been standing close enough to overhear her and Carmen's conversation, but he didn't comment. Aidan had stayed closer to Eloise and Betha, her attention on them as much as their surroundings.

Aidan was acting a little odd, too, and Angie suspected it was because the older hunter knew more about what was going on with Betha and Eloise than Angie did. But they had one more portal jump to make before they could discuss that.

In the distance, Angie heard a sound that was a cross between a screech and a strike of lightning. That was the only way she could describe it. The ground under her trembled briefly then stopped. The volcano in the distance sent up a larger bloom of smoke.

"We need to leave, don't we?" Angie asked.

"Next realm," Betha said. She drew in a visible breath and said, "We should be able to wait in this next one for a bit. The demons are overall weaker and stay away from me."

"Too close to the human realm?" A lot of the weaker demons lived in the outer levels. Though "weaker" was a very relative term for any demon.

"No," Betha said. "This one is a deeper realm. Just one that's got weaker demons in it."

Angie frowned but kept her questions to herself. They had to move again. She didn't want to risk the beautiful monsters chancing the darkness realm and tracking them here before they could jump again.

Betha opened yet another portal. Beyond, the realm reminded Angie of the lava realm, the one she most often opened into. The one she'd been trapped in twice and where she thought she'd die.

Like that realm, this one had black sands and rocky ground. Red spewing lava volcanos lined the horizon. There were even a few strange black trees just within view. But this place didn't have a red sky overhead. The sky looked black with a scattering of gold, almost like stars. Except very very bright. Bright enough to cast a golden glow over the realm, giving a shimmer to the black sands and black rocks.

When Angie got closer to the portal, she saw that the "sky" wasn't even a sky. It looked more like the roof of a ginormous cave, complete with stalactites hanging from the roof. The golden sparkling stars were likely actual gold or a similar mineral, but glittering with its own light. And running through the black sand and rocks, lines of phosphorescent blue. Angie couldn't tell if those blue lines were microscopic organisms or a mineral like the ones overhead. But they added an additional blue glow to the place.

The different colored lights taken together, gave the realm a weird, almost purple tone. And the minute Angie stepped close to the portal, something inside her drew her onward, almost eagerly. As if this realm was a place she actually *wanted* to go.

She'd had a similar reaction looking for Betha. A giddiness that was as strange as it was spooky. That she was *excited* to step through the portal into this new realm was downright horrifying.

She paused long enough to look at the threads of her web. And sure enough, the demon magic lines, those two red lines bracketing her demon witch thread, were tugging toward this new realm. Eager to go through the breach.

That alone was enough to make her hesitate. Going anywhere that made the magic born of demons happy seemed a bad idea. But she had little choice. And Betha said this realm would be safe. Or safe enough anyway.

She glanced back at Sebastian, then Aidan. Aidan's gaze was narrowed but she gave a little chin lift of reassurance.

Sebastian took Angie's hand again and said, "We'll go through together."

That helped. Having him right by her side through all this helped. A lot.

They faced the breach together and stepped through without more prompting.

The others followed quickly while Angie tried to figure

out why this new realm felt so comfortable to her. It wasn't the place where she'd pulled in the demon magic. So it wasn't like-power calling back to like-power. She hadn't felt this in the lava realm when they'd passed through it.

The air had a musty, minerally flavor to it, and a coolness that seemed at odds with the volcanos on the horizon. There was also a river running past not far from where they stood, but unlike the lava realm, this wasn't a boiling red lava river. It was a river of something thick and viscous, though. Not water. Whatever the substance was it looked a bit like gold, but with a purple sheen over it. The musty, minerally scent seemed to come from that river.

"You okay?" Sebastian said, his voice quiet, but it still had a strange echoing quality as if they were in a really large room. He was frowning at her, the concerned frown that he'd worn way too often on this little adventure.

"I'm not sure," she murmured. Her voice had that same weird echoing quality, almost didn't sound like herself, and that made her hesitant to say more. But she did say, "Something weird about this realm. I'll figure it out."

He moved closer, close enough that he could protect her if something went upside down. She wanted to smile, wanted to hug him. Almost did. Only stopped herself because the giddiness of being in this realm freaked her out so much and she didn't want to risk hurting him with... whatever this was.

Betha spun the portal closed, and they were all left staring at their surroundings. Carmen nodded to the river. "Is that... liquid gold?"

"Liquid gold with magic wrapped into it," Betha said. She was frowning at their surroundings, and she looked…

Angie wasn't sure how to describe Betha's expression. She looked resigned. But resigned to what? Staying here for any length of time maybe?

"Pretty," Carmen said. "The blue lines? What are those?"

"Bugs," Betha said. "I wouldn't touch them, if I were you."

"Wasn't going to." Carmen raised her hands, palms out. "You said this place is one of the deeper realms? You can get here from the human realm though."

Angie glanced sharply at Carmen.

"You can," Betha said, either not noticing Angie's reaction or ignoring it. "If you know where you're going, you can get here directly."

"You've seen this place before?" Angie asked Carmen.

She shook her head. "The Molder just talked a lot. He spoke of a place like this. In weirdly hushed tones. He wouldn't have admitted to being afraid of anything, of course, but I got the impression he didn't like this particular realm."

"Even though it's full of supposedly weak demons?" Angie glanced at Betha when she said this, her brows raised.

"It is mostly just weak demons here," Betha said. "Now."

"Now? What does that mean?"

Betha's mouth flattened. She glanced at Eloise. Eloise was staring into the distance, like she was thinking something and not paying attention to the conversation.

Aidan had moved up behind Eloise, and was watching

her, also frowning. The hunters gaze moved from Eloise to their surroundings and back to Eloise.

"Now," a voice said from behind Angie, "means now that I live here."

Angie turned at the new voice, which sounded surprisingly human. Her heart had started to thump hard as adrenaline surged into her blood. She had a shield spell on the tip of her tongue, her fingers raised to begin forming the spell, only to stop mid-motion. And stare. Shock freezing her in place.

"I wondered how long it would be before you came here," the stranger said, smiling. "We've been waiting for a very long time."

Angie blinked, trying to make sense of what she was seeing. Because this didn't seem possible.

Another human in a demon realm.

One who looked just like Eloise.

CHAPTER TWENTY

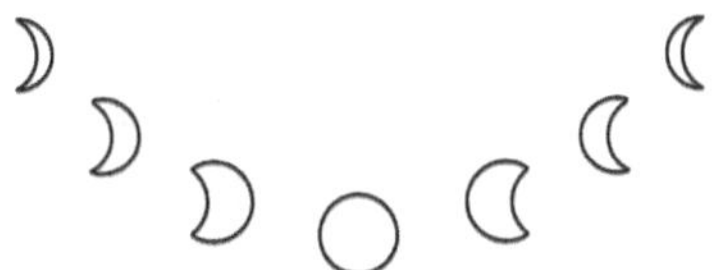

$\mathcal{A}$ngie looked at both the Eloise she'd met earlier and this new one standing a few feet away, her brain refusing to reconcile what she was seeing.

The new woman was almost identical to Eloise. Both with light brown hair, the new woman's a little shorter but still generally long. Where Eloise had worn her hair in a braid, the other woman's hair hung in loose waves. Eloise was dressed in a light-colored purple skirt and long-sleeved t-shirt. The new woman wore a vest made of golden scales that shimmered and black leather trousers with calf-high leather boots. Eloise's features were a little plumper, not cut as sharply as the other woman's, but that was really the only difference in their faces. Take away everything else, all the superficial, easily changeable details, and they looked identical.

Right down to the glowing red eyes.

"Twins?" she said aloud, because it was the only explanation.

But in all the visions and conversations, no one had thought to mention that Eloise had a twin? Eloise didn't think about her twin once in the vision? Betha never thought about Eloise's twin?

She supposed the visions she'd had from each woman's perspective had been during very intense circumstances. It probably shouldn't be that surprising that they weren't thinking of another person. Yet Eloise had never mentioned a twin in her diary. And since arriving in the demon realm, arriving at Betha and Eloise's home, discussing having to run away because of the beautiful monsters, neither woman had once said anything about finding refuge with Eloise's twin?

Who was also capable of moving in and out of demon realms…

What the hell was going on?

"Not quite twins," the new Eloise said, her smile more of a smirk as she glanced at Betha.

Betha was scowling at the other woman, her brows lowered, looking uncomfortable and upset. "You weren't supposed to show up until I said it was time," Betha said.

"I get impatient," the other woman said. "And you were taking ages."

"We had things to discuss."

"Did you get around to discussing me yet?"

"No."

"Well. No time like the present." The woman chuckled. Her voice was very similar to Eloise's but also different. A little scratchier maybe? Like this new woman was a smoker and had roughened up her vocal cords.

Angie glanced at the Eloise she'd already met. Her gaze was turned toward the ground, but she was glancing between Betha and the new woman from under her lashes.

"Alright," Angie said, "what the hell is going on?"

"You're the new demon witch, right?" the Eloise-look-alike said. "The one who can also kill demons?"

Angie gave a curt nod.

The woman glanced at the others, her eyes widening slightly. "Wow. Never thought I'd meet demon hunters quite like these. Interesting." She frowned at Carmen. "Even more interesting."

Carmen lifted her chin defensively and the other woman smiled. It was a sly sort of smile, though. A knowing one.

"Well," the look-alike said, "the gangs all here. So to speak." She looked back at Betha. "If you thought you could make this easier by not telling her everything, you were fooling yourself." She gave a little nod. "I have a safe spot to talk this way. The Aminore and the Helavitee won't come here unless they're forced to. And I think we have some time before anyone forces them to."

"What about other demons?" Angie asked.

The woman laughed. "Oh, no other demons here will bother us. I promise. They know better."

She turned her back on them and started to walk away, in the general direction of a small hill of black rocks topped with some of the strange looking black bark trees. One of the rivers of gold ran past the hill, circling it on one side. And the lines of blue luminescent bugs streaked across the hill and circled the base of the small tree copse at the top.

Betha and Eloise followed the woman without question and without waiting for the rest of them. Neither woman even looked back to see if Angie and the hunters would follow.

Angie frowned at Aidan and Sebastian. "Is this bad or good?"

"Yes," Aidan said. A typical Aidan answer. And then she started after the new woman who looked like Eloise's twin.

Sebastian gave Angie a hooded look and waited for her before moving.

Carmen came up close to Angie and said, "I don't like any of this."

"Me neither. But answers are that way."

"They are," Carmen said with a resigned sigh. "Let's go."

The rocky hill hid a dwelling of sorts buried into the rocks. On the side Angie hadn't been able to see at first was a door made of rock, but there was a deep purple light around the stone, and when the Eloise look-alike pushed it inward, it swung easily on rock hinges. The inside was, like Betha's place, a lot larger than it looked to be from the outside. The hill was only a little taller than Angie and Sebastian on the exterior, but on the interior, the ceilings were high and comfortable, decorated in shiny, multi-colored stones that winked and twinkled like stars. The ceiling was painted a light blue, so it resembled an earth sky, but with all the colored stones it was obviously not a sky at the same time.

Like Betha's home, this one opened into a huge single room, much larger than Betha's house, and the furniture, though made mostly of stone, was elaborately carved and topped with thick, velvet wrapped pillows. Was that velvet? Angie realized she wasn't sure. The shine and shimmer on the material reminded her of Betha's scaled jumpsuit and the Eloise look-alike's scaled vest. Not that the pillows and cushions looked like scales, but they all had a similar shimmer.

The light inside seemed to come from a hidden source. It was a lot brighter inside the house than outside. Which took some adjustment when she walked in. Near what Angie assumed was a back wall, there was a circular staircase going down into the earth. Not huge like the one in Betha's house that took up the entire center of the main floor, but still large enough that even at a distance, Angie could tell they were stairs. That part of the room was dark, a dark hole into which the stone steps vanished.

There was an unlit hearth to one side of the large room. But most of the chairs and seats were in the center, away from the fire. There was a table and what looked to be the ingredients for making tea right next to the hearth.

Everything was stone, but faintly shimmering in either purple magic or glowing from internal light. The purple magic was strange because it sort of reminded Angie of Fae magic, but when she opened her senses to it, it didn't feel Fae at all. It felt like that purple magic that she'd integrated into her own magic web, purple born of her witch magic and demon witch magic blending.

Was that what this was? Was the Eloise look-alike a witch? But… She couldn't be a demon witch. Could she?

Angie had so many questions, more now than she'd had when they first entered the demon realms through that tree in Central Park. Felt like that happened a month ago even though it had only been a few hours. Well, even that she wasn't sure of. Given how many different realms they'd been in, and that time worked so differently here to how it worked in the human realm, she honestly had no idea how long they'd been here, or how much time had passed at home.

She did know she was starting to get hungry, though. Hungry seemed like a bad thing when she might need to fight at any moment.

Except she wasn't exactly sure who she might have to fight. But any fight would cost her energy and that meant she needed food. Without a word, she pulled a protein bar from the depths of her oversized purse and started eating as she looked around the house. No one who knew her even commented, not even Carmen. But the Eloise look-alike glanced at her curiously.

"We have food if you need something to eat," she said.

"I'm fine. This is good. Just get low blood sugar if I don't eat regularly."

"Ah. Fair enough."

"You know what that means?"

"I was a…" She glanced at Eloise. "What were we called then? Not chemist or doctor. Well, I suppose witch, but we weren't a witch then. We just knew folk medicine. And I liked the topic so I continued to study it after. All the new inventions and information. Really fascinating."

"That raises more questions than it answered," Carmen said.

"It does," the Eloise look-alike said and smiled. "Please, sit. We can talk in comfort here."

Everyone settled into one of the various stone chairs or couches, with their shimmering cushions that looked sort of like they were velvet covered. Angie's hands *felt* velvet when she touched them, but her eyes watched the material swim and shift and change if she tried to look at it while also touching it.

"Better just to ignore all that," Eloise look-alike said. "It'll make you dizzy."

Angie frowned and raised a brow at the other woman.

She shrugged. "Soft material is hard to come by in this realm. I use a little magic to adjust what I can get."

Angie nodded, but said, "I was under the impression Eloise wasn't a witch or magic wielder...before. You can wield magic?"

The woman smiled. "You could say that."

Betha grunted something under her breath that drew the other woman's stare. Betha stared back, her brows raised, not backing done under the intensity.

Finally, the new woman blinked and looked back at Angie. "My magic is of this place, mostly. Well, not this realm specifically. But it is of the demons. So here, yes, I wield magic."

"Your magic is the wrong color for demon magic," Angie said.

This made the other woman sit up a little straighter. She'd

chose a seat that essentially put her at the head of her gathered guests. Carmen sprawled in a single chair. Angie perched at the edge of the couch, and Sebastian sat on the arm of the couch next to her. Betha and Eloise were sharing the other end of the couch, which was a huge piece of furniture. Aidan leaned against the wall near the door, with her arms crossed over her chest, her thoughts and mood hidden behind a neutral expression.

"Interesting that you can see the colors of the magic," Eloise look-alike said. "I can't. But I learned…after, that some witches see magic in colors."

"Mostly blue for witch magic," Angie said. "Red for demon magic or demon witch magic."

"Makes sense. And purple?"

"Fae magic is purple."

"I'm not Fae." The woman smiled though, as if delighted by the idea.

"It can also be a blending of blue witch magic and red demon witch magic." Angie hesitated a beat, then said, "I had some of that blending happen, so I have some magic that, to me, appears purple."

"Fascinating," the other woman said, her eyes rounding. This made the red flare, and brought more attention to the fact that she had demon eyes. She didn't seem to notice or care, though. Unlike Betha, she didn't attempt to hide that red. "What does your *purple* magic do?"

Angie wasn't really sure. It added strength, it added power, but she had been avoiding it. Especially since pulling in actual demon magic. She was afraid of what the blended magic might do. "I don't access it," she said, which was honest.

"You think that's what my magic is? A blending of ordinary witch and ordinary demon witch magic?"

"I don't know," Angie said. "I assumed you'd know."

"Oh, there's a lot I don't know. I try to learn everything of course. But there's a lot to learn."

Angie gave a non-committal nod. There was a lot to learn. Finding out there were basic things that the other woman didn't know about her own magic was disturbing.

And if she were honest, a little scary.

"You're wondering how I don't know more about my own magic," the woman guessed, smiling.

"Don't," Betha said in a warning.

"We need to tell them," the look-alike said with a shrug, though her focus was on Angie. "After all this time, the wait, she's finally here. I think she deserves to know the truth."

"What truth?" Angie asked, her own gaze caught in the look-alike's red gaze. She wanted to glance at Betha, but was worried if she looked away now, she'd break some kind of bond forming between her and the other woman and that would result in no answers.

The woman smiled, an almost triumphant expression that made Angie leery. "It's quite simple. You see, in her attempt to cure her love, Betha made one tiny mistake. She didn't attend to the possible complications and side effects of the spell she used. She did, in a way, cure Eloise. But she did it by separating out the magic Eloise had absorbed into an entirely different entity." The woman's smile grew. "Her spell created me."

CHAPTER TWENTY-ONE

ngie nodded, her head bobbing of its own accord, because her thoughts were racing and she wasn't even sure what her physical body was doing in that moment. Her voice quiet and a little hoarse, she said, "Yeah, that's going to require more of an explanation."

Betha snorted and when Angie finally glanced at her, she was rolling her eyes and shaking her head. "So fucking dramatic," Betha muttered to herself.

Dramatic? That's what she was calling this. Angie raised her brows and Betha sighed.

"*That* night didn't go as planned," Betha said.

"Yeah." Angie glanced at the Eloise look-alike. "Think it might be important to tell me the specifics."

"The spell had unintended consequences," Betha said. "Isn't it obvious."

"No. At least not what actually happened. How can you have two Eloises when there was only one?"

"It was all very exciting," Eloise look-alike said. "I go by Lisa, too, if that helps. It can be hard, with us having one name, so I chose Lisa for mine as a distinguisher."

"I like the name Lisa," Eloise said with a shrug.

That was the first time she'd commented, the first thing she'd said. Angie faced her, looking for… She wasn't sure. Something in Eloise's expression to explain all this. She was hoping in vain. Eloise looked at Lisa with a sort of resignation but also a little friendliness. Unlike Betha, who seemed exasperated by the other woman, Eloise didn't seem particularly bothered now.

"How did Lisa come to being?" Angie asked, again.

"The spell I used?" Betha said. "Typical demon, it had loopholes and unforeseen consequences. It got rid of the part of Eloise she seemed to have picked up in the demon realm alright. Separated it out into a completely different person. The… The sand I used from *that* realm twisted things and made a simple stanza in the production of the potion literal instead of figurative."

"You can't blame the spell entirely," Lisa said. "Remember there were other things happening that night. Your concentration was diverted." Lisa looked at Angie. "It wasn't really Betha's fault. She had to finish the potion immediately, but she had trouble getting all those portals closed. It resulted in some…escapes."

"From *that* realm?" Angie was appalled. How was their

world even still standing if something had gotten out of the god realm?

"No," Betha said quickly. "Not… Some power of some kind shot out. It cut through my protection spells and hit Yosuf in the chest. I'm still not sure how he survived. We later decided the…brand wasn't intended to be fatal. Just a mark. The mark drew demons from another realm to him, and it took all Yosuf's considerable strength to keep them controlled, to send them back. While I finished the potion and Eloise drank it."

Eloise shivered.

"It didn't taste bad," Lisa said. "It tasted like heaven. That was a problem later. We both crave it a little now. But more would require reaching into a realm that nearly killed her before." She gave Betha a gentle look. "It really wasn't your fault."

"I got you permanently…damaged. I got Yosuf branded with a demon god mark. And I didn't fix the original problem at all."

"We're not dying anymore," Lisa said.

"And I can tolerate the human realm now," Eloise said. "A little bit."

Lisa looked at Angie. "But I can't. I'm all the demon world 'stuff' that was inside Eloise, made into its own entity. But that means I can't leave the demon realms. My body doesn't have any of the human stuff."

Angie watched Betha closely as Lisa said all this. Betha's eyes narrowed slightly, but she wiped the expression away, leaving hers neutral and unreadable.

"We're still connected, though," Lisa continued, seemingly unaware of Betha's stare. "So I feel when Eloise is in the human realm. It…stretches the bond between us and makes us both uncomfortable. She can stay longer now, but still not permanently, because the part of ourselves that is still intertwined gets very unhappy and stretches beyond tolerance."

"And there's no way to break the bond or reverse the process?" Angie asked. She realized about a beat late, she was asking Lisa if there was a way to end her existence, and winced.

"Centuries of searching haven't turned anything up," Eloise said, exchanging a look with Betha. "We have looked."

"I don't mind living here," Lisa said, "because I am of this place, even if I look human. But Eloise is stuck here still and none of us like that."

"If we could just break the bond holding them entangled," Betha said, "they could separate and Eloise and I could go home."

"But everything we've tried has failed," Lisa said with a shrug, not seeming particularly bothered by that. "And because Betha changed the mark on Yosuf, again to protect him, she can no longer open *that* realm." This Lisa said quietly to Angie. "We'd need a new potion and that potion would require sand from *that* realm. But we can't open that portal anymore."

"Because you can't be in the human realm?" Angie asked Betha.

"Because I can't open it," Betha said, sounding almost defensive. "The process…doesn't work for me anymore. I can't crack it open. Not even a little."

"Why?" Angie's gaze jumped between the three women. "What changed?"

"The mark on Yosuf," Betha said. "I was trying to fix one of my mistakes, to keep him from being a demon target. I… altered the fresh brand so that it became a triangle inside a circle. I was hoping to protect him from the damage I'd done, and the danger I put him in. Thought the protective symbols would keep him safe."

"They didn't?"

"They did," Lisa said.

"For a little while," Betha corrected. "And then he was killed in a demon fight. So not for very long."

"That happened several years after your dealings with him," Aidan said, her voice sounding odd in the open space. Maybe because she hadn't spoken before this. "How could that have had to do with the brand?"

"And demon hunters die in fights," Sebastian added, his voice low and quiet. "That's how we die. In a fight. It was bound to happen and probably had nothing to do with the brand."

"It didn't protect him, though, did it?" Betha said.

"It did," Sebastian insisted. "For years. He survived that night and went on to remain a powerful demon hunter for years after. That was…not common at that time."

"Or any time," Aidan added.

"Whatever change you made to that brand," Angie said, "must have been good."

"Not good enough," Betha said. She waved that away their continued attempt at protest. "It hardly matters anymore. The issue at hand is the split that happened between Eloise and Lisa."

"When did that happen?" Angie asked. "Immediately?"

"After we returned to a demon realm," Lisa said. "After drinking the potion, things didn't happen immediately, and Betha thought it hadn't worked. Eloise was still sick. She brought her back here to where she wasn't as sick. And… then things happened."

Betha snorted, a very cynical sound.

"We both felt better after," Eloise said. "I felt more myself. Lisa was…herself. It wasn't a horrible turn of events."

"Except that I somehow created someone who shouldn't exist and you two are still entangled so we can't go home," Betha snapped.

"She still wants to reverse what happened," Lisa said quietly to Angie. "She's still trying to fix things instead of accepting what's happened."

"What about you?" Angie asked. "You…exist now. And have for a while. What do you want?"

Lisa tilted her head a little and frowned at Angie, then glanced at Betha and Eloise. "I haven't thought about it," she said.

But that was a lie. Angie could hear it in her voice. She had thought of her own existence and what she wanted. And

Angie doubted it was what Betha wanted, which would have meant oblivion for Lisa. Making her just a part of Eloise again.

Or killing her since she was made of a part of Eloise that Eloise hadn't always had. The demonic part.

"This is all..." Angie shrugged. What could she say? Interesting. Horrible. Tragic. She said, "Thank you for the explanation. But all three of you have said you've been waiting for someone like me." Her gaze cut to Lisa, then shifted back to Betha. "Why?"

"Ah," Lisa answered. "That's so you can help us."

"Help you...what?"

"Destroy the god realm," Betha said.

Angie blinked at the women all staring at her. Expectantly. Did they think she'd just enthusiastically go along with something that...wasn't possible? Just say, Sure. No problem. Then we'll have tea.

Because, yeah, no that wasn't going to be her reaction here.

"First," she said slowly, making sure her words were crystal clear, "that's not possible. Because...god realm. Second, why? How would that solve anything? Betha can't open the realm anymore. You two crave the potion made from the sand there. Wouldn't destroying the realm... I don't know, be bad. Why would you want to do that?"

"Killing demons is lots of fun," Lisa said, her red eyes flaring. "And destroying the god realm will leave the rest vulnerable."

Betha's eyes narrowed. "That," she said carefully neutral.

"And it will break the entanglement between the two women. Making them each able to go their own way without being tied and limited by the other."

Angie frowned at Betha. She was lying again. Angie had heard the little, almost imperceptible pause before break. She wasn't hoping to separate the two women permanently. Was she trying to…bring them back into one person again? That meant basically destroying Lisa. But then they'd be right back to where they started with Eloise suffering with the demon magic she wasn't meant to hold.

And none of this really made sense. Angie wasn't sure why she thought it should. This was demon magic, and demon realms, and demon rules. Those rules didn't apply to humans because humans shouldn't even be here—at least not alive—and they definitely shouldn't be able to do what Angie and Betha…and apparently Lisa could do.

Angie frowned at that. Lisa could kill demons too. Lisa had said she enjoyed killing demons. Her expression was… happy when she thought about it. One might even say, she savored it.

But…

What Angie was thinking wasn't possible. According to what Betha told her, an apocalypse witch, a witch who could become a human capable of killing demons, that human had to be a witch and a touch psychic. And Eloise was neither of those things. Before this, she hadn't even had the sort of small kitchen magic that Angie's mother had. She used folk knowledge and herbalism to make medicines for her community, but that wasn't "magic" the way Angie and Betha wielded it. Even the way Angie's mother wielded it. No magic power was required for what Eloise had done.

And she wasn't a touch psychic either. Or hadn't been.

Betha had insisted that was necessary for an apocalypse witch. The reason that long ago witch, who'd had the right amount of anger, hadn't been right to be the second demon killer. She hadn't had the psychic gift necessary.

Either Betha had been lying this entire time—and Angie suspected there had been a *lot* left out of the conversation so far—or Betha had been telling the truth and just left out some of the important information about Eloise.

Eloise might not have been a magic wielder, but she could have been psychic. There were witches who weren't psychic, and psychics who weren't witches. Different powers. Different techniques to use them—or not use them as the case may be. She'd asked if Eloise had been a witch before.

She hadn't asked if she'd been psychic.

Angie held Betha's gaze, watched when Betha realized Angie had figured something out that hadn't been said aloud yet. Her gaze flicked to Eloise and then she nodded slightly.

If they'd understood each other, Eloise was a psychic.

And Lisa was actually the second apocalypse witch.

Which made Angie the third. And according to the demons' legend, with three of them together, they would destroy all the demon realms.

Including the god realm.

"You won't be able to recreate the potion," Angie said,

trying to make sure she understood all this. Afraid she did understand it better than she was supposed to.

"No. But then we can't do that now." Betha shrugged.

"Two of you together can't open the god realm?"

"Lisa couldn't go to the human realm to help me," Betha reminded her. "And I can't do it anymore." She paused. "But you could."

"Lisa can't be there, though. How would that be possible without all three of us in one place?"

"We can link all our powers," Lisa said. "Temporarily of course. It's part of the strength that comes from being three and complete. Two of us alone could never even attempt this. But with three…" Lisa's grin widened.

"Okay." Angie glanced at them all. "But I still don't really understand the why? How does it help? How does destroying the god realm break the entanglement between Lisa and Eloise?"

"It's what created us," Lisa said.

"What bound us," Eloise said.

"Recreating the original potion wouldn't help them, just make things worse," Betha added.

"The addiction," Eloise said. "We'd crave more, drink more, as much as we could get."

Lisa finished, "And the more we drank, the more linked we'd be."

"There would never be an option of untangling them," Betha said, her jaw tight as her gaze flicked to Eloise.

"Destroying the thing that created us," Lisa said, "eliminates the possibility of the potion permanently. And it breaks apart our bond. We'd be completely autonomous afterward. Free to do as we please." Lisa's expression was almost feral as she said this last, her gaze turned inward.

It was an uncomfortable expression to look at. Because it reminded Angie of the killers she'd met. The people who savored killing, not just did it because it was expeditious. Lisa enjoyed killing. A lot.

And even though she enjoyed killing demons, the blood lust in Lisa's expression left Angie extremely leery, and a little sick to her stomach.

She met Betha's gaze again, narrowing her eyes slightly. Another subtle head nod.

Yeah. Something wasn't right with Lisa. And it wasn't something to be discussed in front of Lisa.

Angie said, quietly, "So…just to be absolutely clear and blunt. You think Lisa is the second demon witch. I'm really the third. And that means we can destroy all the demon realms. But the only one you want to destroy is the god realm."

She wasn't sure they'd have a hope anyway. She wasn't particularly interested in the whole destroying-realms part of the legend. Let the demons fear them. Maybe they'd leave her alone. But she doubted that. With demons, they usually wanted to kill what they feared. And that kept the target on her back. And it looked like Betha didn't have answers for this curse. All they'd discussed. None of it had pointed Angie in a direction that helped her get rid of the demon magic.

"I do need somewhere to live," Lisa said with a grin. "And something to do. But it's better if Betha and Eloise aren't bothered about what I do." She glanced briefly at Betha, a look that was difficult to read but didn't look friendly.

It was the first time Lisa had shown any animosity toward the other two women.

"You're sure this process," Angie continued, skipping over the part where Lisa's life goal was to continue murdering demons, "will untangle them and not destroy Lisa? Send her back into Eloise? Start the problem up all over again?"

"We're different people now," Lisa said before Betha could answer. "There's no going back to being a single person. That…" She frowned. "What's that phrase? Oh, that ship has sailed. That's right, isn't it?"

Lisa looked weirdly innocent and eager as she asked, so Angie felt compelled to answer. "It's the right phrase, yes."

Lisa grinned. "We can't be reintegrated into a single person. The only way forward is to finish the process and separate us completely. Then everything will be fine."

"And all we'd need to do that would be to destroy a god realm?"

"Yes," Lisa said.

Angie felt her stomach drop. They hadn't brought her here to give her answers. They'd lured her here to help them do something that was…

Impossible.

CHAPTER TWENTY-TWO

ngie made an excuse to get out of that house for a few minutes. Ensured there'd be no trouble from demons first. Lisa said, "No they don't come here anymore. Mores the pity."

Angie had decided not to touch that comment. She made a beeline for the door and stepped out into a space that felt more like a giant cave and didn't provide anything like fresh air. But she needed a few minutes alone. Away from Eloise's hopeful expression, and Betha's frowns, and Lisa's bloodlust. She needed to think and process everything.

Because everything was a lot. And she just wasn't sure how to deal with it.

No answers. There were no answers here. If there were, Betha would have discovered them a long time ago.

Well, maybe not. She hadn't been looking for something to help herself, not for a long time. It was obvious she was more preoccupied with fixing the mistake she'd made with Eloise, creating Lisa. Their hope for that fix rested in the third apocalypse witch. In Angie.

In doing something that Angie didn't believe they could do, even with three of them.

And that there was *already* another apocalypse witch! She wasn't the second but the third. Betha had lied about her being the second. But that explained why Betha had been so eager to find the last witch now. The second would have done her no good, except as a person with whom she needed to form an alliance. Only two wouldn't have had a hope of destroying any demon realms.

They'd needed her for this. Needed the third witch. Needed Angie to open the god realm portal because the other two couldn't.

And once again, someone was asking her to be a murderer. Because it was expedient. True, it saved Eloise and gave Lisa a sort of real life that was separate from Eloise. But at the cost of an entire realm of beings?

Even if the beings were demons. Demon gods at that.

There was so much about this that felt just wrong. Everything. All of it.

She wanted to go home. Forget she'd ever tried this. It hadn't helped. Maybe made things worse.

As she paced around the back of the rocky hill that was Lisa's home, she realized the worst part wasn't just that she'd gotten no answers, but that she'd dragged the others here with her! Put them all in danger for what?

She paused mid-step. Yes. For what?

Betha had said the two hunters and Carmen *had* to come with Angie or they'd all die. But *why*? Why Carmen? There was nothing for her to do here. No reason for her to be here. There was no reason for Aidan or Sebastian to be here either in this realm destruction plan. But they would have come no matter what, just to have Angie's back. She was glad to have them here, to have someone on her side.

But…why Carmen?

Betha was a touch psychic but she'd never even seen Carmen except as the face a demon had taken to trick Angie. She didn't know anything about her. And she hadn't touched anything in the human realm to gain a premonition that might have given her reason to say Carmen should join the group.

Why the hell was Carmen here?

She turned to see Aidan leaning against the rocky hill, her hands pressed against the stone behind her, her gaze out over the black sand landscape.

"Why is Carmen here?" Angie asked aloud.

"Yup," Aidan said.

"How much of this have you known or suspected this whole time?"

"Not this. Exactly. But I…sensed something wrong with Eloise when she started up those stairs."

"She's not whole. Will she ever be whole again?"

"No idea. Never seen anything quite like this. And that they managed to…create from thin air an entire apocalypse witch on accident. That's an interesting turn of events."

Angie leaned against the rocky hill next to Aidan. "Where's Sebastian?"

"Keeping an eye on things. On Carmen. I think she suspects there's something wrong with her being here too."

"They want her as a kind of sacrifice, don't they?" It was the only thing Angie could think. But she also wasn't sure why still. Lisa might be blood thirsty. But she wasn't a demon, even if she was made of demon stuff. Or was she? "Is she a demon?" Angie asked quietly, and wasn't surprised that Aidan followed the topic jump.

"Lisa isn't technically a demon. She's not technically human either. She's created of the stuff from a demon god realm. There probably isn't anything quite like her to ever have existed. Not something the demon gods would do, creating a demon killer and realm destroyer from a human base. If they'd done it, they'd have used something like the Animore, maybe the Helavitee. Another demon."

"Except they wouldn't create something that could destroy their own realm."

"True enough. And I doubt that's what's happened here. For all the legends and myths, the idea that three human—or humanish—witches could destroy entire realms out of existence is pretty far-fetched."

Angie tried not to wince at the "humanish" part. She wasn't like Lisa, even a little. But she was like Betha, and like Betha, not quite as human as they'd been before absorbing demon magic. "So you think, even if we tried, we'd fail?"

"I don't know."

Aidan didn't admit to not knowing very often and it was a little terrifying. Angie realized she had counted on

Aidan knowing more than everyone else did for a while now.

"What if we didn't fail? What if... What if we could destroy the realm of the demon gods?"

Aidan let out a long breath. "Here's the thing. Even if the realm could be destroyed, it's...it's the sort of thing that is supposed to exist. If it stops existing, the consequences could have a knock-on effect that damages our own world. I'm not certain about that. This is way beyond my pay grade. But I don't trust this situation or what the others are trying to do. And I wouldn't recommend going along with the plan."

"I didn't want to anyway," Angie admitted. "I don't want demons in my life. I don't want a target on my back. But I also don't want to go around destroy entire realms without knowing what that means. It all feels..." She huffed. "I don't know. Killing demons doesn't feel wrong exactly, but it also isn't the way I want to spend my life. I just wanted to go back to being a witch."

"Not the answers here you were hoping for."

"Not sure there are answers."

"There are," a new voice. Betha. She walked around the hill.

Angie straightened a little, prepared to defend the conversation she and Aidan had been having. Aidan remained where she was, not moving even to look at Betha.

"From everything you've said so far," Angie said. "There are not. Not the answers I was looking for. I don't want to be a demon killing witch. I don't want to be an apocalypse witch. I want to go back to just being a witch. Unless you can tell me that's possible and how to do it? Then you don't have the answers I need."

"I never promised that." Betha stopped a few feet away, her gaze steady. She'd continued to hide the red, even now, so that her brown eyes were really quite human. "I just said we had things to talk about."

"And we did," Angie acknowledged. "But I didn't come all this way to participate in…whatever it is you really have planned. And I won't endanger the people who traveled with me for this."

Betha gave a little jut of her chin. "The problem is, now that we're all together, all three apocalypse witches, there's no going back. We're linked. And that link doesn't end unless one of us dies."

"What?" Angie moved away from the hill so she was standing fully.

"I hadn't meant to just force this on you," Betha admitted. "I would have asked you to come here first, let this be a choice you could make. So much of what's happened to me and Eloise has been someone making choices for us. Me making choices for her. Hunters making choices for me. The mayor, all those men… And now, Lisa. I don't particularly like it. So I would have given you a choice." She shrugged. "But it's too late for that now."

A rumble in the distance that sounded like a cross between thunder and an earthquake. No ground tremors, so Angie thought it might be a storm. A storm inside a huge ass cavern. Appropriate.

"It's never too late," she said.

Betha nodded off in the distance. "That was the demons arriving. The Aminore and Helavitee. They'll be here soon. You have two choices. Join us and we all work together—on all of it—or get devoured in the stomach of an Aminore. In the end, I guess you do have a choice."

That was no choice, Angie thought. Not when both options were bad.

But one at least let her live longer.

Long enough to make sure the people with her were safe.

CHAPTER TWENTY-THREE

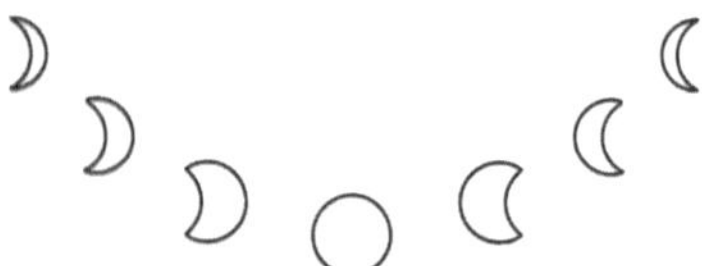

$\mathcal{A}$ngie turned to Aidan. "How long do we have?"

Her gaze traveled out over the landscape. The rolling black sands and rocky outcroppings. The lines of blue iridescent bugs streaming through the black sand. The golden river with its musty, minerally scent. Overhead the stalactites with their dots of golden light seemed very far up.

She couldn't see the demons, those beautiful monsters, yet, but she believed Betha when she said they were here now. That the rumble of thunder in the distance was demons arriving.

She didn't trust Betha enough to tell her when those demons would reach them.

Aidan lifted away from the rocky hill that was Lisa's house finally, her gaze also on the distance where the sound of the demons' arrival lingered in the air. "Not long. But long enough to get out of here." She looked at Angie. "That's still a choice. To run."

"They'll follow," Betha said. "There are three of us now. They'll follow wherever we go. Even back to the human realm. They will sacrifice power to get there and destroy us."

"We were able to run before," Angie said. But, she realized, the running had gotten them here and locked in a fate that she didn't want to follow. Again, other people were dictating her future. Not just the demon hunters now. In fact, their machinations to turn her into a hunter looked pretty tame compared to Betha and Lisa's desire to destroy entire realms.

Rather than whine about it—which was very tempting—Angie said, "We couldn't have beat them back near your home. Can we beat them with three of us? *Can* we fight them?"

"With all three of us?" Betha sighed. "We can destroy them. But they aren't the only ones who will come for us now."

"Helpful," Angie muttered.

"If we destroy the god realm," Betha said with an impatient huff, "then none of them will ever come after you again. They'll be too terrified. They will leave us *all* alone. You need to make a decision. Quickly."

"You mean...go destroy the realm now! Just...now?!"

Betha's mouth flattened. "We'll have to get rid of them first. Opening the god realm will take time they won't give us. So we fight first. Then we do what we need to do to gain freedom for all of us."

Angie almost growled at the pressure and assumptions, but something in Betha's voice stopped her. The way she said "all."

A suspicion started niggling at Angie's subconscious. But a distant howl, an ominous sound that left her deepest instincts desperate to run away, cut through her thinking and made capturing that niggling idea impossible.

Later, she promised herself. There was something there. And it was important. But they had to survive the approaching demons first.

"We need to get—" Angie started, but cut herself off when both Sebastian and Carmen came around the corner of the hill.

"Demons on the way," Sebastian said quietly, coming to stand close to Angie, putting himself partially between her and Betha.

"Unfortunately. Betha says they're the demons who chased us out of her realm."

"And they'll be here in another few minutes," Aidan said, her gaze still on the distance. "Approaching fast. Had to stop and kill something along the way." She sighed. "This'll be fun."

"What's with the sigh?" Angie asked.

"Killing gives them strength. They're…powering up."

"Oh good." Angie sighed too. "Where's Lisa and Eloise?" This she asked Sebastian.

"On their way." He held her gaze for a moment. Long enough to know something had happened inside while she'd been out here with Aidan and Betha. And it was obviously something he couldn't speak about in front of Betha. Another something for later, then. After they survived the demon fight.

If they survived.

Angie could hear the approaching demons now. Her heartbeat started to thump harder with the fear. Her instincts screamed to run away. Or at the very least build another protective circle and triangle. That had worked the last time. Running away had worked.

Except it hadn't because they were here again. And now Angie was apparently trapped in this triad of legendary destruction which she didn't want to belong to.

Survive now. Regrets later.

But she had so so many regrets.

"What do we do?" This to Aidan and Sebastian.

But Betha answered. "You and Lisa and I can destroy them. But it will require combining our powers. We have to agree to do that."

"And if we don't?"

"We fight as individuals. Maybe we die." She shrugged. Her nonchalance and resignation were almost like a real infection. Her expression barely changed. She showed so little emotion.

It was painful to look at, painful to see that hollowness.

Painful for Angie to wonder if she'd turn out that way, too.

Again, she glanced at Sebastian and Aidan for help making this decision. Sebastian's mouth compressed and she was certain he wanted to object. She could see it in the flare of red in the depths of his eyes and the way his jaw muscle jumped and his hands fisted and relaxed. He was agitated and showing her that agitation. He wanted to protect her from all this the way she wanted to protect him from all of it, too.

And yet he wasn't arguing against it. Wasn't telling her they'd find another way or that they'd just fight individually and it would be fine.

Which meant it wouldn't be fine. They couldn't fight these demons and survive. Even with all their varied strengths.

"We survived so much without…this," she murmured to him.

"Nothing like this," he said quietly. "Even inside the lava realm. Even all those swarms of demons. The Molder demon… They aren't like these. These are demons who can go into the god realm and survive. We've never faced anything like them before."

"I hate to say it," Aidan said, also quietly. "But he's right. The others…horrible. Dangerous. Deadly. Like Sokolov's demon. But all things we as hunters are trained to handle. Have a chance of surviving. Even if so few of us do against demons like Sokolov's boss. But just one of the demons approaching would be a stretch for all of us. We could… maybe succeed. With all of us. Against one. Or two. Betha has, on her own."

Aidan hesitated as she said that last, though. And Angie realized Aidan distrusted Betha's stories even more than Angie did. Maybe Betha hadn't fought off the beautiful monsters, even one of them, on her own. Maybe she hadn't actually killed one?

But Aidan continued as if she hadn't paused. "The number that are approaching… To survive would mean to run again. So that's our choice. We run again. Try to out pace them, escape them. Or we fight here. And probably die here."

"Unless I allow this shared power thing with Betha and Lisa," Angie said.

Aidan's gaze flicked to Betha and her eyes narrowed just slightly. She didn't confirm Angie's comment. But she didn't deny it either.

Angie had come to Betha, gotten herself into this situation, gotten the others into this situation, drawn the attention of these horrible demons, trying to make things better. Trying to fix what had happened. She'd endangered her friends and the love of her life coming here to try and undo the very thing that now made them all targets of monsters that were this fucking powerful. All that effort to learn how to reverse what had happened, to make herself less of a target and to keep those she loved safe, had backfired. Completely.

Just as what Betha had tried to do to save Eloise had backfired.

This was going to lock Angie even more tightly into a position she didn't want to be in. But she couldn't see a way around it. They couldn't just…leave. And hope these demons didn't follow them back to the human realm. A realm where *even more* people would be in danger. At least here, there was only them. And there was an option, if she gave in and combined her powers with the other two witches, she could at least—maybe—save the people she loved here. And also Carmen.

"Fuck it," Angie said. She had people to protect. The consequences could be dealt with later.

In the distance, she saw the first signs of the approaching demons, looming large and horrible over the black sands. They were difficult to see, still dark shadows against the strange background. But they were approaching fast.

She was out of time.

CHAPTER TWENTY-FOUR

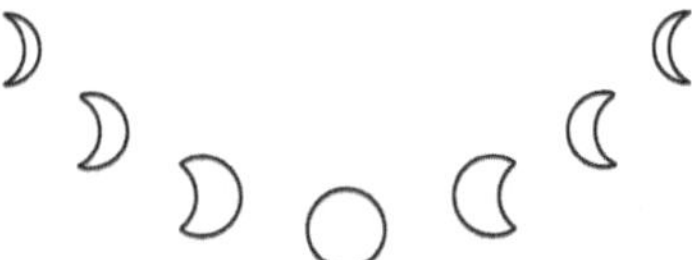

isa came around the corner of the hill at that exact moment, smiling. Behind her Eloise hovered next to the black rocky mound that made up Lisa's house. And behind her, Carmen stood watching both women. She'd stayed behind with them inside the house this whole time. Angie had to wonder what had been said, what Carmen had learned, or done.

But she didn't have time to grill the other woman. Didn't have time to warn her that she was probably here to be some kind of sacrifice.

There were monsters bearing down on them.

The rumbling sound of their passage over the black sand moved ahead of them, like the roll of distant thunder. The shadows of demons so powerful they were beyond even Aidan and Sebastian's skills to overcome. Angie was a little surprised the demons hadn't initiated that silence thing that had been so terrifying outside Betha and Eloise's house. Maybe that was still coming.

She looked to Betha and then past her to Lisa who walked up behind Betha. Betha didn't exactly wince when the other woman approached, but there was a subtle straightening of her shoulders, a subtle tension that settled around her. Lisa didn't seem to notice. Her attention was on the distant demons. Her red eyes brightened. And she smiled.

"This will be fun," she murmured.

"No," Betha said with a sigh. "It will not."

"There are three of us now," Lisa said, sounding as if she was trying to sooth Betha. "And you've handled these demons for years."

"One at a time. With a lot of effort. Never like this." Betha didn't look scared, though. She hadn't, even when all these demons had approached and circled her home. She still didn't look scared. Mostly just annoyed. Resigned.

The resignation worried Angie.

"With three of us, this will be a doddle," Lisa said, reassuringly. She glanced at Angie, her eyes flaring even redder. "And now we get to see the true power of the apocalypse witches. They'll all fear us after today."

Angie didn't want demon fear. Demon fear led to demon attacks. "What do we do?" This to Betha since Lisa's bloodlust was so obvious and off putting, Angie didn't trust her answers.

Betha, her gaze on the approaching monsters, their rumbling footsteps now echoing, shaking the ground, said,

"Make sure your ability to read by touch is shut down. Then we'll have to hold hands."

One of the gold sparkled stalactites above dropped to the ground with a crash that made Angie wince. Eloise and Carmen duck back behind the rocks. Neither the hunters nor the other witches reacted. The enormous dagger of rock had fallen at least half a mile away, nowhere near close enough to hurt them, and yet it made Angie very aware of all those sharp, pointy rocks overhead.

She ensured her psychic senses were shut down—she'd kept them locked down this entire time and they hadn't slipped yet, but she wanted to make sure before touching Lisa—and then stretched out a hand to Betha. Betha after a hesitant pause, put her hand out to Lisa. Lisa was smiling as she reached for Angie's other hand.

The instant they completed the circle power surged through Angie. Like nothing she'd ever felt before. Strong enough to light her up inside, to make the image of her web in her mind's eye flare so brightly, for a moment she couldn't see. Nothing but blue and red and purple light suffusing every part of her.

"Ang?" Sebastian's voice, cutting through the rush and noise of all that magic.

"Fine," she said, but she didn't recognize the sound of her own voice. It wasn't...hers anymore. Not just deeper, the way it got when her magic rose. This time her voice had an echo to it, as if more than her voice was coming out of her mouth.

She blinked hard, trying to see around the flare of power.

Only then realizing the bright light wasn't just something happening in her mind's eye but had really happened. There was a bright glow surrounding her and the other two witches now. A strangely colored light that seemed to be a mix of colors and was also, weirdly…black. A black glow. That didn't seem like it should be possible.

Spells spilled into her mind, things she'd never learned, magic that she'd never experienced. There was a sigh from one side—she thought that was Lisa—and a deep breath from Betha. More poured into Angie that she wasn't sure came from either of the women. Images of destruction. Death. Lands laid waste. The bodies of demons strewn across an open field of red rocks. Green-leafed trees sprouting from the ground. Then turning black like they'd been set alight.

And then a golden light that made Angie flinch, though she wasn't sure if she did that with her body or just her mind. The light reminded her of the moment in her vision when Betha opening the god realm. The way even looking into the swirling vortex of light had made her entire body ache and her brain hurt and she hadn't even been experiencing it in real life.

One of the women muttered something out loud, but Angie couldn't understand the words. Her brain swirled with a combination of pain and pleasure and energy and ache. She wasn't entirely sure how to describe it. Her brain seemed to have collapsed to its most basic self with no real thought or focus. It wasn't like being drawn into the void— which she'd experienced once before when a Molder demon tried to take over her body—and it wasn't like being overwhelmed with magic. It was like…watching herself as she ceased to exist. Watching herself as she died and not really caring about that.

Suddenly it all collapsed. The golden light, the knowledge pouring in, the visions, the sense of dying. All of it dropped down into a single dark light.

Angie blinked her surroundings into focus. The demons on the horizon were close.

And Sebastian's hand was on her shoulder.

He leaned in and whispered, "Stay with me."

She gave her head a shake and then quickly a nod. "Not going anywhere," she said.

She didn't look away from the approaching demons because they were too close now, but she turned her head enough to press her cheek to Sebastian's. Whatever had been happening to her, he'd brought her back. With a simple touch. This was the best she could do to offer her thanks right now. But her heart swelled with love in that moment and she intended for all of them to live so she could make sure he knew just how much she did love him.

He let his hand fall away from her shoulder and she settled into the power coursing through her. Finally looked away from the demons to the other two women still holding her hands. Betha glanced at Angie at the same time as she turned toward Betha. The other woman's eyes were red again, glowing and bright. And there was a halo of silver light around her now, making her skin and hair and even her dark blue scaled jumpsuit glow. She gave Angie a little nod. Angie glanced down at herself and realized she was glowing silver too, which meant her eyes were probably red. A glance at Lisa confirmed they were all glowing.

Lisa wasn't looking at their silver halo, or any of the changes that seemed to have encompassed them. She was watching the approaching demons with a hungry expression that sent a little shiver of dread through Angie.

Angie looked back toward the demons, now very close. In her head, she wondered what they should do now, and the answer popped in as clearly as if someone had spoken. A spell started. She wasn't sure who's voice rose above the sounds of the ground tremors first, but within three words, all three of them were speaking the spell. This one didn't require hand gestures, didn't require them to release their grip on each other. It was made up of words she didn't know. But her mouth formed the spell as if she'd been studying it all her life.

All three of their voices rose in the spell. Not a single voice, though. A harmony of voices. Chanting into an almost song. The repetitive refrain at the center of the spell almost music. She felt the power building even though she didn't understand the words.

The demons, at least six of the ones that had surrounded Betha's house, started to run toward them, the two Helavitee with wings rose into the air, flying. The four Aminore on the ground picked up speed, moving as fast as the winged Helavitee could fly. All of them charging.

She realized even as she continued speaking the spell that Aidan, Sebastain, Carmen, and Eloise, all remained behind Angie and the other witches. She was grateful for that.

Because the power that coalesced around their triad was blinding.

And when the spell ended on an abrupt, strong note, the demon at the front of the pack exploded.

No bolts of power shot from them. Not like using the demon magic to kill a demon. They finished the spell and a demon died.

Not just that one, though. They repeated the final word again. And another demon vaporized. A third time, and a third demon died.

The three remaining stopped charging forward. One winged beast above two without wings. They roared and screeched. And then the silence that was their weapon in the other realm washed over Angie.

She could no longer hear the demons. The trembling in the ground had stopped because they had stopped moving. And all the surrounding sounds that Angie hadn't been aware of—the crinkle of rock, the slight whistle of air through the stalactites, the sound of faint dripping, the thick gurgle of the golden river flowing by, all that sound dropped away, leaving Angie's ears ringing in the silence.

Tightening her hold on the other two witches, wondering if they'd hear her if she spoke, she opened her mouth to say something, and realized that would break the spell. They'd have to start over, with the demons so close the monsters might reach the triad before they could complete the death spell again.

As if they'd all come to the same conclusion at once,

Angie heard all three of their voices, quite clearly, repeat that last word. The death word.

The winged demon flapped around in a circle, its head thrown back, obviously making noise. And then it shattered like dropped glass, a thousand sparkling pieces of red glass raining onto the black sand.

The remaining two demons also gave the appearance of roaring or screeching, even though Angie could no longer hear them. And then suddenly a bolt of lightning dropped from the ceiling, a bolt that opened wide to create a rip in the realm's reality. The remaining two demons dove through. The lightning tightened again into a bolt and then zipped away into the ground. Leaving a space of crinkling black glass in the sand.

A crinkling Angie could hear now.

All the surrounding sounds came rushing back, loud and echoey after the silence. Angie was breathing hard, though she didn't know why because she didn't feel tired or exhausted.

She felt recharged. Energized. Like she'd been fully fed and had slept a solid eight hours and was ready to go. Her magic felt the same. Strong, powerful. Right there and ready for her to use.

In her mind's eye, her spider web was bright, the blues, purples and reds all brighter than she'd ever seen them before. And each thread was encircled by a sheath of glowing silver light.

Abruptly, she dropped the hands of the other two women,

while still watching her web. The colors didn't change. The silver didn't fade away. The power didn't dim.

And she still felt like she could conquer the world.

She let out a slow breath and turned to face Sebastian. He was watching her through narrowed eyes, the red in the depths of the deep brown a bright star now.

"Your eyes are red," he confirmed quietly. "And you look…like a goddess."

She blinked at that. Not his usual compliment. Also, she got the feeling he wasn't giving her a compliment.

She glanced down. She was glowing a little still, though not as brightly as she had been when she'd been holding the other witches' hands. But she realized her ordinary jeans and her simple corduroy jacket that she loved, and that she could still feel on her body, next to her skin, seemed to have been replaced by a glowing gown that sparkled with red and silver light. A hand to her head confirmed some sort of weird diadem in her hair.

The other two women both had similar gowns on, both had diadems in their hair, sparkling with silver and rubies shaped like blood drops. Their hair flowed around them in long, full masses that shimmered silver, and their skin glowed from within, like they were alight.

Lisa laughed, raising her hands to admire the glow and the way the gown's red and silver sparkles shimmered with movement. Betha's mouth was tight and she was staring hard at Eloise who took one step toward her before stopping.

Angie looked back to Sebastian and the others, all of

whom were frowning at her. Even Carmen looked… concerned.

A spell she'd never known before popped into Angie's head, fully formed. She murmured it and made a twist of her fingers into three distinct shapes. The whole spell coming together as if she'd practiced it for years and knew it well. With the last word and a flare of her fingers, the illusion of red gowns and crowns and glowing skin snapped out. Leaving all three of the witches looking as they had before combining their powers.

Angie stared at her hand for a long moment after completing the spell, at the ordinariness of her human hand without the glow and without all that illusionary dress and jewelry.

"Better," Betha said with a sigh.

Lisa, however, pouted. "I liked the gown."

Angie met Sebastian's gaze. Time to reckon with the consequences of what they'd just done.

CHAPTER TWENTY-FIVE

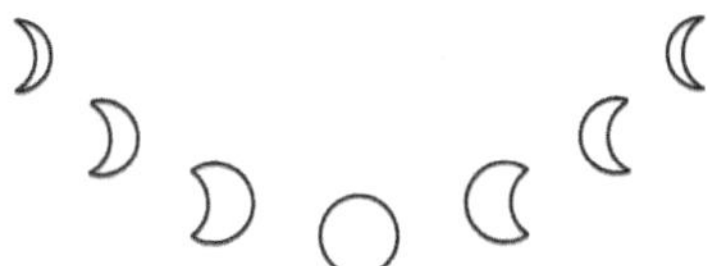

*A*ngie used the excuse of wanting to check on the spot where the demons had vanished, to make sure they were gone and the ones they thought they'd killed had been killed, to walk away from Lisa and Betha for a few minutes. She needed to think, but actually wasn't sure she could just then. She was overwhelmed with the power that had poured in, the strength she felt now, even after the magic had stopped flowing between them, the ways she felt energized and, weirdly, normal.

That last, the way this felt normal and like something that she should have been experiencing all along, was absolutely the scariest part.

Like absorbing demon magic and integrating it had felt normal. Like all that magic had felt like *her* and not foreign or wrong or intrusive. What had happened to her after they'd formed their triad of power had felt like *her*.

And she didn't like it.

Aidan stayed with the others, nominally to be their backup should some demons arrive, but really just to keep an eye on Betha and Lisa. Angie was grateful because Lisa seemed entirely too overjoyed by this turn of events. Angie had *felt* her elation when they'd killed the demons, a disturbing level of savage satisfaction that frankly left Angie nauseated. Even if Lisa's joy did come from killing demons, it wasn't the demon part that excited her, it was the killing part.

Sebastain came with Angie, which didn't surprise her and she was glad of it, because she wanted to talk with him about all that had happened. More surprising was that Carmen joined them. And that this didn't irritate Angie. She wanted to talk to Carmen too. Especially after realizing that Betha had brought Carmen here for potentially nefarious reasons.

Angie wasn't sure how to feel about any of this. And they needed to discuss their options.

"So that was interesting," Carmen said when they were out of earshot of the others.

"Interesting," Angie said. "Good word."

"You ever think you'd be walking around a demon realm this at ease?" Carmen asked, glancing around casually, as if there truly was nothing to fear here.

"I did not." In fact, that was another disturbing thought. They'd had the big bad demons from Betha's realm attack, following them here, but they hadn't seen any sign of this realms demons. Not even a hint of them on the horizon, or high up at the top of ginormous cavern they seemed to be in.

"She kills them all," Carmen said. "Lisa. She kills anything she can kill. With such enthusiasm even the demons have learned to stay away. She slaughtered everything here that was powerful enough to be challenging to her. They all died. Entire species of demons wiped out."

Angie stopped in her tracks to look at Carmen. "That's impossible."

"You'd have thought, wouldn't you?"

Angie looked at Sebastian. "Is this...true?"

He glanced at Carmen, then back to Angie. "I left just as the 'war stories' were getting started, but Lisa had started to talk about all the demon killing before I came out to talk with you and Aidan. She was...excited to talk about the deaths."

"The second savors," Angie said, the disgust making her already churning stomach flip.

"They are just demons," Carmen said. But even her usual callus pragmatism seemed forced.

"This is what you and Jacob want me to become," Angie said, tossing her anger and confusion at Carmen because she was a convenient target, even if the accusation wasn't entirely deserved.

"Not like Lisa," Carmen said. "I don't give two flying fucks about demons being killed. I don't care about demon realms being destroyed. That shit has nothing to do with me. I'll find other ways to...do what I do without demons. But the way that...whatever she is, the way she relished the death and destruction? That's serial killer shit. I've seen that expression in the faces of some of the human trash I've...

dealt with over the years. They love the killing. And if Lisa runs out of demons to kill, she won't stop there."

"And now I'm linked to her." Angie ground her teeth together, frustration and fear a thick weight on her shoulders.

"'Fraid so, chica," Carmen said. She smiled slightly. "And you can't even blame me for this one."

"Mores the pity." Angie tried to keep a straight face with that comeback but it dissolved into a half smile.

Carmen chuckled.

They reached the place where the sand had been turned to glass by the lightning strike.

"That lightning wasn't you, was it?" Sebastian asked.

"No. Not me this time. That was their portal. Their way of moving between realms."

"Good to know we'll hear them coming."

That was true. The thunder claps after the lightning strikes had been loud and echoed across the landscape, before they'd even seen the demons approaching.

"They probably won't be back," Carmen said. "Not after you three so easily killed them."

"What drove them after us in the first place, though?" Angie asked.

Sebastian toed the still crinkling circle of glass. "Betha said it was having two of you together."

"I'm not sure Betha is a reliable source of information," Angie said quietly.

Carmen snorted. "That would be a good assumption."

"You think someone might have…sent them after us? Betha said they're a species of demons that can be harnessed to work for the demon gods. Maybe…there's a god out there that wants us dead?"

"Or you just have two crazy witches who want the power they can only get with three of you," Carmen said.

That was the pragmatic vigilante Angie expected. "Possible," she admitted. "I'd still like to know why those demons were so keen on following us here. Even when 'here' put them in the way of three of us."

"And how they found us here," Sebastian said quietly. "That they converged on you and Betha in the realm where they already exist is one thing. Traveling between realms, even for species like Aminore and Helavitee isn't simple. It takes energy. They'd only chase us because they had a reason to. And maybe that reason was to prevent you three from combining your powers. Maybe that's all it is. But…how did they find you all here so fast?"

"Maybe they've known this is where Lisa was the whole time," Carmen suggested.

"Then why not come here and kill her?" Sebastian said. "Why not gang up and kill Betha? Betha said they only ever came after her one at a time, normally. And though she could kill one, it took a lot of effort. She admitted that had she ever been attacked by a hoard of these demons at once, she'd have been in trouble." Sebastian glanced back toward the mound of rocks that disguised Lisa's home. "Everything from Betha's invitation to find her, to this moment when all three of you combined your magic… This could have been prevented. Demons all know this legend. They must have realized there were two of you already. Why not kill at least one of the three? Even before Angie became…what she is now, that still would have meant only two of the three."

"Lisa is of this place," Angie said. "Made up of demon magic. She's literally cleared out this realm of powerful demons, right?" She looked to Carmen.

"According to her retelling, yes."

"Then the demons have to be afraid of her. And Betha. You saw Sokolov's demon," Angie said to Sebastian. "He was scared enough of the apocalypse witch that he was prepared to burn down everything he'd built in the human realm to escape her. And he only ever talked about *one* witch before me. He said there were two of us now. Maybe the demons don't know about Lisa."

"Or Betha," Carmen said quietly.

Both Angie and Sebastian turned to look at her. She raised her brows. "Lisa is the one who relishes the killing. Lisa is the one who's decimated an entire realm of powerful demons. Lisa is the one who kills for pleasure not just survival. What if that witch who stepped out of the breach was Lisa in disguise? Not Betha. Maybe the demons have thought there was only one apocalypse witch before you. Maybe they thought Betha and Lisa were the same…entity."

"Why would Lisa show up as Betha to us, though? We weren't expecting…any witch to step out of that breach. Why not just appear as herself?"

Carmen shrugged. "Look, I'm guessing. But you said you read Betha's blood for the visions of her, right? And Eloise would have known about Betha leaving that blood for the next demon witch who could become an apocalypse witch.

Lisa is made from Eloise and the magic of the demon realms. Lisa would know what Eloise would know. And Eloise would know everything Betha has done."

"Before they were separated, maybe. But after?"

"You're assuming they're not still linked mentally as well as physically," Carmen pointed out. "You've seen Eloise. She's not…right. There's something about her bugging both the hunters." She cut her chin at Sebastain and he nodded. "We already know the separation wasn't…complete. That Eloise can't go into the human realm without it bothering Lisa. They're entangled. That's what Betha called it. Lisa could still know what Eloise knows. And Eloise knows what Betha knows. Unless Betha's been keeping things from her."

"I have."

The sound of Betha's voice made Angie and Carmen both startle and turn sharply to face her. Sebastian didn't show his reaction to the sudden appearance of the other witch, but Angie felt him straighten taller and move up closer to her back in a protective way.

Betha stood a few yards away. Angie couldn't tell where she'd come from, or how she'd reached them without any of them, even Sebastian, knowing or hearing her.

"What haven't you told us?" Angie asked. "There's a lot more here than just…legends and myths and the demons' fear of the three of us."

"The potion I made for Eloise didn't just…split her in two. Didn't just create Lisa. It created a monster that looks exactly like the love of my life. A monster who feeds off Eloise's energy and knows everything she thinks. Lisa is…

not sane. But I can't destroy her. Not on my own. She's too strong."

"Was that you? Or Lisa? In the church?"

"She's learned some very tricky magic in the centuries we've hidden here. But that was me."

"Why? Why…all of this?"

Betha looked at Carmen, then Sebastian, then settled her gaze finally on Angie. "To destroy the god realm."

"No." Angie shook her head. "That's not why we're here. That was never your goal."

"It's Lisa's."

"Why?"

"Because once the gods are dead, she can replace them."

CHAPTER TWENTY-SIX

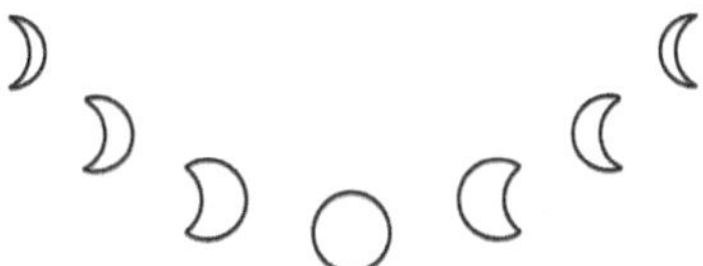

Angie straightened back, bumping into Sebastian. He steadied her with his hands on her shoulders. "What?" she breathed.

Shock making her doubt her own hearing. But the crinkling of black glass behind her and the faint dripping, the quiet breeze whistling through the stalactites high overhead, the distant sound of the glugging river of gold were all still clear.

"She wants to rule as a demon god," Betha said, with such a matter-of-fact tone, it made Angie's head spin. "And she hasn't been able to do that without us. Now, she can."

"Not if we don't cooperate." Angie scowled. Her heart was hammering and she found herself leaning into Sebastian for the support. "Not if we don't destroy the god realm."

"She has a way of wearing you down. Give it time."

"No. No. That's not happening. I'm not replacing demon gods with… I'm not doing any of this."

"Then you'll help me kill her."

Angie blinked. The shift in subject from Lisa becoming a demon *god* to them killing Lisa stopped Angie in her tracks. "Wait, what?"

"I have to destroy Lisa. It's the only way."

"Only way to what?"

"To save Eloise."

"Won't that kill Eloise?" Angie was so horrified by every aspect of this conversation she wasn't even sure what appalled her the most.

"She's dying now," Betha said. "They live in two bodies but they're still bound. The stronger Lisa grows, the weaker Eloise gets."

A sudden lightbulb went off for Angie that nearly stole her breath. "Lisa is even stronger now, with all our magic combined."

Betha nodded. "And it will kill Eloise. Very soon."

"I don't get it," Carmen said. "Why bring us all here if combining all three of your powers only made things worse for Eloise?"

Betha glanced at her, then back to Angie. "I needed a show for Lisa. I needed to…promise her things. To get to this point, I had to hide my real intent from Eloise and play along with Lisa's plan. I never had any intention of revisiting the god realm. I never want to get anywhere near that realm again. But I had to make Lisa believe finding you, combining our powers, would be a good idea. And when she decided she wanted to replace the demon gods with herself, that made things easier."

Betha ran a hand through her hair, the braid loose now and falling out. Somewhere in their escape through the realms, she'd lost her hair tie. Angie wasn't sure why that was drawing her attention. Maybe it was shock. She needed something mundane to focus on.

Betha sighed. "We've waited for you for centuries. And I've watched Lisa grow more power hungry and Eloise grow weaker with each passing year. We can't go on like this. We need you. We've needed you. But not for the reasons Lisa thinks. I need you to help me destroy her. Before she latches onto our powers and strips them away. Once she's done that, it'll be too late."

"She…" Angie blinked hard a few times. "She can do that?"

"Look closely at your magic."

Frowning, Angie let her eyes half close, trusting Sebastian to have her back, and looked at the magical web of her power. The two lines of demon magic vibrated and stretched. One toward Betha. One back toward Lisa's house.

She cursed under her breath. Then, with her eyes still half closed, said to Sebastian, "Remember how I told you my demon magic lines were…pulling toward Betha? Well now one is drawn to her and one to Lisa."

"The demon magic…is leaning into the bond?"

"That or just attracted to the other two apocalypse

witches. Either way, that magic is happy to have all three of us together." She searched deeper into the depths of her web, looking at all the strands, the blue witch, the single original red thread of her demon witch power, the purple blended magic that was scattered throughout…

"The blended magic…" she murmured. "That strange purple magic is…" It was hard to explain, but it looked to be seeping out of the web, dripping out into the black aether surrounding her web on the metaphysical plane. Dew drops on the threads, dripping off like purple blood. Slowly, but it was leeching away.

Angie's eyes popped open and she stared hard at Betha. "She's taking some of my magic now, isn't she?"

"Mine too. She's trying to be subtle. Is being subtle. If I wasn't looking out for it, it would have taken me longer to realize what was happening. She doesn't know how much I know of her intentions. Fortunately, Eloise talks in her sleep. Otherwise, I'd have been none the wiser."

It wouldn't have occurred to Angie to look for this either. At least, not immediately. At that moment, she felt strong, powerful, full of magic and potential. The silver coating around her web made her feel almost…indestructible. But that purple blended magic was still slowly, very slowly dripping away. Despite the silver glow around it all.

There was no telling what that would do to her powers eventually.

"Your magic isn't the kind that should be shared," Carmen said, her expression serious. To Betha, she said, "You can feel it, right? How strong she is?"

Betha nodded. "And so can Lisa."

"How do we stop this? How do we fix it?" And how did Angie keep ending up in situations that were worse than the ones she'd been trying to fix?

"We kill Lisa," Betha said with a shrug. "That'll also break the bond, and we won't be a triad anymore."

"But we'll still be…what we are? Able to kill demons. Stuck with the target on our backs."

Betha's gaze narrowed. "I'm not absolutely certain about this, so don't get your hopes up. But, I think, if we can break the bond now, if one of us dies… It'll destroy the things that make us apocalypse witches."

"Destroy…us? All our magic? Or just the magic that lets us kill demons?"

Betha licked her lips. "I'm not certain. I *think* just the part that lets us kill demons. But… I'm not certain."

Angie closed her eyes again, let out a long breath. She didn't know what to do. What information to believe. Who to trust besides Sebastian and Aidan. And they didn't know any more about this than she did.

"If we don't break the bond," she said slowly, opening her eyes again, "Lisa will try to steal all our magic and become a demon god, or something like it, after using us to destroy the demon god realm?"

Betha nodded.

"And if we do break the bond, we could all be left without any magic at all. Stuck in a demon realm."

Another nod. "Or we could die. The severing, if it's violent, could kill us all."

"Including Eloise?"

"Including Eloise."

"Why try?"

"It's either that risk," Betha said, "or risk what Lisa will become."

Angie shook her head. "There has to be another way."

"There isn't. I've looked. I've considered. Our only hope, Eloise's only hope of surviving, of keeping her sanity, is for us to kill Lisa. I can't do it alone, but *we* can. Together. It's the only way."

"It can't be. There has to be something we can do. Some other way to fix this."

"How would you feel," Betha hissed, suddenly intent, getting so close to Angie's face, Carmen stepped forward to block her. "How would you feel if you knew you'd trapped the love of your life, gotten them permanently bound to someone who was insane? Eloise can *feel* when Lisa goes on a killing spree. It destroys her every time. And as the years pass, Eloise loses more and more of herself, the insanity infecting her as surely as her first trip into the demon realms infected her with magic her body wasn't designed to contain. I am *losing her*. Painfully. Slowly. And I cannot stand it."

"There has to be another way," Angie said, snarling. "This isn't it."

"It is the *only* way. I have spent centuries searching, learning, studying, hunting. I have been trying to fix my...oh so many mistakes for so so long. This is the only way I can do that. But if Lisa discovers the truth..."

"I won't cooperate?" Lisa's voice from out of the shadows.

Lisa, who had just heard everything.

Shit.

CHAPTER TWENTY-SEVEN

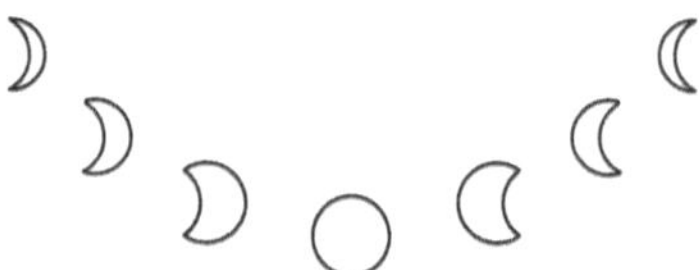

A ngie spun to face the new witch, stepping forward to place Carmen and Sebastian behind her, though both resisted the move. Lisa stood a few yards away, smiling pleasantly as if Betha hadn't just been talking about killing her. Neither Aidan nor Eloise were with her, which set Angie's alarm bells ringing.

The ginormous cavern around them was quiet but for the crinkling of still cooling heat blasted sand and the burbling flow of the golden river. The scent of sulfur in this realm was so faint, she'd almost lost track of it, forgotten it was there under the more dominant musty mineral scent given off by the gold river. But with Lisa standing even a few yards away and her eyes glowing demon red, the scent rose enough for Angie to notice it again.

Though Lisa smiled, there was something brittle and

sharp in her expression. Something that sent Angie's pulse thudding. Where were Aidan and Eloise? Were they okay?

She wanted to ask but after what Lisa had just overheard, she was afraid to speak first.

"So *my* plan," Lisa said, as if they'd all been discussing what to do next and Betha hadn't just been talking about killing her, "is that we should start with one of the smaller realms, destroy it, and work our way up to the god realm. I think they might be afraid of us now, because they sent their favorite pets after us. And that was pretty easy, don't you think? I mean, we killed *four* of them without any effort, just that spell. That was strange, though, right? Using a spell instead of the raw power we use normally? What do you think that's all about?"

Lisa dropped into silence, waiting for an answer.

No one spoke up.

"Does this mean we'll be following my plan or Betha's?" she said after a moment, that brittle smile never cracking. "Or! Or. We could kill Betha. I'm obviously overwhelming Eloise, which is fine. She's weak and a drag on me, like an anchor, you know? And then it'll be just the two of us." She made a gesture, flicking her fingers back and forth between herself and Angie. "And that'll be enough. I mean, not for the god realm, but until another apocalypse witch arises, we can spend the waiting time decimating demons. That'll be fun, right?"

"No." Angie wasn't sure what else to say. Lisa's idea of fun sounded horrific to Angie and she wasn't going to pretend otherwise. "Also no to killing Betha and Eloise."

Though she now understood why Betha wanted to kill Lisa. They seemed to be in a survivor takes it all situation. With Angie caught in the middle.

"But you'd agree to kill me?" Lisa asked, not sounding angry or offended.

"I didn't agree to anything. Not even destroying the god realm."

"Oh, we'll get to that eventually. I'm destined to be the only god here. That's part of the legend. Did she tell you? No. I bet she didn't. Why would she? She wants me dead before it can come to pass, but you can't destroy destiny. Even if she killed me, I'd just rise again. It's fate, if you will. I will be the destroyer of worlds, the bringer of death, the harbinger of doom. All that fun stuff. And I will be the One god for the demons."

Well. Lisa seemed pretty insane. Just as Betha had said. An insanity that was leeching at Eloise. Angie thought about what she might do if Sebastian was in the same position. If this was happening to him and some doppelganger of him was stealing his sanity. She'd want to kill that doppelganger too. He probably wouldn't even hesitate to do the same for her.

The problem was, she and Betha and Lisa were all connected now. Would killing one of them now destroy the other two?

"No," Lisa said with another grin. "Killing one of us won't destroy the other two. In fact, it'll just drop the power balance back to what it was between Betha and I." Her grin turned feral. "Or at least, that's what Betha thinks."

Was Lisa able to read their minds now? Angie didn't seem capable of reading either Betha or Lisa's minds, which was good because she did *not* want to hear what was going on inside Lisa's head—she had a great deal of sympathy for Eloise. But Lisa had answered Angie's question as if she'd said it aloud. Either Angie's thinking was very obvious, or Lisa could do something that she and Betha could not.

"I can," Lisa said. "Remember, I will be the One god, destroyer of worlds…blah blah." She waved her hand in the air, looking amused by her blah blah comment. "We each have slightly different capabilities. Complimentary, but different. At present. Until I absorb everything and take over. Then I'll have it all. You'll both be dead, but that's fine. I'll miss the company. But I'm sure I'll figure it out. I've been alone here for a long time."

Angie's thoughts weren't her own now. That was bad. But she wasn't sure how to lock Lisa out. Because she needed to lock Lisa out of her head.

"Oh, I wouldn't try," Lisa said, and her grin turned brittle again. "Doing so will only hurt. You. It will hurt you."

"What are you expecting from us now?" Angie asked, stalling. She couldn't think without Lisa in her head, but she needed to think. She needed a way out of this.

Carmen moved a little closer to her, just at her back, and gave Angie a little poke. Angie had no idea what the poke meant, but hoped it meant Carmen and Sebastian had some idea of what to do here since the insane witch wasn't reading their minds.

"I'm expecting us to complete our mission," Lisa said.

"The legend says we three destroy and lay waste to all who oppose us, killing demons in piles and piles."

The glee in Lisa's voice and expression made Angie nauseous.

"But when the dust clears," Lisa continued, "there will be only one witch remaining. And that one will have all the power. They will make the hoards bow down before them and control all the evil in these realms. Won't that be nice? Having someone who's not a demon in charge of all the demons? I think that sounds like a lovely idea."

Angie's gaze flicked to Betha even as she tried to keep an eye on Lisa. "Only one witch will remain? Couldn't have mentioned that earlier?"

Betha's mouth flattened, but she didn't comment.

"She's very tight-lipped about the information and knowledge she's gained over the years. Even with my link to Eloise, there was *so much* she wouldn't tell me, teach me. And I needed to know it. All of it. But now, with this link of ours, I do know it." She gave Betha an almost feral snarl. "Didn't expect that, did you? That I would be able to read your mind after the power bond? That Eloise's psychic powers would manifest this way once we formed the triad. And how very much you've hidden from me."

Lisa took a step toward Betha, and Angie moved, stepping between the two women. Not even sure what she intended, but knew she didn't want Lisa getting close to Betha.

Angie didn't want to be too close to the other witch either.

The move meant Carmen and Sebastian were no longer right behind her, though. But since most of Lisa's attention was on Angie and Betha, Angie hoped the others would be safe. Keeping Lisa's attention on her would also give the others time to think of something.

All of this ran through the background of her mind, where she hoped Lisa wouldn't "hear" it. Unfortunately, Lisa's connection meant she read a lot more than Angie thought possible. She turned her feral smile on Angie.

"They can't do anything to me now," she said. "I can destroy worlds now. What can a paltry hunter and your pet telekinetic witch do to me?"

"Hey!" Carmen said.

Angie waved her quiet. This was not the time for her smart mouth.

"Oh no," Lisa said. "Let her talk. Let her try something. Please. I'd love to see what she can do?"

Carmen snapped her mouth shut and stood her ground, staring hard-eyed at Lisa but not rising to her bait. Which frankly, Angie found impressive.

"Where is Eloise and Aidan?" Angie asked, trying to pull Lisa's attention back to her.

"They're fine. I put Eloise to sleep. She's happier when she's sleeping. Makes things easier."

Betha's lip lifted in a little snarl.

"Aidan?"

"Agreed to watch the sleeping Eloise while I came to find you. Such a nice demon hunter. She'll make a very good servant in my empire. Her will is very powerful."

It took a great deal of will power on Angie's part not to mentally comment on that assumption. Keeping her mind blank was almost impossible. Thoughts scattered across her brain without effort, rushing forward for Lisa to clearly see. And knowing the other witch *could* see her thoughts was unnerving.

"So now." Lisa clapped her hands together like an eager tour guide. "Let's settle things, shall we? You two are not going to attempt to kill me because I've already taken too much of your magic. You missed your chance at killing me in the few moments after we vanquished the Helavitee and the Aminore. Took me a minute to figure out how to siphon off the magics. At that point, you could have killed me. Now. No. *But* together we are still a triad of power like no other. We will finish this destiny of ours. And then I'll release you. No need to worry anymore about…any of this."

She grinned like she'd offered them a present.

Angie felt the spell building under her skin without her even having to think the words, felt the power flowing through her, her fingers twitched and started to form the shapes even before her conscious brain knew which spell was rumbling from her mouth.

Lisa narrowed her eyes and said, "You will not do that," and her voice was deeper than it had been a moment ago.

Angie didn't stop reciting her spell. She spoke the words aloud, clearly, and snapped her fingers together to set it.

Lisa lunged toward her, and Angie's hand shot out. The sizzle of lightning shooting from her palm, right into the other woman. Sent her flying backward at least a hundred yards. She landed hard, sprawled in the black sand.

Betha made a move, though Angie couldn't tell if it was toward Lisa or toward her. Carmen murmured, "Good shot." Sebastian moved closer to Angie's shoulder. From the corner of her eye, she saw him open his mouth to say something.

Lisa rose from her sprawl, suddenly, straight up, moving in a way that wasn't possible for a real human. She laughed. "Is that all you've got sister? Would you like a taste of mine?"

Angie started the spell to raise a shield but too late.

A flash of white-hot pain streaked through her head. She might have screamed, but she couldn't be sure. The pain twisted so sharply, she fell to her knees, grabbing her head.

And then the world around her went black.

CHAPTER TWENTY-EIGHT

*A*ngie came to suddenly. The realization that she'd been unconscious, in a *demon* realm, hitting her like a bucket of cold water in the face. She launched upward from a prone position, jerked back by something wrapped around her wrists, and hissed in pain. Everything around her was dark, and warm, and her heartbeat so hard it was the only thing she could hear.

Panic kept her frozen, listening, trying not to scream though a scream crawled up her throat. She could smell dampness and faint sulfur. She could feel rocks beneath her. Despite blinking hard a few times, she still couldn't see anything. When she moved, she heard a clanking sound, like chains. And once the panic settled enough for her to feel her body more, she realized her hands had been encased in something hard, fisted so she couldn't move them.

She couldn't form the hand gestures she'd need to do most of her witch spells.

But she wasn't dead. She ached everywhere. Especially her head. Her body felt bruised too. And the pain in her hands, now that she noticed it, was sharp.

A groan from nearby had her gasping and jumping away. But something about the sound…

"Sebastian?" The sound of her own voice was loud and rough, like she hadn't had liquid in days. And it echoed. Wherever they were, it was inside a place with walls and a ceiling, but those seemed to be far away based on the bounce of her voice.

"Ang?"

Something moved up next to her. She'd swear she saw an outline of darker shadows against darkness. And then a soft touch on her cheek. And a very faint glow of red. She tried blinking harder, but outside of the red in his eyes and a faint outline, she couldn't pull Sebastian into view.

"I'm okay, I think," she said, trying to reassure him. "You? Your hands are free?"

"I've a manacle around one wrist," he said. "I'm not sure what its chain is attached to yet. I just came to. Heard you gasp."

"My hands are encased in…something. There are chains too." She tried to lift her arms. "Weighted whatever is on my hands. They're hard to even lift. And my hands are stuck in fists."

"You can't do spells."

She nodded against his hand, knowing he'd feel the gesture. "The others?"

"I don't know yet. Could do with some light."

"I've got you," a very scratchy voice from somewhere to Angie's left.

It took a few beats before Angie recognized that voice. "Carmen? Are you hurt?"

"One wrist chained. Head hurts like hell. Not sure what she hit us with, but she hit us all at once. I saw you go down about a blink before my world went dark."

"Fucking hell," Angie muttered.

"She didn't kill us," Carmen said. "So we live to fight another day." She murmured something quietly, and then a faint blue glowing ball swirled slowly into being above Angie.

She watched the light grow, listened to Carmen recite the spell. Realized it was the first time she'd heard Carmen do proper magic. Not summoning demons or even the telekinesis she'd revealed to Angie so far. This was the kind of magic Angie did. And she'd had no idea Carmen could actually do this much.

When she looked down, she could see. Everything was still dark, and tinted blue, and a little fuzzy at the edges because of the pain in her head. But she could see.

They were inside a large cavern-like room of black stone. No windows or views to an outside space. And if it weren't for the metal door closing off the only opening, she'd think they'd been buried inside the rocks. There were no rugs or cushions or even straw on the ground. Just the hard black surface and solid rock walls. Not even any stalactites with speckled golden minerals to look like stars. A faint drip she couldn't see in the dim light still came from somewhere, but the ground beneath her and the wall at her back were all dry and warm to the touch.

The chains on her hand manacles connected to a large metal ring fixed into the stone wall. Same with Sebatian's and Carmen's chains. Unlike Angie, they both had a thick band of metal around one wrist attached to the chain. No ankle chains or anything to bind their hands.

Angie's hands, however, were encased in rough, thick metal that, when she was able to look at it closely, without the panic swamping her senses, she could see was glowing faintly purple. So, not just a physical block for her hands, but also a magical block.

A series of curses bubbled up but she bit them down as she asked, "Aidan? Betha? Eloise?" They weren't in the large cave room with them.

Sebastian scowled and shook his head.

"Could they have gotten away?"

"Betha went down with us," Carmen said. "Lisa took you both out. That's…"

"Fucked up?"

"Terrifying." Carmen let out a sigh. "Can't say exactly how much power is coursing through the three of you right now, but it's a lot if those demon explosions were anything to go by. And yet one of you could still knock out the other two?"

"She can read my thoughts," Angie said, still annoyed

and feeling frankly more violated by that than getting knocked out.

"Didn't seem able to read mine," Carmen said. "Or she might have bound my hands too."

Angie glanced up at the light. "I didn't know you could do that. That you had that kind of magic."

"There's a lot about me you don't know." Carmen forced a smirk and a half chuckle, but her usual arrogance wasn't there.

"In this case, that's probably good since I think Lisa officially knows everything I know."

"Do you know her thoughts?" Sebastian asked. He scooted around to lean against the wall and then pulled her closer so she was in his arms.

Angie leaned into him, grateful that if they had to be in this fucked up situation, at least they were together. "No. At least, I wasn't getting anything when she was reading me. I don't have that kind of psychic skill normally."

"Eloise must have before the split," Carmen said.

"Never picked that up from her during the vision where I was in her perspective. But that seems to be what Lisa implied. To be fair, Eloise wasn't thinking about herself during that vision."

"And Betha did say she was a psychic before the split, even if she didn't have witch magic."

Angie tried to lift her hands to study the magic infused metal encircling them. The weight of the covering kept dragging her hands down to the ground or her lap. She tried to wiggle her fingers inside the binding, but the best she could do was dig her fingernails farther into her palm. She closed her eyes to see what was happening with her web of magic.

Overall, her web looked the same. Pulsing with the magic she'd gained when the triad had formed. Silver light coating each strand. The purple magic that had been woven into her web looked a little dimmer. But the blues and three red threads were still bright. And when she gave the blue magic, her witch magic, a metaphysical brush of her fingertips, it pulsed, powerful and steady.

She wasn't losing that magic. Not yet. But the purple, that magic that had formed when her witch and demon witch magics had begun to bleed into each other, that was leeching away. Slower than she'd have expected. But it was dripping away steadily.

The red demon magic threads that surrounding her single demon witch thread were pulling in different directions. One to the left, one just in front of them. Since each of those threads seemed to react to and pull toward the other two witches in the triad, she had to assume Lisa was somewhere outside the door, and Betha was to the left, maybe in another chamber?

She said as much to Sebastian and Carmen.

"Wonder if she's alone or if Aidan and Eloise are there?" Angie said.

"And what's the endgame here," Carmen said. "She wants your magic. Fair. But she can't destroy the god realm on her own, right?"

"I don't know," Angie said, sighing. "I'm not sure I can

trust anything we've learned since we got here. Especially since we were brought with promises of information and all we got was chains and dangerous magic."

Carmen settled back against the wall next to Angie, on the opposite side to Sebastian. "So let me see if I got this right. Betha did show up in that church-warehouse and killed Sokolov and his demon."

"Sounds like."

"And she told you to find her. To bring the two hunters and me."

"Yes."

"And that was really Betha and not Lisa in disguise."

"If Betha wasn't lying, again, then yes."

"So she brought you here, knowing that this… doppelganger of her girlfriend, who she created while trying to heal her girlfriend, wanted to form the apocalypse witch triangle thing and destroy all the gods so the doppelganger could take over. And instead of thwarting that shit by just ignoring you, she purposefully brought you here."

"To kill Lisa."

"To save her girlfriend. Or kill her. Whichever."

"I think that's the general idea."

"So, all of this is a grudge match between the two of them, and the winner gets to kill the other. One hopes she'll get her girlfriend back whole and sane. The other wants to be a god and rule over the demons." Carmen shook her head. "That's some fucked up shit."

"It absolutely is," Angie agreed. "Can you imagine what the hunter council would think of all these machinations?"

Carmen chuckled. Then barked out a laugh.

Angie found herself trying to laugh, too. She wasn't even sure why. None of this was funny. But it was all so absurd and horrible, her only option was to laugh.

"Did you figure any of this out before I did?" she asked Sebastian, leaning back against him and turning her head to see his expression.

"I wouldn't have agreed to all this if I knew this was where we were going." He lifted his cuffed hand and rattled the chain.

"What about Aidan? You think she had a clue what was going on?"

He was quiet. Then, "If she's with Betha and Eloise, no. If she's not—"

Before he could finish, the metal door slammed open, hitting the stone wall hard enough to rain dust from the stone roof onto their heads.

CHAPTER TWENTY-NINE

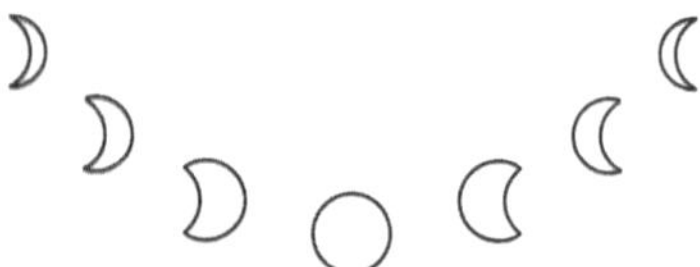

A haze of sulfur-scented smoke billowed into the cavernous prison cell, followed by a very angry looking Lisa.

Angie leaned back against Sebastian, trying to put herself between both Sebastian and Carmen at the same time, though she wasn't in a position to do much protecting with her hands bound.

"Where are they?" Lisa demanded, her voice deep and loud enough to echo in the large cavern.

And wasn't that an interesting way to start this conversation.

"Don't toy with me." Lisa snarled at Angie. "You know I know what you're thinking."

"Then you also know I don't have any idea what you're talking about." Light from several flickering fires inside metal drums outside their prison room cast orange light into the room and haloed Lisa in red. The light made her red eyes even brighter, glowing like a demon's, without any visible human pupil or iris beneath.

It took Angie a beat before she realized that the blue light Carmen had magicked up for them had disappeared the instant the door banged open. But she focused on Lisa's question to keep Lisa from picking up on that thought.

"Who is *they* in this conversation?" she asked aloud.

"You know." Lisa's hands fisted at her sides. "That other hunter. And Eloise. Where are they?"

"I thought you could read Eloise's mind, and she yours. I thought you two were linked." But wasn't it so very interesting that Aidan had not only gotten away, and taken Eloise with her, but wherever they'd gone, Lisa couldn't find them.

Lisa snarled and stuck her face in Angie's as sparks of purple magic danced around her fisted hands. Sebastian tightened his hold on Angie, trying to move her behind him, even though there was nowhere to go.

"That *woman* is somehow blocking me. How? How can she do that when you can't?"

"Magic," Angie said with a shrug. Or in this case, a will so strong it looked like magic from the outside.

Lisa rose to her full height, staring down her nose at them. "You can reach her. You know how to find her."

"I don't even know where I am. Why the hell do you need Eloise anyway? Thought you were just going to kill her."

"She's part of me. I don't want to kill her."

That was a lie.

"It's the truth," Lisa hissed.

"She needs her," Carmen said, her voice low but direct. "They're still too entangled. If Eloise dies now, part of Lisa will die before she can consolidate her power."

Lisa backhanded Carmen across the cheek. Angie cursed and tried to lunge toward Lisa, though she didn't know what she thought she'd do. Sebastian held her back.

Carmen touched her free hand to the cut on her cheek, the drips of blood on her fingertips. Then she smiled up at Lisa and licked the blood off her dirty hand. "Thanks," she said. "I was hungry."

Lisa made a noise that sounded somewhere between a hiss and a snarl and paced away from them toward the metal door. "You have an hour to decide to cooperate, or I will kill the man. Then I will kill the stupid sacrifice you brought." She turned to stare at Angie. "And then I will drain you dry, until you're nothing but a husk. And kill you."

"Got a watch so we can keep track of that hour?" Carmen asked.

Lisa didn't even glance at her, her burning red gaze fixed on Angie. Then she swung out the door and it slammed shut behind her without her having to touch it, plunging the prison cell into darkness.

"Telekinesis?" Angie asked Carmen.

"That or some serious magic skills." A blue glow lit the sudden blackness, coming up slowly as Carmen reactivated the spell she'd extinguished when Lisa barged in.

"That was both terrifying and…informative," Angie whispered.

"Aidan can block Lisa's ability to read Eloise's mind," Carmen said.

"She's got the will to fend off demons," Sebastian said.

Angie looked at him. "Did you know she could do something like this, though?"

His lips flattened. He tugged at his goatee then scratched the scruff now covering his cheeks with his free hand. "I did not," he admitted.

"The less we know right now the better," Carmen said. "At least, the less Angie knows." When Angie turned toward her, Carmen said, "The less Lisa can pick up from you, the better."

True enough.

Angie gave Sebastian a considering look. "If Aidan can do that for Eloise, can you do that for me? It'd be helpful if I didn't have to basically stop thinking with Lisa around." And maybe even when she wasn't around. Angie had no idea if distance mattered to Lisa's ability to read her thoughts.

Although, if it didn't, there wouldn't have been much reason for Lisa to come storming into their prison to demand answers. Angie had a feeling that, at least when it came to reading Betha and Angie, Lisa had to be close.

"I've never tried anything like that," he said. "But next time she's here, I can try. We'll only know it's working though, if you say something to piss Lisa off in your head and she doesn't react. Might be a dangerous experiment."

"Worth it," Angie said. It wasn't like things could get

much worse. Well, things could get worse. She could imagine all kinds of worse if she let herself. Not least the idea of being trapped in these demon realms without any more magic so she'd have no way to get herself or the others home.

"We've got an hour," Carmen said. "Maybe consider that our plan B. We need a plan A—a get out of here before she comes back plan."

"I'd like to find Betha and get her out of here, too," Angie said.

"She's only brought you problems," Carmen said. "You sure you don't just want to leave them to their family squabble?"

"If we leave, without settling things with Betha and Lisa, Lisa and her army will come to our realm and wreak havoc. We can't afford to run away this time. The bitch will follow."

Carmen rolled her eyes, but nodded. "I like this cursey side of you, by the way. I know there's some good magic shit going to happen when you get all cursey."

"Shut up. What can your magic do to get my hands out of these metal bowling balls?"

"Not sure." Carmen looked at the metal encompassing Angie's hands. "The actual spell stuff isn't my strongest suit."

"Or you would have shown it off more?"

Carmen flattened her mouth but didn't comment. "Lisa's not going to leave an easy hole in that spell, knowing you might find it."

"But what would I be able to do about it with my hands

bound? Maybe she didn't consider any holes in her spell because she didn't know you could do magic."

"Sounds like wishful thinking," Carmen said ruefully. "But let me look."

She half closed her eyes, her attention turned down toward Angie's hand where it rested on the ground next to her. Angie did the same. She might not be able to break the spell but she could certainly look at it.

It wasn't a particularly good spell, she realized. Not as stable as something Angie herself might have set. There was a lot of power in it. A *lot*. A lot of brute force magic that, for most, would have been enough. But the spell itself did have weak points that could be exploited.

The longer she studied the spells construction, the results of the binding, the more she realized... Lisa wasn't a very good witch. She had a lot of magic. And she'd figured out how to do a lot of things with that magic. She'd probably learned things from Betha about how to wield all this magic. But...

Lisa hadn't been properly trained. Eloise hadn't been a witch. Lisa had witch-like magic and power, but not the knowledge to make it work as well as it should. The sheer amount of magic she could wield hid that, and to most probably wouldn't have made a difference. But even after centuries of time to study, Lisa obviously hadn't bothered to learn enough about witchcraft and spell casting.

Or Betha had purposefully misled her in her training.

Whichever it had been, the result was that the spell binding Angie's hands was something Angie could have broken with a little concentration and…well, the use of her hands.

"You seeing the weak points?" Angie asked Carmen quietly. "Want me to walk you through the spell to break them? Do you have the magic for that?"

Despite the weak spell, the magic itself was still strong, and Carmen had done an outstanding job of hiding just how much magic she had, so Angie really had no idea if she was seeing this spell the way Angie saw it.

"Think I can," Carmen said, sounding a little amazed. "Sloppy spell. Untrained…"

As Angie watched the weave of light that was her mind's interpretation of the spell, she saw little flashes of blue popping into the center of the weave. Magic that felt very unfamiliar and yet…she'd encountered it before. Once. A memory of a spell on a house in New Jersey that ensured Angie would find that house and all others would stay out… Last October when Carmen had set up a bunch of very dangerous situations that forced Angie into realizing she could open portals without trees. She'd thought at the time that spell had been set by the residents of the house, and maybe Carmen had just taught them how to do it.

But this magic, sparking here and there through the complex but weak spell Lisa had created, was the same magic as that pretty impressive spell that had been on the house's gate.

Carmen had been hiding quite a lot about her skills.

The sparks of blue settled into three distinct spots on the spell, three of the weaker points. The light seemed to burrow into the purple magic, one of the blue spots disappearing completely. Carmen cursed and more blue sparks danced into the spell, around it, coalescing in that place where the previous spot of blue had vanished.

"Tricky bitch," Carmen muttered under her breath.

Angie kept her opinions to herself, barely breathing as she watched Carmen work at the spell. Watched a thread of the intricately woven binding snap. The broken thread tried to reinsert into the original spell, but a tiny ball of blue light attached to the end of that thread like a bead and blocked the purple thread from rejoining the weave of the spell.

The quiet murmur of Carmen chanting, the faint movement of her hands at the edge of Angie's vision, all a background hum as Carmen poked and prodded at those weak points in the binding spell. More of the threads popped out of place. Angie felt the spell weakening. Felt the whole thing starting to fall apart.

And realized they'd made a horrible mistake.

With no time to warn Carmen, Angie wrapped a shield around the ball of binding magic. No spells. No finesse. Just brute force power. The move kicked Carmen out of her work abruptly and resulted in a sharp curse from the other witch.

All cut off when the collapsing spell shattered with a flash of blinding light and a release of energy that made the prison walls tremble.

Angie hissed at the backlash pain that trembled through her bones. She'd been connected to the magic she'd used to build the shield, so felt when the spell exploded against it.

But better that than the spell exploding without that barrier and killing them all.

Only as she let the shield fall away did she realize she'd instinctively grabbed some of the purple threads of power in her web to force up the barrier. She'd never used that magic before. That she could use it without needing a spell was…

Good to know.

She blinked her eyes open to see Carmen scowling at her. "Could have warned me," she said.

"No time."

"Did I fuck up with breaking the spell?"

Carmen sounded almost hesitant, almost chagrinned. Which Angie found a little unnerving. "No. It was…a trap. In case I figured out a way to get around the inability to move my hands. I should have looked for that before sending you in to break the spell. My fault."

"No one's fault. Bitch is just tricky. We'll have to remember that."

Angie looked at her hands, still encased in rough silver metal. But the metal was no longer glowing purple.

"Are you hurt?" Sebastian asked, still holding her.

His arms had been around her during all that. He must have felt her wince. "No. At least, I think I'm okay. I just need to get these metal mittens off."

He readjusted his position and motioned for her to set her hands in his lap. Then he studied the metal wrapped around her fists. "Pretty basic lock here. Don't suppose you have something thin. Piece of metal? Hair pin?"

Angie looked at her hip and realized her ever present bag was gone. "Bitch took my purse," she snapped.

Carmen chuckled. "Don't tell me. You had a lock picking kit in there."

"Not quite." Angie made a face. She did carry a lot of things in her oversized purse. But she just liked to be prepared.

"I got you," Carmen said. She was still wearing her leather jacket and when she pulled it open, she revealed a series of pockets. She gave a few of them a pat and nodded. "Yeah, she searched me too while we were out. But I don't keep all my tricks in obvious places." She raised her brows at Angie.

Which made Angie scowl more. "Purses are handy," she grumbled.

Carmen pulled up the bottom hem of her jacket and worked her nail under some of the threads, cutting through them easier than Angie would have expected. Separating the outer leather from the inner silk liner. And revealing a hidden pocket.

"Very clever," Angie said begrudgingly.

Carmen grinned. She pulled out a four inch long, very thin knife, the blade so thin it couldn't have been more than a quarter inch wide. The hilt was also narrow, silver and etched with symbols she didn't let Angie see as she passed the little knife to Sebastian, hilt first.

"Careful," Carmen said. "That point is sharper than it looks."

Sebastian studied the blade. "Poisoned tip?"

"Not that one." Carmen winked.

"Where were these poisoned-tipped pokey sticks when we were fighting demons?" Angie asked as Sebastian went to work on one of the locks holding the manacles closed.

"Useless against demons so they remained safely hidden in my jacket. Those are more for…human-type situations."

"Hmm." Angie wasn't sure she wanted details about what sort of "human-type" situation Carmen might feel required a poisoned knife.

"Haven't actually had to use the poison one in years," Carmen said, still conversationally. "Last time was…on a demon hunter."

Angie snarled at her. "You sure you want to bring that up right now?"

"What do you think that hunter was up to when I killed him? Hmm?"

"Trying to keep your *protege* Grant from unleashing a demon." Barthalomew Grant had been a horrible person who Carmen had gone after, playing a long game to destroy him by using his own hubris against him. She'd taught him how to summon a demon, knowing he'd one day end up getting destroyed by that demon. But in the meantime, Grant had caused a lot of damage and endangered a lot of lives. Including his own child's.

"That was the story, anyway," Carmen said. "Except that hunter wasn't trying to stop the demon. He was negotiating with it. And Grant. For money."

"I don't believe that." Hunters knew better than to negotiate with demons. Certainly not for something as superficial as money. They're jobs were to stop the people making those bad deals.

Carmen shrugged, her gaze moving around their prison cell. "You ever wonder why someone like me had a friend on the council? Why one of the hunters had been protecting me?"

Angie had as a matter of fact. But she didn't say so out loud.

Carmen smiled as she settled her gaze on Angie again. "We kept the truth quiet. Even from the other council members. Bad for hunter moral, right? Learning one of their own had tried to betray everything and join the dark side." She wagged her eyebrows.

"You still killed him."

"Well. He was about to fuck up my plan. Give Grant more protection and knowledge than I wanted him to have. And it helped ingratiate me more with Grant. Win-win for me."

"You are a liar."

"Sometimes." Carmen nodded, her gaze moving around the cavern again.

"Why should I believe you? Why even tell me that?"

She waved a careless hand. "Just telling stories to pass the time. I don't give two fucks if you believe me or not."

Angie heard the lie in that statement, though. She wasn't sure what to believe. She had witnessed Carmen doing horrible things. Carmen wasn't a good guy.

But she also wasn't what Angie had thought either.

Did it make a difference? Knowing Carmen's reason for

killing that demon hunter all those years ago? Angie glanced down at her hands, then at Sebastian. He hadn't lifted his head or stopped picking the lock on her cuffs. She couldn't tell how he felt about what Carmen had said. She knew he hadn't known because if he had, he would have told her. Did this change his opinion of Carmen?

A click and snapping sound broke through her chaotic thoughts. One of the heavy balls of metal fell off her fist and wrist, freeing her hand. She sighed and groaned a little as she stretched her fingers out, flexing them to get the blood flowing again.

"Better," she said, and handed Sebastian her other hand. Watching the top of his head, she said, "When did you learn to pick locks?"

"In my misspent youth," he said, glancing up to give her a small smile before returning to his work.

She smiled, but thinking of his youth reminded her of the turbulent time that led him into being a demon hunter. A heartbreaking story of loss that made her ache for him.

Thinking about that now, though, would distract her, so she focused on loosening the fingers of her freed hand. She studied the metal door across from them as Sebastian made shorter work of the second cuff. When she had both hands free, she rubbed her wrists and palms, getting the blood flow moving again.

"There's no magical spells on that door," she said. "Not that I can see. Just thick metal."

"She probably didn't think she'd need the door spelled," Carmen said.

Angie moved out of the way while Sebastian picked the lock on the cuff around Carmen's one wrist. Then Carmen returned the favor by getting Sebastian's handcuff off.

Angie went to study the door, relieved to hear the sound of chains clattering to the hard rock floor. Sebastian came up beside her. But she kept her attention on the door. "Definitely no spells," she murmured. "And Lisa hasn't come running. So she isn't reading my thoughts at this exact moment. If she was, she'd know we're free."

"Maybe she does know and this is all another trap," Carmen said.

"Maybe." Angie let her eyes narrow and looked at the threads of demon magic that pulled toward the other two witches in the triad. The one that tugged toward Lisa was more stretched than the one that tugged toward Betha, somewhere to their left. "I think Lisa is...not very close at the moment. At least, Betha is a lot closer."

"Doesn't mean this isn't a trap," Carmen said.

Given that the binding spell had had a trap built into it, Angie thought Carmen was probably right. But they had to get out of here. And they had to get to Betha. The only way to take down Lisa was for Angie and Betha to work together.

And hope they didn't kill themselves or Eloise in the process.

CHAPTER THIRTY

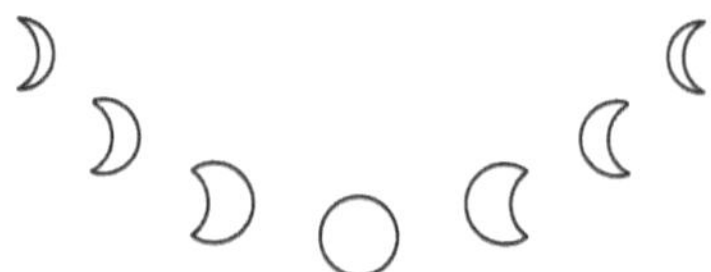

The outer chamber was similar to the cavern that had been their cell but larger. Lots of black rock and sharp edges. Solid surfaces with no windows or openings onto the outside. The scent of sulfur was stronger here, which made Angie think they might be closer to one of the volcanos than they'd been before Lisa trapped them. The air was muggy, so there had to be water around here somewhere, too. The rocks themselves were warm, but not too hot to touch.

The fires in metal drums that Angie had spotted behind Lisa when she'd barged into the cell were gone—likely an illusion of some kind. Leaving the outer chamber as pitch black as the cell had been. But Carmen's little ball of blue magic followed over their heads, lighting the way.

There was a single corridor leading out of the chamber. And a second metal door a few yards from theirs.

Moving carefully, with Carmen at her back and Sebastian

at her shoulder, Angie went to the other door, the demon magic thread that drew her toward Betha pulling her in that direction. She studied the door before touching it, though, looking for spells or traps. She didn't trust her own magic at the moment, because it was tied to the other two witches, but she still seemed able to sense and see magic. And use it, though in ways she hadn't known possible.

She listened at the door for a long time, studied the metal from her peripheral vision, even closed her eyes to try and see if anything came up on the metaphysical plane.

Nothing.

"Do you pick up any magic?" she asked Carmen.

"Can't see anything. I'm not as powerful a witch as you, but I can generally see spells. Nothing there. Like our door."

"Then Betha probably has cuffs on like I had. And she doesn't have a fellow witch with her to break the spell."

"Wow. Did you just give me a compliment and include me in your ranks of friends?"

"No," Angie said, but she smiled faintly at Carmen. Carmen chuckled.

"We need to hurry," Sebastian said. He was standing at the tunnel which Angie hoped led out of wherever they were. "There are other things in these tunnels to worry, not just Lisa."

"Fuck." Angie closed her eyes.

"We need to find Aidan and Eloise before Lisa does, too," Carmen said quietly. "She'll kill them both if she finds them before we reach them."

Angie held in another curse because it wouldn't help and

studied the lock on the door—just in case. Discovered that, like their own, this door wasn't actually locked. Betha must be chained and confined the way they'd been. Lisa thinking her helpless.

She eased the door open slowly, carefully, waiting for any hint of disaster. Searching with her magical senses wide open for any hints of a trap. She was tempted to open her psychic sense too, but was afraid what she sensed would overwhelm her, so kept that part locked down, instead relying on her normal senses and her awareness of magic.

Nothing snapped, triggered, or jumped out at them when the door eased open. The interior of the cell was pitch black, as dark as their own had been. Carmen's blue light floated forward as Angie and Carmen eased into the room, leaving Sebastian to guard their backs.

It took Angie a moment to see the room's interior, the bouncing ball of blue magic had to rise high enough and move far enough inside before much of the cavern was illuminated. Betha was laying on the floor, unconscious, her hands bound exactly as Angie's had been. She was alone in her cell. No longer wearing the scaled jumpsuit, instead wearing in an ordinary t-shirt and cargo pants.

And there was blood on her shirt, near her waist.

Angie rushed to her side. "Betha? Betha, can you hear me?" She hovered her hands over the woman's wound. There was a slight magical residue, but the injury itself seemed to be mechanical—something caused by a weapon. Lisa had had a weapon beyond magic? Or was this something she did to Betha after she'd already locked Betha in here?

Unfortunately, Angie wasn't a healer. Her magic didn't lean into that particular skill. And she didn't have her purse with all her handy items that could help bandage the wound.

She lifted Betha's shirt to get a better look, all the while murmuring to the other witch. Two slices cut an X across Betha's stomach. The cuts were jagged and rough looking, but not too deep. They were still bleeding though. So either they were fresh, or the magic residue Angie was sensing was keeping the cuts from clotting.

If magic was interfering with the clotting, even pressure on the wounds wouldn't help. Still, she pulled off her jacket and bunched it into a makeshift compress, pressing the corduroy over the cuts in an attempt to stop the blood flow.

"I need some proper bandages," she muttered.

"Try some of that magic you used to make the shield," Carmen said.

"What?"

"It helped you build a shield without a spell. Maybe it'll help here? It's a mix of witch and demon witch, right?"

"But not healer. I'm not one."

"Try it," Carmen said. "Carefully of course, but you never know. I'll get to work on the cuffs. If your magic doesn't help with the wound, maybe the two of you can work together to fix the injury or at least staunch the blood after she's free."

Angie had no idea how, but with the triad mixing of magic, maybe they could fix the wounds. In the meantime, she let Carmen focus on the bespelled cuffs, and she turned her attention to the wound. She might not be able to heal the cuts, but maybe she could figure out the magic that was keeping the wound from clotting and closing itself. If she could stop the bleeding, that would help a lot.

Focusing down on the faint magic she sensed, she studied the elements, the pattern. It wasn't a spell, per say. The wound had been created by something bespelled. The spell on the weapon acted a bit like a poison, seeping into the wound. So she just needed some sort of antidote to that poison.

Damn it she wished she'd learned more healing arts. Okay. If she just…created something that worked in the opposite way. Maybe a reversal spell? She had one of those. A reversal spell might work.

She started to murmur the spell, letting her magic build under her skin as she made the necessary hand gestures. She let the magic flow with her words, her eyes half closed as she studied the residue and how her spell affected it. Remembering what Carmen had said, Angie, very carefully, touched a metaphysical finger to some of that remaining purple magic in her web. That magic had been dripping away, but there was enough still woven inside her web to send a jolt of strength and power through her body.

She felt the change in the spell she'd been creating the instant she touched that magic. Felt the slight variation, the pulse of something…more.

The reversal spell lifted out the magic residue, gathering it on the stone floor the way Betha's blood had formed a small pool under her. And then the wound reversed itself too. Knitting closed, sealing up.

Leaving only faint red lines to even indicate the wound had been there.

Angie blinked down at the healed injury, stunned. "Uhm."

"Purple magic, right?" Carmen said, sounding smug. "Told you so."

Angie didn't have the energy to snap back. "How are you doing on the cuffs?" Betha was still out cold. They needed to revive her somehow. That would be a lot easier after they got the binding metal mittens off.

"Almost there. Not falling for the trap this time, though." Carmen's voice was quiet in the cavern room, not even loud enough to bounce off the low ceiling. "See it this time. Should have spotted it with yours." This last she mostly muttered to herself.

Just in case, Angie prepared to raise that shield she'd raised earlier, though she still wasn't sure how she'd done it. And because she wasn't, she murmured the shield spell she'd known for years, automatically forming hand gestures and whispering words she knew would work. Getting the spell to the last moment before triggering it, waiting for Carmen to finish.

In the end, Angie didn't need to trigger her own spell as Carmen sat back with a satisfied sigh and the glowing purple light around Betha's cuffs melted away, leaving only an ordinary metal barrier. Rather than undoing the threads of her own spell and letting it melt away, Angie "stored" it, in case she needed to activate it quickly as they escaped.

"Need your boyfriend to pick the locks," Carmen said,

gesturing to the metal gloves. She was frowning, though. "I'm not used to doing this kind of magic much. It's fucking exhausting."

"Can be, yup."

"Doesn't do that to you anymore, though."

"Nope. I'm feeling very energized right now." She was, too. All the strength and power flowing through her. Even without food and water for who knew how long, she was full of energy and strength. She felt like she could keep going for hours.

Which was good because she didn't have her purse and any of her handy protein bars to feed her ravenous body at the moment, and she couldn't afford to pass out.

"Still unnerving, though," she said to Carmen. "It's… stronger now since forming the triad." She looked at the chains on Betha's hands. "I'll get these. I don't want us all distracted in here."

She set a finger to the lock on one of the cuffs and murmured the reversal spell again, without touching the purple magic this time. The spell reversed the position of the lock and the cuffs dropped open, freeing one of Betha's hands.

Betha sat up suddenly, dragging in a deep, gasping breath. She roared a curse, looked at her one still bound hand, and started a spell of her own.

Angie looked across her to Carmen, who was also wide eyed, and they both dove away from Betha as Betha brought the metal binding glove down hard and the rocks with the last word of her spell. It shattered into pieces that sprayed everywhere like shrapnel.

"Hey!" Carmen barked. "Careful with that! We're here to help you."

Betha, her eyes glowing red now, looked at Carmen, then snapped her head around to see Angie. The glow settled, fading back to an ordinary level of red, her expression clearing. She gave her head a little shake. "Sorry," she murmured. "Sorry about that. A knee-jerk reaction to waking up confined."

"Fair enough," Angie said, "but don't do anything like that again. We don't have time to heal more injuries before we get out of here."

"Eloise? Where's Eloise?" Betha lunged upward, the clanging of her chains dropping to the rock floor loud in the confined space. She reached upward when she wobbled, balancing herself on the low ceiling.

"We don't know," Angie said, raising her hands in a soothing gesture as she also stood. "Lisa doesn't have her. Lisa is currently looking for her and Aidan. But she doesn't have her."

"That bitch." Betha snarled. "I'm gonna kill her."

"Okay, well, yeah, we might have to do that. But it will not go easy on us if we do. So we need a plan. She can read our thoughts. And she's out there waiting to kill us and steal all our magic. Mine is still dripping away—some of it anyway. Yours?"

Betha pulled in a deep breath, seeming to calm down more. She closed her eyes briefly and said, "I can still feel it.

Kinda wish I had your visualization. I can't tell what she's taking. Just that there's a…drain somewhere. But there's so much there, it's hard to feel."

"Yeah. We're all still tied so the magic is pretty immense right now. We'll have to be careful."

"Lisa should have been more careful," Betha said, her eyes narrowed.

"Hey, hey!" Angie snapped, forcing Betha to look at her. "Calm down. Eloise is safe with Aidan. We need to keep it together and focused. Lisa is insane and dangerous and we're linked to her. We go off on anger and panic, she will win. And kill all of us. I am *not* dying in this place. Not any demon realm. So we are going to do this with at least some logic to guide us, and we're going to calm down long enough to listen to our instincts. Got it?"

Betha's mouth flattened into a grim line, but she nodded and pulled in another deep breath.

"Okay. Let's get out of here. There's a tunnel. Sebastian says there are other things besides Lisa down here. So we need to move. Are you okay with walking? You lost a lot of blood."

Betha finally looked down at the pool of blood that had formed beneath her. She snarled at it, and leaned over to run her fingers through it. She rubbed her fingers together, the glow in her eyes coming up. "I don't do proper blood magic, despite what the mayor and his followers claimed," Betha said quietly. "I've used blood to protect my home because everything in this fucking place is about blood. But I don't do proper blood magic." She glanced up from her fingers, meeting Angie's gaze. "But Lisa does. Lisa has attempted to study all different kinds of magic."

"You held back knowledge, though, didn't you? Some of it anyway."

"What I could. I knew she was not…mentally capable of ethically handling the magic she already had. Knowledge would only make it worse. For a long time, her only victims were demons and I couldn't care much about that. But she won't stop there."

"Is she using blood magic now?" Angie asked as they started out of the cell, joining Sebastian in the antechamber. She kept her voice low, not wanting to draw the attention of whatever else was in these tunnels. A quick glance at her demon magic threads confirmed that the one that linked to Lisa was still stretched and tugging her in Lisa's direction, but that Lisa was not nearby.

"She's using it in the mix of what she does. But she's using our knowledge now to…fix what she was never able to do before. She's extremely dangerous now."

"You think?" Angie snapped under her breath. "So she can read our thoughts and she's stealing our knowledge and she's hunting for Eloise and Aidan. How the hell do we stop her?"

Betha's mouth worked but she didn't answer.

Given that Betha had been thinking about this for centuries, planning for it, had come to find Angie just so Angie could help Betha kill Lisa, and now she didn't really know how to do it, was a terrifying reality to face.

Her panic and worry ratcheted up. "Okay. One thing at a time. First, we get out of here."

A screeching sound echoed down the corridor, distant, but loud enough to make Angie wince. The sound made the hairs on her arms stand up.

"The other things in the tunnel?" she asked Sebastian.

"The other things in the tunnel." He glanced at her, looking grim in Carmen's magical blue light. Then he started down the tunnel.

Angie and the others followed, Angie's heart pounding hard in her chest. A thick blanket of fear and worry settled heavily on her shoulders.

Another loud screech filled the corridor in front of them.

CHAPTER THIRTY-ONE

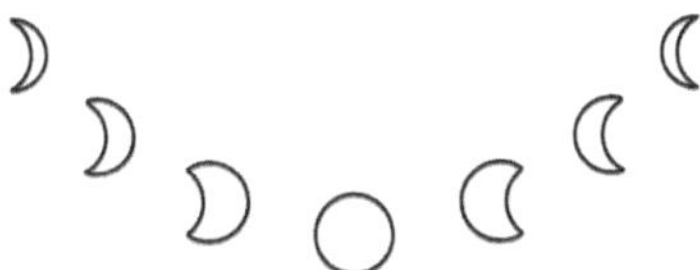

The tunnel was as dark as the chambers had been, with only Carmen's little blue light floating overhead to show them any obstacles in their way. Betha used the walls to brace against as they moved forward, her fingers scraping over the hard rough rocks. Angie had tried that too, but the warmth in the rocks kept sending tremors of strange sensations through her, and they were too uncomfortable and distracting. She couldn't explain them. Just a sense of excitement and foreboding and fear, and the knowledge that if she searched long enough, she'd be able to sense blood from centuries past.

She did not want to risk touching centuries old blood of who knew what creature. Her nerves were stretched far enough.

Another of those hair-raising screeches echoed down the dark corridor. Somewhere in front of them, but still at a distance. Maybe. It was impossible to tell. The sound sent another rush of adrenaline through Angie's system and set her pulse to pounding harder. She had her shield spell set and ready to go with just a word and gesture. And she went ahead and stacked up her illusion spell. Because her magic felt so strong and easy at the moment, she stacked a third spell—a water spell—and a fourth spell—her lightning spell. If she had to call on any of these, it would only take a word and a single twist of her fingers to get them going.

By the time she had the additional three set up, they'd gone deep enough into the tunnels that Angie was lost and had no way how they might find their way back to even the cells they'd been in. She was relying on Sebastian to lead the way. And it was only when she had the spells set and worry about being lost set in, that she thought to check on where Lisa was again.

The red thread in her magic web that leaned toward Lisa was stretched more than it had been while they were inside the cells. As if Lisa was even farther away now. And it was stretched at an angle. Her magic wanted her to head in that direction, go toward the other witch.

Her logic screamed that that would be a bad idea.

"Wish you had your purse," Carmen grumbled from her spot between Angie and Sebastian. "Could use a drink."

"Wish I had my purse too." She was feeling edgy and restless without its reassuring weight at her hip. She always had her purse with all the things she *might* need in it. Without that, she felt almost naked. A sensation not helped by having her corduroy jacket—now covered in Betha's blood—wrapped around her waist.

The combination of being lost and having no purse kicked a memory forward. "The charm!" The present from her mentor, the charm that helped them find Betha when they were jumping around demon realms. She'd tucked that into her jeans pocket. Had Lisa found it and taken it too?

She patted her pants, and found the little charm still securely hidden inside her front pocket. Pulling it out, she rubbed her thumb over the little silver medallion, owl engraving on one side, butterfly engraving on the other, and a sense of settling calmed her racing pulse. She hadn't lost it. The gift had stayed with her.

"We can use this to find the others, I think," Angie murmured. "But I don't want to lead Lisa to Eloise." She glanced at Betha. "I know you want to reach her, and I can sense your desperation to find her. But Eloise is safe with Aidan. Safer than she'd be with you since Lisa can read your thoughts. It's better if we leave them hiding. Deal with Lisa first."

"You're assuming we can," Betha said.

"You assumed we could, or you wouldn't have lured me here."

"What else can that charm do?" Carmen cut in to ask.

"As far as I know, just find people."

"Shame it can't find the exit," Carmen muttered.

Another screech from somewhere ahead of them.

Angie tried not to jump at the sudden noise, and failed. She gripped the charm tight in her fist, felt the tingling of its magic, stronger it seemed than the last time she'd gripped it. That was odd.

"I've never used it to try and find a location," Angie said, "just a person. But maybe that would work?"

"Worth a try," Sebastian said, without turning to face them. "The creatures moving through these tunnels are closer than they sound."

"More than one?"

"More than one.

Shit. "How close?"

"It would be good if we knew which way the exit was."

That didn't answer her question. Which meant the answer to her question was terrifying and he didn't want to scare them all more.

"The demons will be afraid of us now," Betha said quietly. "More afraid of us than we are of them."

Angie found that hard to believe, even when she'd seen the fear in Sokolov's demon when he realized he'd been killed by the "apocalypse witch."

"Demons attack when they're afraid," Angie said. "And if we draw on the magic that links us all, that will definitely get Lisa's attention. I'd rather not fight her and demons at the same time."

Betha shrugged. "She'll just kill the demons."

"Then why are there demons in these tunnels?" Angie asked. "If that's all she ever did, why are there monsters here?"

Betha didn't comment.

Yeah, that's what Angie thought. Lisa wanted to be a god

among the demons. That didn't involve *just* killing them, or even just being able to kill them. That involved being able to control and rule them. That involved being able to *use* them.

And Angie had a feeling Lisa was using the creatures in these tunnels as guards for her prisoners.

They might have been able to get out of their cells, but getting out of the prison would be far trickier.

"Try the charm," Sebastian said. "I'm not seeing anything that will lead us out of the tunnels. We could be walking here for hours, days, before finding the exit.

"And if the charm doesn't work?" Angie said, trying to keep her voice from rising with her panic.

"We try something else."

"Maybe we go right to Lisa and kill her," Betha said.

There was more emotion in her voice than Angie was used to hearing. An anger and resentment and rage that Betha had kept hidden beneath indifference and resignation since Angie had met her. Betha wasn't hiding her anger anymore. And it was all focused on Lisa.

"Charm first," Angie said. One problem at a time.

Since she was looking for a location instead of a person this time, she flipped the charm so the butterfly side was facing upward and focused on the words "way out" as she recited the spell. Whispered her desired result along with the spell to activate the charm. When she murmured the very last word of the spell, and drew the fingers of her right hand over the medallion in the last gesture, she felt a little tremor of…

Magic.

It was the kind of magic she associated with being a

witch, with her mentor, with her mother. Comforting and settling and familiar. She smiled. She loved witch magic.

The little medallion started to vibrate and lean in one direction, the direction ahead of them. It wasn't rising up above her palm and rushing forward, so they probably still had a ways to go, but it was at least leaning in one direction. She tested it by walking forward, a little past Sebastian. After a brief pause, he hurried to her side and kept pace with her.

The charm continued to pull them forward, no hesitance or changing its mind. That was good.

"Working?" Carmen muttered. She'd come up close to Angie's back and it meant the little blue witch light overhead was closer, better illuminating the charm and the path right in front of Angie.

"Working." Angie glanced back long enough to make sure Betha was still with them, then she put her full focus on the charm.

Up to this point, the tunnels had branched off and turned a few times, and they'd been relying on Sebastian's instincts to take them toward an exit. When they reached the next branching tunnel, everyone leaned toward the charm to see which direction it chose. It angled to the right.

"The direction you would have chosen?" she asked Sebastian as they headed down that tunnel.

"I would have," he said. "But I would have been worried I was getting us lost."

"Are your instincts leading you…toward something?" This whole place was a big demon fight waiting to happen, so she wasn't sure what his instincts were feeding him at the moment.

"They are, but not like toward a fight. Or… It's hard to say. Maybe a fight. But it's not intense enough for that." He paused as the charm chose another direction for them at the next tunnel branching.

Left this time. They followed, though Angie's gut was tight. In the distance, the sounds of the screeching creatures echoing down the corridors seemed a little farther away. Was that good or bad?

"They're hunting us," Sebastian said, as if reading her mind about the creatures. "And their sense of smell is better than ours. But they're having trouble picking up the scent for long."

"You?"

He nodded. "As much as I can. I can do more now that the charm is leading us out."

She gave him a look. "You should have said earlier."

"I didn't realize you still had the charm," he said giving her a look in return. "Your bag was taken. Everything is always in your bag."

Carmen snorted, not even trying to hid that she was laughing when Angie turned to scowl at her.

"Fine," Angie said to Sebastian. "Can you focus on distracting the demons more now?"

"These demons, yes," he said.

"These? There are more in here?"

"The ones hunting us are more of a distraction. Hunters.

And they'd tear into us if they found us. But they're…not the worst demons in these tunnels. The silent ones are the worst."

"Silent ones." Shit. "The beautiful monsters from Betha's realm?" They couldn't be here, right? How would those have found them? How were they here? She'd thought the triad had scared those away back to their home realm.

Sebastian gave her a grim look, all he had to do.

Shit. There were Aminore, and maybe Helavitee, in these tunnels somewhere? Maybe not Helavitee because of their wings. But the Aminore would be enough. How? How were they here? Why?

"We need to get out of here," Carmen said, the panic in her voice banked but there. "Now."

"Yup," Angie said, feeling Carmen's panic in her bones.

They weren't just running away and trying to avoid the ordinary demons, but the monstrous super powerful demons that had chased them across realms. And it took combining the powers of all three apocalypse witches to stop them last time.

Angie considered their triad as they moved deeper into a tunnel that felt like it was going down instead of up and left her gut churning, worried they were going in the wrong direction.

Everything about the apocalypse witch situation was weird and she wished she knew more. Information she could actually trust. About Lisa and what she could do. About the kind of psychic Eloise had been before she and Lisa were separated. The kind of magic Lisa had access to now. Was Lisa even a demon witch? Did she count as one? Could she open portals and move around realms the way Betha and Angie could? She was obviously an apocalypse witch, she could kill demons. Had killed many.

But could she open portals?

When Angie asked Betha this, Betha was quiet for long enough to make Angie nervous. She kept her focus on the charm because it was starting to hover over her hand now. The sign that they were close to the exit sent Angie's adrenaline rushing and her stomach dancing. The need to *get out get out get out* thrummed through her veins.

They angled around a corner, taking a middle branch where four different tunnels angled off their path. The charm rose higher over her hand and started pulling forward so hard, Angie had to make sure the chain was wrapped around her fingers to keep the charm from getting away.

Finally, Betha said, "Lisa cannot open portals the way we do. She can…see into other realms. Her psychic abilities surpass mine by a long way, and are only worse now that she's got the power of our bond, but until that bond, she wasn't able to open a portal without help."

"Your help."

"She can't open anything at all without a tree," Betha said, skipping past Angie's comment. "But with a little anchoring help, she can open a portal in a tree's V."

"She uses a spell?"

"Brute force magic. But her strength is the psychic part of our bond."

"You said the apocalypse witch had to be a touch psychic. Was that Eloise's skill before the…split with Lisa?" Because

Lisa's psychic powers seemed to be quite different to anything Angie did or could do with a touch.

Betha was quiet a moment. Then said, "Eloise could read people. Sometimes with a touch, but sometimes without. For her, touch was not vital."

"And Lisa inherited that." Great. "So Lisa's strength is the psychic part of our bond and she doesn't need touch. What's your strength?" Angie moved down a tunnel that finally felt like it was moving upward, which was a relief. Though it occurred to her that there was no reason to think these series of tunnels were "below" ground level. They could be tunnels in a mountain side and going downward was heading toward an exit.

The screeching demons screamed then, but they sounded very far away now.

"I've got them chasing shadows," Sebastian murmured quietly.

She glanced at him. His eyes were half closed but the red glow in the depth was bright enough to see in the dark. "Thank you. You okay?"

"So far, yes."

She didn't push for more explanation.

"Back to my question for you," she said to Betha. "What's your strength in our bond?"

"The portals," Betha said. "Jumping around different realms takes very little effort for me, even before the bond."

"I can move between realms pretty easily," Angie said. "And with trees, the portals are too easy to open."

"You resist, though," Betha said—guessed?—"and you've only just started opening non-tree portals?"

Angie grunted her answer.

"Opening even into the god realm took focus and concentration and power, but it wasn't…difficult for me. The portals are my strength. I'm the first."

Angie decided Betha was probably telling her the truth about that. She probably could open portals easier than Angie. Because Angie *had* spent a lot of years trying *not* to open them. She certainly hadn't studied them and how to use them to go into a variety of realms. That information was only in Angie's head now because Betha had put it there in the blood she'd left on Yosuf's document. Without that, Angie wouldn't have known precisely how to open a portal into different realms. She wouldn't have known she could *choose* which realm to open a portal to.

"Okay," Angie said as the medallion moved a little faster forward and she had to pick up her pace to keep up with it. "So you're the portal witch. And you burned. Lisa is the psychic witch. And she savors. That makes me the witch that blooms, whatever that means. What's my strength in all this?"

"You're the witch."

Angie scowled and looked back at Betha briefly. "We're all witches."

"Your strength is the witch power. The actual magic use. Neither Lisa or I have the same level of magic wielding skills as you do. Lisa's is untrained brute force. Mine is trained but not as strong as yours at the basic power level. Since our combining, it's been obvious. You're the one with the magical skills."

Okay. That was… Information. She wasn't sure whether to call it good information or not. "What does the 'bloom' part mean?"

"I don't know," Betha answered. "I felt the burn. I've witnessed Lisa savoring the kills. I haven't seen the 'bloom' yet. So I don't know what it will mean."

Given how all the rest of this was working, Angie wasn't sure she wanted to know.

CHAPTER THIRTY-TWO

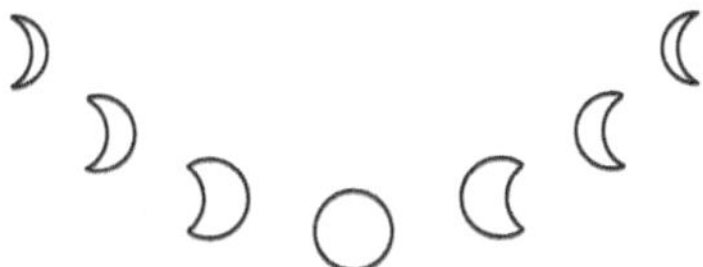

The exit to the tunnels came up so suddenly Angie almost didn't realize the way out was ahead. The air currents didn't change much, maybe a brush of movement that was a single degree cooler than the tunnels. The light change wasn't obvious because of Carmen's blue witch light bobbing over their heads and the exterior beyond the tunnels was almost as dark as the tunnels. As Angie approached the exit, she thought they were just stumbling into another place where the tunnels branched, even though the medallion was hovering well above her palm and moving forward so fast only the chain wrapped around Angie's hand kept it from flying away.

Then suddenly they were outside the tunnel and looking into the grand, dark landscape with a "sky" made of stalactites and golden sparkling minerals. A distant river of gold carved across the land. Several lines of iridescent blue bugs cut patterns through the black sand close to the river. The moisture and humidity from inside the tunnels dropped significantly, leaving Angie cold even though it wasn't cold outside. And the sounds of distant crinkling and movement opened up, making it obvious how muted sound had been inside the tunnels.

They were standing about half way up a rocky hill, not quite big enough to count as a mountain, but still far enough above the plain below to give her a much wider view of this realm. There was no end in sight, no wall to show the border of this cavernous space. It was as if the entire realm had a ceiling instead of a sky. And maybe it did. Or maybe there were just tunnels inside caverns inside tunnels.

She didn't care, so long as they could rescue Eloise and Aidan and get out of here.

But they couldn't do that without facing Lisa first.

The charm dropped back into her palm, no longer tugging her one way or another. She gave the little medallion a rub with her thumb and thanked it for leading them out. Then she tucked it back into her pocket as she scanned the hillside below them. Black rocks, a little loose looking. They'd have to scramble down and be careful not fall.

"How the hell did she get us up here?" Carmen asked, stepping up next to Angie. She made a small hand gesture and the blue witch light snapped out of existence.

Angie glanced up, then back at Carmen. "Thanks for that. It was really helpful."

Carmen waved away the thanks, not looking at Angie.

"Lisa didn't get us up here this way and down into those cells on her own."

"No. So either she had another way in and out. She used magic…"

"Or she had help," Betha said.

Angie looked at Betha, who'd come up to stand on the other side of her. "Help from who?"

Betha's mouth worked but she didn't answer.

"Continuing to keep secrets will not save Eloise," Angie said bluntly.

Betha shook her head. "I don't know. And if Eloise knows, she never told me."

"Can you trust Eloise?" Angie asked, again bluntly.

"Can you trust him?" Betha snapped, pointing back at Sebastain.

"I can. But he's also not psychically linked to a killing machine who wants to murder us all. That's the same reason I can trust Aidan. I do not really know either you or Eloise. Lisa came from something in Eloise. Is Eloise hiding things from you to save Lisa?"

"No," Betha said, firmly, snarling at Angie. "She would never."

"Then why do you keep her in a room with psychic locks on the doors?" Carmen asked.

Angie glanced at Carmen, then back to Betha. Carmen had seen something when she'd gone to get them out of their house's basement level. They hadn't had a chance to talk about that yet. Seemed like now might be the time.

"We need to get down this hill," Betha said. Her jaw was

tight and she refused to meet Angie's gaze, but her eyes were glowing brighter red than they had been even inside the tunnels.

"I still want to save Eloise," Angie said. "I understand how much you love her. I felt it, during the visions. But we both know the link with Lisa is a danger. To Eloise. But also to us."

"We destroy Lisa, Eloise will be free. That's all I want."

Angie wanted to believe that would be the end of it. That would fix everything. But since none of this had been straightforward, and Betha had lied to her multiple times so far, Angie wasn't holding her breath. Especially because it was obvious Betha was *still* keeping secrets.

"We'd better hurry," Sebastian said. He still stood at the tunnel opening, his attention focused back into the caverns. "The hunters have realized they're being redirected. And I'm too far away now to impose enough will to keep them moving away from us. They'll pick us up soon." He glanced at Angie. "I can't sense the other ones anymore."

That wasn't good. "They could be anywhere."

She started down the hill, taking the first few steps easily, testing the ground. The rocks and sand crumbled beneath her feet, making each step treacherous. Carefully, her hands out to the side to balance herself, she half slid, half trotted down the hill, rocks and pebbles from the others tumbling down next to her, making a small avalanche of debris. Angie slipped once, but someone caught her by the arm before she hit the ground. She thought it was Sebastian, but when she looked up, she realized no one was holding her.

She glanced back at Carmen, who had her hand out. Holding her up with her telekinetic powers until Angie got her feet back under her.

"Thanks," Angie said.

Carmen grunted her response.

Betha slipped next and slid toward Angie. Angie caught her just before she passed. The ordinary cargo pants and t-shirt Betha had on now showed a few tears from the slide through glass-sharp rocks.

"Hurt?" Angie checked. After Betha's earlier wound, Angie was worried about her losing more blood.

A screech from above had them all looking back toward the tunnel opening.

"Nothing that will slow me down," Betha said. "We need level ground if we're going to face them."

Angie agreed. The rest of the descent was a haphazard mix of running and controlled falling. Angie hit the level plain below the hill at a run, and had to jog a few yards to slow down without falling. She spun to face the hill as the others came up next to her.

Above them, just exiting the cave opening, a series of dark shadows, so black the only thing she could make out were the red eyes and an impression of size.

"The ones that were trying to herd us?" Angie whispered to Sebastian.

"The ones that were tracking us in the tunnels. I still don't sense the silent ones."

Angie dragged in a deep breath then let it out slowly. There was nowhere to run now. They could leave this realm and go somewhere else, come back after the demons lost track of them. But the beautiful monsters, the silent ones as Sebastian was calling them, might just follow. And even though Lisa wasn't good at moving between realms, she still might be able to follow now that they'd formed the triad of power. Angie's thread of demon magic still pulled toward Lisa, somewhere still inside the hill, but Angie couldn't tell how far away she was.

"Okay, witch," Carmen said to her. "Now what?"

Angie watched those dark shadows start down the hill, flowing over the dirt and gravel like black fog, rolling toward them. An avalanche of death and destruction made of darkness instead of snow.

She turned to Betha. "If we kill them, will that bring Lisa out to face us?"

"Maybe. She needs us to find Eloise. But maybe she'll just track us to Eloise."

"Aidan won't reveal where they are until Lisa is no longer a problem," Sebastian said, his gaze fully focused on the approaching demons.

"We're running out of time," Carmen snapped. "Do something?"

Angie faced the demons again and, because it was her instinct, she grabbed hold of her witch magic and built a circle around all of them. The spell spilled out of her, the circle closed up around them, the blue light spreading fast, the protective magic coming up with an almost audible snap. She blinked a little at how easy and quickly she'd been able to make the circle. And the surge of energy she felt after using her magic.

"Impressive," Carmen said.

Angie didn't answer.

"Now what?" Betha said. "We just stand here and wait for Lisa?"

"Yes," Angie said. "She needs us. This circle might not cut her off from our magical bond, but it will keep anything she throws at us from getting in." Angie closed her eyes and studied the circle. Then frowned and looked at her web.

On the metaphysical plane, her web had stopped dripping magic. The purple pieces of threads woven throughout the web were not as long as they'd been, but where they'd been draining away, Angie realized her own blue magic had filled in the gaps, glowing brighter blue than she'd ever seen it. The silver encasing her magic, that sparkling energy that increased everything when the triad formed, glowed and sparkled. But her demon magic thread was no longer pulling toward Lisa. Everything in her web was settled. Pulsing with power. But no longer being drained. And no longer calling to the other witch.

"Weird," she muttered. She opened her eyes and said, "I think I accidentally built a shield that, at least somewhat, blocks Lisa from accessing our magic. At least, I'm not still dripping away magic the way I was before. You?" She turned to Betha.

"I feel fine. I…" She frowned. "Better than fine. Stronger even than I did a few minutes ago."

"Good. That's useful."

She turned back just as the approaching demons slammed up against her shield, igniting an explosion of bright light and sizzling demon skin. The stench of fried meat and burnt ozone only slightly worse than the screech of outrage so loud it made Angie wince.

Closer, she could see more of the details of the demons now. There were three of them, somewhat ironically. With areas that could sort of be called wings of stretched membranes, though there didn't seem to be any bones holding those membranes out, so that the wings looked as much like smoke or cloaks flapping behind the dark bodies. The bodies themselves were still amorphous, even up close. An amoeba shaped fog that shifted and changed with their movement. Their heads were wedges of dark fog and red eyes, but when they screeched, they revealed a mouth rimmed with rows of teeth moving back down into their gullet.

They tested her protective circle, punching at it and screeching with each sizzle of contact. Angie hadn't consciously separated herself from the circle, which she usually had to do, but this time, the circle she'd built so swiftly wasn't linked to her, so she didn't feel the hits. Fortunately. Because the demons were relentless and persistent.

The shield held, though. Sturdy and safe.

Angie let out a deep breath when she was certain the demons wouldn't get through and that she wasn't going to feel each and every test and hit against the protective barrier. Her knees wobbled a bit as the adrenaline wavered. But she caught herself and ensured she wasn't going to fall down before Sebastian noticed.

Then she took another assessment of herself. Everything felt...fine. Her magic surged through her, stronger even than it had felt before closing the shield. And that surprised her. "I'd have thought putting a kink in the link between us all would...dampen the magic," she murmured aloud. "With Lisa cut off, or at least unable to keep draining us, I thought all that strength from the triad would be diminished."

She blinked at Betha. "It's not, though. I still have all that power that came with combining our magic."

Betha's gaze jumped to the attacking demons, then back to Angie. "I'm feeling strong, like I did after the magics combined. But also...pretty ordinary. I feel like my access to the magic is much like what it was before the bonding. I still feel good, and stronger than I should after our ordeal. I feel like there's a lot of magic there to access. But also like I can't quite access it."

"Is that because the circle limits our bond with Lisa? Or because you never had full access to it?" Since Betha said Angie was the witch, it made sense that she'd have a stronger bond to the actual magic of their triad.

"Not sure," Betha said. "Didn't have enough time to study it before she knocked me out." She glanced again at the attacking demons. "They could do this for a while."

"Got somewhere else to go?" Angie asked.

"Eloise."

"Is fine for now. We need to deal with Lisa."

"Who may decide just to leave us here until we wither or grow impatient."

Impatience was going to be a problem. Angie was happy to be safe inside her circle. But she wanted the confrontation with Lisa over sooner rather than later.

"She might also decide to send bigger demons at us," Carmen muttered.

"There aren't that many left here," Betha reminded her. "Nothing that we can't handle like this." She gestured to the enclosed circle.

"What if she imports them?" Carmen said.

Angie glanced at Carmen with a frown. Remembered the beautiful monsters somewhere in that hill. But before she could voice her concern, her suspicion, a voice from above them echoed across the plain.

"Angela Jordan, we have a reckoning!"

CHAPTER THIRTY-THREE

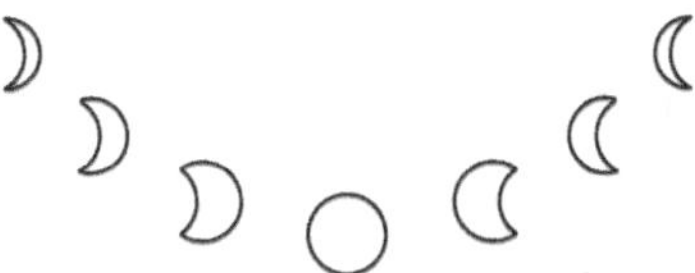

"Using your full name?" Carmen said, leaning in close to Angie. "Must be pissed."

"So am I," Angie said.

She looked up the hill to where Lisa stood above them at the tunnel entrance, staring down. Lisa was glowing now, a reddish gold halo around her that lit up the mountainside and spread all the way down to the valley floor, touching against Angie's protective circle and making it steam. The light should have made it difficult to see Lisa in the midst of the glow, but by some trick, Angie could see her clearly, wearing a gown now, made of the same golden scaled material as the vest she'd worn previously. It shimmered with pearlescent light and the scales looked more prominent on the dress. Her dark hair was wound up on top of her head and pinned with jewels. Her pale skin glowed almost as brightly as the light surrounding her, lit from within.

She looked like a woman trying to be a goddess and doing a passably decent job of it. But mostly, all Angie saw was someone who had forced Angie's hand. Again. Again, Angie found herself in a dangerous and deadly situation at the center of *someone else's* game. Someone else's machinations and goals. Someone else's purpose for her.

Someone else creating a mess. Leaving Angie to clean it up.

She was getting really tired of cleaning up after everyone else's messes.

"You're glowing," Sebastian whispered to her.

Angie glanced down and realized he was right. That same reddish gold glow that was surrounding Lisa was creating a halo of light around her now, too. She glanced at Betha. Same light. Same halo.

Angie looked back up to Lisa. They hadn't done this inside the caverns. But then her magic and Betha's had both been bound by the metal mittens Lisa had put on them. And Lisa had been draining away their combined power.

Without that constant drip in the background, the triad powers seemed to have only increased.

Good or bad? It meant Lisa had more power, but not all the power she'd been trying to steal. It could only be good that Angie had access to so much of the magic now.

Lisa started down the hill. But unlike their running, tripping, slipping descent, she floated down, using the magic that circled her like wings, flapping them gently as she dropped slowly to the plain.

"Could have used that earlier?" Carmen said. "Why did we risk a broken neck coming down the old-fashioned way?"

"Didn't know I could fly now," Angie said. She actually wasn't sure she could do what Lisa was doing. Maybe that was something Lisa learned before the triad formed.

Lisa alighted onto the black sand and the bright glow around her faded back a little as the light she'd been using for wings folded onto her back.

"You are really making this more complicated than it has to be," she said to Angie. "Give me Eloise, and I won't drain all your powers. I'll let you keep…something."

Angie raised a brow. "Really? Threatening now? When we have the advantage?"

Lisa laughed, a happy, trilling sound that was at complete odds to their situation and the dark demonic shadows still testing Angie's circle. That laugh had echoes of Eloise's chuckle, but it was higher, and there was a slightly discordant note at the edge that made it a little difficult to listen to. Like there was an echo Angie couldn't quite hear.

"What advantage?" Lisa said, smiling, looking happy and friendly. "You're stuck in a circle."

"From which you can't read our minds anymore." Angie was mostly guessing, but it seemed reasonable since Lisa wasn't able to drain their magic now either.

A little twitch of Lisa's mouth, a slight tic in her cheek confirmed Angie's guess and gave away that Lisa was not happy with this turn of events.

But Lisa kept her smile in place. "Oh. That was just a bit

of fun. I don't have to read your minds. We share a bond. It will follow us wherever we go. Won't that be lovely."

"I will not let you kill Eloise," Betha said.

"But you're willing to kill me. I came directly from her, look just like her. You could say I was her child. So you want to kill your lover's child? Is that it?"

"You are insane."

"I am what you made me."

The shadow demons flowed forward and crashed repeatedly against Angie's circle. Angie kept her gaze on Lisa, ignoring the attack. Ignoring the sound of Betha's hiss and Carmen attempting to shut Betha up.

Angie watched Lisa so closely, she knew the moment something changed. Without having to read her mind, she could tell the instant Lisa had called in more demons.

A slight glow, a silvery sparkle around the edges. Almost like reading her aura, Angie realized. Well. Laura, her friend and aura reading teacher, would be really proud of her. Even if Angie was reading the aura of a non-human entity. Maybe more proud of her for that.

And with that slight silvery sparkle, Angie also felt a little tug at the magical link that connected the three of them. She thought something rude at Lisa, just to make sure the circle was still keeping them separated. Lisa showed no reaction to the thought. In fact, most of her attention was still on Betha, a smirk on her face as she stared at the other witch.

Their magic was still definitely linked then. But Lisa couldn't access Angie and Betha's enough to steal it. And she couldn't read their minds. Not while they were inside the circle.

Could Angie reach out and tug at Lisa's magic?

The thought hovered in the back of her mind, but took a back seat when she felt the ground beneath her tremble.

Betha cursed. Carmen cursed. Sebastian moved up close to Angie.

He whispered, "The Aminore and the Helavitee."

"From inside the tunnels?" She continued to stare at Lisa.

"Thees arrived by the lightning strike, the way they left last time."

"There are still some of those in the tunnels, then."

Sebastian was quiet a moment. Then, "Yes. But they're heading this way. They're close enough for me to sense them now."

Angie nodded. "How long have you been controlling the gods' pet demons?" she asked Lisa.

Betha spun and stared at the side of Angie's head, then at Lisa. "She can't control them. No one but a god can."

Lisa giggled. "I am a god. Remember. I just need to get rid of the others to take my rightful place. It's a small inconvenience. Unfortunate that I need help, but…well, even the gods themselves can't destroy their own realm." She shrugged as if this was all perfectly ordinary.

Something in the potion Betha had made, using sand from the god realm, must have given Lisa certain powers over other demons. That it gave her power over *these* kinds of demons was…horrifying.

"Have you kept them from attacking Eloise and Betha

this whole time?" Angie asked. "That wasn't the forest or the circle of blood Betha had drawn. That was you."

"It was. I needed her and Eloise alive until you got here. Until we could form the bond. Until I had enough power to rise up to my rightful place. Now, though, the rest of you are really no longer needed. Well, except for destroying the god realm. Once we do that, you're no longer needed. And if you cooperate, I'll make your deaths quick and easy."

"What of Eloise?" Betha said.

"What of her?"

"You just called yourself her child. Yet you're intent on killing her."

"Yes, well, having to stretch my self across two entities can be a little…much. I'd rather just be me." She waved a hand in the air. "It doesn't matter. An inconvenience. I'll get to her as soon as I've killed you both. Then you and Eloise can finally rest. Angie will have her freedom from all this 'demon stuff,' and I'll take my place in the demonic celestial pantheon as was always meant to happen. Everyone will be so happy."

"Yeah, no," Carmen said.

"Oh don't worry," Lisa said. "You aren't here just as demon fodder, I promise. Your glorious sacrifice will seal my ascension. That's the whole point. That's why I nudged Betha to ensure you were brought along on this mission. She was going to just have the hunters join Angie, but really, what good would they be? No, I needed someone properly corrupted by demons for the sacrifice. That's where the real power is. And you don't have the will to control your fear the way they do, and I need your fear."

"You're one crazy bitch," Carmen muttered.

"I am what I was made to be," Lisa said. Her smile was more brittle now. Less light and fluffy and happy.

The ground trembled again. Angie knew the beautiful monsters were closer. She could almost see their shadows reflected in Lisa's red red eyes.

If the shadows of the approaching demons hadn't been enough to confirm these were the Aminore and Helavitee, the silence that proceeded them would have been. The sound of the screeching shadow demons dropped suddenly. Lisa's laughter. The sizzle as the shadow demons tested Angie's shield. The crinkling rocks and the skittering sand and pebbles dropping down the hill behind Lisa. Angie could no longer hear any of it.

She glanced up long enough to confirm that two Animore had come from the cave above and were moving down the hill, as beautifully horrible as they'd been around Betha's house, though now Angie didn't find them fascinating or alluring. Now they were just one more problem to deal with. The hail of rocks and sand in front of them built up at the base of the hill into little mounts of debris.

The smell of sulfur and the sickly sweat detritus scent form their home realm filled the surrounding area now. The slim light that came from the golden rivers and the sparkling golden stars in the stalactites and cavern roof above were blotted out as deep shadows fell across Angie's circle.

Through the silence, Lisa's voice floated to her. She

watched Lisa's mouth move, but the sound reached her ears strangely, at a different time to Lisa's mouth moving. Making it look like Lisa was an actor in a dubbed movie.

"This will be easier on you if you just give up," Lisa said, shifting her gaze from Carmen to Angie. "I promise, I'll make it easy. The demons would love to extend your deaths, to really drag out the pain and torment. Being able to kill an apocalypse witch is, oh so very rare. It would make them feel better to be able to do it as slowly and painfully as possible. But I promise, if you cooperate, I won't let them."

Angie dragged in a deep breath as she let her magic build under her skin, the strength of it filling her up and making her nerves tingle. She let out the breath slowly, carefully.

"No, Lisa. That's not what's going to happen here."

CHAPTER THIRTY-FOUR

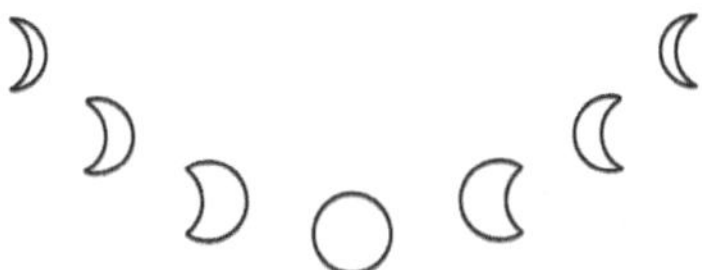

Angie didn't have to hear the crash of the demon fists above her. She watched Lisa's eyes gleam as she smiled at Angie. Then the surprise when those silently pounding hands couldn't break Angie's containment circle. If she could hear anything beyond the circle, she was sure she'd hear the sounds of the demons screeching and growling. The frustrated howls as they attempted to break her protective bubble and only got shocks and singed skin for their trouble. The stench of burnt meat got stronger. And under that and the sulfur scent, a faint hint of blood.

Blood around demons was dangerous. That one of the demons was bleeding could lead to some chaos.

That was fine. Angie didn't care what the demons did to each other. She only had eyes for Lisa.

Lisa snarled at her. Her voice once again floated through

the air, hitting Angie's ears out of sync with the movement of her mouth. "You can't hold them off forever. They are the minions of the gods. They will not be denied."

"Still just gonna hang out in here all day?" Carmen murmured.

"You in a hurry to get out when she just confirmed she wants to sacrifice you?"

"Not really. No."

Angie might have snort-laughed if she wasn't so focused on calling up more power. All the witchy blue power, coated in silver, felt like bubbles of potential in her chest and stomach. All the possibilities filling her head. Magic unlike anything she'd ever wielded. And that was after accessing demon magic. And that purple magic.

Now, suddenly, Angie could see how the web all wove it together. Not just individual threads for her to grasp. She sat in the center. She *was* the web. The power. And there was so much of it! The spell fell from her lips, her voice that deep, guttural tone that took her when her magic rose. Her fingers and hands moved to the rhythm of the words, forming the backbone of the spell.

This wasn't a spell she'd known before. Not something she'd studied. It was just there in her head. But it hadn't been something she'd gleaned from either Lisa or Betha. She was certain neither of them knew this spell either. This was something else, something that arose from the triad link.

Betha's voice joined her, and the strength of that added power filled Angie's vision with light, impossible to see what was happening beyond the circle. Didn't matter. She wove the last few gestures of the spell together. And when she said the last word, hers and Betha's voice sounded as one perfect harmony.

Somewhere, through the silence that surrounded them, Angie heard thunder boom.

She blinked away the light that had filled her vision during the spell, taking in her surroundings with a satisfied nod.

The shadow demons were pinned to the sand under an invisible weight, not dead. Just immobilized. If they'd been able to make noise, she still wouldn't have heard it, but they couldn't make noise now either. She and Betha had trapped them inside a frozen moment. They couldn't escape, couldn't move, couldn't act. Trapped in a condensed bit of time and now harmless.

That was a very handy spell.

"You could have just killed them." Lisa's voice, once again floating to them in that strange dubbed way that was out of sync with her mouth's movements.

"That's the only thing you know, isn't it?" Angie said. Her voice had a deep, echoing quality to it that was a little distracting, but she tried to ignore it. "That's what you'd have us be. Killing machines. Nothing more."

"What else is an apocalypse witch but a bringer of death and destiny?"

"What else?" Angie raised her hands, murmured a small spell, and let little balls of swirling pink light form in her palms. The light twirled into the shape of flowers, then butterflies, then two owls, and then vanished back into hands. "This. This is what else."

"Somone weak and afraid to kill?" Lisa laughed. "Someone who plays at illusions and can't think beyond small power?"

"Someone in control of her own power."

Lisa stopped laughing abruptly and snarled at Angie. "I am a god!"

"A god of death? I will have no part of that."

"We are linked now. You can't escape. Join me or die."

"Your offer earlier was join you until you killed me. Are you saying you'd let us live now?"

Lisa shrugged. "You could prove useful." She glanced at the trapped demons. "A neat trick."

"Not a trick," Angie said. "Witch magic."

Above and around her, Angie was aware of the giant demons still trying to break into her circle. More had reached them from the plane, the lightning strike that brought additional beautiful monsters. The new Aminore pounded at her shield, and some of the Helavitee now flew above them. All of them testing and battering at the barrier Angie had created. The two that had moved down from the tunnel now stood behind Lisa, flanking her as if they were her guard. She made a sharp gesture and they rejoined the others, attempting to shatter Angie's shield.

The ground shiver. But the shield held.

At the edge of her awareness, Angie could feel the power in the shield. The strength of her circle. There was always a tiny worry at the back of her mind that something would go wrong and a circle would break. But this one…this one felt like a titanium casing. Breaking it would take more than a few demons, even if they were extraordinarily powerful ones.

That was so reassuring, it made her brave. Brave enough to try this new magnificent spell on the them. She chanted again, moving her fingers, heard Betha's voice join in, watched Lisa scowl. Watched her mouth form the "No!" without hearing it this time. Angie's head was filled with magic and the power of the spell.

She cast it toward one of the demons at the edge of her circle, one at a time for these monsters. They were larger and stronger than the shadow beasts. She turned to see one of the winged Helavitee momentarily wrapped up in a shimmer of silvery blue light. And then it was pressed into the ground, flat on its back, unmoving.

She repeated the spell, letting all the magic that flowed freely between her and Betha inside the circle increase its power. Cast it against another demon. And again.

Until she had all six of the giant beasts pinned to the ground in their bubbles of frozen time. Two Helavitee. Four Aminore, including the two from the tunnels. All incapacitated by her spell.

Sound came rushing back in, ending that weird silence that was their weapon. The tinkling slide of pebbles and rocks down the hill behind Lisa. The distant rush of golden rivers. An echo from air movement that filled the ginormous space.

It only occurred to Angie after she'd finished her spell, after the sound returned and she let the glow of power dim and sink back into her body, that she'd been casting magic out of a protective circle…without breaking the circle.

That shouldn't have been possible. The protective circles she usually built were designed to keep things out, to keep things in, or both. When she worked magic that was new and potentially dangerous, or she didn't want interference, she drew circles to keep the outside world out and her magic in. To keep both her and those around her safe. When there was an outside danger, she built a circle to keep those dangers out. But if she stepped over the line or sent magic out, she broke the circle and it would have to be reset.

The point of the protective circles was to prevent the movement of magic and other supernatural things over the barrier. She could even keep most mundane things from crossing her particular circles—except for cats who didn't seem to be bound by such things—but if she used magic and cast it *outside* the circle, it broke the circle.

That hadn't happened this time.

She glanced at Sebastian, but his attention was on Lisa. Angie was afraid to say anything aloud and give Lisa any bit of leverage. But casting magic to affect things outside her circle without breaking the circle was…

Well, it shouldn't have been possible. And that it had happened meant whatever this magic she was that she was wielding was even more powerful than she'd guessed.

And if Lisa figured out that what Angie was doing shouldn't be possible, they were all in trouble. Lisa wasn't a trained witch. She might not understand that what Angie was doing was generally impossible. That casting these spells should have broken open Angie's circle. Really, Angie should have realized sooner. But the power had just come, the spell had spilled out.

Power that Lisa had access to, as well.

Betha had joined Angie to make this spell work, though. And Lisa didn't have that. She was alone, cut off from their combined powers enough that she couldn't use Betha or Angie. Angie had to hope that her ignorance of proper witch magic and spells kept her from realizing…

She might be able to use her magic to cast through Angie's circle.

Angie's sense of security in her circle, that sense of bravery that came from being encased in titanium, fled. So much for bravery and immutable security.

But she held Lisa's gaze and bluffed her way past the horrifying realization.

Lisa was snarling at her, and curls of purple magic encompassed her hands. "I am a god! I will not be denied."

A smart ass reply leapt to Angie's tongue, but she kept it to herself. Now that she worried Lisa's magic could get through her shield, even if she couldn't tap the combined triad magic, Angie didn't want to tempt the other witch. She did quietly check the shield again, and she poured more power into it. Reflective power.

Wait. Reflective power.

She smiled. The ways she could use magic now were astounding. She wove a new spell into her shield, a spell to reflect any power thrown at it. She'd never done this before, never even thought of it, but the minute she'd thought "reflective" power, she knew exactly the spell to use. The shapes to make with her fingers, the words to weave into the shield.

Betha didn't join her this time, though she felt Betha move up closer to her. When the spell was done, Betha asked, "What did you just do?"

"Reflective spell," she murmured. Because it would be better for Lisa to know she shouldn't throw magic at this circle now.

"How?" Betha asked.

Angie shrugged. She wasn't entirely sure. The knowledge was just there. That she was the "witch" of the triad now made more sense. Whatever spells were hidden in the depths of the apocalypse witch bond, they were obviously Angie's to control and access.

Lisa stalked close to the edge of the circle, her snarl distorting her face so that she no longer looked quite so much like Eloise. A blessing for Betha, Angie hoped.

"You cannot hold me out forever. I will have the prize I have been waiting for. I have worked for. For centuries! It is my destiny and I will not be denied."

"I wouldn't recommend throwing that at the shield right now." Angie nodded down to Lisa's hands, now glowing brightly with purple light, so much that her hands were no longer visible.

"Who do you think you are?" Lisa slammed her hands against the circle's barrier, hard, letting the purple magic she'd built up loose.

The magic spread across the shield, a purple rush through

the flaring blue light. Angie narrowed her eyes as the light brightened. The blue light swirled in eddies like liquid, surrounding the purple light, gathering into whirlpools, spinning and spinning and coalescing into one big storm of light.

"I'd step away if I were you," Angie said to Lisa. The people inside the circle with her, moved closer to her, even Sebastian, as that light twisted into a storm that filled the entire outer edge of the circle.

And then the purple magic lashed out from the shield, arrowing right into Lisa. Knocking her fifty yards backward so that she landed in a heap against the side of the hill, rocks and pebbles rushing down around her as sand mushroomed up into the air, settling like black glitter around her.

"That had to hurt," Carmen said.

"Is she still even alive?" Betha said, her voice quiet.

"She's alive," Angie said with a sigh, watching Lisa's hand twitch. "She hit the shield with enough power to incapacitate us, not kill us. She needs us alive to finish her *ascension.*"

"That was a pretty big jolt backward," Carmen said.

"Rebound spells are like that." The one she'd added to the protective circle wasn't anything like the rebound spells she'd used before. This one reflected all the power back at the user. Sometimes, rebound spells could bounce around and cause innocent bystanders to be hurt. Angie liked this one better, that it just hurt the person casting the dangerous magic.

Lisa sat up, shaking dust out of her hair and off her scaled dress. The purple shimmer over the golden scales had increased, and Angie realized it had protective elements too that must have absorbed some of the backlash. Lucky for Lisa. She might still be unconscious.

"Well done," Lisa said, chuckling. "That'll be useful when it's mine."

Angie didn't comment.

Lisa pushed up to her feet, remaining above them on the hill. The glow around her increased, a show to impress and intimidate. "But magic isn't my only talent," she said. "And not my primary skill."

"Except that you can't read our minds through the protective circle," Angie pointed out.

"I don't need to," Lisa said. "Because I've already got everything from you I need." She turned her gaze on Sebastian.

Angie stepped in front of him without thinking, because something about the gleam in Lisa's red eyes and her sly smirk sent a wave of alarm through Angie.

Lisa walked down the hill with seeming ease, despite having just been blown backward by her own magic. She kept her gaze on Sebastain as she did.

"Would you like them returned?" Lisa murmured to him. "After all this time. Would you like them back?"

What the hell was Lisa talking about?

A pair of shapes formed close to the protective circle, materializing out of the air, swirling in dark sparkles of light and purplish shadows.

It took Angie a beat, maybe two before she realized what

Lisa had been implying. Too late to react. Too late to warn Sebastian…

The shapes coalesced, came together, grew solid. Formed two humans, a man and a woman, both staring at the circle.

Angie spun to face Sebastian just as he murmured, "Mum? Dad?"

CHAPTER THIRTY-FIVE

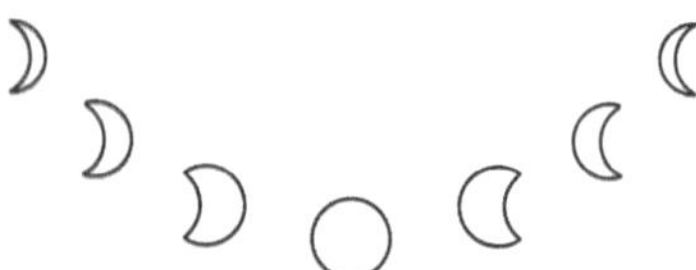

Heart thumping, Angie took Sebastian's face in her hands, his beard scruff rough against her palms. "It's an illusion," she said, desperately trying to get him to meet her eyes.

The shadows that looked like his parents stood silently on the other side of her circle, but Angie could almost feel their stare. The faint golden light from the sparkling minerals far above them reflected in Sebastian's dark eyes right over the top of the faint red glow.

"Listen to me, Seb," she said urgently. "It's not real. They are not real. You know this. Don't let another demon use them to fuck with you. Do you hear me?"

His gaze remained fixed on the two shadows that looked like his parents.

Angie had no idea what his parents had actually looked like. He'd lost them to a demon realm when he was just a teenager. He'd tried to chase after them, been dragged out by Aidan, only to have a demon latch onto his young mind and two years later convince him that his parents were somehow still alive and he had to rescue them. It was a horrible story. Painful and heartbreaking. And he'd only told her about it a couple of weeks ago. Demon hunters didn't talk about when and how they became hunters, and she hadn't pushed him for those stories. He volunteered this one. And she still hurt for that child, the young man who had lost both parents at the same time so horribly.

He'd become a demon hunter then. But he'd essentially had to deal with losing his parents twice thanks to a demon manipulating his mind.

And now another monster was trying the same fucking thing.

His breath left him on an exhale that Angie felt in her own chest. The pain. The loss. All at once. Suddenly. Unexpectedly.

When he wouldn't meet her gaze, she glanced back at the two illusions. They looked solid enough. A man, about Sebastian's height, maybe a little taller. Dark skin, hair cut short, clean shaven. He was dressed in a pair of dress slacks and a button down shirt with thick cuffs and collar. The woman beside him was smaller, thin, almost too thin—his mother had been sick at the time—dressed in a long white nightgown, her black hair curling loose around her shoulders. They both stared at Sebastian with dark eyes, the woman's actually reminded Angie of Sebastian's eyes. And it was disturbing to see the resemblance to him in both the ghosts.

To know that they looked like the parents Sebastian carried in his memory.

She snarled at Lisa. "Stop this. Enough."

"What are you going to do about it? From the safety of your little cage."

Angie felt the magic beneath her skin, building again. And there was a spell there at the tip of her tongue, dancing along the tips of her fingers. But she ignored it. She needed to pull Sebastian out of this illusion.

She returned her attention to him, panic and pain filling her chest. "Seb. Sebastian. Please. Listen to me."

"Mum?" he murmured again, and tried to move around Angie.

Damn it. If he walked out of the circle, he'd break it. And if he broke the circle, Lisa would be back inside her head. She shoved herself in front of him again. He was physically stronger than her, but she was no small woman and he was so off balance, she managed to shove him back the step he'd taken toward the shadows that looked like his parents.

"Sebastian," she barked in his face. "Those aren't your parents. Your parents are dead."

He blinked. The red in his eyes flared briefly.

She tried again. "Decades ago. They couldn't have survived. They didn't survive. Remember. The demon who fucked with you and made you think they were here? This is the same thing. Lies. All lies."

"No, this isn't," Lisa said, suddenly standing right next to the circle. "I saved them. When they got into the demon realm. I saved them. I've been protecting them all this time.

Don't you miss them. They've missed you. Why aren't you going to them?"

Angie felt a tear track down her cheek. She could almost feel the pain Sebastian was in, and Lisa, that *bitch,* was making it worse.

"Shut. Up." She glared at the witch and realized how deep her voice was, how much magic was building with her anger. She controlled it. She didn't want to accidentally hurt anyone inside the circle. But she had never hated another person more than she did in that moment. Hated. From the depths of her soul. Because of the pain Lisa was inflicting on Sebastian.

"Dad? How?" Sebastian tried to move around Angie again.

"Damn it, damn it. Listen to me." She pushed him backward, and then took his face in her hands again. There was a glow around her hands, the magic building. And she was terrified in her panic she'd hurt him. She had to make him see her. See through the lie. "This is a trick. Lisa is tricking you. She will kill you."

He tried to move around Angie again.

"Damn it, Seb, if you go to those lies you will break my circle and Lisa will kill us all."

Sebastian didn't stop moving, but his expression changed. A tic next to his eye. His mouth worked into a different kind of a frown.

"Sebastian," Angie said quieter. "She will kill me. If you break the circle, Lisa will kill me."

He blinked hard and gave his head a shake. He was still

looking at the shadows, but his forehead creased and his jaw tightened. "Why aren't they speaking?"

The man who was supposed to be his father said, "We've missed you, son. Join us."

Even Angie heard the accent was wrong. She'd never heard his parents speak, of course. But she knew what Sebastian's original accent sounded like. The burr and deep rolling cadence of Manchester, where he'd been born and raised. He rarely sounded like that these days, unless he was teasing her or playing a part. His accent, though still with the lilt of England in it, was softer and less pronounced most of the time. A subtle flavor of England rather than the bold original.

Though she might be wrong, she would have assumed his parents sounded similar to that original accent. Had similar speaking styles. But the shadow father had spoken with an almost American flatness. No real accent at all. Barely similar to the way Sebastian sounded now.

"See," Angie said, her voice intent and quiet. "Those aren't really your parents. They can't be. You know that. Deep down. You know that."

He gave his head another shake and squeezed his eyes shut, opening them suddenly. Looked directly at Angie when he did. "They're shadows. Not real."

She smiled as the panic started to ebb. "That's right. Not real. A cruel trick. To get you to break the circle. So Lisa can kill us. A monster's trick."

"I'm not a monster," Lisa said, pouting and sounding hurt. Then she laughed. "I'm a god."

"You're a bitch," Carmen said.

And Angie nodded. On this, she and Carmen were in agreement.

"Even I wouldn't have pulled out the dead parent card," Carmen muttered. "Well, maybe in my youth."

"I don't need to know about that right now," Angie said, her gaze still intent on Sebastian, holding his gaze. The flare of red in the depths of the brown was stronger, but he was looking at her, and she could see he was *there*. Not living in the past. Not lost in that horrible, futile hope.

"Lies," he said, shaking his head. "More fucking lies."

"Yup. Just lies. That's what monsters do."

"Not a monster," Lisa sang again. "Though you could call me a demon if you really wanted to. I will be their god. I suppose it's appropriate."

Angie ignored her. "You with me," she murmured to Sebastian.

"Mostly," he said. "That hit harder than I would have expected. Even the…that first demon who made me see my father in dreams, didn't show them to me so… They weren't standing right there while I was awake."

Angie wrapped her arms around him, kissed his temple, his cheek, the scruff rough against her lips. "I've got you. You're okay now. Just a bunch of lies. Not real."

She'd been about to say the lies couldn't hurt him, but they had. She could feel it. They'd hurt him a lot. And she very much wanted to hurt Lisa in turn for that. Make her suffer, too.

She swallowed down that impulse. Revenge, seeking

repayment for wrongs… That led a witch down a dangerous road. One she'd chosen not to take more than once. She'd avoid that path again this time, if she could. But the siren song of vengeance still sang in her blood.

And she knew her eyes were more red now than green.

Hugging Sebastian, his arms tight around her, she ignored Lisa continuing to try and taunt them. Angie put her full focus into Sebastian, into settling him and bringing him back to her fully. When he'd finally told her this story, it was a warning, a warning Aidan had wanted him to give her, that Sebastian would go to great lengths to save Angie. She'd already seen him do that. And he wasn't stupid. He hadn't done any of the things she'd feared right after hearing his story, including coming into the demon realm looking for a cure for her all by himself.

He wouldn't do anything stupid now. At least, not anymore.

She glanced back to see the shadows were still standing there, solid and horribly real looking. With a half snarl, she muttered a spell and flung her hands out at them. They faded back into the darkness around them, disappearing. Leaving no trace. Not even footprints in the black sand.

Never there. Always just shadows.

The illusion was half witch magic and half that strange purple magic that Lisa wielded best. A mix of that and her psychic skills, conjuring Sebastian's parents from deep in his memories. Maybe using what she'd picked up of the story from Angie's thoughts to make things worse. That Lisa had gotten into Sebastian's head at all was worrying. But he could hardly be expected to will away Lisa's powers while he was unconscious, and Lisa didn't apparently have any scruples.

With the shadows gone, Angie looked back at Sebastian. He was staring at the spot again. "Very easy to erase," he murmured.

"Never there in the first place," she said. Again. "Just shadows. Drawings on the air."

He nodded, but there was a deep, painful sadness in his expression that hurt Angie just to look at. She cupped his cheek and he met her gaze. "I'm sorry she did that. I'm sorry you had to experience that."

"I'll be okay. Mostly just shock. Haven't seen them in…a long time."

She wasn't sure what to say to make things better, probably couldn't make things better, so she just pulled him back into a hug.

"So sweet," Lisa sang. "Such love. Such weakness. Just like Betha and Eloise. So much love. So much weakness. You'd think humans would learn. Though that's probably why the gods don't love. Can't be weak as a god. Wouldn't do."

"Can we kill her now?" Carmen asked. "Or really, will you two kill her now. She's fucking irritating."

"Can't," Lisa said with another giggle. "They'd need to drop the circle. We have to be bonded. Fully. No blocks. And I'll be in their heads then. Won't be able to get around that. Once I'm there, I'm in charge. I'm the strongest. The one who will be the god. You're my servants." She glanced at the still trapped demons. "Though maybe you'll be more useful to me alive?" She bobbed her head around, almost like a bird, as she considered that possibility. "Or maybe not. I'll have to consider that. Carry on."

She did a little dance on the mountain and spun in a circle, the light of her magic glowing brighter around her.

"That woman is not well," Carmen said.

"She's insane," Betha said. "She's never been fully sane, but this is the worst I've seen her."

"She's got the bond she's been waiting for now," Angie said. "She's not hiding anything from you anymore."

Betha's mouth flattened. "Probably."

"So," Carmen said, almost casually, "our choices are to continue hanging out inside the circle until she finds some psychological pain point that gets one of us to break. We run away to another realm, where she will just follow or send her pet monsters to kill us. Or…we attack her and try to kill her before she kills all of us. I got that right?"

Angie let out a rough breath. Carmen was right. Their choices weren't great. She wasn't sure what she'd been hoping for at the end of this. How she'd thought this would go. They had to stop Lisa. But they weren't going to talk her out of the god delusion. They either fought her, and hoped they'd win. Or they ran.

But there was nowhere to go. Lisa might not be as good at portaling as Betha, or even Angie. But she did know how to. And now with all their combined powers, she'd be able to find them. Eventually. The destruction she'd leave in her wake wasn't something Angie wanted to think about either.

She released Sebastain and held his gaze. "What do you think?" she asked quietly.

"Not a lot of choice now."

"I know. But I was hoping for another way. Especially after…"

"I'll be okay now," he said. "She can't get in. And she just showed me the worst she could."

She studied his face. The flare of red in his eyes was dimmed, his jaw was tight. But he looked okay. Grounded here in their current reality. She'd trust him to tell her the truth about his state. Because they were about to go into battle.

Glancing at Betha, she said, "You ready for this?"

"I've been waiting for this as long as she has," Betha said.

Angie wanted to ask if Betha was prepared for the consequences to Eloise, but they'd been over this all before. Angie was stalling. For a lot of reasons. She didn't want the others in danger. She didn't want to have to kill Lisa, even with her demon god delusions. And she didn't want to open her mind to Lisa again.

But maybe…maybe there was another option.

Lisa had been draining their magic. Slowly dripping it away. What if they did that to Lisa? What if between them, Angie and Betha drained her until she had no power left? Or at least not enough to cause any more trouble. They'd have to find a way to break the triad, so that Lisa couldn't just regain her powers. Or separate enough that they were too far away for Lisa to make a power grab. But at least it would mean they didn't have to kill her.

Betha was watching her closely. So Angie mouthed, *Drain her instead of kill her?*

Betha frowned. Her gaze jumping between Lisa and Angie. Draining Lisa would minimize the damage to Eloise, too. And it might give Betha more time to…fix the mistake that resulted in Lisa. Without Lisa fighting back or threatening to destroy Eloise, Betha might be able to find a solution. Angie could help. They might be able to save both women.

Slow, Betha nodded. Two against one. They'd have to work fast, and Lisa would fight back. But Lisa herself had proved it was possible. Their bond meant they shared things. Thoughts. Powers. History. Knowledge. Lisa would know the minute the circle dropped what they were trying to do. But if they acted fast. Coordinated what they did…

"Might work," Betha said so quietly her voice was almost inaudible. She glanced at Lisa again.

Angie looked back to see Lisa still spinning in circles on the side of the hill, her gaze turned up to the cavern roof high overhead, with its golden star dotted stalactites. As if sensing her gaze, Lisa looked down and smiled at Angie, looking friendly and harmless and sweet.

"It's a beautiful place, isn't it?" Lisa said.

"Sure," Angie said.

Lisa's grin grew. "This will be the new god realm. I'm looking forward to my ascension." She faced them fully, her glowing halo brightening around her.

Angie moved with Betha to stand in front of Sebastian and Carmen. She had to trust them to take care of each other —and she did trust Sebastian at least to take care of Carmen and Carmen not to stab him in the back. This time.

If this was going to work, Angie and Betha would have to focus on Lisa completely, and also keep Lisa's attention entirely on them.

And hope Lisa hadn't thought of a way to stop them before they got started.

Lisa tilted her head to one side and her smile softened. "I will miss you when you're gone."

Angie raised a hand, prepared to cut the circle.

Just as Lisa shot a bolt of purple magic.

Right through the protective barrier of the circle.

CHAPTER THIRTY-SIX

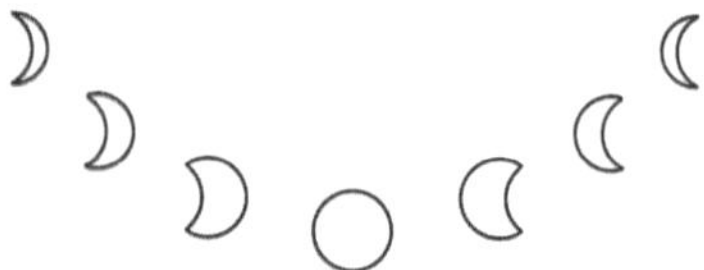

Angie dove to the side as she realized her protective circle wasn't going to stop Lisa's magic. It all happened so fast, she didn't have time to scream a warning, didn't have time to make sure Sebastian and the others reacted. She hit the ground as the purple bolt of power flew over her head, so close, she felt the tingling bite of it against her cheek.

She rolled to make sure Sebastian hadn't been hit. He was still standing, but to one side, staring hard at a spiraling ball of purple magic. Carmen had hit the ground next to Betha. Sebastian made a grunting noise and then flipped his hand out. The ball of magic continued on its way, flying harmlessly past everyone, deeper into the black sand landscape, where it slammed into a rocky hill, exploding the rocks into a shower of golden light.

Angie flipped back to face Lisa, rolling to her feet. Just as Lisa flung another bundle of purple light at her.

Prepared this time, Angie grabbed hold of her own purple magic on the metaphysical plane, then caught the bolt in between her cupped hands. Instinct. Knowledge from Lisa, she realized. The purple magic was Lisa's specialty. But Angie had absorbed her knowledge of it with the bonding. It was almost more like wizard magic. Instant. No spell required to use it with brute force.

Useful.

Angie collected the magic in a bundle of swirling power in between her hands, and before Lisa could throw more, beamed the magic right back at her. Lisa laughed as the magic hit her in the chest, sizzling over her scaled dress, swirling around it, before sinking back into her skin.

"Tickles," she said.

"Scary bitch," Carmen muttered.

Betha came up next to Angie, both of them facing Lisa.

Lisa moved down the hill, walking this time instead of flying. Her red eyes glowed brightly and her smile was now a smirk. The giddy, laughing, mad woman act fell away with each step.

"Took you two long enough," she said.

Angie took hold of all that magic that flowed through her, infused her web, filled her with knowledge and strength. Lisa started to run toward them.

Angie yelled, "Now!" And sent a rush of demon magic from her palm at Lisa even as she grabbed at the power they all shared and pulled it toward her.

Lisa stumbled as the demon magic hit her, magic that she was made of. Unlike demons, this didn't kill her, but she didn't roll through the hit the way she would have with the purple magic. Angie made note of that and threw more demon magic at her, a red stream of pure power arrowing toward Lisa's chest.

She felt the presence of the others in her head now. Not just Lisa, but Betha as well. Their thoughts shared. Their knowledge shared.

It was almost enough to distract her. Almost enough to make her stumble.

Lisa tossed some of the demon magic she held back at Angie and Angie had to raise a shield from the purple magic to stop it. Lisa's laugh echoed around the flare of light.

Beside her, Betha was murmuring a spell. Angie sent a pulse of her witch magic to Betha to aid the spell, then shot a mixed magic bolt of power at Lisa. She did it on instinct, the combination of demon magic and purple magic she'd been using mixing into a spiraling stake of power that slammed into Lisa's chest.

This jolted the other woman back a step. She snarled and flung more demon magic at Angie. Angie didn't have the scale covered clothing to absorb the power so when it hit her, it hurt like hell, burning through her limbs and over her skin.

She looked down to see the power sink into her, leaving no outward evidence of harm. The burning sensation cooled almost instantly. But she wasn't keen on taking another hit like that.

Betha finished her spell and flung her hands out. A

whirlwind of black sand rose up around Lisa, encompassing her, swallowing her up so that she was barely visible.

Angie used the distraction to grab at more of Lisa's power. Not just dripping it away. Pulling it into her in huge gulping swallows. A waterfall of magic, directed into her web.

More lines of magic speared out through the web, an intricate pattern growing as she dragged in Lisa's power.

There was more here than she'd realized. Not just the demon magic or that purple blended magic. There was something else, something she'd never encountered before. It wasn't the silvery glow that encompassed all their powers after the bonding either. It was…shimmery with no real color that her mind could interpret.

And when she touched it, it hurt.

She felt blood dripping down her nose. The more she pulled in, the more that magic without color tightened around her brain, increasing the pain exponentially.

"What the hell is that?" she shouted over the sounds of the whirlwind.

Purple magic shot out from the storm of black sand, pocketing the ground around Betha and Angie.

"It's from the god realm," Betha said, gasping. She was pulling that magic in too. "It's part of what made her."

"How the hell has she survived with that?"

"I am of that." Lisa's voice from the whirlwind. "It is me. I am a god."

Her voice was an echoing boom. And for a moment, Angie could believe Lisa was a god. Believe that this magic she'd carried inside her from the god realm really had turned her into something beyond her outer appearance.

But it had also taken her sanity.

With their thoughts blended, with the echoes of other things in her head, Angie was certain of it now. Lisa hadn't been acting insane. Betha was right. The other witch wasn't in her right mind. There was only lust for power and a certain knowledge that she was destined to rule everything. There was no logic there, though. Delusions and imaginings, but nothing that smacked of awareness of the real world. Nothing Angie could latch on to and talk sense to Lisa.

Angie wondered if it wasn't just that Lisa had come into being this way because of the potion that broke her off from Eloise. Angie wondered if the magic she'd been carrying with her this whole time might have actually caused the break in her mind.

And if that were the case, what the hell would this stuff do to Angie and Betha?

Too late now. She dragged in more of Lisa's magic. Shot power back at the witch when she broke through the sand storm. Kept pulling in that magic, despite the pain.

And suddenly, her mind filled with…well things her human mind couldn't comprehend. There were images there. Lights. Movement. Shadows. Impressions of things that, had she been another kind of being, she thought she might be able to understand. But as it was, what filled her head was nothing she could make sense of. It hurt to try. It hurt to have those images in her head.

More blood dripped from her nose.

She clenched her jaw against the pain, focused on pulling in more of the magic, even as she murmured a spell and let it loose. Lightning dropped around Lisa, pulling her up short as she rushed toward Angie and Betha. The lightning fell fast and in rapid succession. A line, holding the other witch back.

Angie drew in more of Lisa's magic.

Lisa fought the drain, though, dragging at the bond, too, trying to claw back what she'd had. Trying to take even more.

With Betha and Angie pulling only at Lisa, and Lisa having to divide her efforts between Angie and Betha, Lisa couldn't take back as fast as the other two were taking away. But the tug and pull, the having to regain some of what Lisa dragged back, kept half of Angie's focus.

Which meant she wasn't fighting with her full attention.

The shock spell hit her suddenly, right in the chest, made her skin sizzle and her arms numb. Damn. No wonder her brothers had hated that spell. And Angie hadn't ever hit them with that powerful a blast. She breathed through the numbness and used the brute force of purple magic to hit Lisa back.

Then a wall of sand rose up, like a wave, cresting over the top of Lisa, burying her in a hill of the soft stuff. Angie blinked, thinking Betha had done that without her being aware of what Betha was doing. Looked past the hill and realized Carmen was standing there. No smile now. Just concentration. She moved her hands and more sand covered over the top of Lisa.

Then she was gone. As if she'd gone invisible. The

demon hunter will thing that Carmen had never been able to do before.

Sebastian must be helping Carmen.

That they were still around and hadn't run away was a momentary distraction, but not enough to pull Angie's focus. She knew they'd stay, that Sebastian would stay, even if she'd wanted him to run.

The hill of sand exploded outward, Lisa roaring as she emerged. She looked around for the culprit, but she didn't seem to see Carmen—or Carmen was long gone—and turned her anger on Angie and Betha.

Where Angie wanted it.

Betha opened a portal next to Lisa then. A sudden swirl of red light. Then blasted Lisa in the chest with the demon magic, sending her careening backward toward the portal.

Lisa hissed and resisted going through.

Angie tried to shout at Betha to stop. They didn't want to send her away. They needed to end this now!

Then the realm pulled Lisa in, sucking her through the opening. The portal swirled shut. Angie felt the snap in the bond, the cutting off of their triad link. Lisa wasn't in her head anymore. The flow of power that Angie had been dragging in cut off sharply.

"Ground as much as you can," Betha said, her voice deeper than Angie had ever heard it. "Get ready."

Another portal started to swirl open. Angie acted, sending some of the power building up in her into the ground. The odd magic she hadn't yet incorporated into her web she could release. Not all of it. But enough arrowed into the sand and rocks beneath her she no longer felt like her body might explode.

The instant some of the building pressure eased, the portal opened again and Lisa ran through.

She snarled at Betha and shot red magic at her. Betha ducked to one side, closing up the portal fast. So fast it made a hissing noise as it collapsed.

Then Betha opened a new portal.

Okay. Angie could work with this. She summoned the lightning. Rained it down around Lisa. Lisa snarled at her, batting the lightning away with a hand encased in purple magic. The new portal opened at her back, and sucked her through again. She screamed as it snapped shut.

Angie hadn't managed to pull anymore magic in during that volley, though. She'd have to focus more on that.

Betha brought Lisa through a portal again. In a different spot. Betha's ability to place and open portals astounded Angie. Different realms, came to her easily. The openings and closings happening faster than anything Angie could conceive. Popping up exactly where she wanted them instead of randomly or in exactly the same place.

Lisa stumbled through, looked around, seemed disoriented. Angie started the pull of magic again, and wove an illusion spell, sending red lights like fireflies dive bombing Lisa. She swatted at the little diving lights, her hand going through them. But there was a sizzle whenever she did drag a hand through the lights. The smell of burning flesh. And Lisa hissed at the pain.

Angie's illusions had never…caused pain before.

She put the thought aside, focused instead on acting. Each thought was Lisa's. But if Angie acted fast enough, Lisa didn't seem to pick up what Angie was about to do. If Angie acted on instinct rather than thought, Lisa couldn't anticipate her.

Dragging in more of the horrible power that had been living in Lisa, Angie brought up another whirlwind of sand as a new portal opened.

Lisa resisted this one longer, though, managing to walk away from it, dragging herself beyond its pull.

Angie heard Betha curse, knew she'd close the portal and try a new position. Then Lisa stopped as if she'd come up against a wall. And suddenly she slid backward. Then flew off her feet through the portal, like she'd been dragged back by an invisible line, fish on a hook.

The portal snapped shut and Sebastian stood there. He gave Angie a small solute, then disappeared again, his solid form seeming to dissolve into the blackness behind him.

"He's a hell of a demon hunter," Betha grunted. Then she spun a new portal open, releasing Lisa into this world in a completely different spot.

Lisa stumbled again, dropping to her knees, cursing in a language Angie didn't know. Lisa tried to push to her feet, but Angie and Betha both took advantage of her disorientation to drag in even more magic.

Angie could feel Lisa weakening. Feel the control she had over the magic slipping through her fingers.

She snarled up at them, her eyes glowing bright red, the golden red halo around her dimmed. "No! This cannot be!"

Still on her knees, Lisa widened her hands and started a chanting spell.

Angie recognized the spell, even though she hadn't known it before. Realized in confused shock…

"She's going to break the bond!"

CHAPTER THIRTY-SEVEN

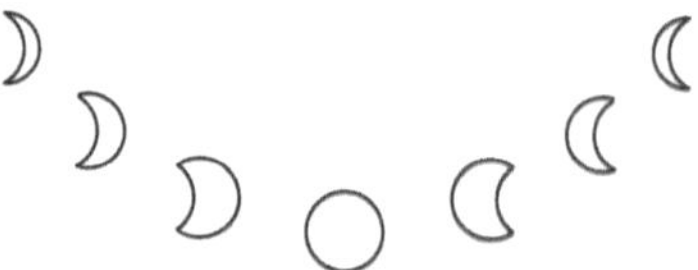

Angie hadn't even known breaking the triad bond was possible now that it was formed. Not with just a spell. She'd thought one of them would have to die to break the bond. But Lisa had known there was another way. And she recited the spell with enough magic and conviction to make it work.

The black sand under Lisa shivered with the power in her voice. The air smelled of burnt ozone particles from all the magic thrown around. The darkness edged in around them, so that not even the golden speckles in the stalactites far above cut the gloom. Angie could feel the power of severing in the warm, dry air.

Once the bond was broken, Angie and Betha would no longer be able to drain away Lisa's magic. They'd taken a lot. And Lisa wouldn't be able to grab it back with the bond broken.

But they wouldn't be able continue draining Lisa.

"More," Betha shouted. "Take it all."

Angie tried dragging more of Lisa's powers while the bond was still there, but she could feel the tendrils of it stretching taut. Feel the strained edges starting to snap.

She cursed and pulled in more magic, tried to think of a way to distract Lisa from the spell. Doing so was dangerous. The backlash of power from a spell interrupted could be deadly under the best of circumstances. And these were not the best of circumstances.

A note in the spell struck Angie, a series of words that weren't…quite right. And she knew in that instinctive witchy part of herself that Lisa had the spell wrong. Wherever she'd gotten it, whatever language she'd translated it from, or whatever well of knowledge she'd pulled it from, she wasn't a trained witch. She missed the mistake.

A mistake that changed the entire nature of the spell.

Angie rapidly dug through the words Lisa had said already, what she was saying… Where would this go. What would it do?

The best-case scenario when a spell went wrong was that it just didn't work. This wasn't going to be one of those spells. Angie wasn't that lucky.

Instinct kicked in when Angie panicked. Her lips formed a spell, her fingers formed the shapes, on the metaphysical plane, she drew in power from all three magics in her web. She stopped trying to drain Lisa. Left that to Betha. She ignored the gory and impossible to decipher images still filling the back of her mind from the golden power she'd dragged in from Lisa.

She focused all her attention on the spell Lisa was creating and her own spell.

So when Lisa cast her own spell out, when the bonds that had tied them frayed and snapped, when the backlash of the broken spell flung unregulated magic across the black sandy plain...

Angie had a massive shield up to block the wave.

A shield that sent the power washing backward. Right over the top of Lisa.

Stalactites from overhead shivered and began to fall. Pummeling the ground around them. The demons that Angie had encased in that frozen moment of time broke through the barriers. Lisa screamed. Betha screamed. Someone shouted behind Angie.

She looked up to see more of the stalactites falling. She poured more power directly into the shield spell, adding layers of purple, adding some of the power she'd sucked in from Lisa, golden magic from the god realm. She chanted the spell again. More strength as high-rise sized pointed chunks of rock dropped around them. The rock hit her shield and shattered, scattering rocky shrapnel into the rising demons.

The area all around them, outside Angie's shield became a rain of rock knives and golden daggers. She couldn't see Lisa through the power she was wielding, couldn't see much of anything as she used everything she had to feed the shield and prevent any of those deadly rocks coming in. Her web brightened so much, she could no longer see the various colors. There was light but so dense and thick she couldn't *see* it anymore.

All of that power, all of that magic.

All of her.

The part of her that wasn't the magic was aware of the three other people inside her shield. Aware that Lisa wasn't inside the shield. Aware that there were demons now free beyond the barrier she'd created and a deadly avalanche of stone and sand.

But most of her was the magic in that moment, the spell she continued to speak to keep the shield strong. The protective conjuring that became her entire being.

And like the instincts that had given her the spell before the bond severed, she only came out of the trance, stopped chanting the spell, when instinct said it was no longer needed.

Her throat hurt, but her body vibrated with all the power still coursing through her. She blinked hard a few times, trying to clear away the residual glow of the magic in her mind's eye. When all that light cleared, she realized her surroundings were pitch black. There was no light. No sound. Wait, no...

She heard breathing.

A dim blue light rose, lighting the immediate area.

Angie kept her hands up, knowing she was still holding up her shield and reluctant to let it down until she knew what had happened. Only once the blue glow lit up her surroundings did she realize her shield was protecting them from...

"A shit ton of rocks and sand," Carmen said. "How the hell do we get out of this?"

Angie swallowed, trying to wet her dry throat. She couldn't talk yet, so she gave her head a little shake.

"Don't drop the shield," Carmen said.

Angie wanted to comment on that obvious point, but couldn't so satisfied herself with an eye roll. She glanced to one side and realized Betha was holding her hands up too. Betha's eyes were wide and red, her breathing fast. Angie wasn't sure she'd seen fear from the other woman before. Anger after discovering Eloise was missing. But even through the entire fight, Betha hadn't looked scared.

She looked scared now.

That was terrifying. Angie cleared her throat and said, "We're holding the shield together?"

Betha nodded, but faintly, like she was afraid to move. "You...pulled me in, I think? I'm not sure. I just started chanting and magic was pouring through me and then... This. I've never handled magic like this before."

Angie hadn't either. Not quite like this.

Sebastian came up close to her and Angie wobbled when she realized he was okay. She straightened her legs to ensure she didn't fall down or screw up the shield that was keeping them safe from the mountain of debris covering them.

"Are you hurt?" he asked quietly.

She shook her head. "But I'm a little worried about how we get out of this now." She glanced at Betha. "I don't think either of us can do anything without risking lowering the shield."

"I'm afraid to move," Betha admitted. "It *feels* like there is a lot of earth above us."

Yeah, it did to Angie too.

Carmen grunted and said, "Do not shift the shield even a little. I'll see what I can do."

"You can move that much telekinetically?"

"I've never tried," Carmen admitted, her mouth a thin line. "This'll be a fun experiment."

For a long moment, it seemed like nothing was happening. Angie watched the gap of air above them, held there only by the shield she and Betha were holding, created with magic she wasn't sure they'd have after this collapsed. Waiting for some sense that the pile of earth was moving.

The pressure of significant levels of rock and sand above them made Angie's arms shake. But she, like Betha, was afraid to move. Collapsing the shield on accident would bury them all alive, a horrifying thought.

"Can you hurry," Betha grunted.

Carmen didn't respond, which was probably for the best if she was concentrating.

After several moments of terrified watching, Angie finally heard some scraping of rock against rock and watched a trickle of sand just above her head shift positions. Then more of the material above her head seemed to move. Tumbling down the domed sides of the shield.

More debris from above them moved down, surrounding the sides of the shield like a wall of rock and sand. Significantly better than having it all over the top of their heads, but it still looked like it would collapse on them if they released the shield.

She risked a glance around. Carmen had managed to clear the entire top of the shield. Only the wall of debris around them remained, like they were inside a deep hole.

Carmen sucked in a deep breath. "Need a minute," she murmured, bending over to put her hands on her knees. "That's a shit ton of sand."

"Are you done? Can you move anymore?" Angie asked, worried at how pale Carmen looked, at the way sweet dripped down her cheeks.

"Fine," she muttered. "Just need a minute."

Angie looked at all the surrounding debris. Then at Betha. "If we blow the shield outward, do you think it'll blast the stuff away, or send it falling back in on us?"

Betha frowned, her gaze moving over the parts of the wall of dirt she could see, then looking overhead. The wall was at least another four feet above them, though no longer covering them. If they didn't send the shield out just right, they'd still be in trouble.

"I got it," Carmen grunted. "Just hold the fucking line for a minute more." She stood to her full height. Pulled in a deep breath, then moved her hands in a way that looked like she was brushing at things.

The ten-foot-tall wall of dirt tumbled away from the shield, like someone had taken a hand and just swept it over backward. It scattered away from them, a dark scar of material over the landscape. The hill of material shrank as it blew outward. Until they stood in a clean area in the center of sand and rock that spread around them like flower petals.

"Impressive," Angie said.

"Fuck off."

"I wasn't being sarcastic." Angie glanced at Carmen who was doubled over again. "Very impressive. Thank you."

"You get to do it next time," Carmen said.

"Deal." Angie just hoped there wouldn't be a next time.

"Lower the shield now?" Betha asked.

Angie's arms were trembling, so she nodded. "First, we need to draw a circle."

Once they dropped the shield, they'd have no protection from any demons who hadn't run away when things started collapsing on them. And Angie and Betha were both at the very edge of their endurance after building the shield. She wasn't sure they could immediately jump into a demon fight. There were still some of those beautiful monsters around here somewhere. Sebastian couldn't fight them all off on his own.

But Angie wasn't sure she could draw a circle while keeping the shield up. She and Betha had built the shield together, so one of them couldn't move away from it without it collapsing. And Carmen was too wiped out from moving a literal ton of rock and sand using just her telekinesis.

She glanced at Sebastian. "I don't suppose you can draw a traditional circle?" There were magical circles built all the time by none magical people summoning demons, using ritual and spell and the right objects. Her magic made the circles she built strong and protected against magic. But magic skill wasn't required to create an analog circle.

Sebastian glanced around and nodded. "Give me a minute. You okay a little bit longer?"

She nodded. Without the stress of eminent burial, holding the shield no longer felt so harrowing, at least not for her. And she found all the magic that was coursing through her was still there, still feeding the shield. She'd be back up to strength sooner than she expected once they dropped the shield. But not fast enough for an instant demon attack.

Sebastian walked around collecting stones from inside the shield and placing them in a circle, walking clockwise and chanting as he went. She hunted their surroundings—now that they could see their surroundings again. No sign of Lisa or the demons yet. But a lot of rock and sand had piled up on the hill and there were mounds of dirt everywhere. Any of those mounds could hide the other witch. Overhead, the cavern roof, so far above them it might as well be sky, was cleared of hanging stalactites. Only black rock with golden speckles of light like stars.

For what Angie thought might be a mile around them, the stalactites had fallen and the ground had heaved and bucked. The hill with the tunnels where they'd been held looked like a part of it had collapsed and other parts were bigger than they'd been. There were three stalactites that Angie could see that had speared into the ground and not dissolved or broken apart. They looked like strangely shaped buildings, fortunately all far enough away that if they fell over, they *probably* wouldn't fall on top of their group.

There didn't seem to be any approaching demons on the horizon, even curious creatures just looking to see what the hell had happened. And there were no signs of the shadow demons, the Aminore, or the Helavitee that had been freed right after Lisa's spell broke. They could be under the debris. Lisa could be under the debris.

Angie had no idea if any of them could have survived.

Once Sebastian was finished building his circle, he murmured a closing spell, one she hadn't heard before. But she felt when the circle closed around them. It wasn't like anything she would build. But it was strong enough to keep demons out.

With a glance at Betha, they both murmured a dissolution spell and lowered their arms in sync, collapsing the shield.

Betha stepped to the edge of the circle without crossing and hunted their surroundings. "Is she dead? Did she kill herself?"

"I don't feel her in my head." Angie tried tugging on the magic that had been part of their bond and found only a connection to Betha that was tenuous at best. A tiny link from one of her demon magic threads to the other witch. The second demon magic thread that linked to Lisa was still inside the web, not moving out or tugging toward anyone else. And the silver sheen that had encased the web of her magic after the bond formed was gone.

"She broke the triad," Angie said quietly. "We're not bonded anymore, even if she is alive."

"We weren't supposed to be able to break the bond," Betha murmured. "Not with a spell. How the hell did she know that spell existed when I didn't?"

"Got me. However she learned that spell, though, she had

it wrong. That's why it did…" Angie waved her hands at the surrounding destruction.

"Are you hurting?" Betha asked.

"No. I feel fine."

"You're glowing," Betha said.

Angie blinked and looked down. "Why am I glowing and you aren't?"

"You took in more of the god magic than I did," Betha said. "I was burning with it and couldn't ground it fast enough."

"Well this isn't good." Angie looked at her hands. The glow was subtle. Not enough to illuminate their surroundings or even cast a shadow beneath her. But there was a faint light just beneath her skin that almost made her skin look transparent.

"Can you ground it or get rid of it or something?" Carmen asked, sounding better now.

"No idea." She closed her eyes and looked at all her magic again. No more silver encompassing the web. No new magics inside the web—she'd expected maybe a new thread of dense colorless magic. Just the one demon witch line, the two demon magic lines, and the rest of her web blue with some spots of purple. More complex than it had been before, more threads throughout. But no new magic.

She frowned at the pattern of the cross threads. And realized they were more sharply angled now so that they made very distinct Vs all the way around the circle. That was new.

"Maybe it's the pattern of the magic now," she

murmured. "There's more there, but it's all just my usual witch magic. Just seems like a lot more of it. And the pattern of my web is changed."

"To what?" Betha asked, frowning.

Angie explained.

Betha nodded. "That would be the effects of the god magic. It's more…pattern than color. For me. But I don't have the visual of my magic the way you do. I just have a sense of it. And that sense is of a lot of triangles and circles now."

"Like the pattern you left on Yosuf's chest," Angie said.

"A protective pattern. I changed it from the V inside a circle to the triangle. If you're seeing a lot of Vs, you're going to have to turn them into triangles or you'll attract the gods."

That sounded super bad.

"I can't believe I came all this way to get rid of magic, only to end up with a whole lot more," she muttered to herself. "Power that will attract demon gods." She should have just stayed home. But the demon magic was already going to attract other demons. There was no way around it once it was known she could kill demons. Attracting demon gods was just one step beyond.

"We need to find Lisa," Sebastian said quietly. He met Angie's gaze. "She might still be alive under all this."

He was right. And if she was, despite Betha bringing her here to kill Lisa, Angie didn't want to leave someone who was still alive buried to die slowly. She suspected that would be bad for Eloise, too.

"We'll have to break the circle to look around," Betha said. She glanced at Carmen. "Unless you can move the debris aside?"

"Not for another few hours," Carmen said. "That took a lot out of me."

"You've done enough," Angie said, trying to make her tone reassuring, even though she wasn't used to taking that tone with Carmen.

"I'll break the circle and we'll all search," Sebastian said. "But we be careful. Be prepared. There might be demons buried under some of those mounds, too."

Angie's heart rate accelerated and she almost wanted to refuse. Would have preferred to just portal away from here and go home.

But they had some clean up to do.

CHAPTER THIRTY-EIGHT

In the end, they found no demon bodies. The shadow demons and the beautiful monsters either escaped the chaos or were so destroyed by it, they left no remains. Angie was betting they got away and were out there somewhere, lurking. But so long as they didn't return before she and the others could leave the area, she didn't care.

The hills and mounds of black sand and rock were mostly just left over chunks of the giant fallen stalactites. Outside of their protective circle the minerally smell of the dirt and debris actually overpowered the faint sulfur smells and burnt ozone scent from the magical fight. The three giant stalactites that had buried into the ground and remained intact and standing, they all gave a wide birth.

And because of that, they didn't find Lisa until they were almost ready to give up.

They found her finally near the base of one of the intact

stalactites. Or at least, they found her body. From yards away, Angie couldn't tell if she'd survived or not.

As they reached her, though, it became obvious she was breathing. Shallowly. And she didn't look well. One leg was in a terrible position. There was blood on her face and a wicked looking cut on her cheek. Angie didn't have to be a healer witch to know Lisa needed a doctor.

Without hesitating, Betha went right to her and knelt beside her, taking one of Lisa's hands roughly in hers. Angie had a moment when she thought Betha would finish off what the chaos had done and kill Lisa. It's what she'd wanted, what she'd been hoping for with Angie's arrival. Angie wasn't okay with watching her murder Lisa right in front of her, but when she reached them, she realized Betha was chanting something, forming a spell.

It wasn't a killing spell.

It wasn't a healing spell either.

"She's binding her power," Carmen murmured, half question, half statement.

Angie nodded. She couldn't see the level of power Lisa had left, what had happened to her during the explosion of the bad spell. If Angie and Betha had managed to drain away all Lisa's power, the binding wasn't really necessary. And maybe it wasn't. Maybe this was a precaution on Betha's part. But if there was even a little magic still in Lisa's control, Angie was certain the wannabe god would find a way to gain more, to resume her efforts to destroy the demon god realm and take over as a demon god.

Had Angie thought about it, she might have considered a

binding spell herself. But then, before, Lisa had been too strong. They wouldn't have had the time, or the power individually, to bind her. Even with their magics combined and working together Angie and Betha hadn't been able to completely overwhelm Lisa's power. With Lisa weakened, and unconscious, this opportunity to bind up her magic—any that was left—was a unique chance they probably wouldn't get again.

Once the binding was done, Betha leaned back on her heels and looked over Lisa's injuries. "She's in a bad state. I can do some healing, set the bone. I'd need Eloise to mix some of her healing potions, get a good poultice together to ensure no infections. Not even sure if Lisa can get infections."

This last she said mostly to herself.

"Was she insane before, when she was first...created?" Angie asked. "Was that something she was driven to by centuries of the god magic in her head? Or was she always like that?"

"Always, but it got more pronounced as the years passed. She didn't try to hide it after a while." Betha looked around. "I need something that will work as a splint. There's not a lot of wood here, but anything straight that I can use to bind her leg."

They spent the next...well, Angie had no idea how much time. Time had lost all real meaning in this place. But they spent some time finding scraps of things that they could cobble together to make a splint—there were some slivers of rocky debris that were thin enough and still strong enough to work. Wood would have been better, but this had to do in a pinch. Betha poured a little magic directly into the injury, something Angie didn't know how to do…or hadn't. She realized as she watched Betha that some of what she was doing was still in Angie's mind.

The bond between them was well and truly severed, though. When she looked, her threads of demon magic still *leaned* toward the two women but not with much intensity, even when she'd walked quite a ways from them in the hunt for potential splint material. She supposed they'd always be linked, the three of them. Until one of them died. But they weren't bonded anymore. And the call to do so seemed to have eased.

At least for Angie. And the logical part of her brain wanted nothing to do with another triad bond. This one had done enough damage.

Lisa murmured and looked like she might wake up in the middle of having her leg set, but Betha murmured a sleep spell that put her into a deeper sleep. A mercy since the leg was badly broken and realigning it took effort and would have been extremely painful. Even unconscious, Lisa broke out into a sweat as they adjusted the leg to get everything as lined up as possible.

"If she'll let me, I'll set it better," Betha said. "Once we get her to her house." She glanced back at Angie. "I really need to find Eloise now."

Yeah, Angie would like to find Aidan too.

There hadn't been any signs of demons the entire time they worked. Not even the beautiful monsters that Lisa had apparently been controlling. But that didn't mean Aidan and Eloise were safe from the demons left in this realm.

Building a stretcher proved a little more difficult than finding something for the splint because all the slivers of rock that might be suitable were either too heavy or crumbled when they picked them up. In the end, they found a couple of long slivers of rock that didn't crumble, but were light enough to carry. Angie encircled them with a strengthening spell to keep them from breaking, and then she and Betha devised a spell to create a cushion between the rocks, a swirling rectangle of light, like a shield, that Lisa could lay on.

They might have been able to scrape together enough spare pieces of clothing to make a sheet stretched between the rocks, but Angie hadn't been confident of their ability to tie the material tight enough to not fall apart. And if they were going to use magic to reinforce the knots, maybe they could just make a magical sheet.

The process of inventing a new spell with Betha came easier than Angie would have thought. She'd memorized hundreds of spells in her life, during her training, and she'd used magic in some pretty unique-to-her ways in the last year. But she'd never sat down to write her own spell, to create her own unique set of words and hand motions, to build something so new. Betha, on the other hand, had had to write and invent her own spells a few times, especially since being forced into the demon realm where she couldn't just consult with a mentor or find the answers in someone else's spellbook.

By the time all was said and done, Angie knew she should have been exhausted. Both Carmen and Sebastian looked like they were walking around half asleep. Angie felt a renewed energy every time she used her magic. Even her usual hollow stomach and need for food weren't nagging at her.

She felt remarkably fine. And after everything it was still a little freaky.

While Angie had no idea where they were in relation to Lisa's house, Betha seemed to know and with each of them taking a different corner of Lisa's makeshift stretcher, they carried her across the sandy plain, back to the house inside the mound. Again, Angie wasn't sure how long it took. But it seemed like they were walking for a while before they reached the hill.

They settled Lisa onto a bed, then Betha reinforced the sleep spell. "She'll be better off unconscious for a few days," Betha said.

"I'm surprised you didn't kill her while you had the chance," Angie said bluntly as they stood over Lisa.

"Me too. But…I'm pretty sure we drained most of her power and what wasn't drained got ripped out of her in the explosion. There's some there. But nothing like what she'd possessed previously. I wouldn't have been able to bind her, even unconscious, if she was still at full power." Betha gave Angie a look and a shrug. "I tried. She fought back instinctively. She didn't this time."

"Why didn't you kill her?"

"I didn't want Eloise to feel it. And I don't know for sure

what it'll do to Eloise. It seemed the only way before. But now… If Lisa truly is no longer a powerful magic wielder, she's less of a threat. And maybe something can be done to severe their bond without harming Eloise. We managed to break the triad bond without all dying. I didn't think that would happen."

"Don't use the spell Lisa tried to use," Angie warned. "She had it wrong."

Betha made a sound that was almost a laugh at Angie's understatement. "I have time now," Betha said. "Time to figure out how to separate them, how to keep Lisa bound, how to keep her from regaining all that power. And if I can't, I can still kill her. I can do that now without your help thanks to how much of the demon god magic she lost in that fight."

Angie wasn't sure how to feel about that last part, so she said, "Let's go find Aidan and Eloise. I'm worried about them."

She didn't have to ask Betha twice.

When they came out of Lisa's bedroom, Carmen was asleep on the couch and Sebastian, though sitting up in a chair, had his eyes closed and his breathing was slow and deep. She thought he was asleep until she got close and he opened his eyes.

"You're still feeling well?" he asked.

"Still weirdly good," she said. "You look exhausted."

"I am. Could do with a nap." He nodded at Carmen. "But we need to find the others."

"Betha and I can do that. You and Carmen can stay here

and keep an eye on Lisa. She's in a spelled sleep so probably won't wake up. But just in case."

He nodded but glanced at Betha with a funny look.

Angie kept expecting the exhaustion to settle in, to feel tired and wiped out from all the magic they'd done. Everything that had happened. Even getting Lisa back to her house should have exhausted Angie. She couldn't remember the last time she ate or drank—and she was still very salty about Lisa stealing her purse—and yet she wasn't getting dizzy or grumpy from hunger. She didn't think she could live off magic forever. She still had a physical body that needed food and rest and water. But at the moment, she felt so normal and fine, it was weird.

"Not tired either," Betha said with a nod as they circled around Lisa's mound house.

"Did you read my mind? I thought the bond was broken."

"It is, and I didn't. But I've spent years studying the expression of a psychopath to ensure I kept Eloise as safe as I could. Your expressions are easy to read compared to that."

Angie snort-laughed. "Fair enough. It's worrying, though, isn't it? That we're not just totally exhausted right now?"

Betha let out a long breath. "Probably."

When she didn't say more, Angie let it go. Neither of them had been through anything like this before. She shouldn't expect Betha to have answers.

When they got to the back of the mound house, Angie pulled the silver amulet from her pocket, let the medallion settle in the palm of her hand, and whispered the finding spell, asking it to find Aidan. Eloise was with Aidan, and

Angie didn't want to risk the medallion getting Lisa and Eloise confused since they had, at one time, been the same person.

Angie used the owl side this time, to find a person, instead of the butterfly side for location. The medallion rose and leaned into a direction that felt random to Angie. Just off into the black sand plains. She headed that way, trusting the little charm completely now after it had led them out of the tunnels. Aidan wouldn't have left on obvious trail, or Lisa would have found them already. So Angie didn't worry that the direction seemed arbitrary and seemed to be very out in the open for an escape route.

"How will you try to sever the link between Lisa and Eloise now that you have time to think about it?" Angie asked quietly as they walked across the warm sands, the crinkling and low whoosh of the golden rivers their only company. The lines of blue bugs curved around in the distance now.

"I'm not sure," Betha said. "They can't be rejoined, and I'm not sure Eloise would want that. She's never talked about it, but I think it bothers her that someone like Lisa came from her. That she had any of that in her."

"It wasn't Eloise. It was the god realm magic in the potion. I could feel it when we were draining Lisa. It's… corrosive. I'm not sure I'd stay sane long with so much of it coursing through me, either. Human bodies weren't meant to hold that kind of magic. Even whatever Lisa is, she's not designed to hold god magic and stay sane."

Betha nodded. "I've tried to tell Eloise that. But with Lisa looking identical to her, and with Eloise feeling everything Lisa feels, I'm not sure she ever believed me."

"How could you heal Lisa now if you couldn't do it before?"

"Lisa didn't want me to 'heal' her before and had the magic to prevent any efforts I might have made. She doesn't have that magic now."

"But you can't heal a psychopath. If that's the make up of her brain, there's no fixing that." Even with magic, there were things that couldn't be fixed.

Betha nodded. "I know. But maybe…maybe that's not really who she is? I don't know. I just feel responsible. For all this. And the fact that I was so intent on killing her to solve the problem was…" She let out a long breath. "I'd like to try to do something to make this better. Maybe even give Lisa a shot at a life without so much delusion. It's a long shot. But it's one that's possible now."

At least someone found answers in all this, Angie thought. She still wasn't sure what to do about what had happened here, how to deal with all this new magic and the after effects of the apocalypse witch bond. But if Lisa was no longer a magic wielding apocalypse witch with the power to kill demons, that was at least something. They couldn't form the triad anymore and that part of the myth wouldn't come to pass.

The problem was there were still two apocalypse witches that could kill demons. And that still kept a target on Angie's back.

And she feared there was no way to get out of that now.

CHAPTER THIRTY-NINE

*J*ust as the medallion in Angie's palm lifted and started to urge her forward faster, she looked across the open sandy plain and spotted two people walking toward them. It didn't take more than a moment to realize those two people were Aidan and Eloise. Angie hadn't seen the demon hunter and her charge just moments earlier. There were no giant rock piles or hills in their immediate area. Just black sand and a small steam of golden liquid running beside Angie and Betha as they walked.

The thick stalactites far overhead with their spots of golden minerals like stars had taken on a new and more deadly beauty since the chaos of so many of them collapsing around her, so Angie couldn't appreciate them as much anymore. But she'd tried not to look up very often as they walked.

The musty, minerally smell of the open plain had fallen into an almost pleasant background scent that reminded Angie of hot springs and overwhelmed the underlying sulfur smell of the realm. That part at least had made the quiet, non-demon infested walk with Betha a lot more pleasant.

Demon danger must have been well and truly absent, too, because Aidan made herself and Eloise visible while still several hundred yards away.

The minute Betha spotted Eloise, she took off at a run to reach her. Eloise did the same and the two women met in an explosive hug halfway between Angie and Aidan. Angie smiled a little, glad they were able to reunite without the still looming threat of Lisa in the background. Lisa was still a small threat and an ongoing problem. But she was unconscious and magically bound so she wasn't able to pour her psychosis into Eloise just then.

By the time Angie and Aidan reached each other, Eloise and Betha were busy murmuring questions and explanations to each other and Angie didn't want to disrupt their reunion so she moved off to the side to greet Aidan.

After a relieved hug of their own, she said, "Thank you for looking after Eloise. Lisa wanted to kill her. And if she had I'm not sure what Betha would have done."

"You're welcome." Aidan glanced at the two women. "Eloise spent the whole time worried about Betha. But to hide her, I had to will a block between her and Lisa, and Eloise told me it was the first time she'd felt at peace since before that first time Betha brought her into the demon realm."

"Lisa is not healthy mentally. I'm not surprised."

She told Aidan what had happened as they all walked back to Lisa's house, explaining how Lisa had broken the bond with a bad spell, because Betha and Angie had realized the only way to beat her was to drag out all her power, the way she'd been trying to steal all theirs. When Angie got to the part where the stalactites had collapsed around them, Eloise wrapped Betha up in a hug that nearly lifted the other woman off the ground. There might have even been some tears.

By the time they'd returned to the house, Aidan had explained how Eloise had realized what Lisa wanted to do and told Aidan. Aidan and whisked her away to keep her safe and thwart Lisa's plan even though it meant Aidan hadn't been able to directly help Angie and the others.

"You did good," Angie said. "We would all have been fucked if Lisa got to Eloise."

Inside the house, there was more reunions and confirmation that Lisa was still unconscious. Then the practical end of things kicked in. Everyone was hungry and exhausted. Lisa's house was stocked with human food, so they prepared a simple meal over a fire in the hearth of roasted beef—Angie didn't ask what the beef came from and just let herself pretend they were eating cow—and some potatoes and carrots also roasted in a pan that caught drippings from the beef and made a nice gravy.

With fresh water from the underground well, that Betha ensured was safe to drink, and enough meet and veg to fill her stomach, Angie finally felt the exhaustion of their day...

days? She had no idea. It felt like they'd been hoping around demon realms for weeks even though it had probably only been a day or two of their lives. She had no idea how much time had passed in the human realm. But she was anxious to get back, not least because she didn't want to be in a demon realm anymore, and also because she wanted to reassure her parents that she was still alive.

But she didn't want to leave Betha and Eloise alone with Lisa just yet. Not until she made sure things were settled. And she couldn't have that conversation until everyone had slept some. Almost as soon as they'd finished eating, Eloise curled up on a blanket on the floor near the hearth and went to sleep. Betha curled around her and also fell asleep quickly.

Aidan sat in a chair that blocked the front door and closed her eyes. Angie wasn't sure if Aidan would sleep, but this was probably as close as she'd get to rest. Carmen curled up in one of the larger chairs in the room, her head resting on her arm on the armrest, her eyes closed, breathing softly and deeply enough Angie was pretty sure she was asleep too.

Sebastian led a finally exhausted Angie to the couch, and they stretched out with Sebastian at her back, his arms around her, holding her close.

In the quiet, she murmured, "Are you okay after…all this? After Lisa showing you your parents like that?"

She felt his lips brush against her temple, and snuggled back farther into him, hugging his arm that lay across her stomach.

"I'm okay," he said quietly. "It was a shock. But an illusion. A picture from the past. And in some ways, it…

confirms for me that my parents are well and truly gone." He sighed. "I've always known they were, of course. Intellectually. But I suppose there was a part of me, a small part, that still held onto that childish belief that maybe they'd managed to survive here somewhere. If they had, I don't think Lisa would have needed an illusion. Not with all the power that was flowing between you all. I think she would have brought my real parents here if she could have. But even powerful witches can't bring back the dead."

Angie nodded. Hugged him tighter. Didn't mention the fact that, deep inside Betha's knowledge and centuries of learning, she'd discovered a way to bring back someone who'd died, using some of that cursed sand from the god realm. What came back, like Lisa, couldn't be predicted, though. The entity that looked like the returned loved one wasn't necessarily the person hoped for. It was a monkey's paw spell. A curse of sorts. The kind of thing no witch in her right mind would use.

And Angie was just glad Lisa hadn't had any of the sand from the demon god realm to use in such a spell or she might just have tried it.

***

ANGIE SLEPT FOR LONG ENOUGH TO FEEL RESTED, THOUGH IT was a restless sleep because she wasn't in her own home and she didn't feel entirely safe because, though there were few demons in this realm now, it was still a demon realm and there were still those shadow demons out there somewhere.

She'd no idea if the beautiful monsters had returned to their own realm yet either. Without Lisa to guide and command them, they were probably gone. But the unknown of that made getting a deep sleep impossible.

Still, she snoozed enough to feel somewhat recovered. Enough for the conversation that needed to happen with Betha. And enough to ensure she could open the portal that would get them all home.

She eased out of Sebastian's arms, hoping he'd sleep more, and went looking for Betha—who was no longer sleeping near the fire with Eloise. Angie checked in Lisa's room first. The witch was still unconscious, but breathing. And when Angie checked on her leg, it didn't seem to be showing any signs of infection yet.

Betha wasn't in the room with Lisa, or anywhere else in the house. Aidan had moved her chair to one side of the front door. When Angie quietly asked about Betha, Aidan confirmed she'd stepped outside and didn't object or even comment when Angie went out to look for her.

Angie found Betha near one of the golden streams, a thin offshoot of the larger river running behind Lisa's house. "Couldn't sleep?" she asked the other witch.

"I slept enough," Betha said, her gaze on the river. She smiled a little. "It was the most peaceful sleep Eloise has had in centuries. No twitching, no nightmares…" She tossed another rock into the stream, like she was trying to skip it, but there wasn't enough room and the rock sank into the golden liquid instantly, making a little slurping noise as it plunked beneath the surface. "It's as close to a happy ending as I could have expected." She glanced at Angie. "And I have you to thank for that."

"You're welcome. I'm not sure what I did, but…"

"Without you, we were in a stalemate that lasted centuries. You were brave enough to come here looking for answers. You completed our triad and allowed the opening to…neuter Lisa. Without killing her. It's better this way. Better than I could have hoped for." She tossed another rock. "I was thinking about that, as I woke, holding Eloise… For a long time, my only goal was to kill Lisa. I couldn't see any other way out. But the fear that killing Lisa would destroy Eloise meant I wasn't sure I ever wanted you to be real. I was very conflicted."

"Understandable," Angie said. She picked up a handful of small black pebbles and tossed them into the river too. Each pebble hitting the golden surface sparked a strong minerally smell that was quite pleasant.

"When I saw you in that church, I thought, okay. This is it. If she finds us, then we would end this, and if Eloise was killed, well, I'd lived long enough. I figured I'd follow her. And it would be done."

Angie wasn't sure what to say to that so she tossed another stone.

So did Betha before saying, "What will you do now?"

She snorted. "Not sure. I came here to find a way to get rid of some of the magic I'd picked up, and now I seem to have even more. The 'cure' I thought you had wasn't actually a cure. I do not want to create an alternate, homicidal version of myself…"

"Please don't," Betha said emphatically. "A psychic homicidal Lisa is bad enough. Someone with your witchy skill and learning… I'm not sure any realm would survive it."

"I'm not sure if that was a compliment or not," Angie said with a sideways grin, "but trust me when I say, I'm not going to use the god realm sand for any cures. One pass with that magic was enough." She thought about how much of it was probably still in her web. She hadn't seen any color changes. No threads that were specifically the crazy-making magic they'd pulled out of Lisa. She hoped she and Betha had grounded enough of it here to keep them both sane.

Betha shivered. "I'm not having weird visions, like we did while we were draining Lisa. I think we grounded enough of it."

Angie nodded. What they'd done had changed them both. Again. Just like pulling in demon magic had changed them. She supposed she was going to have to learn how to live with all this now.

"I think I finally know how we've all pulled in the demon magic," Betha said quietly. "Including Eloise. The apocalypse witch bond seemed to come with…knowledge that none of us had had before."

"I noticed." Angie faced Betha, clenching the remaining stones in her hand. "What do you think happened?"

"I think it's the reason we had to be touch psychics. We *touch* the magic here. Instead of reading it, the way we might do an object or a person, when we touch this magic, we pull it in. That's why Eloise absorbed it even though she's not a witch."

"Because she was a touch psychic in a demon realm. Someplace she'd have never normally been. Since she wasn't a demon witch who could open portals." Angie closed her eyes. She hadn't learned that through the link but she'd learned a lot of other things. Knowledge she'd never be able to get rid of now.

"Why did she get sicker going back to the human realm?" Angie asked. "That didn't happen to me. Or you."

"She wasn't a witch." Betha shrugged. "I don't think someone who didn't also have magic of their own was ever meant to contain that demon power. Being here, where everything is demon magic, she stays in balance." Betha shrugged. "It changed her. As much as it changed us. Just in a different way."

"It didn't kill you," Angie said.

"No. And it won't kill you."

Angie nodded and turned back to the golden river. That was one answer at least. Not the main thing she'd come here to learn. And it didn't help her rid herself of the demon magic. But at least it was an explanation. She knew how this had happened. Knew she wouldn't die. She supposed she'd have to be satisfied with that.

But it meant there would still always be a target on her back, demons after her, and the demon hunter council wanting to use her against demons. Half to herself, as she tossed another stone, she murmured, "I just wanted to be an ordinary witch. For once in my life, just an ordinary witch."

Betha gave her a speculative look, rolling some of her

remaining pebbles in her hand, and said, "There is a way to… bind it all."

"Bind it? The way you bound Lisa?" Angie shook her head. "No. That would bind all my magic. I don't want to give up being a witch if I can help it. I would have gotten one of my mentors to bind my magic years ago if I wanted that."

"Not all your magic. Just the parts you don't want to tap into. The magic from Lisa, the magic from the demon realm that lets you kill demons, even the magic that lets you open portals. I can help you isolate and lock those magics off so you no longer have access to them."

"I've never heard of that." Her mentor in New Mexico, Esmerelda, had said she *might* be able to cut the demon witch magic thread from her web if she moved quickly enough. But then Angie had absorbed magic from the demon realm, and Esmerelda said, in the end, they'd lost the window. There was no cutting those threads now. No getting rid of any of the powers. She was stuck being a demon witch.

At least, she thought that's what her mentor had said. Esmerelda had used words like "likely" and "probably", though. Which meant maybe it was just that she didn't know *how* to cut off specific magics without damaging Angie's witch magic anymore.

"You can get rid of the magic I don't want and allow me to keep the magic I do want?"

Betha shrugged and tossed another black pebble into the golden stream. The minerally scent was tinged with something warmer, like cinnamon now. "You'll never be rid of it," she admitted. "That's not how power works. It's there.

Once you have it. It's there. But because of the triad bond we formed, if you allow it, I can bind what you don't want, tie it up so you can't access it, so it doesn't work anymore. Hide it. From you and from everyone else. So that to all outside observers, as well as for yourself, that magic will be gone."

Angie felt hope swelling in her chest. But… "You can do that with specific parts of the magic? You're sure? Not just bind everything the way you did with Lisa?"

"I'm sure," Betha said. She gave Angie a look. "Another piece of knowledge that was there after we bonded. I couldn't have before the apocalypse triad. I didn't know it was possible to selectively lock down parts of someone's magic. But the knowledge is in my head now, just like knowing how we absorbed demon magic." She narrowed her eyes. "I actually thought it might have come from you, since it's a witchy spell."

"Not me. And not Lisa?"

"Not Lisa. If Lisa had known how to do that all these years, she'd have bound my magic long ago so I couldn't stop her. Left my ability to portal and cut off everything else."

Angie blinked at the golden water. "There was a lot of knowledge gained in that triad bond that none of us knew before."

"It was something bigger. It…exists. The apocalypse triad is a thing. There have probably even been other apocalypse triads in the past, though I can't be sure of that. But it makes sense, doesn't it? That they existed and we shared their knowledge when we formed."

"No wonder the demons were terrified of this myth."

Betha nodded. "I don't think there's anything I can do about the knowledge, or the memories of what the god realm magic showed us."

Angie shivered.

"But I'm not sure I'd want to get rid of the knowledge. I think I'd like to explore that more."

"Lisa will want to too," Angie warned. "Even with her powers bound, if we have more knowledge, she will."

"Did you have the information about the binding?"

Angie frowned and searched her memories. "No. I don't. Though I do have more spell information than I did before. And…a better understanding of portals."

"We got more of what we didn't have. But we didn't get the same information I think." Betha faced her. "I *know* this would work. It would lock down the magic you don't want to use. Leave you with only your witch magic. But it would be essentially permanent."

"Essentially?"

"The binding will take time. Undoing the spell even more time. And I get the impression that the process is uncomfortable."

Angie thought about what Betha was saying for a long moment as they continued to toss small pebbles into the golden water. The plunk and slurping noises remarkably soothing.

Finally, Angie said, "Even if we go through with it, that doesn't solve the problem of demons continuing to come for me. Might not solve the demon hunter problem either."

Betha gave a little head tilt. "If they don't know who you are…"

"How would they not?"

"A spell I learned centuries ago, after what happened to me and Eloise. When I was hunting for the cure but hadn't found the potion that required god realm sand yet, I discovered this spell. Once I found a cure, I was going to use it to wipe us from the memories of our townspeople. Then we could move and be safe. We'd have had to move. Being around the people who had once known us would have eventually worn through the spell. They'd know us again eventually, know what had happened, how they'd felt. But if they didn't encounter us and we didn't encounter them, they'd forget we ever existed and we could have lived the rest of our mortal lives unmolested and safe."

She faced Angie, turning away from the river and their little game of tossing pebbles. "What I'm offering you is what I had planned to do for myself once Eloise was cured. A fresh start."

Angie's heart thumped hard, her brain latching onto those three words. *A fresh start.* No more demon hunters. No more demons. What she'd always wanted. What she'd come here hoping to gain.

What she'd thought was forever beyond her reach.

A fresh start. Hope and fear and elation and terror all mixed into a soup that made her a little nauseous.

"Can you limit who forgets me?" She glanced back at the mound that was Lisa's house. Thought about Sebastian. Aidan. Even Carmen. She could live with Carmen forgetting she existed. Maybe even Aidan, though that would be a loss. But Sebastian…

"I can't…" She swallowed hard and looked back at Betha. "I can't lose him. I did once. I can't again."

Betha nodded. "Believe me, I understand. I can limit the people who forget you. It can be very specific. But…" Betha raised a hand when Angie opened her mouth. "There's a trick. Like I said, if you spend too much time around the people you do not want to remember you, the spell will eventually break down. Their memories will get through. You want the demon hunters to forget you, right?"

Angie nodded.

"But he is one. Which means, you will encounter the others if you're around him too much. I can exclude him from the spell. The people here will remember you." She nodded toward the house and Angie knew she meant Aidan and Carmen as well as Sebastian.

"My family?" she asked, just to be sure.

"Your family will remember you if you like."

"I like."

Betha gave her a wistful smile. "Must be nice. Having a family you love and that accepts you."

"It is. I don't want to lose them."

"You don't have to."

"And the people at my work place? I don't want to lose them either."

Betha's eyes narrowed a little. "They won't have to forget you. But if you stay in New York, you'll encounter the hunters. Eventually. The ones you know. That's their enclave now. If you stay in New York, live there, work there, keep openly seeing Sebastian… Eventually, the other hunters will come across you often enough to remember. They might even break through the spell faster than ordinary humans would because of that blasted will of theirs. And then you'll be right back to where you are now. Only the powers they want to use will be bound and inaccessible. Which will put your life at great risk."

Angie rubbed a spot on her chest that had started to ache when Betha said "if you stay in New York." She shifted away from that painful thought for a moment to say, "You said the magic would be bound essentially permanently?"

"For all intents and purposes, yes. I can unbind it, if necessary. In an emergency. If I'm still alive when you need it. But it's not an easy spell, not an easy process. It's not something you'll want to do and undo every few weeks. I won't be able to do and undo it all the time. It takes too much power. So if you want to bind some of your magics, that needs to be something you really want, something you can live with. As if it's permanent."

Angie nodded, pulling her lips into her mouth. "So…I can do one or the other, or both. Right? Different spells."

"Different spells. But if you do the forgetting spell without the binding, the demons will still come after you. I can't make them forget. Not without an intact triad. And frankly, I could wait another four hundred years without going through that again."

Angie suppressed a shiver. She agreed wholeheartedly.

"So the demons will still remember me, no matter what?" That wouldn't solve her problem.

"If you can't open portals, or kill them anymore, they won't be able to find you. They'd have no idea where you were. Even if you they had known you in the past. And demons who haven't encountered you won't be able to sniff you out without the demon witch magic to make you obvious. So long as you avoid demons, they won't find you."

"All the more reason to stay away from the hunters," Angie murmured.

Betha nodded. "The only way this works, the only way you get some semblance of a life back and can live as a witch and only a witch, is if we do both spells, at the same time, and you move away from the demon hunters. Never get into a situation where you end up meeting them. Especially not regularly. And avoid all demonic activity."

Avoiding demonic activity sounded excellent to Angie. It was absolutely what she wanted to do. What she'd wanted for years. Except for one sticking point. "What will that mean for me and Sebastian? For Aidan? They'll know me. But I won't be able to see them? Ever?" That was unacceptable. Especially for Sebastian.

Betha sighed. "If you spend time with them, it will draw attention from the other hunters. They'll look into it, into you. Eventually the forgetting spell will break."

"You're telling me to give him up. I can't. I don't want to. I won't. Not again." Even when she'd tried, she couldn't give him up. Whatever else happened, she would walk through fire, through the demon realms, through the god realm itself, to keep him.

"Then you'll have to keep your relationship secret," Betha said. "From everyone. Or the hunters will get wind of it. They'll look into it. Into you. They do that with all of the hunters. And if they look close enough at you, they'll remember."

Angie closed her eyes briefly, let out a long breath. Betha was offering her everything she'd wanted, everything she'd come here looking for. More even. A fresh start. A new life. Without the burden of the demon world at every turn, through every V in a tree trunk. She'd be free.

But she'd have to leave New York. Leave Dana's Cauldron. And to keep Sebastian, they'd have to keep their relationship a secret. No one could know.

Could she live that way? Could she give up the home she loved, the work she'd found fulfilment in, the life she'd built...

If it meant a fresh start and no demons?

No more demons. For the first time in her life, she saw something like a light at the end of the dark tunnel that was her particular skill set. And she wanted it. She wanted it very badly. Even if it meant giving almost everything else up. She wanted that freedom. She wanted to be rid of the demon world for good.

Most of it anyway. She glanced back at the rocky hill hiding Lisa's house, knowing Sebastian was waiting for her in there, probably wake now, but giving her space. She could still keep Sebastian, if she did this. Secretly. But she could love him still.

If he was willing.

"I need some time," she said, her gaze still on the hill that was a house. "Just a little time. To talk with him about all this."

"Good. I made that mistake, multiple times. Thinking I knew what was best for me and Eloise. Not asking her before I acted, just acted. Trying to save us both. It only made things worse and took…hundreds of years and the help of someone else for things to finally get mostly fixed. At least as fixed as I could have hoped for. Don't make my mistakes."

Angie glanced back at her, smiling faintly. "Thank you. For the offer. The advice. After what happened with Lisa…"

"That was my fault. Don't…" Betha made fists around the remaining pebbles in her hands, then relaxed her grip and tossed another one into the river. "You don't have to thank me. For anything. This offer, this is to repay the enormous gift you gave me. You saved my love. I can never express how much that means to me." She glanced past Angie to house, then back to Angie. "But I think you understand. Which is why I make this offer."

"I do," Angie said. "I'll have an answer soon."

Betha nodded. "The offer stands whenever you're ready. I would try not to wait too long, though. The demons will return and come for you sooner rather than later."

Angie took Sebastian for a walk along the thin stream of gold to tell him everything Betha had offered. His response was quick and adamant. "If we can start fresh, if you'll be safe from all this but we can still have each other, I will do whatever it takes." He stopped and took her face in his hands. "I will love you in secret, steal time with you when we can manage, do whatever is necessary. If it means you will be safe and living the live you *want* to live? I will do everything in my power to make that work."

She smiled, the expression a little watery from the tears she was trying not to let loose. "A secret relationship won't be easy. Being apart a lot... You might get tired of it."

"I won't. I love you, Angie. I will love you in whatever way I can. Forever."

She nodded. "You too. Same." And kissed him. Hard and for a long time.

CHAPTER FORTY

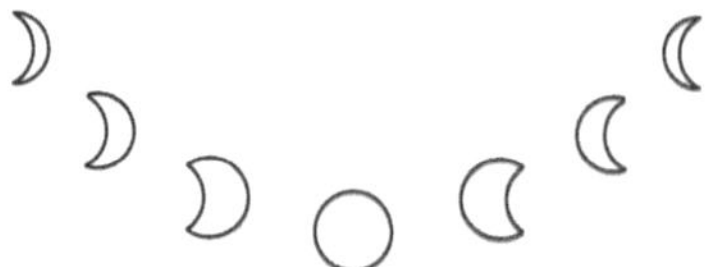

*A*ngie hung a wind chime near her sliding glass back door and looked out on the small backyard of her new home. With a little help from her parents and a short-term loan from her former bosses at Dana's Cauldron, she'd been able to buy the small house in Portland, Oregon with a reasonable mortgage. She intended on running her own psychic business out of the house eventually, but for a year or two she was going to need to work through a business in the city center as well. Dana and Omar had given her an outstanding reference and pointed a few of their former clients who'd moved to the west coast to Angie.

She'd been very sad to say goodbye to Dana's Cauldron and all her friends there. The farewell party had been fun, relatively quiet—to avoid the demon hunters being aware of it—and filled with a lot of tears. Laura was coming out to visit in a month. A few of the other witches had promised to come visit soon. She hoped she wouldn't lose touch with any of them and planned to make the effort not to.

But she also had to be careful. Too much contact with anyone from her former life risked drawing the attention of the demon hunters and breaking the spell that now kept her safe.

One of the few things she regretted about the spell that had wiped her from the memories of the demon hunters, though, was that she hadn't been able to say goodbye to Gabriella. Or even thank her for everything she'd done. She couldn't risk it, not even a text or a brief random meetup in the city. Gabriella had, in the end, been a strong advocate with the council. And Angie hoped the older woman was able to hold her own in the future with the others, with Marty. In fact, Angie kind of hoped Gabriella was the one to take over the council, maybe even get it back to what it had been before Marty and his allies.

But demon hunters and their politics were no longer her issue.

She studied the yard with a critical eye, gaging the wooden fence and currently basic lawn. Among other things she still had to do to settle into her new home, she needed to set a permanent circle around her house, set into the ground, seeded with salt. Her neighbors might hate that. It would affect their grass. But needs must. She was certain they'd prefer dodgy lawns to an influx of supernatural shenanigans.

She rubbed the little pentagram on her bracelet, smiling softly at the gentle tingle of magic. She wasn't going to need the bracelet charm to keep her grounded so she wouldn't open demon portals anymore. But like Esmerelda's second present, the medallion, Angie intended on keeping the bracelet with its dime sized pentagram dangling from it. A good luck charm now instead of a necessary protection.

So far, her witch magic and even her psychic touch had functioned exactly as they had before the binding. Betha had done what she'd promised, bound up the magic Angie didn't want. The demon witch ability to open portals. The demon magic that let her kill demons. Whatever it was they'd both absorbed during the triad bond didn't seem to be something they could isolate enough to bind, though. It had blended in with Angie's ordinary magic, making her witch powers even stronger than they'd been before. Something she'd have to concentrate on training properly. But she could manage that. It was all witch stuff. No demon stuff.

Aidan had shown up at Dana's to wish her well on her move and then left before Angie could say goodbye. She had no idea when or if she'd see Aidan again. But she had a feeling the hunter would be around if Angie needed her. Carmen had not shown up at Dana's and Angie was a little worried about that. She hadn't commented one way or another on Angie getting her powers bound. And after Betha had gotten them all back to New York safely, Carmen had vanished without even much of a goodbye. That was a little worrying. Carmen remembered her and Carmen was mixed up with the hunters. Angie had to hope that after all they'd been through, Carmen didn't decide to stab her in the back.

But if she did, well, Angie would deal with that.

She put her hands on her hips and assess her new kitchen.

So far so good. There was still a lot of decorating to do, furniture to buy, things to unbox. But she had her little cactus garden set up in the kitchen window. Once those little plants were settled into their new place, the house had really started to feel like home.

The doorbell rang, which made her frown. She wasn't expecting her family for another two weeks—they were giving her time to move in before rushing up here to see the new place—and she hadn't had a chance to meet any of her new neighbors yet. She wasn't due to start work until next Wednesday. She hadn't booked an appointment with any new clients.

A lifetime's worth of caution had her building a shield spell as she headed to the door. The spell fell out of her lips and fingertips easily, with a lot of power, so that by the time she reached the door, she had it in place in front of her. When she opened the door, she was glad she'd taken the trouble.

"Carmen," she said. "How the hell did you find me here?"

Carmen leaned against the railing that surrounding Angie's small front porch. Past her, the lawn that bracketed a narrow walkway needed to be mowed. The sidewalk was empty but for some cars parked on the street. And the Portland afternoon was cloudy but dry, the air warm as summer crept into the Pacific Northwest.

Carmen had her arms crossed and was smirking. An expression so familiar, Angie realized it was a bit of a relief to see her that way. "I missed you, chica. Isn't that enough reason?"

"Right. Try again."

Carmen chuckled. "Gonna invite me in?"

"No."

"I'm not a vampire."

"Still no. I don't know why you're here. Or how you found me."

"And you're worried I'll lead the demon hunters right to your secret little love nest?" She shook her head. "No. It's to my benefit to have you out here keeping all our secrets. And I think I might be done with the demon hunters. Kinda need to disappear myself, stay out of their way for a bit."

"And give up using demons to do your dirty work."

Carmen shrugged but didn't answer. "I did want to thank you."

"For what? Taking you into demon realms where a delusional entity wanted to sacrifice you so she could become a god?"

"That was fun," Carmen said with no little sarcasm. "No, I wanted to thank you for the interesting ride. Never thought I'd live long enough to see an actual demon witch at work. Nonetheless encounter an apocalypse witch. Learned a lot. Useful things. And it's been a wild time." She gave a little shrug. "And you also took care of a few of my enemies along the way. For that alone, I should thank you." She paused as if waiting.

Angie didn't say anything because she wasn't sure what to say to all that.

After a moment, Carmen said, "And don't you want to thank me?"

"For what?"

"For helping you unearth your powers? Hey, without me, none of this happens and you are still accidentally opening tree portals and fending off the hunters."

"You think *you* are responsible for this? Not, like, the actual witch who was able to provide a real answer?"

"You wouldn't have found her without me. Without me opening up your powers. Without me pushing you to become the witch you had to be for all this to happen."

"We're gonna have to agree to disagree on that point."

Carmen shrugged. "If you say so."

"What are you going to do now?"

Carmen pushed away from the railing and glanced out over the quiet neighborhood. "Got a lead on someone who might need to be taught a little lesson."

"No demons," Angie said firmly.

Carmen ignored that. "Gonna be changing my name, too. I've burned this one. Too many people know it now. What do you think about the name Teresa?"

"You came all this way to ask my opinion on a new name?"

"No. I came to force you to thank me. But it looks like I'll have to wait on that."

"We are done now. We don't need to have anything to do with each other at all, ever again."

"Ah, chica. You know you'll miss me." She tapped the railing and then winked at Angie. "Have a good life, witch. Sorry we won't be killing more demons together."

"I am not."

Carmen sauntered off, like she didn't have a care in the world. She climbed onto a motorcycle parked at the curb that Angie hadn't paid any attention to, put on her helmet, and gave Angie a little solute before she drove off, the motorcycle's powerful engine loud on the quiet street.

Angie shook her head, and found herself smiling though she wasn't entirely sure why.

"Everything okay?"

She turned to see Sebastian standing on the stairs, his expression concerned. She closed and locked the front door and went to him, meeting him at the base of the stairs and wrapping her arms around him. "It's fine. Just Carmen saying her goodbyes in a very Carmen way. She's changing her name now."

"Probably for the best. Whoever her supporter on the council was, they aren't keeping her safe anymore. It'll be best for her to disappear."

"Do you think she was being honest, when she said that the hunter she killed had been about to make a deal with a demon?"

"It happens. Not often. But it's possible. Then again, Carmen is a consummate liar. Hard to know what's the truth and what's part of a con."

"Not sure there is anything but the con for her."

And yet, Angie did find herself not as…angry at Carmen as she'd once been. But that was a chapter of her life she wanted to put behind her. With luck, she'd never see Carmen, or Teresa, or whoever she became, again.

"I'd rather talk about something more pleasant," Angie

said. "Like what's for dinner." She wagged her eyebrows at him, and Sebastian chuckled.

He'd come here the long way, not following her immediately after she moved, and showed up when even she hadn't been expecting him. She wasn't sure how long they'd be able to keep their relationship secret, but she was prepared to live this way for the rest of her life if it meant she could still have him and also not have to live in the demon hunter world.

"How about we order in some Mexican food. Might as well try the local places right away and make sure you can feed your habit."

She laughed. "Mexican food it is." She leaned into him, savoring the press of his warm body against her. "Though, you know what we're going to need with that, right?"

"Tequila?"

"Tequila." She kissed him, deeply, savoring this moment of peace, of having him to herself. The moments together would be fleeting, she knew. Every meeting, every minute precious. Like the kiss, she intended on savoring these times. Knowing she could love him freely.

When she leaned back, she was a little breathless. "You order the food. I'll go find the nearest liquor store and see what I can get. I'll be back soon."

He pulled her in for one more kiss before she could leave. "I love you," he murmured against her mouth.

"I love you, too," she said. Grateful to have a way to love him in peace.

THE LIQUOR STORE A FEW BLOCKS AWAY HAD BOTH excellent tequila and some good wine. She stocked up, figuring she and Sebastian would probably want to avoid leaving the house much over the next week. Once she started at her new job, he'd have to go. There were demons to hunt, and a council of demon hunters to convince he wasn't seeing anyone. There were still hunter machinations and politics for him to navigate. And she'd have to settle into her new life pretending to be alone. But until then, they were going to hole up in her new house and enjoy some much earned time together.

At the counter, as the clerk rang up her order, she felt someone come up behind her. She half turned, adjusting the strap of her new oversized purse across her chest, to see a ridiculously handsome blond man with blue-green eyes and sharp, angular features standing behind her.

He grinned and gestured at all the bottles she was buying. "Looks like you're due a fun night."

She frowned. Something about him…

He gave a little nod, and she blinked and turned back toward the clerk as he gave her the total. After paying and taking the large box with all her liquor safely separated and packed, she turned to leave. The blond man stepped to the door and held it open for her.

She was about to tell him she was seeing someone and he was wasting his time, but he stopped her with his next statement.

"It's good to meet the new witch in town," he said. "And a strong one at that. I don't suppose you'd be available for helping me with a little…problem we're having with a local magic wielder?"

"We who? Who are you?" Angie leaned away from him, and almost automatically started to murmur the shield spell, but her hands weren't free for the gestures.

The blond man pressed a hand to his chest. "So sorry. Forgot all about the introductions. My name's Jaxer. I work with some of the local Fae. And I spend a great deal of time keeping humans here in Portland safe."

Angie stopped murmuring her spell and looked closer at the man, attempting to use the aura reading Laura had taught her. He was surrounding by glamour, the purple Fae magic hiding his real appearance, which was pretty typical for one of the High Fae.

He was also telling her the truth. He really was looking for help to protect people.

"What's your name again?"

He grinned. "Name's Jaxer. It's nice to meet you, Angela Jordan. What do you say? Got some time to work with the good guys?"

Angie frowned. Then raised her brows at the offer. Nodding to herself. Huh. Yeah. She might. She just might.

"So long as it has nothing to do with demons."

Thank you so much for reading APOCALYPSE WITCH! I hope you enjoyed the final journey in this series! And that it answered *most* of the questions posed by the series. There are, of course, some things that aren't dealt with here, but that's because my muse has decided there's an entire *other* series where all that stuff happens. I'm not sure when I'll write that series. The muse is a bit fickle about which stories she wants to write when. But it's possible there's a demon hunter series in my head somewhere. A demon hunter series with more of Aidan. And maybe more of Carmen.

As a side note, Carmen was one of the series surprises for me, and I loved writing her. Someone irreverent and maybe not entirely a good guy but also not entirely a bad guy but definitely with a bent moral compass who still managed to make some sense in a strange way but was also definitely wrong about a lot of things and did some pretty bad stuff during her life… Yeah, she was really fun to write. And she made a great foil to Angie.

In general, I'm not a planner when it comes to writing fiction. I sit and I write. The story goes where it's going to go. Writers have a lot of names for this type of writer and writing: pantser, writing into the dark, organic writer. All of them will do but I like organic writer and writing into the dark as explanations. Simply put, I don't outline. And if I try, my imagination takes me off the rails pretty quickly. So my imagination has the reins and I enjoy the journey, discovering the story as I go. (I know that sounds a little woo woo but it does work, and it's the way a lot of long term writers actually create stories!)

But in this case, I knew I had to end up in a certain place. That place was established in another series, already published, out there in readers' heads. And mine! I *knew* where Angie landed in the future in the Cary Redmond series. I knew she dropped hints and kept herself away from the demon things Cary ended up mixed up in. But I didn't know why. Angie let things slip in the Cary Redmond books. And she had demon hunter contacts. But she was also never *there* when Cary had to face off against some of the biggest threats in her series. Why?

The Demon Witch series arose out of my desire to answer those questions, for myself and for readers. And when I started, I knew I needed to get Angie to the place she ended up in Cary's series by the end of this series. To explain how she got to be that person based on the events of her younger life. So I was writing toward that destination, an end point that was well established. But without being entirely sure of the route to get there!

About two-thirds through writing the first draft of this final book, I thought there was *no way* this could be the last book. There would probably have to be one more to get Angie and Sebastian to the right place. And I sighed. Because I thought when I got to Apocalypse Witch, which I *did* know was a book in the series, I thought it would be the last book. With a name like Apocalypse Witch, it really should have been, right? I just couldn't see how that would work out, though, even so far into the book, because so many things were happening that I didn't expect.

And then…it all worked out! The story was longer than I assumed it would be when I started writing, the longest novel in the series, but it needed that time. And when I got to the end, to the point where everything fit together and Angie got her answers, and the life she'd always wanted… That was a very satisfying moment in the writing.

Knowing where a series character ends up and then going back and telling the story of how she got there was really fun. There were things I thought would happen that didn't. And things I didn't expect that did happen. Some easter eggs popped out while I was writing, especially in the last two books. And now I have a hint about the backstory of a bad guy in the Cary Redmond series. Actually, there might be two easter eggs in this story that speak to bad guys in the Cary Redmond books, but I'm still mulling one over. It may or may not be what I think it is. (How's that for a mysterious tease! This is the problem with organic writers. LOL) This is all still mostly in my head, although astute readers of both series might spot at least one of the easter eggs, but I suspect it'll all come out in a story at some point.

Especially since the Cary Redmond series is still going (that's one I thought I'd finish and then…didn't. Oops.). Angie will be back with Cary soon, too. And there are more stories to tell. But for now, the Demon Witch gets to rest.

If your first foray into this bigger world was this series, and you haven't read the Cary Redmond series yet, but you want to see all the ties with Angie to that series, here's my suggested reading order. Start with the novella *When Cary Met Angie*. There's another novella called *Cary and the Demon Witch* that takes place after that with more Angie and references to her history. And then start the Cary Redmond main series of novels starting with THE TROUBLE WITH BLACK CATS AND DEMONS. You'll see where Angie ended up with the added bonus of knowing where she started! (I didn't even know that!)

And if you'd like to see a little more Aidan, she also makes an on-page appearance in the Cary Redmond series as well as the novella *Anger Management*. And and! If you'd like to read a little about the witch collecting demon witch histories, and the mysterious demon witch who had to be killed by her own coven, there's more on her in the novella, *Demonic Dates*.

For those who like a lot of intertwined storytelling and books that link into other books, I've got you covered!

And if you'd just like to know more about my books, there are several ways to do that! The best way to keep up with what I'm doing is to join my author newsletter. It goes out monthly for the most part, unless I have something special going on and then there might be a few extras sent. But mostly it's a monthly newsletter with all the news and updates and occasionally some free books, excerpts, and special discounts to my store. New subscribers get two exclusive stories that are only available to newsletter people, including one in the Cary Redmond series.

If you get too much email and prefer to check on things in your own time, the best places for that are my website and my store which are both updated regularly. My website at katsimons.com has listings of all the books and buy links, and the front page is updated once a month to announce new releases and upcoming news.

The store, KatSimonsBooks, is a great place to get updated reading order lists and be able to easily see all the different series. You'll see what's coming out in the near future. And I have a section there called The Café at KatSimonsBooks were I post free-to-read short stories on the 1st and 15th of the month. You also have the added bonus here of being able to support the author directly by buying books directly from the store.

You can also follow my author page at BookBub, on Facebook, or at your favorite vendor. And I can be found on social media if you're interested in chatting all things fiction. Mostly Bluesky and Instagram as I write this. I love hearing for readers, so don't be shy about emailing either!

And finally, I'd like to give a very special shout out to the people who backed and supported the Kickstarter I ran to launch APOCALYPSE WITCH! That support was invaluable and really made getting this book out to readers super fun. Thanks everyone!

And thank you, once more, for reading Angie and Sebastian's story! I hope you enjoyed the entire Demon Witch series!

Bye for now. At least until the next linked series...

Happy Reading!

~Kat

BOOKS BY KAT SIMONS

Demon Witch Series

Howling Dreadful

Moonlit Strange

1-Bone Lantern Witch

2-Spiderweb Witch

3-Storm Shadow Witch

4-Darkling Mist Witch

5-Apocalypse Witch

Urban Fantasy

The Cary Redmond Series

Cary Redmond Short Stories and Collections

Joan of Kerry Series

Friday's Curious Shop Series

Paranormal Romance

Dragon Thief Series

Seven Families: Wolf Series

Tiger Shifters Series

Destiny Cats Series

Romancing the Leopard: A Tiger Shifters-Cary Redmond Crossover Novel

ALSO BY KAT SIMONS

Contemporary Fantasy

Haunts and Howls Collections

*Tombstone Wizard * The Unshattered Sword * Going Out of Business: Everything's for Sale * Anger Management * Demonic Dates * The Museum of Small Art's Everyman * Burning Inside a Stone Circle * Bored Questless * I Just Ate a Bug * Ting Ling * Sophie Saves the World * Black Water Hawthorns * To Dance in Fallow Fields at Midnight * The Troll and the Dressmaker*

Stories from the Café

The Café Collections

Stories from the Café: Volume One

Pick Your Genre Collections

Who Steals a Dragon

Contemporary Romances

Designed for You

Poinsettias and Possibilities

Mystery and Thriller

ROSS AND O'NEILL ADVENTURES

Galileo's Pendulum

ABOUT THE AUTHOR

Kat Simons earned her Ph.D. in animal behavior, working with animals as diverse as dolphins and deer. She brought her experience and knowledge of biology to her paranormal romance and urban fantasy fiction, where she delights in taking nature and turning it on its ear. She writes urban fantasy, contemporary fantasy, and paranormal romance in series which combine action adventure, the otherworldly, and a frequent dose of sexy romance.

The newest book in her bestselling romantic urban fantasy series about Protector Cary Redmond, The Trouble with Shifters and Fae Courts, sees a new direction for the intrepid Protector, her sexy leopard shifter mate, and the entire crew. Kat also launched a new novella length Urban Fantasy Romance series that follows the adventures of a magical thief and the dragon shifter prince she just can't seem to shake—and really doesn't want to. The first season of the Dragon Thief series released throughout 2024. Season Two begins in 2025 with The Crown of Kingship Job.

For something a little different, Kat also publishes fantasy, science fiction, and the occasional hockey romance under the name Isabo Kelly (https://www.isabokelly.com).

After traveling the world, living in places like Hawaii, Germany, and Ireland, Kat now lives in New York City with her family and a library's worth of books.

For more on Kat and her future books

Website: https://www.katsimons.com/
Newsletter: https://bit.ly/KatSimonsNewsletter

KatSimonsBooks

https://www.katsimonsbooks.com
https://www.TheCafeatKatSimonsBooks.com

Social Media

Facebook Page: https://www.facebook.com/
KatSimonsAuthor
BookBub: https://www.bookbub.com/authors/kat-simons
Bluesky: https://bsky.app/profile/katsimons.bsky.social
Instagram: https://www.instagram.com/isabokelly/
Threads: https://www.threads.net/@isabokelly

KATSIMONSBOOKS

Mystery

URBAN
FANTASY

Romance

And More!

KATSIMONSBOOKS.COM

www.ingramcontent.com/pod-product-compliance
Lightning Source LLC
Chambersburg PA
CBHW031158010826
48971CB00012B/905